# WESTERN

*Rugged men looking for love...*

## A K-9 Christmas Reunion
Lisa Carter

## Bonding With The Cowboy's Daughter
Lisa Jordan

# MILLS & BOON

K-9 CHRISTMAS REUNION
© 2024 by Lisa Carter
Philippine Copyright 2024
Australian Copyright 2024
New Zealand Copyright 2024

First Published 2024
First Australian Paperback Edition 2024
ISBN 978 1 038 92178 9

BONDING WITH THE COWBOY'S DAUGHTER
© 2024 by Lisa Jordan
Philippine Copyright 2024
Australian Copyright 2024
New Zealand Copyright 2024

First Published 2024
First Australian Paperback Edition 2024
ISBN 978 1 038 92178 9

MIX
Paper | Supporting
responsible forestry
FSC® C001695

Published by
Harlequin Mills & Boon
An imprint of Harlequin Enterprises (Australia) Pty Limited
(ABN 47 001 180 918), a subsidiary of HarperCollins
Publishers Australia Pty Limited
(ABN 36 009 913 517)
Level 19, 201 Elizabeth Street
SYDNEY NSW 2000 AUSTRALIA

Cover art used by arrangement with Harlequin Books S.A.. All rights reserved.

Printed and bound in Australia by McPherson's Printing Group

# A K-9 Christmas Reunion
Lisa Carter

# MILLS & BOON

**Lisa Carter** and her family make their home in North Carolina. In addition to her Love Inspired novels, she writes romantic suspense. When she isn't writing, Lisa enjoys travelling to romantic locales, teaching writing workshops and researching her next exotic adventure. She has strong opinions on barbecue and ACC basketball. She loves to hear from readers. Connect with Lisa at lisacarterauthor.com.

For I know the thoughts that I think toward you, saith the Lord, thoughts of peace, and not of evil, to give you an expected end.
—*Jeremiah* 29:11

# DEDICATION

To Leslie-Jean—thank you for praying me through.

# CHAPTER ONE

RUNNING BEHIND SCHEDULE had become the story of Nate Crenshaw's life.

From the start, his day—like most of his days since his wife died two years ago—had gone heels over head. First, he discovered the downed section of fence. The cattle had escaped from the grazing pasture into his neighbor's property.

He spent the morning rounding up the cattle into a temporary holding pen, but he didn't have enough materials to properly secure the breach in the fence. Which meant driving into town to acquire the necessary wire from the agri-supply store.

With each tick of the clock, today's to-do list faded further out of reach. Tires kicking up a cloud of dust, he steered around the bend of trees on the graveled drive of the High Country Ranch. Barreling under the crossbars, he took the secondary road leading over the mountain to his hometown of Truelove, North Carolina.

The blistering heat of summer had long since given way to the crisp coolness of mid-November. The blaze of autumn color, for which the Blue Ridge was famous, now carpeted the forest floor. The hardwood trees lifted stark, bare branches to the Carolina blue sky.

With his father having one of his good days, when Nate returned with his supplies, he didn't stop to check on his dad. He gathered his tools from the barn and headed to the pasture on the far edge of the ranch to make the repairs. He'd have to hurry to make the appointment the agency had set up for him and his dad.

It was important the meeting go well. Their future depended on how well his father took to the new, specially trained dementia service dog. As soon as his dad had gotten his diagnosis, Nate had put him on the list to receive a dog. They'd waited almost eighteen months for this day to arrive.

With his father in the early stages of the disease, this was the optimal time to pair him with a service animal. Nate had high hopes the dog trained by Juliet Melbourne's canine agency, PawPals, would make a real difference in alleviating some of the worst symptoms of his dad's heartbreaking and progressive illness.

Clearing his mind of everything else, Nate got to work. By the time he finished, his head was pounding. He probably shouldn't have skipped lunch. When he looked up from the wire he'd strung, the sun sat much lower on the horizon. The repairs had taken longer than he'd anticipated.

He took a deep breath of the tangy scent of evergreens lining the perimeter of the pasture. He loved ranching. He'd never wanted to live anywhere else or do anything else.

Not exactly true. He frowned. There'd been a brief time, long ago, when he'd believed he wanted something quite different in a place far from here.

A temporary insanity from which life—and a particular girl—had soon disabused him. This was his life now, and he loved it. Except when the loneliness got to him.

Bone weary, he put his tools and what was left of the wire roll into the back of his pickup. He climbed behind the wheel. Scrubbing his forehead, he willed the headache to subside. These days, he stayed tired. It had been a while since Dad had been able to help on the farm.

Cranking the engine, Nate jostled down the rutted path toward the barn. The boys would be wondering where he was. He liked to be there when they got home from school. Yet despite how hard he tried, he'd failed them once again.

Not for the first time, he thought how much better Deanna would have coped as a single parent. But she was the one who died, and he was the one left to pick up the pieces of an unimaginable future spent without her.

Holding the leash of a medium-sized, sable-colored rough collie, a woman with indistinct features emerged from the shadows cast by the barn.

Gut churning, he suddenly realized he was late for the appointment with the trainer from PawPals. He braked sharply, sending gravel spinning. The woman jerked.

Nate threw himself out of the vehicle. *Way to make a terrible first impression, Crenshaw.*

He hoped his dad had stepped into the gap due to his lack of hospitality. The boys had been looking forward to the dog coming to live with them. Probably lively five-year-old Kody and seven-year-old Connor had more than made up for his absence and provided a most cordial welcome.

From a distance, his first impressions of the

dog trainer were of her even, pleasing features. She was pretty in an outdoorsy way. Compared to his six-foot height, she wasn't tall. Maybe only five foot five. Casually dressed in jeans, brown ankle boots and an oversize beige sweater, she wore her hair in a pale golden braid, which hung over her shoulder.

Tromping across the yard to meet her, he raised his hand. The dog yipped a greeting. "I'm so sorry I'm late, Ms. Spencer. I meant to be here to greet you, but the time got away from me."

She stepped out of the shadows and into the slanted light of the sun. A slight breeze fluttered the blue silk ribbon tied around the end of her braid. Once upon a lifetime ago, he'd known a girl who wore her hair the same way.

Hand outstretched, he got his first glimpse of her face. A face that teased at the edges of his memory. "Welcome to—"

The pieces of an all-too-familiar puzzle clicked into place. His heart skipping a beat, he came to a complete halt.

"Gemma?" He blinked at her. "Gemma Anderson?" Dropping his hand, he went rigid. "You're the dog trainer Juliet sent?"

She stiffened. "It's Spencer now. And yes, I'm here to help your father bond with Rascal."

He flicked a look at the collie sitting quietly at her feet. "Rascal?"

The dog cocked his head.

She flipped the end of her braid over her shoulder. "It suited him in an entirely endearing way."

He folded his arms across his chest. "I'm sorry you came all this way for nothing. This isn't going to work out."

Gemma's heart skipped a beat. "You can't be serious?"

Rascal rubbed his nose against her hand. The collie always sensed when his humans needed emotional support. It was this sensitivity that made him such a great service dog.

Nathan's blue eyes glinted. "I've never been more serious."

She threw out her hands. "But why?"

He lifted his Stetson off his head and placed it again on top of his short, dark hair. "I think you know why."

As seventeen-year-olds, they'd met as 4-H camp counselors. During that unforgettable summer, they fell in love.

"I wasn't sure you'd remember me," she rasped.

When the summer ended, they vowed to love

each other forever. But after she returned to her home near Greensboro in the Piedmont, her world fell apart.

She immediately ended her budding relationship with him, stopped answering his letters and refused to take his phone calls. Later, she'd heard through the 4-H grapevine, he and a former girlfriend got married.

"No one ever forgets their first love." He threw her a piercing look. "Nor the Dear John left in my voicemail the very next day."

Because the next day after she returned home, her mother was dead and her father in prison. The shame had been too much. Recalling that terrible day brought only darkness. A downward spiral into an abyss she'd barely managed to survive.

She couldn't—wouldn't—go back to that time in her life. Better for him to believe her coldhearted than to ever learn the truth. With an effort, she steadied her rioting emotions.

"That was a long time ago. Today I'm here to help your dad." She raised her chin. "The program would be a godsend for your father. A dementia service dog could potentially extend his independence several years beyond what most patients with his condition experience. Rascal will also help you and your wife shoulder the day-to-day burden of caring for him."

His ruggedly handsome features creased. "My wife is dead. It's only me, the boys and Dad."

She reared a fraction. She hadn't realized he was a widower. She'd assumed... Wrongly as it turned out.

"I'm sorry." She bit her lip. "I didn't know."

"How could you know?" He peered at the evergreen-studded mountain range that enfolded the ranch like the worn but comforting arms of a beloved grandmother. "I haven't heard from you in fifteen years." His gaze locked onto hers.

She flushed. "There were reasons..."

His eyebrow arched.

She could feel the heat creeping up her neck. "Reasons I'd rather not discuss."

Nathan's lips—such a handsome mouth—tightened. "Look, I don't want to cause problems for you with your boss. I'll tell Juliet we weren't a good fit. And request a different trainer to acclimate my father to Rascal."

Hearing his name, the collie woofed.

For a split second, Nathan's tense features relaxed. A tentative smile lurked at the corners of his lips. Like her, he'd always loved dogs, but too soon a weight settled upon his countenance once more.

Her heart fluttered against her rib cage at the brief glimpse of the warm-hearted teenager she'd loved so deeply. Judging from his broad shoulders, Nathan the man had fulfilled the physical potential of the adolescent she'd known. Otherwise, probably little remained of the boy she recalled. Little enough remained of the girl she'd been.

Life had a way of doing that. After their glorious summer together, she'd had to grow up fast. But Gemma wasn't ready to give up on the PawPals program, which she and her best friend, Juliet, had piloted.

"I'm afraid it doesn't work that way." She glanced at her dog. "Stay." Dropping the leash, she moved closer to the thirty-two-year-old rancher.

"There are only a few facilities in the nation that train dementia assistance canines. And there are even less trainers than there are dogs. Without me, there can be no service dog for your father. He'll lose his place on the waiting list to another family in desperate need of help." She pursed her lips. "By the time another dog and trainer become available—"

"Another eighteen months?"

She nodded. "Possibly two years. At which point, your father might no longer benefit from the program."

A bleakness clouded his gaze. "You mean he could have slipped too far from us?"

Her heart pinged inside her chest. "Dementia companion dogs typically make the biggest difference with patients in the early-to mid-stages of dementia. After that..." She sighed. "I'm sorry."

"You and Rascal are a package deal." He scoured his face with his hand. "Got it."

"The training only lasts a few weeks. Just until your father is comfortable with Rascal. Just until I'm sure Rascal has bonded to him, and we establish a routine."

"What kind of routine?"

She smiled. "You'll be amazed at what Rascal can do for your father, once I identify what would be of most help to your dad. In the application, you mentioned sundowner events. Late in the day confusion and sleep issues are fairly typical of a patient with your father's illness. Once attuned to your dad, Rascal will be able to reduce the severity of the agitation your fa-

ther experiences and sometimes divert an episode altogether."

He pinched the bridge of his nose. "Those
episodes are the worst. Upsetting not only for
my dad, but the boys, too. They don't understand why their granddad suddenly…" His Adam's apple bobbed in his throat.

She put her hand on the sleeve of his tan Car-
hartt jacket. "If you'll give me the chance to
work with your father, I believe Rascal could
enrich all your lives."

He searched her face.

Not entirely sure why this mattered so much,
she held her breath. There were lots of other
families in need of Rascal's services. If he sent
her away, she and Rascal would become a blessing to someone else.

She tilted her head. "Surely you can put up
with me for two weeks?"

For a second, something she couldn't decipher
flitted across his features. A muscle ticked in his
square-lined jaw. She let go of his arm. Touch-
ing him had been a mistake.

She prided herself on her professionalism, but
Nathan Crenshaw was far from being just another client. For a multitude of reasons, she'd
sensed seeing him would be hard, and she'd

steeled herself for the upcoming training. Yet being with him again… The intensity of feeling was far more than she'd anticipated.

Rattled, she preferred not to examine too closely why she so badly wanted this to work out for him. She wanted the dogs she trained to work out for every family. What she was feeling was probably nothing more than the emotional equivalent of an aftershock. What else could it be?

"My father's happiness and well-being are the only things that matter." He touched a finger to the brim of his hat. "We'll give it a try."

A shaft of sheer joy pierced her heart.

SHE THREW NATE a dazzling smile. "You won't be sorry."

Bits of the Gemma he'd fallen in love with that long ago summer sparkled in her soft brown eyes.

To his ultimate heartbreak, he'd discovered she wasn't the girl he'd believed her to be. But according to the credentials Juliet Melbourne forwarded, prior to specializing in the training and placement of dementia service dogs, Gemma Spencer had an extensive résumé of working with patients in memory-care facilities. The program at PawPals provided families an at-home care option for their loved ones.

He didn't delude himself about what his father's future would hold. Nate had done his research. Diagnosed in his late sixties, his dad could live for many more years.

The progressive disease, this most terrible of illnesses, would eventually rob Ike Crenshaw of everything that made him who he was. If his dad lived long enough, one day permanent placement in a care facility would become a necessary reality.

But if Rascal could truly improve his father's quality of life... Nate would be a fool to turn down this opportunity.

His sons had already lost so much. He needed to do everything in his power to ensure their granddad was there for them—in every sense of the word—for as long as possible.

Nate wasn't a lovesick teenager anymore. He was an adult. A son and a father in his own right. A privilege and a responsibility he didn't take lightly.

He'd find a way to work with Gemma. Yet forewarned was forearmed. She'd proved she couldn't be trusted. It would be best to keep her at arm's length.

Leash in hand, she walked the service dog forward. "Rascal, meet Nathan. Nathan, this is Rascal."

Something bittersweet pinged inside his chest. He'd forgotten she always used his full given name. She was the only one who ever had.

Rascal lifted a paw and placed it atop Nate's hand.

"Go ahead. Shake his paw. He's waiting for you." She smiled at him in such a winsome way, for a moment his earlier resolve wavered.

Arm's length might prove easier said than done. He gave the collie's paw a tentative shake. Rascal dropped his paw to the ground, and brushed his head against Nate's leg.

"If you rub the spot below his ears, he'll love you fur-ever." She winked. "Get it? Fur-ever?"

Despite his intention to remain aloof, his lips twitched. He'd also forgotten how she used to make him laugh. Usually at the lamest, silliest things.

It was reassuring to know something of the girl he'd once fallen for so hard still remained in the coolly sophisticated woman standing in front of him.

He stroked the dog's fluffy fur. "It's great to finally meet you, Rascal."

The collie licked his hand.

He smiled. "Rascal seems like an extraordinary dog. I'm surprised you're willing to let him go."

"Rascal is special. And believe me, I've trained a lot of service dogs over the years." Her smile became strained. "But it's because of his specialness I'm able to let go. Rascal will make such a significant difference to your family."

Nate stuffed his hands in his coat pockets. "How did Dad respond to Rascal?"

Her forehead puckered. "What do you mean?"

"Earlier, when Dad and the boys met Rascal."

She shook her head. "When we arrived, nobody answered the door. That's why we were in the barn looking for you."

"Nobody's home?" He stared at her. "That can't be right. I don't understand."

His eyes drifted to the sprawling white clapboard farmhouse. But the home he shared with his father and sons lay dark and shuttered. He glanced at his wristwatch. Five o'clock.

She wrapped the leash around her hand. "What's wrong?"

"Where's my dad?" A sick feeling coiled in his gut. "By now, the boys should've been home from school, too."

Like every other afternoon since school started in September, his second cousin Maggie brought his sons home when she picked up her own children. Where were Connor and Kody?

His gaze darted to the sky, swathed in swirls of golden pinks and apricots. But there was no time to appreciate the sunset. Once the sun slid below the ridge on the horizon, darkness would descend rapidly.

Breathing heavily, he dug his phone out of his jean pocket. His eyes widened.

While mending the fence in the back pasture, he'd missed a half-dozen phone calls. In rural areas outside town, cell reception was notoriously spotty.

Chest heaving, he scrolled through the calls. The school had called four times. Maggie had left three messages for him to call back ASAP.

What had happened? What was going on? Panicked, he hit Redial on the school number. Had there been an accident at school? Had his father taken the call and gone to the hospital to be with them?

His call to the school went unanswered. Everyone must have gone home for the evening. Frustrated, he disconnected.

"Would your dad have left a note?"

Cell pressed to his ear, he hurried toward the house. She kept pace with him. Rascal loped alongside.

Beyond the curve in the drive around the cluster of trees, he heard the sound of an engine.

Nate released the breath he hadn't realized he'd been holding. "Finally."

His relief was short-lived.

It wasn't Maggie's hunter green Outback or his dad's bronze GMC. Instead, a white cruiser, belonging to Truelove's chief of police, rounded the bend.

Fear robbing the oxygen from his lungs, Nate raced forward.

# CHAPTER TWO

Jumping out of the police cruiser, his cousin Maggie intercepted him a few feet from the vehicle. "Everything's okay, Nate."

He craned his neck, trying to get a better look at the occupants inside. "Where are my sons?"

"They're in the car with Bridger."

"I want to see them." He tried to step around her, but she held his arm in a firm grip.

"Let me explain before they get out."

"What's happened, Mags? When I realized you'd called so many times and the boys weren't home yet—"

"Bridger's got everything under control." The slim brunette squeezed his arm. "But the state you're in, you'll spook the boys again."

He cut a look over her shoulder at the police chief—also her husband—sitting behind the wheel. The law enforcement officer gave him a small nod.

Nate's eyebrow arched. "What do you mean 'spook' them again?"

"There was an incident at school this afternoon."

His mouth went dry. "A shooter? In Truelove?"

"Not that." She shook her head. Her ponytail whipped back and forth. "Your dad showed up at the school office to collect the boys."

He frowned. "But Dad knows you take them home from school."

"Ike had it in his mind he was taking them home today." Her bottom lip wobbled. "He became agitated when Principal Stallings refused to call them out of their classrooms. Ike's name wasn't listed on the consent-to-release paperwork. By law, the school cannot relinquish physical custody of a child to a nonauthorized adult."

Nate slumped. "His name used to be on the form. This school year, out of concern for the boys, he agreed it would be better for you to take over carpool duties. Why would he take it into his head to do this?"

"Ike couldn't be reasoned with, Nate." Her brown eyes watered. "When the situation escalated, Mrs. Stallings phoned Bridger at the police station. I was already en route to the carpool line."

Nate scrubbed his hand over his face. "I'm so sorry you got dragged into the nightmare that has become our lives." He lifted his head. "Are Austin and Logan with you?"

Her twins were a year younger than Connor.

"Bridger's mom took the boys to her house. But what happened at school is not the worst of it, Nate." Her voice hitched.

Dread dropped like a stone into the pit of his stomach. "It gets worse?"

"Before Bridger could arrive, Ike grabbed Connor and Kody off the playground. They were scared, but they went with him because—"

"Because he's their grandfather and they love him." Nate rubbed his forehead. "Was there a car accident? Is my father dead, Mags?"

"Ike is shaken but all right. He became disoriented and couldn't find his way home. He'd been driving around for thirty minutes before Bridger and his deputies were able to locate the SUV."

"Dad's been okay driving to Truelove to see his buddies, or I never would have let him keep the keys to his car."

At the image of his dad driving erratically on the winding mountain roads surrounding

Truelove with his precious sons in tow, Nate's heart plummeted.

"Anything could have happened, Mags. They could have plunged over the edge into the gorge," he whispered.

"But they didn't." She gave him a fierce hug. "God watched over them."

He jerked his chin at the police cruiser. "Is my dad in the car, too?"

She dropped her gaze. "Bridger believed it might be best if my father drove him home in Ike's SUV. We'll give Dad a lift back to his house when we pick up Austin and Logan."

Nate's dad and his first cousin Tom Arledge, Maggie's father, had been best friends since they were children.

"Dad and Ike should be here in a few minutes." She looked at him. "I wanted to give you a heads-up and the chance to speak to the boys before they arrived."

He swallowed past the lump in his throat. "I can't thank you and Bridger enough for what you did today for my family."

"We're family, too, cuz." She swiped a finger under her eyes. "We love you guys."

Taking a deep breath, he opened the back door. "Connor? Kody?"

Strapped into the seat, five-year-old Kody reached for him. "Daddy?" His small, forlorn face bore the unmistakable signs of tears.

Beside his brother, seven-year-old Connor's lower lip trembled. "I... I took care of Kody, Daddy. I made sure he was okay. But Granddad got lost." The child's face crumpled. "Why couldn't he find his way home? We tried to help him, but he wouldn't listen to us."

His heart broke. "You've been very brave, but it's my job to take care of Kody and you. I'm sorry I wasn't there when you needed me."

Leaning in, he released Kody's seat belt and opened his arms. Both boys flew into his embrace. He gave them a tight hug. "I'm so sorry this happened, guys."

He helped them out of the car.

Kody tugged at his arm. "Is that our new doggie?"

Standing near the porch holding Rascal's leash, Gemma smiled at his sons.

"Hi." Striding forward, Maggie stuck out her hand. "I'm Nate's cousin, Maggie Hollingsworth." She motioned. "This is my husband, Bridger."

The police chief tipped the brim of his regulation hat to Gemma. "Ma'am."

Maggie cocked her head. "You must be the dog trainer lady. Ms. Spencer, right?"

"I am." She smiled. "Please call me Gemma."

"What a lovely name." Maggie flashed her eyes at him. "An unusual name I recollect only hearing once a long time ago."

He toed the dirt with his boot. "Mags..." he warned.

The collie barked.

"And this is Rascal." Gemma waggled her fingers at the boys. "That's his way of saying hello."

Connor stuck his thumbs into his belt loops. "Kind of a silly name for a dog."

She grinned. "Rascal can be a silly kind of dog. When he's not working, though, he loves nothing better than hanging out with silly boys. You wouldn't happen to know any silly boys, would you?"

Kody thrust his hand into the air. "Me! Sometimes I'm a silly boy."

Nate ruffled his hair. "Just sometimes?"

Connor took a cautious step forward. "Is Rascal working now? Daddy said we mustn't pet Rascal if he's working with Granddad."

"Thank you for asking first." She led Rascal forward. "I'm so happy your dad explained the service dog rules. Rascal's off duty until your grandfather gets here. He would love to get to know you better. It's okay to pet him if you want."

The boys looked at him. He nodded. Gemma showed them where Rascal liked to be petted.

Connor stroked the dog's head. "You have to be gentle, Kody," he admonished his younger brother.

Not unlike Nate, the second-grader had an overly developed sense of responsibility. Since Deanna died, Connor had taken it upon himself to act as a surrogate parent to his kid brother. It pained Nate that his too-serious firstborn had borne the brunt of taking care of Kody. Connor deserved to be a kid, too. .

Kody gave the collie a pat. Rascal licked his hand. The kindergartener's blue eyes widened. "He licked me, Miss Gemma."

"That means he likes you."

Giggling, Kody put his hand over his mouth. "I love Wascal."

Nate jammed his hands in his pockets. "Kody sometimes has trouble with his *r*'s."

She winked at his son. "Don't we all?"

His lips quirked. This was exactly how he remembered her dealing with the young campers in her capable charge that long-ago summer. Defusing the gravest cases, from mosquito bites to homesickness, with her offbeat humor.

Just then, his dad's bronze GMC rounded the bend. At the wheel, Maggie's dad, the silver-haired former police chief, pulled alongside his son-in-law's cruiser.

Nate took a breath. "I need to help Grand-dad, boys."

Connor stuck his hands into his pockets. Just like Nate did. "We're okay, Daddy. You take care of Granddad."

Gemma touched Kody's shoulder. "Guys, Rascal needs to work now. I'm going to put on his PawPals vest so he knows to switch gears."

Tom Arledge unfolded from the car and shut the door gently behind him. "You need to be prepared, Nate. I've tried to calm Ike down, but…" His dark brown eyes, so like Maggie's, were sad. "Why didn't you tell us his condition had gotten so bad?"

Nate's gut knotted. "The good days were out-weighing the bad. At breakfast, he was in good spirits. We were coping. I hoped with the ar-rival of his assistance dog…" He squeezed his eyelids closed and opened them. "Dad's a proud man. He didn't want people to know the extent of his problems."

Gemma and Rascal moved next to him. "It's natural for families to cover over the increasing deficits in order to save a loved one from awkward or embarrassing questions."

Nate looked at her. "Until they can't anymore?" But he appreciated her attempt to console him. Despite what had happened between them later, she was as kindhearted as he remembered.

Rascal rubbed his coat against Nate's leg. He found an extraordinary amount of comfort in the canine's touch.

"Nathan, I think it would be a good idea to get your dad into more familiar surroundings." She glanced at his cousins. "However, too many people right now might overstimulate him."

Bridger took off his hat. "Maggie and I can take Connor and Kody home with us for a sleepover."

Nate threw a look over his shoulder at his small sons, huddled next to Maggie. His heart twisted in his chest.

Gemma took a half step toward the boys and then as if checking herself, she stopped. "Connor and Kody have had a frightening experience.

I'll do everything I can to ensure they're able to stay in their own home tonight." Compassion shone from her dark eyes. "If we're able to get the situation under control with your dad."

He nodded, grateful for her empathy for his sons. Bracing for what he might find, he opened the SUV passenger door.

Nate was taken aback by the disheveled old man glaring at him. "D-Dad?"

Looking far older than the spry, alert man he'd last seen that morning, his father was agitated and his pale blue eyes darted wildly.

"I want to go home," his father shouted.

"Dad, it's me." Anguish clawed at his throat. "It's Nate."

Lurching forward, his father would have fallen out of the vehicle if Nate hadn't grabbed his arm. "Dad, you *are* home."

"This isn't my home." His dad glowered at him. "Who are you? I want to go home. Why will no one take me home?"

He blinked rapidly. Did his father not recognize him? He'd known this moment would eventually come, but he'd never believed it would happen this soon.

Other than the ever-increasing forgetfulness, he'd believed—hoped and prayed—he and his dad would have months, if not years, together. But the disease had taken a precipitous and frightening turn for the worse.

Sudden grief rocked him. His eyes watered. He started to shake.

"Nathan." Gemma's gentle voice cut through his cloud of misery. "Don't argue with him. Go along with his reasoning. Let him know you're going to help him get home."

The steadfastness in her gaze gave him the courage to do what needed to be done.

He swallowed the sorrow he was only just keeping at bay. "I'll take you home, sir. Come with me. Okay?"

The confused old man bore no resemblance to the strong, confident rancher he had known and admired his entire life.

Eyes narrowed with suspicion, his father scrutinized his face. "You'll take me home? You promise?"

"I… I promise." In an act of sheer will, Nate quelled the quavering of his chin. "It's this way, sir." He held out his arm. "I'll show you the way home."

"Gotta get home." His dad placed his gnarled hand on Nate's coat. "Pamela's waiting supper on me."

Nate tried not to flinch. His mother died two decades ago when he was in middle school.

"If there's anything we can do...?" Tom opened his hands. "We're here for you, Nate. You're not in this alone."

On Tom's features, he caught a glimpse of the same, nearly unbearable pain welling inside himself. With slow, halting steps, he led his father toward the house.

"Connor and Kody, you come, too." Leash in hand, Gemma beckoned. "Maybe you could have a snack in the kitchen while we get your granddad settled?"

Maggie gave each boy a quick hug and nudged them toward Gemma. "Go with Rascal." She mouthed a thank-you to Gemma.

"I'll give you a call later," Nate said over his shoulder.

He helped his suddenly fragile father climb the steps to the porch. With Maggie and Tom in the cruiser, Bridger drove away.

Behind one of the posts, Gemma retrieved a small purple shoulder pack with the PawPals logo. She must have left it on the porch earlier when she'd gone in search of him.

Inside the house, he assisted his father to his favorite recliner. "Here you are, Dad."

His father's hands shook as he lowered himself into the leather chair.

Gemma ushered the boys into the kitchen. There was a soft murmur of voices, the muffled thud of a cabinet door closing, the crinkle of what had to be a potato chip bag and the clink of a glass upon the countertop.

"Where's Pam?" His dad scowled at him. "Who are you? Why are you people in my house?"

Feeling helpless, he gaped at his father.

Rascal at her side, Gemma appeared in the doorway separating the den from the kitchen. "You don't know me, Mr. Crenshaw. My name is Gemma."

She kept her voice low and soothing. "This is Rascal." She ran her hand along the collie's fur. "He's been looking forward to meeting you."

Tail wagging, Rascal barked a greeting.

A hint of something lucid—something that still belonged to the essence of the man Nate had loved his entire life—sparked in his eyes. Nate's heart jackhammered.

"Rascal?" His dad huffed, but the beginnings of a smile tilted his lips. "Earned that name, did he?"

"Well and truly." She and the dog took a single step into the room. "I'm thinking you might have more than a little in common with him. Am I right?"

Some of the strain eased from his rigid features. "Got that right. Gemma, was it?" He cocked his head.

Gemma smiled. "Yes, sir. That's right. I'm sure you have a few rascally stories you could tell."

Sticking his tongue in his cheek, his dad propped his elbows on the armrests. "I don't like to brag, mind you, but when I courted Pammie—the purtiest girl in Truelove—I gave her quite the run for her money."

Nate's mouth dropped.

Gemma threw him an amused look. "Of that, Mr. Crenshaw, there can be no doubt."

His father grinned like the mischievous charmer he'd been once upon a lifetime ago.

"I also hear you're good with dogs, Mr. Crenshaw."

His dad jutted his jaw. "I've raised a few ranch dogs in my time."

She sent Rascal toward the recliner. "Would you do me a favor and groom Rascal while I see if Miss Pamela has dinner going in the kitchen?"

Nate held his breath.

Reaching into the purple shoulder bag, she withdrew a small brush. "Rascal loved exploring your ranch this afternoon, but his coat is in need of serious attention."

Making herself small and nonthreatening, she crouched beside the collie and the chair.

She held out the brush to his dad. "Would you be a dear and help me out?"

This was the make-or-break moment. Would his dad accept Rascal into his rapidly diminishing world? Or withhold his trust?

Fear flitted across his father's face. "They're watching us, you know. They've got eyes and ears everywhere, Gemma," he hissed.

Wanting to weep at the paranoia in his dad's voice, Nate sagged heavily against the wall.

"Is it safe for Rascal here?" Brow constricting, his father's gaze pinged from Gemma to Rascal. "Safe for *me* to be here?" he whispered.

She laid the brush on the armrest next to his hand. "Rascal is here to keep you safe, Mr. Crenshaw," she whispered back.

"You promise?"

"I promise, Mr. Crenshaw."

His dad peered into her face. Slowly, the terror eased from his eyes.

"Call me Ike, short for Isaac." His father

picked up the brush. "Come here, boy. Let's see what we can do to get you back to the handsome fellow I suspect you are." His dad went to work smoothing the tangles from Rascal's coat.

Getting to her feet, Gemma moved to Nate. He crammed his hands into his coat pockets. "What do we do now?"

"We let Rascal do his job to calm your father." She turned her head toward the kitchen. "Corn chips was the quickest, if not most nutritious, snack I could find for your little guys. Why don't you get supper going while I keep an eye on your dad?"

He hunched his shoulders. "Are you sure?"

"Food would do all of us a world of good." She gave his arm a small push. "And your boys need you right now more than your father."

With his dad momentarily appeased, he joined his sons in the kitchen. He put together the most comforting, quick meal he could remember—a variation of his mother's tomato soup and grilled cheese sandwiches with thick slices of Virginia ham.

While he stirred the pot on the stove, it did not escape his notice Kody plastered himself to his side. Connor, too, attached himself like an unshakeable shadow to his every move. It had been a scary afternoon for them.

He hadn't seen them so clingy since those early weeks after Deanna died. Taking a cue from Gemma, he put the boys to work setting the kitchen table. He said a quick grace over their meal, and thanked God for bringing them home safely.

Connor picked up his sandwich. "Aren't you going to eat, Daddy?"

"You two go ahead." At the stove, he ladled soup into bowls. "I'll eat with Miss Gemma and Granddad." He placed a bowl in front of each boy.

Gemma returned to the kitchen. "That smells delicious. I think your father is ready to eat, though maybe just the soup."

He spooned a small amount into another bowl and placed it on a serving tray. He carried the tray for her. "Is Dad bonding with Rascal?" He lowered his voice. "Or is it too late? Have we already lost Dad?"

"Take a look for yourself." She took the tray from him. "Your father is a long way from lost."

His pulse pounding, he ventured into the living room. Rascal's head lay in his dad's lap. His father crooned to the collie in the baby talk people employed with animals and children. His liver-spotted hand rhythmically combed through the fur of Rascal's coat.

Both dog and man looked utterly content. His dad appeared as peaceful as he'd seen him in months.

Smiling, his father looked up. "Have you met my new friend, Rascal?" The confusion had cleared from his gaze. "Rascal's coming to live with us. Isn't that great news?"

Tears misted Nate's eyes. "The best news, Dad."

His father sniffed the air appreciably. "Is that your mother's tomato soup I smell?" He grinned at Nate. "It's not as spectacular as hers, but your version is good, too. I can't believe how hungry I am. Must have been a busy day on the ranch. What did we do today, son?"

How many more chances would he get to hear his father call him "son"?

Emotion welling in his heart, he shot a look at Gemma. "We mended fences, Dad." In more ways than one.

His father wasn't lost to them. *Thank You, God.* His dad was back. At least for now. And for now, it was enough. More than enough.

Nate's relief was so great, it nearly brought him to his knees. "Thank you, Gemma," he rasped.

She set the serving tray on a folding table next to the recliner. "Thank Rascal. He's the real hero." She stroked the collie's head.

Rascal removed himself from the older man's lap, but didn't drift far. He settled into a furry heap on top of his father's feet.

His dad chuckled. "Such a rascally pup."

She moved the tray table within easy reach of his father. "Let's leave your dad to his supper. After dinner, I promised he could feed Rascal, and we'd unpack his toys."

A lump settled in Nate's throat. "Does this mean you're staying?"

"Of course. Like Juliet told you over the phone. PawPals provides a training camp for clients."

"I don't know how we would've gotten through this afternoon without you."

"By the end of two weeks, it'll seem like Rascal has always been a part of your family. He'll aid your father in keeping his independence for as long as possible."

"Two weeks?" Suddenly, that seemed far too short a time. "After that, what will you do?"

She gave him the most curious of looks.

"I'll train another neuro-service dog for the next family."

Of course. What else would she do? Their lives would go in separate directions.

He tried not to dwell on how lost he'd feel after she left Truelove.

# CHAPTER THREE

THAT NIGHT, GEMMA was awakened by the sound of a faint, tiny beeping. Concerned, she grabbed her robe and headed out of the guest bedroom next to Ike's. At the end of the hallway lit only by the single bulb of a solitary night-light, in a T-shirt and pajama bottoms, Nathan gazed into the darkened kitchen. Moonlight cast a silvery glow through the window over the sink.

She laid her hand on his shoulder blade so as not to startle him. "Is everything all right? What's going on?"

Bare arms crossed, he leaned against the door frame. "Dad wanders at night. I installed an alarm to go off if his bedroom door opened," he whispered. "I'm sorry it woke you up."

"That's why I'm here," she whispered back. "To help you work through real-life scenarios with Rascal."

Gemma peered over his shoulder. The collie had inserted his body between Ike and the outside door. Making soft, wuffling noises, Rascal nudged Ike's pajama leg with his head.

She smiled. "Looks like Rascal has got the situation under control."

Nathan sighed. "Should I guide Dad back to bed?"

She shook her head. "Let's not intervene. This is one of Rascal's primary jobs—to ensure Ike doesn't wander outside unaccompanied. Let Rascal redirect him." She put her finger to her lips.

Whining, Rascal butted his head gently against the older gentleman until Ike appeared to rouse as if from a stupor.

Bending, Ike rubbed Rascal's head. "Are you thirsty?"

Finding Rascal's bowl, the older man carried it to the sink and filled it with water. Setting it in place beside the kitchen island, he returned to the sink and removed a glass from the cabinet. "I'm a mite thirsty, too, Rascal, my boy."

Ike took a long swig of water and placed it in the sink. He wiped his hand across his mouth. "I'm ready for bed. How about you?"

Rascal gave him a quiet woof.

With the dog by his side, Ike headed toward the hall. Gemma pulled Nathan through the open door of the bathroom. As the older man passed them, Rascal turned his head toward her. She gave the dog a small thumbs-up—the non-verbal equivalent of "good boy."

Seconds later, there was the soft snick of Ike's bedroom door closing.

"Your father will probably sleep through the rest of the night, but if not, Rascal will be there to make sure he's okay. When is the last time you had a full night's sleep?"

Nathan threw her a sheepish look. "I look that bad, huh?" He dragged his hand through his already mussed hair.

Her heart did an uptick. Nathan Crenshaw looked the opposite of bad. His bare feet poking out from his pajamas, he looked impossibly handsome.

Before the idea could take root, she squashed it.

Pulling the cords of her robe tighter, she gathered her professionalism around her like a shield. "With sundowner syndrome, it's as if the patient is in a fevered delirium from which they must be awakened. You'll find Rascal a vigilant protector of your father, keeping him safe from himself."

They moved into the hallway.

Nathan scrubbed his hand over his five-o'clock shadow. "I don't function too well when I'm sleep-deprived. Today was a perfect example of how there's never enough of me to go around—the downed fence, forgetting the appointment with you, then what happened with Dad and the boys."

The night-light shone upon his features. Exhaustion etched itself across the lines of his face.

"What happened at school wasn't your fault. You don't give yourself enough credit." Without conscious thought, she took a step closer. "You've done everything right by your dad to ensure he's happy and safe. Installing the electronic devices... Getting him a service dog."

He looked at the closed door of his father's bedroom. "I haven't coped as well as I should. It's been overwhelming at times. The never-ending responsibility for his welfare and for the boys." His voice thickened. "I've felt so alone."

"Not anymore." She shook her head. "You have Rascal on your team now."

"And you," he rasped.

Her gaze locked onto his.

Pinpricks of awareness danced down her spine. "For two weeks…"

His gaze never left hers. "Then you'll return to Greensboro and Mr. Spencer?"

There was something unfathomable in his eyes. She felt on the cusp of throwing herself headlong into the liquid blue fire of their depths.

She pursed her lips. "There is no Mr. Spencer."

His eyebrow cocked. "Divorced, or widowed like me?"

"Neither."

He waited, as if willing her to explain. Not something she had any intention of doing. Not if she wanted to preserve his image of the Gemma she used to be. The Gemma he used to love.

After a long moment of silence, thick with unasked questions, he nodded. "I see."

But he didn't. He couldn't. Even after all these years, she only half understood it herself. There was a handful of people, including her longtime friend Juliet, who knew what happened the day she returned from summer camp that long-ago August.

A story she never intended Nathan to know. It was the reason she'd ended their relationship. She had borne so much, but the one thing she couldn't bear would be to see her shame reflected in Nathan Crenshaw's dark blue eyes. Anything but that.

"Just to be clear..." Something in his face shifted. "You're not married."

It seemed of such monumental importance to him. As if the fate of the world rested on her answer. Something raw, powerful and vulnerable rose palpably between them.

Her heart drummed in her chest.

"No," she said at last, conceding the point. "I am not, nor have I ever been married."

Clutching at the tatters of her self-respect, she spun on her heel and fled to the relative safety of the guest room. Gasping for breath as if she'd run a marathon instead of a short sprint down the hallway, she leaned against the closed door, her palms pressed flat against the panels.

She heard the muted slap of his feet as he retreated to the back of the house and the master bedroom.

Gemma struggled to capture her careening thoughts. But as her breathing gradually slowed, she wondered if what just happened was a hurdle that needed to be crossed between them. So she could finish the job she'd come to do.

She'd known when Juliet first showed her

Nathan's application for a dementia assistance dog, the unresolved situation between them was likely to be fraught with dangerous undercurrents.

Yet she was good at what she did. The dogs she'd trained over the years provided such life-changing services. She'd been unable to walk away from helping his family.

Lying on the bed unable to sleep, she went over the events of the tumultuous day.

She was pleased Rascal's training had paid off. Pleased for Rascal and Ike. Pleased for Nathan, too. It was obvious the burdens he carried were crushing him.

After eighteen months of scent-training Rascal to bond with Ike, she'd believed she was ready to walk back into Nathan's life, albeit temporarily.

Now after her visceral reaction to him and the fool she'd made of herself in running away from him, she pondered if fifteen years had been enough to get over her first and only love, Nathan Crenshaw.

*Would thirty—or a lifetime—have been enough?*

She stared at the ceiling above the bed. "Two weeks, Lord."

It wasn't so much a statement as a plea for help.

THE NEXT MORNING, she let Rascal out of Ike's bedroom. The collie padded down the hall with her. In the kitchen, she found Nathan dressed for his day on the farm in jeans, his stocking feet and a long flannel shirt worn over a gray Henley.

She spied a pair of work boots by the door. He'd already been hard at work with morning chores and returned to the house. She supposed a rancher had to be an early riser. So did a dog trainer.

According to the schedule Nathan shared with her yesterday, Ike wouldn't be awake for another hour or two. Ike's midnight wanderings must have been playing havoc with Nathan's stamina.

Despite the late night, he looked far too handsome for her good. He poured water into a coffeemaker. "Gemma." His voice had an early-morning gravelly quality to it.

A sudden awkwardness sprang between them. "Nathan."

Opening the kitchen door, she let Rascal out to do his morning business. It was one of the items on her training list for Nathan to take over after she left. She reminded herself rather forcibly that she would be leaving.

Standing on the wraparound porch with its

amazing three-sixty views of the mountains, the large red barn and various outbuildings, she wrapped her arms around the heather-purple sweater she'd donned. Rascal headed toward a bush.

High Country Ranch felt like such a happy, wondrous place, where nothing bad could ever affect the people who called it home. That couldn't be true, or else Rascal's services would never have been needed. Yet the feeling persisted.

With Rascal by her side, she ventured inside the farmhouse again. Minutes later, any lingering tension was broken when Connor and Kody, like two cowboy tornadoes, rushed into the kitchen.

Heading straight for her, Kody wound his arms around her waist. "Mornin', Miss Gemma."

Surprised and touched, she hugged him back. He smelled like soap and toothpaste. Just like a little boy should. Not that she'd ever had much to do with children. Unlike Juliet. Over the last few years, her dearest friend had managed to acquire a stepdaughter and a baby son of her own.

Hands crammed in his jean pockets—so like his lanky father—Connor cleared his throat. "We love having you and Rascal here, Miss Gemma."

Nathan's oldest son wasn't as exuberant a personality as his brother, but she felt the sincerity of his affection. Yet the look of anxiety on his face concerned her. A niggling spur of worry for Nathan's eldest lodged itself in her heart.

As usual, Rascal sensed the one who needed him the most. It was to Connor he went first, not Kody. The collie pushed his head under the little boy's hand. A shy smile broke across Connor's face.

For a second, the anxiety receded in his eyes. She wanted Connor to laugh and play like other little boys. She decided to make it one of Rascal's jobs to banish the concern from the child's face.

Of course, she wouldn't see it happen because she was only here two weeks. Her insides did a nosedive. Usually, she was more than ready to move on to the next dog and the next family.

"Coffee?"

Her eyes flicked to Nathan. He held a mug out to her. Something as delicate as a butterfly's wings flitted inside her chest.

The blood pounded in her ears. "Thanks," she managed to gasp. Taking the cup, she took an appreciative sip of the aromatic brew in an effort to regulate her heartbeat.

He returned to the stove. "How do you like your eggs?" His brow creased. "You like eggs for breakfast, don't you?"

Despite the charged, intense summer they'd once spent together, she realized they actually knew little of the practical things about each other. Nor anything at all about the adults they'd become.

"Gemma?" Spatula in hand, he angled toward her. "Eggs?"

"Eggs are great." She hid her face in the mug. "Any way is fine."

Kody set the table. Connor inserted bread into a toaster.

She put down the mug on the counter. "What can I do to help?" It wasn't in her nature to be idle.

Watching the eggs sizzle in the skillet, Nathan had his back to her. "I wouldn't be too quick to offer. I might put you to work shoveling cow stalls."

She heard the grin in his voice.

"As a dog trainer, I'm not afraid of hard work or a little poo."

Kody held his nose. "Too much poop, Miss Gemma."

"Thanks for the warning." She laughed. "I

like all animals, although I don't know much about cattle."

"If you like, I could give you a proper tour of the ranch later."

Her eyes flitted to Nathan's and held. "I... I'd like that."

The bread popped up out of the toaster. They jerked. He turned to stir the eggs. Covering her confusion, she picked up her cup again, warming her hands around the mug.

Kody slathered butter on the slices and then cut the bread into triangles with a butter knife. Connor poured milk into glasses. The Crenshaw men were a well-oiled, breakfast-making machine.

Connor held out a chair for her. "Miss Gemma."

So well-mannered. Like every other properly reared Southern child, the "Miss" was an honorary title of respect bestowed on any elder lady. No matter if the "Miss" was elderly or not.

Due to their mother's early influence? With their short, dark hair and blue eyes, both boys were incredibly like Nate. Not that she'd ever ask, but she couldn't help wondering what had happened to their mother.

"Miss Gemma?" the little boy prompted.

Woolgathering again. The High Country

Ranch and the Crenshaw men in the plural were having a completely deleterious effect on her concentration.

Since she wasn't going to be allowed to help, she sat down. "You have quite the team, Nathan."

He placed a heaping platter of scrambled eggs in the middle of the table. "They're good boys."

They were incredibly sweet boys.

Everyone sat down. The boys bowed their heads. Nathan said grace.

Between bites of eggs and toast, she tried to get to know the boys better. She asked the usual questions about their teachers, who were their best friends and what they liked the most about school.

As she watched the loving interaction between Nathan and his sons, a strange longing tugged at her heartstrings. Sitting at the table, sharing their lives with each other, it was the kind of family she always wished had been hers.

If her world hadn't fractured that long-ago August and she hadn't ended things with Nathan, a family like this might have become hers.

Connor and Kody would never fully comprehend how blessed they were to have a man like Nathan as their dad. A man the exact opposite of her own father. Remembered shame burned her cheeks. She kept her head over her plate.

No child of hers would ever endure a childhood like she'd endured. Because she would never put herself in the same situation as her mother. Her eyes strayed to Nathan. No matter how handsome or winsome the cowboy rancher.

*Best to keep a professional aloofness.* After two weeks, she'd never see any of the Crenshaws again. Which, given her conflicted feelings for Nathan, was just as well. Yet somehow the idea of not seeing any of them again failed to cheer her as she'd hoped it might.

At the end of the meal, she insisted on cleaning up the dishes. With his nose, Rascal pushed a small red ball across the linoleum to Connor's chair.

The boy looked at her.

Scraping plates, she smiled at him. "Until your granddad gets up, Rascal would love to play with you."

"Yay!" Kody fist-pumped the air.

Connor's blue eyes flickered. "We need to make our lunches, Kode. So Daddy doesn't have to, remember?"

The kindergartener's face fell. "I forgot."

She handed Nathan the plates. "Let me make the lunches."

Frowning, Nathan stacked the plates in the dishwasher. "Gemma…"

"No, really." She held up her hand. "I want to."

And she did. Truly. More than was sensible. But suddenly, she didn't care. Not if it brought happiness to Nathan's little guys.

She tilted her head and looked at him. "Please?"

He gave her a bemused smile. "I never could refuse you anything when you turned those big, puppy-dog brown eyes on me."

Gemma's heart skipped a beat.

He ruffled Connor's hair. "Go ahead, son. Have fun with Rascal."

Kody did a silly sort of happy dance.

"Thank you, Daddy." Connor included her in the ecstatic smile he threw his father. "Miss Gemma."

His tail wagging like a flag in a stiff breeze on the Fourth of July, Rascal appeared to know playtime was on the horizon. To Connor's and Kody's delight, he covered their faces with doggy slobber. They chortled.

She opened the fridge and examined the contents. "Turkey, cheese, lettuce and mayo work for you guys today?"

Kody grabbed the red ball. "Yes, ma'am. Please."

Her heart warmed. They'd done their Southern mama proud. Good boys. Such good, sweet, dear boys.

Nathan pulled two insulated lunch boxes off a shelf in the pantry.

"Guys, roll the ball along the floor and Rascal will retrieve it." She spread mayonnaise on slices of bread. "He loves nothing better than playing fetch." She glanced at their father.

Leaning against the countertop sipping his coffee, Nathan was quiet, quieter than the pay-for-every-word boy she recalled. A slight smile curved his lips as he watched the boys play with the collie.

She felt his eyes drift in her direction. A curiosity about her gleamed in his dark blue gaze. A curiosity she didn't intend to satisfy.

Outside, a green Subaru drove up. A horn tooted. The boys grabbed their backpacks off the back of their chairs. There was a sudden stampede for jackets. An onslaught of frantic hugs for Rascal and their dad.

Stepping onto the porch, she handed them

their lunch boxes, which resulted in equally fervent, if unexpected, hugs for her, too.

Calling goodbye, the boys dashed toward the vehicle. A window scrolled down. Maggie stuck out her hand and waved. Gemma made out the silhouettes of two other little boys in the back seat. As befitted his position as eldest cousin, Connor got to ride shotgun in the front.

Then, doors closed, seat belts secured, Maggie steered the car back the way she'd come.

As the red taillights of the Subaru disappeared in the early-morning mist, Gemma stared after them, a trifle gobsmacked.

She sensed rather than saw Nathan at her elbow. She possessed a weird sort of radar whenever he moved into close proximity.

Gemma shook her head. "How does Ike manage to sleep through this ruckus every morning?"

Nathan chuckled. "Connor and Kody are a lot." But the fatherly pride in his voice was unmistakable.

"They're wonderful," she whispered.

"Yeah, they are." He smiled. "We've got time before Dad stirs. How about that ranch tour?"

She really ought to get to work—the sooner

she did her job, the sooner she could return to PawPals. But when he looked at her like that…

For once, she decided aloofness might be overrated.

# CHAPTER FOUR

ON THE PORCH, Nate wished almost immediately he hadn't offered to show her around the farm.

Earlier, she'd indicated interest. He flushed. Interest in the High Country Ranch. Not in him, of course. Which was exactly as it should be.

His resentment at how she'd dumped him fifteen years ago—even now with no explanation—rankled.

She'd been so good with the boys this morning, for a second he forgot how clear she'd been about maintaining professional boundaries. A reminder he'd do well to heed. How had he already managed to overstep?

He had neither the time, energy or inclination for anything beyond his responsibilities to his sons, his father and the ranch.

Just as he was working his way to a clumsy retraction—

"Let me grab a jacket…" She gave him a faint smile. "I'll leave Rascal to watch over Ike in case he awakens while we're gone." The hinges squeaking, she eased through the door.

Hunching his shoulders, he stuffed his hands into his jean pockets. Hinges creaking, she closed the door softly behind her and joined him on the porch.

She held out his coat. "You might need this."

Blinking, he took his coat from her. "Thanks."

She rubbed her hands together. "It's colder here than Greensboro."

"We're at a higher elevation." He slipped into his coat. "The mountain peaks will get the first dusting of snow soon, but it will be several weeks for those of us in the valley."

She studied the mountain range in the distance. "I won't be here to see it."

He felt the gentle, altogether necessary, admonishment like a kick in the gut.

*Stick to business, Crenshaw. She wants to see the ranch, not reconnect on a personal level.* Jerking his mind from golden blond hair and silk ribbons, he set his jaw and moved down the steps.

"How many cattle do you have?"

Nate led her toward the livestock buildings.

"We have over a hundred and fifty cows on our four hundred acres."

"Wow." She took in the acreage as he pointed out the hay storage sheds, water tanks, feeding facilities and calving barn.

Beyond the small pond, he drew her closer to one of the grazing pastures. At the fence line, he opened the gate, stepped into the paddock and beckoned her.

She gave the herd of cattle a hesitant look.

"It's okay. The cows are used to people. Hand raised, they are my first and last stop every day."

She ventured into the pasture, and he shut the gate behind her. Taking a few steps, he held out his hand and gave a low whistle. One of the cows disengaged from the herd and ambled over to them.

He grinned at the expression on her face. "The cattle are trained to follow us so we're able to move them from pasture to pasture every day or two without stressing them with chasing or herding." He rested the flat of his hand on the cow's broad black shoulder. "Go ahead and touch her if you want."

Biting her bottom lip, Gemma laid her hand on the cow. A smile teased at the edges of her lips. The breeze ruffled wisps of her hair.

For a second, time went sideways. He'd come home at the end of that summer imagining her eventually joining him on the farm. Surrounded by these mountains. Raising cattle and a family. By his side. And now, here she was.

His heart clenched painfully in his chest. It hadn't been Gemma who joined him on the ranch. It had been Deanna with whom he'd made a life. A pang of unanticipated grief assailed him. Followed by a wave of guilt.

"What kind of cattle do you raise?"

Startled out of his painful reverie, he dragged his attention to the present.

"It's a mixed-breed operation. Red and Black Angus. Hereford. And Charolais."

Shading her hand over her eyes, she peered out over the hilly terrain and the distant fallow fields. "I didn't realize cattle ranching involved farming the land, too."

"We take pasture-to-plate seriously. Our cattle are pasture fed year-round. Raised on high-energy, high-protein sweetgrasses. No feedlots. Hormone free. Antibiotic free."

He moved among the herd, doing his daily check to make sure each one was in optimal condition. She strolled after him.

"We grow our own forage. Last month, we

harvested the last crop. This time of year, they feed on rye grass, crimson and red clover."

"This is quite the operation." She smiled at him. His chest squeezed. "I'm impressed."

"High Country Ranch is a fifth-generation farm. It's about sustainability and good stewardship." He gazed toward the mountain vista. "I'm always mindful of our impact on the land. I want to be able to pass on to Connor, Kody and future generations the option to farm like my father passed on to me."

"You enjoy working the land, don't you?"

He looked at her. "I do." He laughed. "When I was in high school, I couldn't wait to get out of Truelove and experience real—" he made quote marks in the air with his fingers "—life."

"You've made a good life for yourself here." She made a sweeping motion. "This is the realest, the best, life can offer."

A good life. Exactly what he and Deanna had carved out here when they took over primary responsibility for the farm. Although without Deanna, it also had become a lonely one.

Nate cut his eyes at Gemma. She had her dogs and her work. Was it enough for her? Did she ever feel lonely, too?

He'd never needed to wonder about his wife's

feelings on any subject matter. They'd been high school sweethearts. A former cheerleader, Deanna had been openhearted, bubbly and animated. He'd never had to doubt where he stood with her.

Yet the spring of his junior year, he'd been restless and dissatisfied with what he perceived as the boring sameness of small-town life. Heading off to work as a camp counselor that summer, he'd broken up with Deanna. Ironic. He'd done to her what Gemma would later do to him.

Gemma was quieter than Deanna had been. The lovely dog trainer wasn't one to broadcast her emotions.

As the sun climbed higher on the horizon, she put her hand over her brow to shade her eyes. "What changed your mind about farming?"

She had.

But they no longer knew each other well enough for that conversation. In light of her subsequent rejection, he doubted he'd ever known Gemma as well as he believed.

That summer changed his life forever. He'd loved her so blindly and devotedly. He was old enough now to recognize there had been moments when he'd sensed she kept parts of herself hidden.

He flicked a glance in her direction. Perhaps the mystery had been a large part of his attraction. Until her secrets drove them apart for good.

After the breakup, he'd thrown himself into the backbreaking work of the ranch. Initially he was hurt beyond belief, but anger at Gemma's treatment of him soon followed. True to her forgiving nature, Deanna had been quick to console him. Her utter devotion had gone a long way toward soothing his pride and filling the hole in his heart. A few months later, he and Deanna got together again.

Gemma blew out a breath. "You don't work the ranch by yourself, do you?"

He squinched his eyes against the glow of the sun. "Dad used to help."

She tilted her head. "It seems a lot for just you and your dad."

It hadn't always been only him and his dad. There'd been Deanna, too.

"Every year, the boys are able to help more." He scrubbed his hand over his face. "I can handle everything else."

Forehead puckering, she gave the red-and-white Hereford steer a final pat. "We should probably check on Rascal and your dad."

Opening the gate, he allowed her to precede him before latching it behind them.

Rounding the corner of the house, she paused beside the small, fenced-off garden area. "What vegetables do you grow?"

"Not vegetables." His jaw tightened. "Deanna liked flowers."

After her death, one by one the flowers she'd loved had faded and wilted from neglect.

Sometimes in the wee hours of the night when he couldn't sleep, he regretted how often he'd taken her for granted. Unable to bear the reminders of her absence, he'd plowed the little garden under. Although for some reason, he hadn't yet dismantled the deer fence around it.

"Your wife's name was Deanna?" Gemma gave him a gentle smile. "A lovely name."

"She was a lovely person," he rasped.

He couldn't bring himself to talk to Gemma about his late wife. It felt too much like a betrayal.

HER FACE FELL as she got a nice view of his back. Message received loud and clear. He didn't want to talk about his wife. He must have loved Deanna so much if he couldn't bring himself to speak of her.

What must it be like to have been loved like that? Not something she'd ever experienced. Her stomach clenched. Not something she would ever experience if the current state of her life—PawPals and her beloved dogs—was any indication of what her future held.

Head down, she trailed after him. Inside the kitchen, he toed out of his heavy-duty work boots. Following his example, she slipped out of her low-ankle muck boots.

Nathan busied himself at the sink. "Dad must still be asleep."

She shrugged out of her coat. "The late night is catching up with Ike."

His broad, muscled shoulders slumped. "With us all." He hadn't bothered to remove his jacket.

She gripped the back of one of the chairs. "If you've work to do, I'll stay here until your father gets up."

He did an about-face, pressing against the countertop. "I've always got work to do, but I should be here in case he wakes up disoriented."

Maybe the ranch wasn't financially secure. Perhaps there was no money to hire someone to help him. It was none of her business.

His lips thinned. "Is there stuff we should be going over while we're stuck—I mean, waiting?"

Stuck with her. Gone was the comfortable camaraderie they'd shared in the pasture. All traces of the easygoing, sweet boy she'd known were gone. Vanished once the conversation had drifted to…his wife?

Or was the stiffness between them about something else?

Her heart slammed against her rib cage. "About what happened last night…"

Nathan stiffened. "Rascal made a real difference for my dad. Won't be long before you can return to your own life."

Leaving him to his? She flushed. *Right back at you, Nathan Crenshaw.*

Irritation burned at her stomach. To him, she was nothing more than an unwelcome intrusion. Another item to be checked off on his to-do list.

*Two weeks*… She'd likely never see the Crenshaws, father, son and grandsons, ever again. He didn't want her gone any more than she wanted to be gone. But until that time—

"Maybe now would be a good time to go over prepping your dad's medication each morning." She squared her shoulders. "That will need to be done before you head out at the crack of dawn to begin your never-ending chores."

He gave her a look that could have scorched milk. "Fine." He yanked out the chair across the table and threw himself into it.

Glaring back at him, she pulled out a chair and plopped down.

Clearly, he wasn't the same boy she remembered. Which was all well and good because she wasn't the same naive, mooned-eyed innocent she used to be, either.

She had a job to do. Her only concern must remain fixed on Ike and on Rascal's ability to help him.

"I think it would be wise to update Ike's doctor on yesterday's events." She laid her palms flat upon the surface of the table. Proud that her hands didn't shake. Nor her voice wobble. "His prescription may need adjusting."

Nathan gave her a curt nod. "I'll make the appointment. It'd be great if you could go with us to the appointment to clarify the role Rascal will have in my father's treatment plan. Not sure if the doc will have an opening this week, though." His eyes darkened to indigo, the color of the sky before a coming storm. "But I know how difficult you find commitment."

Was his chip-on-the-shoulder attitude about their history with each other? About that summer—their summer? He'd moved on. She had, too.

Hadn't they?

Juliet had warned her. This had been a mistake. A bad idea for Gemma to take on this case. Yet she was here now. There was no one else. What was done was done.

She darted a glance at the set, closed expression on his face. Done in more ways than merely the present.

Gemma took a deep breath. "If I'm unable to be here for the appointment, maybe the doctor and I could teleconference."

A muscle throbbed in his cheek.

"The program will not succeed if we don't work as a team. If that isn't something *you* can commit to, tell me now."

Their gazes locked. And held for a long, long moment. She didn't dare breathe or break eye contact. She mustn't back down. For Ike's sake, this was too important.

Plowing his hand through his hair, Nathan was the first to look away. "I apologize. I'll do everything in my power to make this work for my dad." His gaze returned to hers. "This won't be a problem again."

This—the energy between them last night? The amiable companionship this morning?

"I apologize, too."

Gemma had learned the hard way it was better to know where she stood with people. She'd been forced to grow up rapidly in the space of one horrific day. With Nathan, now she knew. Boundary lines had been drawn. She would respect them.

Scraping her chair across the linoleum, she retrieved Ike's medicine bottles and went over what he needed to do to help Rascal do his job. She also hammered out what the rest of Ike's day should look like.

True to his word, nothing further was said of the electrifying moment between them last night. For which she was grateful.

Later that morning, he was able to secure an appointment with Ike's doctor, who specialized in neurodegenerative disorders, for the following Monday.

Over the next few days, she worked with Rascal to be of most service to Ike. By unspoken mutual agreement, she and Nathan kept their distance. A painful politeness.

When forced to interact on Ike's behalf or at dinner with the boys, they remained cordial. Otherwise, the farm was a big place. It wasn't hard to avoid each other.

Each morning, Rascal acted as Ike's canine alarm clock, urging him out of bed. At the sound of an electronic timer, Rascal brought a bag of medicine to Ike, which included a note reminding him to take the pills with a glass of water.

Thankfully, Ike was still ambulatory and took care of his own hygiene needs. Yet she trained Rascal to wait for Ike outside the shower and taught him how to trigger a specially installed alarm should the older gentleman experience a problem.

Most of all, Rascal provided a constant source of encouragement and companionship that was truly making a difference in Ike's slowly returning self-confidence. Putting a larger harness on Rascal to aid Ike's balance over the rough terrain of the ranch, she instituted midafternoon walks around the pastures. The exercise was good for Ike's mental and physical well-being. The timing of the walk served to tire him out enough so that sleep came more readily at bedtime.

Sometimes she caught sight of Nathan near the grazing herd or by one of the barns. He'd assured her winter was his slower time on the ranch, yet out of necessity he was out on the farm most of the day. If she hadn't been at the farmhouse, Ike would have been left on his own.

Rascal was trained to respond to a caregiver's commands, but between the demands of the ranch and his children, Nathan wasn't always available to direct Rascal or perform the tasks only a human could do.

Ike's illness had reached the stage where the lack of a full-time caregiver was a growing concern to her. Ike's doctor should be aware of how much time he spent on his own, but she wanted to address her misgivings with Nathan first.

He would accuse her of interfering. He'd be angry, but Ike's safety was paramount. Her apprehension wasn't only for his father. Nathan's long-term well-being was at stake, too.

Illnesses like Ike's often took the greatest toll on their caregivers. And if something happened to Nathan, what would become of his motherless sons?

Living with a loved one's dementia meant

endless hard conversations between everyone concerned. But the coming confrontation threatened to sever her tenuous truce with Nathan.

IKE EXPERIENCED ONLY one other episode that first week. The structure of the daily routine she'd implemented was working.

The outdoor air and the healing benefits of nature countered some of the sundowner syndrome triggers. As soon as Rascal sensed an oncoming bout of agitation, the dog refocused Ike's attention by bringing him the brush. It helped Ike to have something to occupy his hands. Gemma hoped to have hit on a strategy to avert another crisis like the one to which she'd arrived.

Ike responded well to the new routine. She posted Ike's schedule on the refrigerator and went over the details with his family.

Each afternoon when Maggie brought Connor and Kody home, she enjoyed hearing about their day at school. It hadn't taken long for the boys to make a special place for themselves within her heart.

Those first few days she'd stuck close to Ike in case she was needed. But later in the week, she let Rascal get on with his job, and she spent more time outside.

While Ike took his afternoon nap, she wandered around the farm. While they did their chores after school, Connor and Kody liked to show her around. She didn't mind in the slightest.

Kody had joined the local 4-H chapter only recently. In one of the outbuildings, he introduced her to his two rabbits. He was raising the fluffy white rabbits with black ears to show at the county fair next spring.

"I helped Daddy build the wabbit hutch." Kody's chest puffed with pride. "'Cause in 4-H you learn by doing."

"And you did a terrific job." Admiring his handiwork on the raised plywood hutch, she smiled at the little boy. "It's a rabbit palace for bunnies."

Kody grinned. "It's my job to feed them and make sure they have enough water." He pointed to the larger rabbit, nibbling on a piece of timothy hay. "That's Sir Hops-a-Lot."

She laughed. "What's the other one's name?"

"Harriet. *H-a…*" He looked at Connor.

Connor's lips quirked. *"H-a-r-e."*

"A hare is like saying, 'wabbit.' Did you know that, Miss Gemma?"

"I did know that, Kody."

Chortling at his own joke, he slapped his hand on his knee. "Aren't I funny, Miss Gemma?"

She tapped the end of his nose. "The funniest five-year-old I know."

"It was Granddad who thought of those names, Kode." Connor dropped his gaze. "Before he got so sick."

Kody's shoulders drooped. "I miss the stuff we used to do with him."

Connor sighed. "Grandad took us to our 4-H meeting every week."

Kody's bottom lip wobbled. "Granddad was helping me keep a wecord of Hops-a-Lot and Hare-i-et's progress for the fair 'cause I can't write yet."

Connor squeezed his brother's shoulder. "I told you I'd help you. It'll be okay, bud. No need for you to worry."

Her eyes misted. They were such good brothers to each other.

"I miss him," Connor whispered. "The way he used to be."

A single, solitary tear rolled down Kody's cheek. "When he gets confused, it's makes me afwaid."

She wrestled with what to say to them. With how to comfort them.

"Your grandad's disease *is* confusing. For grown-ups, too. And scary."

Crouching, she put an arm around both boys and hugged them. "But no matter what, I know your granddad loves you so much."

Kody burrowed into her. "Granddad is going to die, isn't he, Miss Gemma? Just like our mom."

Her heart clenched.

Connor frowned. "Don't talk about stuff like that, Kode. It's too sad."

She shook her head. "It's okay to feel sad about what your grandfather is going through, guys. If you're feeling scared or sad, it helps to talk about it."

Connor's brow furrowed. "How do you know?"

She swallowed. "Something scary happened to me when I was younger. I didn't tell anyone how confused and afraid and angry I was."

The boys looked at her.

She took a deep breath. "I believed I was being brave by never crying or talking about it, but now I think it would've been better if I had. I would've felt better sooner."

Connor nodded slowly, and she could tell he was thinking through what she had said. Very much like how his father processed everything.

Kody rested his head against her shoulder. "I like talking with you, Miss Gemma."

Her lips brushed against his forehead. "I like talking to you, too, Kody."

Connor leaned into her side. "Rascal is helping Granddad feel better."

She gave him a bright smile. "I'm praying with Rascal's help, you will make many more happy memories together."

Kody straightened. "Would you like to hold Sir Hops-a-Lot while I clean his cage? He's really soft."

She smiled at Kody. "Until I go check on Rascal and your granddad, I'd love to hold Sir Hops-a-Lot."

Gemma took a seat on a nearby bale of straw. At a sudden creak, she looked over her shoulder at the shadows near the door. There was no one there. Probably just the wind.

Opening the hutch, Kody extricated the rabbit and gently deposited his pet into her lap. He handed off Hare-i-et to Connor, who sank down beside her.

She ran her fingers through the silky coat of the bunny's fur.

Kody got busy cleaning out the hutch. "Sir Hops-a-Lot is a buck." Going into professor mode, he wagged his finger at her. "That's a boy wabbit. Hare-i-et is a doe, a girl wabbit."

"You are a bunny expert, Kody."

Connor groaned. "Don't encourage him."

She laughed. "I don't mind."

Connor brushed the tip of his finger along the rabbit's head. "My ultimate goal is to some-day raise alpacas."

Alpacas? She smothered a grin.

"But until then, Daddy says the next calf born will be my 4-H project." He jutted his chin. "I can show calves next year because I'll be eight."

"Absolutely."

Connor gave her a rare smile. "I'm so happy you came to help Granddad, Miss Gemma."

Her eyes misted. "Me, too."

Despite the awkwardness between her and their father, she wouldn't have missed getting to know his sons for the world.

As for Nathan?

She buried her face in the soft fluff of Sir Hops-a-Lot.

Gemma learned a long time ago it was less painful to not dwell on what couldn't be changed. Like once-upon-a-time-dreams that could never come true.

# CHAPTER FIVE

NATE HADN'T MEANT to eavesdrop.

He'd gone in search of the boys and heard their voices in the barn with the rabbit hutch. He'd been about to step out of the shadows when he caught wind of their conversation with Gemma.

It killed him to hear the sadness and confusion in their little voices. He'd tried so hard to make sure they didn't suffer the lack of anything during his dad's illness and after their mother's death.

One more thing at which he'd fallen short. When the discussion took a lighter turn, he decided to beat a hasty retreat. He didn't want her to feel uncomfortable.

When he took a backward step, the floorboard creaked. He froze. Silence fell for a second, but his sons soon picked up the conversation with Gemma again.

Breathing a sigh of relief, he slipped out the door. Trudging to the house, he checked on his dad. At his approach, Rascal lifted his head from a recumbent position outside his father's bedroom. With the situation under control thanks to Rascal, he moved to the porch to wait for his sons.

From her talk with the boys, it appeared she had suffered a traumatizing loss of her own. At the time, he'd assumed she broke things off with him because she'd met someone else.

Nate scrubbed his face with his hand. Had something else happened after they returned from camp that summer? Even after all these years, it pained him to think of her being hurt. Though from what, he had no idea.

He'd always heard a person never quite got over a first love. He wasn't ready to go that far, but if he was being honest, he'd admit his feelings for her weren't as nonexistent as he'd like to believe.

Might there have been extenuating circumstances to explain why she'd broken off their relationship? But then there was the added mystery of why she'd changed her name…

For the first time, the long-simmering anger he'd felt at her treatment of him diminished, leaving in its place compassion for whatever it was she'd gone through. Giving him a different perspective on their mutual past.

At the sound of footfalls, he looked up.

Catching sight of him on the top step, Gemma paused. "Is everything okay with Ike?"

He rose. "Still resting. Rascal's got everything well in paw."

Either not getting his joke, or failing to appreciate the humor, she made as if to move past him. "That's good."

Something pinched in his chest. He hadn't enjoyed the strain between them this week. "Gemma…"

She stopped.

"I accidentally overheard you talking with the boys."

She crossed her arms over her black puffy vest.

He put up his hand. "I wasn't spying on you, but you addressed their concerns so well I hesitated to interrupt. I've said as much to them before, but perhaps they needed reassurance from someone besides me."

She frowned.

"Thank you for talking with them. You knew just what to say. You're great with children."

"You think so?" Dropping her defensive posture, she looked down and then up at him. "I wasn't sure what to say. I merely spoke from my heart."

"Exactly the right thing to do with kids. They can spot phony or insincere a mile off." And because he couldn't resist probing a tad, he continued, "You must have experience with kids."

She shook her head. "I don't. Other than spending time with Juliet and her brood."

*Ah. Never married. No kids.*

"Good instincts then." He smiled. "You'd make them a good mother."

She threw him a startled look.

"I didn't mean Connor or Kody… Um, kids of your own. One day."

*Open mouth, insert boot.*

She blinked at him.

Nate flushed. "I wasn't trying to…imply… presume…"

*Stop talking, just stop talking.*

He was a grown man. Why did Gemma always reduce him to a stammering teenager?

"I didn't think you were—" her gaze went everywhere except to him "—implying anything."

He jammed his hands in his pockets. "Good."

"I don't have kids in my life." Her eyes found his. "I have dogs."

"Right. Of course."

Nate loved a dog as good as the next guy, but he wouldn't trade his sons for anything else in the world. He hoped her life wasn't as lonely as she'd made it sound.

He exhaled. "Okay."

She took a step, but stopped again. "Can I ask you a question?"

"Turnabout is fair play." But he braced. For what he wasn't sure—a question about Deanna or their summer?

"First, let me say I'm amazed at what you do around the ranch." She fluttered her hand in the direction of the pasture. "The boys. Your father."

He sensed a *but* coming. "I'm a jack of all trades. Master of none."

"Would you consider hiring someone to help with your dad?"

"You mean a full-time caregiver?" He started to bow up. "Now that we have Rascal, he's doing fine."

"Just one of the three enormous responsibilities you deal with on a daily basis would overwhelm most people." She ticked off the items on her fingers. "Running a cattle business. Raising two kids. Taking care of an ailing parent. You are stretched so thin. As for the stress... I'm worried about you, Nathan."

He bristled. "That was the whole point in having Rascal—to look after Dad. Are you telling me Rascal isn't up to the task?"

She stiffened. "Dementia assistance dogs are trained to work best under the direction of a care manager."

He narrowed his eyes. "Which would be me."

"But you're not in the house with Ike or Rascal. You're not available most of the day."

He went rigid. "I'm always available whenever he needs me."

"Due to the nature of this illness, your father's judgment about his own abilities will become increasingly impaired. He's going to become dependent on having someone on hand to safeguard him from himself. I don't know your financial situation—"

"No. You don't." He gritted his teeth. "Yet after fifteen years, you think you know me well enough to tell me how bad I'm failing my family?"

"That's not what I meant. No one is blaming you for any of this."

"Your job is to train dogs." He jabbed his finger. "It's my job to take care of my family."

She tossed her braid over her shoulder. "If there's an emergency, the system with Rascal breaks down. When he can't locate you, Rascal can't do his job of safeguarding your dad."

He scowled.

"Caring for a dementia patient takes a tremendous toll on the caregiver's mental and physical health. The impact can be long-term. It's okay to ask for help."

"I've asked for help," he growled. "Maggie has been a godsend in getting the boys to and from school."

She touched his sleeve. "Would you at least consider taking on help around the ranch? It would free you to spend more time with your father and the boys."

He wanted to hold on to his anger, but standing close to her, he felt the sincerity of her concern. He wasn't good about asking for help. No more so than his dad. Pride? A misplaced self-sufficiency?

She wasn't wrong about his boys needing him more. Not wanting to burden him with their fears, they'd reached out to her, a virtual stranger, instead of their father.

He was struck by the kindness and empathy in her eyes. No judgment. Only a desire to help. "I'll… I'll give it some thought."

"I know you'll do the right thing. You always do."

Her smile lit up her face. And places in his heart he'd believed forever numb.

Nate didn't always do the right thing. The right thing would have been to follow up with Gemma. After the Dear John voicemail, he should have checked to make sure she was okay. Especially when she refused to answer his phone calls or letters. She hadn't been okay. After they left camp, something had happened to her.

But he'd been seventeen, insecure and unsure of himself. He let her down. Was he doomed to always fail the people he loved? He'd failed Deanna. Would he fail his father and the boys?

"How about letting me make you guys my world-famous tortellini soup for supper?"

Nate shuffled his boots on the porch step. "Gemma—"

"You didn't ask." She wagged her finger at him. "I offered. Since this asking-for-help business comes hard for you. Baby steps, Crenshaw. Baby steps."

He threw her a sheepish grin. "If you insist."

Smiling, she opened the door. "I insist." She headed into the house.

His grin fell. When it came to the lovely K-9 trainer, he couldn't help wondering what else baby steps might lead to.

AFTER THE CONFRONTATION with Nathan, the tension between them lessened.

To a degree. Yet like an unscalable boulder, the past—their shared past—loomed large and immovable between them.

Since she would only be here a little over a week longer, it was probably best not to address it. As a K-9 trainer, she knew the value of letting sleeping dogs lie. Admitting what happened would serve no purpose other than to bring up painful memories she preferred not to recall.

On Monday, she, Rascal and Ike rode with Nathan to the doctor's appointment in Asheville, an hour's drive from Truelove. She laid out the PawPals program with the doctor. Ike testified to the difference Rascal was already making in his life. Nathan expressed his concerns about the latest incident.

When she explained the need for a full-time caregiver, both Ike and Nathan became indignant.

The doctor listened carefully to each of their

views and changed Ike's medication in the hope of avoiding future incidents like what happened at the school.

"For now, let's agree to monitor the situation." The neurologist cleared his throat. "If further changes are necessary, please don't hesitate to contact me."

The return trip to Truelove ride was far less pleasant than the ride to Asheville. Nathan and Ike were irritated with her. Yet later that day, Nathan contacted his friend Clay McKendry, at the nearby Bar None Ranch.

They worked out an agreement to share the fellow rancher's part-time ranch hands, splitting mornings and afternoons between the ranches. It took only a day for her to see a tremendous difference in the workload Nathan previously shouldered alone. Already, he appeared less stressed and better able to cope with his father's situation and his sons' boundless energy.

Ike wasn't one to hold a grudge. They soon returned to the easy camaraderie they'd shared before the appointment. To her relief, Nathan got over his resentment at her interference, too. But no more was said of hiring a full-time caregiver.

Despite her best intentions to steer clear of

him as much as possible, she got into a routine of sorts with Nathan. She looked forward to the early mornings before the boys joined them for breakfast, when it was just her and Nathan, sharing the details of their upcoming day over coffee.

By mutual unspoken agreement, their conversations revolved around the people they'd become, rather than the teenagers they'd once been. She concentrated on getting to know the adult Nathan better. There was much to admire about a man determined to take care of his ailing father, raise his sons and run a cattle ranch.

He hadn't lost his sense of humor. He was a man of faith. A man who honored his commitments.

They talked about everything, except the past and his late wife. On some level it would have pained her to hear details of his blissful life with Deanna. But his unwillingness to talk about her at all felt like a hugely significant omission.

When Maggie brought the boys to the ranch each afternoon, Gemma liked being the first person to welcome them home. She and Maggie also got into the habit of chatting a few minutes. She'd never been one to make friends easily, but she felt she'd made a friend in Nathan's second cousin. Several years ago as a sideline, Maggie's police chief husband had started a training kennel. Sometimes if a particular canine turned out to not be suited for law enforcement work, he referred a dog to Juliet and PawPals. Gemma hadn't made the connection at first, but several of Bridger's dogs had become incredible service companions.

During the first week of training, her goal had been to help Ike and Rascal acclimate to each other. Now she was ready to tackle how Rascal might benefit Ike outside his home environment. An active social life went a long way toward diminishing the sense of isolation and bouts of depression.

One morning while the boys were at school, she, Nathan and Ike sat down to discuss what could be done with Rascal's help to give Ike a fuller life. Or at least, she and Ike sat down. Nathan leaned against the doorframe leading to the kitchen. He wasn't a man who knew how to relax.

Her job was to listen to a client's felt needs and if feasible, create a plan to meet those needs. One of the things Ike mentioned was how much he missed the weekly lunch gathering at a local diner with a group called the ROMEOs.

She glanced at Nathan.

"Retired Older Men Eating Out." He grinned. *"R-O-M-E-O."*

She laughed. "That sounds like fun."

Ike chuckled. "We're a fun group."

Folding his arms across his green-checked flannel shirt, Nathan propped against the wall. "The men have been a part of Dad's life long before any of them retired."

Ike nodded. "It's really an excuse to get together. And eat at the Mason Jar, of course."

Gemma smiled. "I'm beginning to see where Kody gets his appetite."

Seated in his recliner, Ike patted Rascal's head. "Some of the guys, like Nash and Dwight, I've known since we were boys. Tom, of course, is family. We do service projects, too." Sighing, he leaned back. "Since my driving privileges were suspended—" he shot a glance at his son "—and rightly so, I guess my ROMEO days are over."

Perched on the sofa, she jotted a few notes on her electronic tablet. "Perhaps not. At this stage in your illness, with Rascal by your side and appropriate safety protocols, I see no reason for you to be continually confined to the ranch, Ike."

A slow smile spread across Ike's grizzled features. "I sure would enjoy the opportunity to jaw with my old pals again." He winked at her. "The Double Name Club may think they run this town, but it's the ROMEOs who provide the elbow grease necessary for it to flourish."

"Double Name Club?" She cut a look at Nathan. "Is that like a garden club? Or a book club?"

Ike hooted.

"Not exactly." Nathan laughed. "The Double Name Club are in a category of their own."

Ike grinned. "The Double Name Club are also known as the Truelove matchmakers."

Nathan nodded. "The seventy-something ladies are infamous for poking their powdered noses where they don't belong. They take the town motto—Truelove, Where True Love Awaits—a little too seriously."

She raised her eyebrow.

Nathan rolled his eyes. "Half the town marriages are the result of their scheming."

His father snorted. "Half and counting. Their tally sheet also includes multigenerational matrimonial mayhem." He threw out his hands. "Not that I'm complaining. Aunt Georgie is the one who introduced Pammie and me."

In his stocking feet, their son smiled. "The

founding members are GeorgeAnne Allen, ErmaJean Hicks and IdaLee Moore."

Southerners, past and current generations, were fond of double names.

Gemma shrugged. "It's nice they care so much about their friends."

"They're a menace." Nathan rubbed the back of his neck. "The matchmaking double-name cronies are determined to help everyone in Truelove find their happily-ever-after. Whether the recipients of their efforts want them to or not."

His elbows on the armrest, Ike sat forward. "My aunt, GeorgeAnne—her family owns the local hardware store—is the de facto leader of the pack."

"Your aunt?" Gemma tilted her head. "If she's in her seventies and you're—"

"Not." Ike chuckled. "Not yet anyway. Back in the day, Appalachian farm families were big of necessity. Like many others, the Arledge clan had nine children, strung out over a dozen years. Tom's daddy was the eldest son. GeorgeAnne is the oldest girl. My mama was a middle daughter." He gestured toward the ridge of mountains outside the window. "The equestrian riding center over yonder belongs to the youngest sister, CoraFaye, who's closer to my age than her own siblings."

Gemma's mouth fell open. "Wow."

Nathan grinned. "Maybe I should draw you a family tree."

"That's a lot of family." She blinked at the men. "You must be related to nearly the entire town. How wonderful."

Ike smiled. "By blood or by marriage, we probably are."

"Not so wonderful." Nathan grimaced. "Growing up, it meant was there was nowhere someone wasn't waiting to report any misdeeds to your parents."

She arched her eyebrow. "I find it hard to believe the ultratrustworthy Nathan Crenshaw ever got up to misdeeds."

"Just the usual high school hijinks and high spirits." Ike tapped the side of his nose. "But don't let his stuffy facade fool you, young lady."

Nathan made a face. "You both make me sound so boring."

She lifted her chin. "Responsible isn't boring."

As a camp counselor, he'd been gentle with the kids. Dashing, handsome. And so reassuringly safe. The exact opposite of her father.

Maybe that's what had drawn her to him in the first place.

"Your mother and I weren't the only ones in this family to benefit from the matchmakers's endeavors." Ike threw his son a look. "I recall Aunt Georgie had a hand in bringing you and Deanna together, too."

Stiffening, Nathan unfolded his arms. "If we're done here, I've got someone coming to install the doggy doors for Rascal."

As a further safety measure, they'd decided to modify Ike's bedroom door and the back door.

She surveyed Nathan's pained expression. Anytime his late wife came into the conversation, he became uncomfortable.

Her gaze dropped to the tablet. "I'll make some calls and see what I can arrange so Ike can resume the weekly ROMEO get-togethers."

"Outstanding." Ike slapped his palm on the leather armrest. "Thank you. Can't wait."

She looked at Nathan. "I'd like to take him to the Mason Jar this week, but after I'm gone, arrangements will need to be made for future transportation."

"Right." Nathan sneered. "Lest we forget, your days with us are numbered."

Gemma reared a fraction. "And *after I'm*

*gone*," she reiterated with some heat in her voice, "going forward the situation will need to be continually assessed per Ike's condition."

She was never sure where she stood with Nathan. Whether he would be sorry to see her go, or if he couldn't wait to be rid of her. His inexplicable moods shifted daily. Like the direction of the wind.

"Got it." He straightened. "Now if you'll excuse me…" He padded toward the kitchen to retrieve his boots and hat. Moments later, the back door squeaked open and then shut with a decisive bang.

She jerked.

"I shouldn't have mentioned Deanna." Ike sounded weary.

She gazed at the empty spot in the doorway. "He must miss her so much."

"Grief and guilt are a toxic combination and until my boy deals with both…"

She threw the older man a sharp glance.

Ike ran his hand over his face. "Deanna's death was sudden and unexpected. She was in Boone, visiting friends. A drunk driver…" His chin sank to his chest.

She put her hand to her throat. "How awful.

The boys were so young to lose their mother. And for Nathan…"

Imagining the excruciating pain of his loss, she blinked away tears. A service van pulled up outside the house.

The older man blew out a breath. "I love my son dearly, but it remains a sad but true fact he never appreciates anything or anyone as fully as he should until it's too late."

Unsure what he meant, she frowned. The buzz of a power tool whined from the direction of the kitchen.

Leaving him and Rascal watching a game show on television, she retreated to her bedroom to make her calls. Tom Arledge was refreshingly agreeable to helping his cousin ease back into circulation. Tom also gave her the number at the Mason Jar.

By law, restaurants were required to accommodate assistance dogs and their companions, but she'd found over the years it best to give owners a heads-up and talk through any potential issues. Eating establishments were often leery about how service animals might impact their health code ratings or pose a danger to other customers.

However, she met no resistance from Kara

MacKenzie, owner of the Jar. Quite the opposite—the woman was extremely enthusiastic and eager to help. Apparently, her father-in-law, a retired fire chief, was a ROMEO, too.

Gemma made arrangements to bring Ike to the Jar for lunch the next day. And she looked forward to getting to know the vivacious Kara better.

Wandering into the hall, she encountered Ike "supervising" Nathan and a handyman. When she shared her news with Ike, he was delighted at the prospect of tomorrow's reunion with his buddies.

The doggy door installation complete, Ike and Rascal escorted the handyman to his vehicle. Avoiding eye contact, Nathan concentrated on putting his tools into a red toolbox.

"Let's see how his first outing goes and then I'll work on enabling Ike and Rascal to join you and the boys at church on Sunday."

No response. *Fine. Be that way.* The emotional whiplash from his mood swings was tiresome. Been there, done that.

Subject to her father's erratic behavior, she'd spent her childhood walking on eggshells. A grown woman, she no longer had to put up with any man's bad attitudes, much less Nathan Crenshaw's.

Miffed, she wheeled, intending to return to her bedroom and answer a few emails from PawPals.

"Gemma, wait."

She halted midstep, but she didn't turn around.

"I have a bad habit of taking out my baggage on those around me."

She faced him.

Contrition darkened his eyes. "I'm sorry. Thank you for everything you're doing to make Dad's life happier." He scoured his face with his hand. "I'm not so great with words, but you've brought life back into this house." His chest heaved. "Into my life, too."

Her heart pounded. "Being here has been a joy. Getting to know the boys…" She took a breath. "Spending time with you."

"Like old times. No. Better." He gave her a lopsided grin that set her heart fluttering. "Gives me hope good times are coming again for all of us."

What those good times would look like, and who they would include, she didn't know. But coming here had set into motion a course of events whose outcome was still undetermined.

She understood what he was saying, though. Nothing would ever be the same for her, either.

Her empty apartment, her work and her friends no longer seemed enough.

She felt on the cusp of a turning point. The new start she so desperately yearned for. Would her new start include the man standing before her?

Gemma didn't—couldn't—know the future. But the small treacherous part of herself—that never let go of the man she'd loved and lost—couldn't help breathing a prayer somehow it would.

# CHAPTER SIX

MIDMORNING THE NEXT DAY, she, Ike and Rascal set off in her car for the ROMEO rendezvous at the Mason Jar.

As they drove down Main Street, Ike enthusiastically pointed out various landmarks. It was her first glimpse of the mountain hamlet of which the Crenshaws were so fond.

He insisted on giving her the grand tour so she drove the long way around the town square lined with oak trees. The river bended around the town like a horseshoe. On the horizon, the Blue Ridge surrounded the town, looming in a perpetual smoky mist from which the mountains derived their name.

"May not look like much to a big-city girl like you." The corners of his eyes fanned out in a lifetime of wrinkles. "But it's home to us."

Home.

She got the attraction of Truelove. The slow

pace of life. The simplicity and goodness of small things. Big city or country crossroads, no matter its location, home was invariably beautiful.

She parked in one of the spaces in front of the café across from the square.

They stepped inside. A bell jangled above the door. The aroma of fried eggs and the yeasty smell of biscuits floated past her nostrils. The diner was jam-packed.

At the sight of Rascal, conversations momentarily halted, but she'd made sure he had on his vest identifying him as a service dog. The Truelove grapevine Ike had bragged about and bemoaned in equal measure must have put out the word. Within a millisecond, everyone returned to their own lunch.

She read through the chalked menu on the wall over a pass-through window to the kitchen. Cherry red swivel stools bolted to the floor lined the long counter edged with chrome.

There was a light in Ike's eyes she hadn't witnessed in her short tenure at the ranch. Unlike his son, he relished the company of people. He pointed to a delectable-looking concoction in the display case by the vintage cash register. "Take my word for it. Kara's award-winning apple galette is not to be missed."

Waitresses in jeans and long-sleeved Mason Jar T-shirts scurried from table to table. Booths lined plate-glass windows overlooking Main Street and the town square. A handful of older gentlemen occupied several tables pushed together.

Tom waved them over. She'd briefed Tom to remain alert for signs Ike might be getting tired or overwhelmed. Since it was his first public foray with Rascal, feeling not unlike what she supposed a protective mother might feel, she walked Ike and Rascal to the table.

As she'd advised, to avoid anything remotely triggering that might cause Ike to spiral, Tom went around the table making the introductions. Not only for her benefit but also by way of a reminder for Ike in case his memory failed him.

Nash's family ran the Apple Valley Orchard. Ike clapped him on the back. "As the crow flies, the High Country's closest neighbor in the valley."

She relaxed a smidgen. Ike was having a good day. Fantastic.

Ike slipped into the vacant chair. Rascal plopped at his feet under the table out of the traffic flow. So far so good. Just as she'd trained the sweet collie at PawPals.

Breathing a sigh of relief, she was preparing

to make an unobtrusive exit when a pretty, petite blonde touched her elbow.

"Gemma?" The woman, a few years younger, held out her hand. "I'm Kara. I'm so pleased to meet you."

Her gaze cutting to make sure Ike and Rascal were okay, she shook Kara's hand and stepped away to talk with the perky chef.

Kara smiled. "We've never had a service dog visit the Jar before. I don't want to distract Rascal from his job, and per health code regulations I'm not allowed to serve him food, but would it be okay if I provided him a bowl of water?"

Her heart warmed. "Not many people think of the animal. Thank you. He'd love a bowl of water."

"Will you stay for lunch? If I do say so myself, the blue plate special—beef bourguignon—"

She couldn't help but smile at Kara's exquisite French pronunciation.

"On a cold November day like today…" Kara kissed the tips of her fingers. "It's simply *magnifique* if I do say so myself."

Gemma threw another glance at the ROMEOs. "I don't want him to feel like I'm hovering."

Kara drew her away to the farthest booth. "Would this work?"

She nodded. "Thank you."

"Training dementia assistance dogs must be so rewarding. I admire the work you do." Kara's remarkable eyes, a shade resembling blueberries, misted. "Maggie has raved about the difference you've made for Ike."

Gemma slid into the booth. "That's why I do what I do. Hoping to make life better for clients and their families. And I love working with the dogs."

"Would you mind if I joined you for lunch?" Kara lingered. "As one out-of-towner to another, I'd love to get to know you better."

"I'd like that." She gestured to the other side of the booth. "But isn't this your busy time?"

Kara laughed. "Actually, other than overseeing menu planning, I've trained my staff so well, I've nearly worked myself out of a job. Tell me what interests you for lunch and I'll bring it to the table myself."

She chose the hearty French stew. Over coffee, she learned Kara's husband was the local fire chief, a position he'd taken over from his father.

"Sort of like Maggie's husband, Bridger, took over as chief of police from his father-in-law, Tom?"

A former city girl, Kara chuckled. "Small towns."

Gemma had firsthand experience with the quirks of small-town life. Everyone knew everyone else, both its major appeal and its primary downside. Once upon a time, she'd been a small-town girl, too, until she could no longer live in the shadow of what her father had done.

In contrast to her own deeply engrained reticence, Kara was remarkably open about the struggles she'd faced as a child living in homeless shelters until she was adopted after her mother died.

She admired Kara's candor, how comfortable and secure she was with herself and where she came from. She wished she could be more like her. She'd learned over the years to share just enough for the conversation to not feel one-sided. She'd become skillful at diverting questions about her childhood.

The bell at the door jangled. Kara straightened. "Here comes trouble."

Several older women trooped past to a vacant table underneath the community bulletin board.

"I'm guessing the matchmakers?"

Kara rolled her eyes. "I see you've been warned. GeorgeAnne and I had a now-resolved issue over pie versus galette, but she helped Will and I find happiness together."

She peered around Kara. "Which one is Ike's aunt?"

Kara took a quick peek over her shoulder. "GeorgeAnne's the skinny, scary one with her back to the wall. No doubt scoping out her next victim. Just don't let it be you."

Lips twitching, Gemma took a surreptitious second look. Nathan's great-aunt was an angular, faintly terrifying woman with ice-blue eyes and a short, iron gray cap of hair.

"She's the bossy one." Kara made a face. "Although, considering the rest of them, that's probably splitting hairs. The pleasantly plump one is a distant relative of mine, ErmaJean. The tiny one is Miss IdaLee, who taught forty years' worth of Truelove children. On the end is GeorgeAnne's sister, CoraFaye, a terror in her own right. If you don't believe me, ask her daughter-in-law, Kate Dolan."

The bell clattered again. Kara's gaze sharpened. "But maybe putting your marital destiny in their hands might not be such a bad idea. Not if hunky Nathan Crenshaw is on the market again. What do you say to that?"

Gemma went crimson. "We're colleagues on

Ike's care team. I'm not looking for… He's not interested in…" She brought the glass of water to her mouth.

"Oh, it's like that, is it?" A shadow fell over the booth. Kara's gaze lifted. "Good to see you, Nate."

Blue eyes sparking with mischief, the chef threw her a slightly wicked grin. "Why don't you keep Gemma company while I bring her a slice of apple galette and get you some lunch?"

Gemma made a grab for her, but too late. Kara slipped out of the booth.

A perplexed frown creased Nathan's forehead. "Okay…" He took Kara's vacated seat.

"What's your pleasure today?" Kara beamed at them. "Interested in trying something new?" She winked.

Gemma gaped at her.

Nathan, like most men *thank the Lord*, appeared impervious to any subtext in conversation. He shrugged. "Sure. I'll like whatever you pick for me."

She could see the effort it was costing Kara not to respond to that leading remark. She glared at her new, maybe not so good, friend.

Kara smirked. "I'll get right on that." She sauntered toward the swinging door with the porthole, separating the kitchen from the dining area.

When Gemma could no longer stand the tension strung between them like a high wire, she said, "I didn't realize you were coming into town today."

Removing his hat, he laid it on the seat beside him. "I didn't know myself, but with Dad occupied I decided to catch one of the rancher association meetings this morning at the county seat. When I got back, the house felt too empty." His gaze dropped. "I thought I'd have a bite at the Jar."

"And check out how your dad is doing, too?"

"Guilty as charged." He met her gaze. "Sorry."

He wore such a hangdog puppy look, she couldn't help but smile.

"Nothing to be sorry about." She took a sip of water. "I was concerned, too, but he's having a great time. As for Rascal? It's kind of like Graduation Day for him and I'm so proud. How silly a doggy mom am I?"

"You're not silly."

Good thing she was already seated—his dazzling smile might have buckled her knees otherwise.

"Here's your French onion soup."

They jolted. Nathan sat back. She pretended an intense fascination with a packet of artificial sweetener.

Kara put a steaming bowl in front of him and a side plate of crusty French bread. "Enjoy."

She motioned to one of the younger waitresses, who brought over a glass of water for Nathan and an enormous slice of the most decadent apple dessert Gemma had ever beheld.

Her eyes widened. "I can't eat this by myself, Kara."

"That's why I gave you two forks. Nate probably wouldn't mind helping you out." Kara batted her eyes. "You can thank me later."

Pursing her lips, Gemma leveled a glance at her. Apparently, the Double Name Club wasn't the only Truelove matchmakers. Kara waggled her fingers at them and headed to the kitchen.

Again, thankfully the subtext was lost on Nathan. Saying a brief grace, the rancher dug into his lunch.

When he came up for air, he asked, "Do you have a dog of your own, Gemma?"

She shook her head. "Training assistance dogs doesn't leave much time or energy for a pet." She shrugged. "Maybe one day. Plus, PawPals headquarters is in Laurel Grove, about a thirty-minute drive from my Greensboro apartment."

Fork midway to his mouth, he paused. "That's where you and Juliet grew up. She was a counselor at camp that summer, too. With your best friend and your workplace there, I'm surprised you don't still live in Laurel Grove."

"Guess I'm a big-city girl at heart. It's nearer the airport." She made an effort to relax her shoulders from where they'd bunched near her ears at the mention of her former hometown. "I'm away a lot, acclimating clients to their new service companions. I'd love a dog of my own, but being cooped up in my small apartment wouldn't be fair."

Eager to deflect the conversation away from Laurel Grove, she handed him a fork. "Want to share?"

He smiled. "Thought you'd never ask."

The galette was delicious.

She savored the crisp sweetness of the apples. "Totally lives up to the hype."

Nathan laid down his fork. "I guess this is the first time we've actually eaten a meal out together."

"Hot dogs around the bonfire at the lake surrounded by little campers doesn't exactly qualify, does it?"

Soon as the words left her mouth, she would have done anything to take them back. Anything personal from the past—the elephant in the room—was one of the subjects she took care to avoid with him.

Instead of being annoyed, he laughed. "Company's just as good." He stabbed his fork into the pie again. "But this time around, the food is a lot better."

She became aware of GeorgeAnne, a woman she'd never met, scowling at her from across the diner. Although why, she had no idea.

"I should go." She grabbed her cell off the table. "Maggie invited me to stop by the Hollingsworth kennel. There's a dog she and Bridger wanted me to meet as a possible future candidate for K-9 dementia assistance training. But I'll be back to the ranch soon. Tom is bringing Ike home."

Nathan picked up the bill before she could get it. "Lunch is on me. Don't worry about hurrying back to the ranch. I'm planning on being there all afternoon."

"This has been nice." She hesitated. "I don't

want to argue again, but it's important someone is with Ike at all times."

He stilled. "It has been nice. We're going to have to agree to disagree on this issue. Dad will be fine. Enjoy your afternoon off."

She couldn't shake a disquieting feeling of looming disaster on the horizon, but as Nathan had pointed out yesterday, she was merely a dog trainer. "Thank you for lunch."

"See you at home."

Gemma blinked at his choice of words. Either *home* didn't have the same connotation for him as it did for her, or he didn't notice the slip of his tongue.

He cocked his head. "Everything okay?"

A stark longing for everything she'd wanted and had never been fulfilled blazed in her heart. If only things had turned out differently for them… But they hadn't.

She swallowed past the boulder in her throat. "See you soon."

Before she lost what little control she possessed over her ragged emotions, she hurried out. Yet she had the uncomfortable sensation of eyes following her to the exit.

Nathan or GeorgeAnne Allen? Friend or foe?

As much as she hated the conflict with him, she feared friendship might prove more dangerous to her hard-won peace of mind.

# CHAPTER SEVEN

NATE LINGERED OVER his coffee. GeorgeAnne plopped into Gemma's vacated seat. From the look on her face, she had something to say. Given her track record, it didn't take a genius to figure out what.

"Don't start with the matchmaking, Aunt Georgie." He folded his arms across his chest. "Gemma is only in Truelove in a professional capacity."

GeorgeAnne looked at him over the top of her horn-rimmed glasses. "I wouldn't dream of it. The girls and I have already discussed it—"

The "girls" of the Double Name Club would never see seventy again.

"We agree you and Gemma Anderson Spencer or whatever she calls herself these days..." GeorgeAnne waved a bony, imperious hand. "You two wouldn't make a good match."

"Oh, really?" Hackles unaccountably rising, he narrowed his eyes. "And why is that?"

His great-aunt sniffed. "She's not from around here."

In Southern-speak, that meant Gemma didn't and never would belong.

He stiffened. "She's from Greensboro, not the moon."

"She's the emotional equivalent of quicksand, my boy." Leaning forward on her elbows, his great-aunt warmed to her theme. "She's an excellent dog trainer. And she's been extremely compassionate with Ike, but she's a city girl. Not the right kind of woman to be a rancher's wife."

Gemma would make an excellent rancher's wife. Though of course, not his.

"She's unreliable. Capricious in her affections. And secretive."

He frowned. "That's not fair."

GeorgeAnne shook her finger at him. "I haven't forgotten how devastated you were when she broke things off with you without any explanation."

"That was fifteen years ago, Aunt Georgie. She's changed."

"What do you know about her? Her family?

Or her background? Did she ever—does she ever—talk about any of that?"

He shook his head.

She raised her voice in triumph. "Exactly."

An unexpected and unwelcome protectiveness for Gemma surged in his chest. "We're both different people."

She gave him a look. "Life has a way of working out for the best. Who knows how your life would've turned out if you'd stuck with her?"

How indeed...

"You certainly wouldn't have enjoyed a rock-solid, thirteen-year marriage to a woman who adored you. Or have two of the most delightful children God ever created." She curled her lip. "You'd probably have ended up in some place like where she's from—"

"Greensboro is hardly the back side of Mars."

"Surrounded by concrete..." GeorgeAnne threw out her hands. "Possibly selling insurance."

He rolled his eyes. "Anything but that."

GeorgeAnne arched her eyebrow. "I thought you'd be pleased with our noninterference pact. You're always accusing the Double Name Club of unwanted meddling. Well, this is us not interfering."

"For once," he huffed.

Then the natural caution that must be exercised when dealing with any of the Double Name Club reasserted itself. "Unless this is some kind of reverse psychology strategy you're trying?"

Her mouth pinched. "I'm crushed you have so little faith in my integrity."

Not buying her affronted sensibilities, he snorted. "You forget I've seen how you operate. The matchmaking shenanigans you've waged against practically everyone I know. Bridger and Maggie. Luke and Shayla. Clay and Kelsey." He jerked his thumb in the direction of the booth where the recipients of the matchmakers' most recent campaign were eating lunch. "Colton and Mollie."

GeorgeAnne gave him what for her passed as a smile. "Successful, happy matches each and every one. You'll find no complaints from any in that quarter."

"Not now, but at the time…"

"Water under the bridge of their eventual domestic bliss." She patted his hand. "Not something you have to worry about."

At his startled look, she squeezed his hand. "No doubt someday when you're ready, you'll find eventual domestic bliss once again." Her mouth thinned. "But not with the K-9 trainer. She's totally unsuitable. You two wouldn't be a good fit. Besides, it's not like she's sticking around. As I understand it, the training ends next week. To which I say, goodbye and good riddance."

He gaped at his great-aunt. "You're serious about not pushing us together, aren't you?"

One for the record books, for the Truelove matchmakers, a match not-in-the-making.

"Absolutely." She eased out of the booth. "You've been through so much losing dear Deanna."

When he returned to Truelove that summer after Gemma broke his heart, his aunt had been a huge, give-hometown-Deanna-a-chance advocate.

"And you're going through so much with your dad... Ike's always been my favorite nephew."

"You say that about all your nephews," he muttered. "Maggie's dad, Tom, too."

His great-aunt lifted her chin. "You've got enough on your plate without dealing with someone like Gemma." She rose. "Although, if your thoughts are once again contemplating romance... I would urge you to take another look at our local veterinarian. Ingrid is the epitome of stability and levelheadedness."

Ingrid might be great with animals, but with humans not so much, and she certainly wasn't mother material for his sons.

"My boys have a mother," he grunted.

GeorgeAnne's wrinkled face softened. "I'm not trying to be cruel, Nate. Deanna would want her sons looked after properly, and she wouldn't want you to spend the rest of your life alone."

"I'm looking after my sons."

Yet after what he'd overheard yesterday, that wasn't exactly true. And Gemma's return seemed to have stirred something inside him. Made him aware of how isolated and lonely he'd become.

GeorgeAnne scanned his face. "If Ingrid doesn't take your fancy, then someone else. We'll keep a discreet lookout for additional blondes." She threw him a wry look. "A preference of yours." With that parting shot, she exited the diner amid a clatter of jangling bells.

He stared after her.

Instead of taking comfort from her uncharacteristic hands-off pronouncement, he was left with a disquieting sense of alarm.

IT WASN'T LONG after GeorgeAnne left that the ROMEOs got ready to leave, too.

Nate headed over to Tom and his dad with Rascal.

At the cash register, his father fished his wallet out of his pocket, but Tom waved his money away. "I've got it this time, old friend."

Nate's dad thanked him. "How about I leave a tip?"

"Great." Tom handed his credit card to the cashier. He and Nate watched his dad return to the ROMEO table to lay down a few bills. "I'm so pleased to see Ike is more like his old self."

The waitress ran Tom's card through the machine.

Nate nodded. "The changes Gemma has made to his routine and the medication adjustment are doing the trick."

"So many reasons to feel optimistic for him." Tom signed his name to the receipt. "When I take Ike to the ranch, I'll stick around until you or Gemma get back."

"I appreciate that, Tom, but I need to head home and do some bookkeeping. I'll take Dad with me and save you the trip."

The waitress handed Tom his receipt. The retired Truelove police chief folded the slip of paper and squared it away in his wallet. "If you've got work to do, I don't mind sitting with him."

Nate made a face. "You've been talking to Gemma, haven't you?" He paid the waitress for his lunch.

Tom's brow creased. "She's concerned about Ike being left on his own and getting confused."

"Which is why Dad has Rascal. Gemma is being overly cautious. Dad wouldn't appreciate a babysitter."

Tom fingered his chin. "When Gemma and I worked out this arrangement to bring Ike to the weekly ROMEO lunches, she was adamant about not leaving him alone."

Nate furrowed his brow. "Like you said, he's more himself than he's been in months. I'll be in the next room. He'll be fine."

Tom didn't appear convinced. "If you're sure."

Fifteen minutes later, Nate and his father arrived at the ranch. The field trip to the diner had taxed his dad. His father didn't protest when Nate suggested he lie down for a short nap.

Nate sat at the large, antique desk that had been his dad's and his grandfather's before him. The pile of paperwork never seemed to diminish. Maybe he could pay a few bills and put in an online order to pick up tomorrow at the agri-supply store. He'd been working about an hour when he remembered he needed to check on a heifer, calving for the first time next month.

Pushing back from the desk, he soon located the heifer in the pasture with the other cattle. Other than being a mite ornery—he grinned at what Deanna would have said to that—the heifer looked to be doing well.

"Won't be long now." He patted the heifer with affection. Deanna would have said not soon enough. He smiled.

It struck him it was the first time since her death, the thought of her hadn't brought an instant stab of pain. Or guilt.

Gazing over the herd, he pinched the bridge of his nose.

She'd been an excellent mother. A wonderful homemaker and rancher's wife. Their thirteen-year marriage had been strong, mainly because of Deanna.

"I'm sorry," he whispered into the wind. "Did you feel loved enough?"

To his dying day, he'd regret not telling her he loved her more often. On their last day together, he'd wasted it by arguing over something trivial. Then it was too late.

His time with Deanna ran out.

The wind and sorrow whipping at his heels, he was on his way to the house when Gemma's car pulled into the drive.

A yearning rose in his chest. Stealing his breath. Accelerating his heart. The aching vulnerability frightened him. Instead of embracing it, he shoved the feelings aside and allowed irritation to replace them.

She opened the door and got out.

Nate stalked toward the car. "I don't appreciate you talking behind my back with Tom about Dad."

Her smile faded. "Where's Ike?"

"In the house. And don't change the subject." He threw out his hands. "What did you hope to gain by dumping that on Tom? Get him to side with you?"

Her brown eyes darkened. "This isn't about taking sides. This is about keeping your father safe."

Nate rocked on his heels. "I'd never do anything to put my father in jeopardy. His care is my number-one priority."

Arms folded, she got in his face. "And my number-one priority—"

The doggy door flew open. There was a

streak of sable-colored fur. Barking furiously, Rascal raced toward them. Clamping his teeth into the sleeve of Nate's jacket, the growling collie tugged hard, nearly knocking him off his feet.

He staggered. "Get this crazy dog off me." He tried to free himself, but the collie's grip was tenacious. "What's wrong with him? Does he think I was threatening you?"

"I don't know what's got into him. I've never seen him like this. He's not an aggressive animal. Rascal," she commanded. "Release."

Ignoring her, the collie continued to forcibly drag Nate across the yard. Resisting, Nate stood his ground. There was a ripping sound. A piece of the fabric from his coat came loose, clenched between Rascal's jaws.

The dog went into a defensive half crouch. Howling, he leaped up and ran in a tight circle around Nate. Rascal barreled into the back of Nate's legs, almost sending him sprawling.

"Rascal!" She tried to pull the dog off him. With a growl, he snapped at her.

She fell against the fence. "I've never had one of my dogs... Wait. Do you smell smoke? Nathan!" Gasping, she pointed. "The house is on fire."

He whirled. Black smoke leaked from around the doorframe. The fire alarm shrieked. He spotted flames through the kitchen window.

The farmhouse was on fire. And inside was his dad.

NATE SPRINTED TOWARD the house, but Rascal raced ahead.

"Don't go in there," Gemma screamed. "I'm calling the fire department. Wait for help to arrive."

"There's no time," he shouted. "Stay here!"

Rascal leaped through the doggy door and disappeared into the burning house.

Without stopping to think, he reached for the doorknob. Thankfully, it remained cool to the touch. Twisting it, he flung open the door. A cloud of smoke assailed his nostrils.

Coughing, he threw up his arm to cover his nose and mouth. "Dad!" he yelled. "Dad, where are you?"

There was no sign of his father or Rascal. Plunging into the swirling, choking darkness, he spotted flames licking at what was left of a pot on the stovetop.

He seized the hand towel they always left draped over the drainboard. With it, he grabbed hold of the pot handle and flung it into the stainless-steel sink. He turned off the stove and turned the faucet full blast onto the contents of the pot. Hissing, steam rose. He sputtered.

From the living room, there came a frenzy of barking. Stumbling out of the kitchen, he found his father crouched behind his recliner with his hands over his ears. Rascal nudged his dad, trying to get him to move.

The alarm continued its deafening shriek.

His father's eyes were wild and frightened. "Make it stop…" His chin trembled.

It struck Nate like a blow to the chest how much he resembled Kody—childlike and utterly dependent. A complete role reversal.

He pulled his father upright. "Let's get you someplace safe."

Bewildered, his father allowed himself to be towed out of the living room. Gemma met them in the kitchen. She'd flung open the window and, using the towel he'd abandoned, she was trying to clear the air by fanning away the fumes and smoke.

His heart contracted. "Gemma!"

She took his dad's other arm, and they propelled him out of the kitchen and into the yard.

His father dropped onto the brown, winter-withered grass.

A siren blared. His dad cringed. Talking to his father in a low, soothing voice, Gemma sat down and put her arm around him.

His heart thudded. He found it difficult to draw an even breath. Bending double, he propped his hands on his thighs. Whining softly, Rascal rubbed his face along his leg.

"If you hadn't come to get me, Rascal..." His voice hitched. "Good boy. Such a good boy." He ran his hand over the collie's coat. If he hadn't been able to reach his father in time, he had no doubt Rascal would have remained with his dad, a faithful, loyal companion to the very end.

Rumbling up the drive, an engine with the Truelove Volunteer Fire Department rolled to a shuddering stop. Friends and neighbors in turn-out gear jumped out of the fire truck. Behind the engine, an ambulance screamed to a halt. Luke Morgan and Zach Stone exited the vehicle at a run.

Fire Chief Will MacKenzie dashed over to him. "The boys!"

"Still at school," he rasped. *Thank You, God.* His nose and his eyes burned. His throat felt raw.

What if the boys had been in the house? What

if the fire had gotten out of control before he arrived? If he'd been in the back pasture, he would have never heard the alarm.

A wave of dizziness overcome him. He swayed and would have hit the ground hard if Will's second-in-command, Lieutenant Bradley, hadn't caught hold of him and eased him to a sitting position.

"The fire's out," Nate wheezed. "A pot was left on the stove."

"My men will do a thorough assessment to be sure." The chief sent Bradley and several other firefighters into the house. Seconds later, the screech of the fire alarm went silent.

Will motioned EMTs Luke and Zach forward. "Nate needs to be checked out."

Nate shoved at the oxygen mask Zach tried to fit over his face. "I'm fine."

The young owner of the Truelove auto body shop wasn't so easily deterred. "Smoke inhalation isn't anything to play with. Take a few deep breaths and let us check you out."

Luke fitted a mask over his dad's nose and mouth. He figured his father would fight Luke, but in his current state of befuddlement, the older man offered no resistance.

Will hovered over Gemma. "Ma'am?"

She fluttered her hand. "I'm fine." Patches of black soot streaked across her high cheekbones. "I wasn't in there long."

Nate ripped the mask from his mouth. "You shouldn't have been in there at all." Black spots danced before his eyes. "I told you to stay outside."

Her lips quivered. "You might've needed my help."

"You might've gotten yourself killed," he growled. The notion of what could have happened to her—to all of them—was like a punch to the gut. Fear and nausea roiled in his belly.

The chief moved away for a consultation with his men and then returned. Will pushed his helmet back on his head. "The fire was contained to the range. The damage was minimal, but the stovetop's a total loss. It'll need to be replaced. But at least we didn't have to go in there with the hoses. Water damage is a whole other kettle of fish."

A distant cousin—one of GeorgeAnne's sons who ran the family hardware store—stepped forward. "I've put in a call to my wife. She's bringing a dehumidifier. That will help a lot. Mom said to tell you not to fret. She and the family will be here ASAP to do a deep cleaning."

Nate shook his head. "I appreciate that, but it's only the kitchen. I can handle—"

"Family helps family." His cousin, closer to Nate's father's age than his own, removed his helmet and held it under his arm. "Smoke penetrates an entire house. All surfaces need to be disinfected with baking soda. Charcoal will help absorb much of the smell. The curtain, rugs, and upholstery must be vacuumed with a special HEPA filter. Clothing and bedding also run through a wash cycle of vinegar."

Nate gaped at him.

Will grimaced. "It looked like something was left too long on the burner."

His dad yanked off the oxygen mask. "I wanted to surprise everyone by fixing your mom's soup. I'm getting a little forgetful." He peered at his Allen cousin. "Who are you again? I know I should remember."

Nate winced. His father and Brian Allen had known one another their entire lives. But Brian's expression never wavered. There was only compassion in his hazel eyes.

Kneeling beside Nate's father, he put his hand on the older man's shoulder. "It's Brian, GeorgeAnne's oldest. Mom will be here soon. She'll soon have you set to rights."

"Brian?" The confusion cleared from his dad's face. "I knew that. Sometimes I just need a reminder."

Sadness engulfed Nate.

Will removed his gloves. "Didn't you smell something burning?"

Nate pinched the bridge of his nose. "Dad was taking a nap. I'd stepped out to check on a heifer."

"It took a while for the liquid in the soup to burn through the pot." Will's gaze cut between him and his father. "How long were you away from the house?"

Guilt smote Nate. "I only meant to be gone a few moments, but time got away from me."

"I don't mean to add to your troubles, but if you understood how quickly things can go wrong... If you saw the things we see on a weekly basis..." The fire chief scrubbed his hand over his face. "This could've easily turned into a tragedy today."

Nate got to his feet. "I know," he whispered. "I'm sorry."

Standing at his side, Gemma slipped her hand into his. At her gesture of support, he blinked away the treacherous moisture in his eyes.

Will's dark brown eyes pinned him in place.

"Perhaps it would be best if Ike was no longer left on his own."

Nate looked at Gemma and then at the fire chief. "I see that now. It won't happen again."

Will gave him a short, decisive nod. He shouted an order to one of his men. "We'll get out of your way and head to the station."

Nate thrust out his hand. "Thank you." The fire chief shook his hand.

"Don't hesitate to call whenever you need us." Will touched the rim of his helmet. "Ma'am. Mr. Ike, sir."

Nate nudged his chin at Luke and Zach. "Thank you, guys."

"Your dad inhaled more smoke than you did." Luke reslung the stethoscope around his neck. "It would make me feel better if you got him checked out at the ER. Better safe than sorry."

"I'll do that."

The EMTs and firefighters packed their gear and departed.

He took out his phone. "I should let Maggie know what's happened. It might be better for the boys to have a sleepover tonight with Austin and Logan."

A caravan of vehicles approached, including GeorgeAnne's GMC pickup.

His father rose. "Reinforcements have arrived." Waving, he and Rascal moved to greet them.

Nate stared after his dad. "It's like the fire never happened. Much less that he started it."

He raked his hand through his hair, only just realizing his head was bare.

She handed him his hat. "It fell off when you bolted toward the house. I kept it safe for you."

"You were right about not leaving Dad alone." He sighed. "I thought I'd accepted the truth about the inevitable, worsening nature of his condition, but I've been in denial."

"There's no blueprint for navigating the emotional fallout for this illness."

"It's going to be a long goodbye, isn't it?" He swallowed. "Losing him, one inch at a time. A thousand little deaths."

She gazed after his dad, chatting with GeorgeAnne and her daughters-in-law. "I hate this disease for what it does, not only to the patient but their families, too."

He pursed his lips. "Once I get GeorgeAnne started in the kitchen, I'll take Dad to the ER."

"Please let me come." She touched his arm. "I won't be able to rest until I know Ike is really okay."

From across the yard, he was aware of GeorgeAnne's stern gaze burning a hole through him.

Broadening his chest, he placed his hand over Gemma's. "Thank you. Your wisdom and company would be most appreciated."

At the hospital, he and Gemma waited in the reception area while his father's doctor, called in by the attending ER physician, did a complete assessment. The doctor had also supplied a list of agencies that provided daily in-home care services. Nate managed to call through the list before business hours ended for the day.

After talking to the last agency on the list and feeling hopeless, he clicked off his cell.

"Bad news?"

"With the holidays approaching, their care providers are already booked with other clients. The lady said she couldn't make any promises, but she hoped someone might be available after New Year's Day." He sighed. "What am I going to do about Dad until then?"

"You're going to let me be there for Ike until you can secure a full-time caregiver."

He looked at her. "I couldn't ask you to do that."

"You're not asking. I'm offering." She squared

her shoulders. "As for any concerns you might have, I have an LPN license. I worked at a memory care facility for four years after high school before I joined PawPals and got into K-9 training."

He shook his head. "But this would require a five-week commitment."

"I won't start training the next dog until the third week in January. I'm totally free to look after your dad." She steepled her hands under her chin. "Please. Let me do this for you, for Ike, for Connor and Kody."

He looked at her. Truly looked at her. His great-aunt was wrong. She had changed from the young girl who broke his heart without so much as an explanation, much less an apology.

Unless that's what this was—a misguided attempt at redemption?

He cleared his throat. "You don't have to make up for what happened in the past."

She blinked. "That's not what this is. I care about Ike. I care how his illness impacts Connor and Kody. I can understand how you might not believe me, but I care about you, too." She half turned away from him. "I always have," she whispered.

His heart jolted. Was that true? If it was, it

completely altered the lens through which he'd viewed that long-ago summer. And perhaps also his perspective on the future.

"Of course, maybe you can't wait for me to get out of your life." She lowered her gaze. "I don't blame you if you never want to see me again."

Never see her again... His gut clenched. "If you're sure about taking care of Dad for the duration of the holidays..."

"I'm sure."

He took a ragged breath. "Thank you."

An odd sense of relief filled him. Her staying in Truelove felt like a reprieve of sorts. Five weeks... He hadn't been ready to say goodbye.

He was beginning to wonder if he ever would.

# CHAPTER EIGHT

OVER THE NEXT few days, GeorgeAnne and her crew did an amazing job restoring the farmhouse to livable conditions.

Yet with so many extra people in the house, Ike was feeling out of his routine. Gemma had her hands full with him, but she pitched in with the Truelove contingent whenever she could.

She also made time each day to call Connor and Kody who were on an extended sleepover at Maggie's. Her little guys were understandably distraught about their temporary exile from the only home they'd ever known.

*Her* little guys?

They weren't her little guys. But it felt as if they were. They'd become so dear to her.

She called her friend and PawPals boss, Juliet, to let her know about her decision to stay in Truelove a while longer.

Her announcement was met with a long beat

of silence. Then Juliet asked, "Is this the right thing to do in this situation, Gem?"

She frowned into the cell phone in her hand. "Ike needs care. The agency can't provide anyone until after the New Year."

"I meant the right thing for you."

Sitting on the bed in the guest bedroom, she tucked a loose tendril of hair behind her ear. "Ike needs my help."

"You mean it's Nathan who needs your help."

She stiffened. "What if he does?"

"Considering how you feel about him, I'm not sure staying on another month is a good idea."

"Nathan and I are friends, Juliet." She clenched the phone. "Friends help friends."

"We both know that isn't what's going on here. This is about your unresolved feelings for him. What is it you're hoping to achieve by sticking around?"

She got off the bed. "Ike—"

"I'm talking about you, Gemma. Is something more than friendship growing between you?"

*If only…* The longing was so sharp, she bit her lip to stem the flow of it. "He's grieving his wife. And grappling with the anticipatory grief of what's happening to his father."

"Then what possible good will come from prolonging the agony of being there with him but not *with* him in any meaningful sense?" Juliet prodded. "I know a thing or two about grief, remember?"

Juliet lost her first husband, a soldier, to combat. Gemma had watched helpless from the sidelines as her dear friend nearly went under from the sheer intensity of her loss. Her complicated grieving had almost cost her a chance at a new life with wonderful Rob and his little girl, Sophie.

Gemma gritted her teeth. "If it's in my power to help them, don't you think I should?"

Juliet sighed. "I don't want to see you get hurt. Again. Last time, it was me and the Spencers who picked up the pieces."

Her memories of those first few weeks after her mother's death were hazy at best. The Spencer family had taken her in so she could finish her last year of high school in Laurel Grove.

Restless, she paced beside the bed. "I'm trying to do a good thing, Jules. I like it here. Connor and Kody are wonderful. Everyone has been so kind."

With the exception of Nathan's great-aunt GeorgeAnne. Coordinating restoration efforts over the weekend, the older woman had been a near-constant presence. More than once, she'd felt the older woman's steely, measuring gaze upon her.

"Please be careful, Gem. Don't forget there are people who love you here in Laurel Grove."

From the window, she spotted a blue sedan approaching the farmhouse. "I need to go."

Kara got out of the sedan with a large cardboard box.

Opening the bedroom door, Gemma walked into the hall. "Talk to you soon, Jules. Bye." She clicked off.

In the kitchen, a beehive of activity, she met up with Kara, delivering a week's worth of pre-cooked, gourmet meals to tide them over. They smelled delicious.

"This is so thoughtful of you. Thank you." Making room in the refrigerator for the covered aluminum trays, she could feel the ever-watchful GeorgeAnne glowering at her back.

She wasn't sure what she'd done to earn the Double Name Club member's disfavor, but disapproval was writ large across the woman's rigid features.

Gemma walked Kara out to her car.

Then summoning her courage, she went into

the house again. Most people liked her. Animals certainly did. Unwilling to admit defeat, she made one last attempt to draw the older woman out in friendly conversation.

She found GeorgeAnne with Ike and Rascal in the laundry room, pulling bedsheets from the dryer.

"With the stove out of commission, it was so nice of Kara to bring ready-to-heat meals." Gemma grabbed the other end of the flat sheet in the older woman's hands to help fold it. "Everyone has been so kind."

"We care for our own." The sheet strung between them, GeorgeAnne brought her ends together. Gemma did the same. "There are a lot of people who care about this family."

Stepping forward, Gemma met the older woman in the middle with her folded half of the bedsheet. "Including me." She locked eyes with the Ike's aunt. Something akin to respect stirred in GeorgeAnne's gaze. She figured few people stood up to the indomitable force of nature.

"I appreciate everything you're doing for Ike." The older woman took possession of the sheet. "I just don't want to see a repeat of what happened the last time you came into my great-nephew's life."

"I never meant to—"

"But you did."

Gemma bit her lip.

"Nothing to say for yourself? Even a poor excuse is better than none."

Ike's eyes went deer-in-the-headlights. "Georgie…"

Gemma swallowed. "I'm sorry, Miss GeorgeAnne."

The Double Name Club member sniffed. "It's not me you should be apologizing to." Pressing her lips together, the older woman stalked away.

Nathan's dad put his arm around Gemma. Rascal licked her hand. "My aunt is a funny old bird. Protective of her family. Deanna was a particular favorite of hers."

"I hope I haven't given the impression I'm trying to take Deanna's place…" She went crimson. "You don't think I'm trying to replace Deanna in the boys' affections, do you?"

"Absolutely not. You have your own place in our affections."

But what about Nathan? Maybe it was hard for him to see another woman fixing meals in Deanna's kitchen…spending time with Deanna's sons…occupying space that by rights belonged to Deanna, never her.

Ike rubbed his hand over his face. "Have you talked with Nate about what happened that summer?"

She wrapped her arms around herself. "I think it's a topic best avoided."

Ike shook his head. "All these years, he's struggled to make sense of why you broke things off with him. All I'm saying is, it would mean more than you can imagine to Nate if you would talk to him about your reasons. It'd bring both of you closure if nothing else."

"I'm not sure I can," she rasped.

He rested his hand on Rascal's head. "Just think about it. That's all I'm asking." He shuffled out of the laundry room. Rascal padded after him.

Closure. An ending. Was that what Nathan wanted from her? Was that what she wanted?

Her eyes cut to the window overlooking the barnyard. Under the shelter of the lean-to, he'd spent a good part of the day changing the oil in various farm machinery. She wished she knew what he was thinking, but he was a man of few words. The endearing shyness of the boy had turned into a man with nearly impenetrable reserve.

Gemma's offer to stick around and help Nathan care for Ike had been spur-of-the-moment. But perhaps it hadn't been as out of the blue as she wanted to believe.

Truth was, she'd leaped at the chance to extend her stay. She had nothing and no one waiting at her cold, empty apartment. She was in no hurry to leave Truelove, the ranch or... Her heart pounded. Or Nathan.

She wended her way toward the lean-to.

Nathan lifted his head from the guts of the machinery. "Everything okay inside?"

"Almost done with the cleanup."

He wiped his hands on an old oil rag. "Is Dad all right?"

"In his element."

Nathan grinned. "The more the merrier with him."

Something pinged in her chest, momentarily stealing her breath. Ike—and GeorgeAnne—were right. They needed to talk about what happened. But as she recalled the terrible day she returned from camp, the words lodged in her throat.

He cocked his head. "Was there something

you needed? Aunt Georgie sent me out here to do what I needed to do on the farm."

Given the older woman's attitude, she suspected it was a ploy to put as much distance as possible between the two of them. She wasn't sure what his great-aunt was so afraid of. She'd thrown away any chance for something more with him long ago. Their friendship was far more than she had any reason to expect, and she was grateful. So thankful to have even a small space in his life.

"Thankful," she murmured.

He stuck his hands in the pockets of his jeans. "Hard to believe next week's Thanksgiving."

"Thanksgiving?"

"Surely you've heard of Thanksgiving?" Raising his eyebrows, he gave her a crooked grin. "The holiday involving turkey and giving thanks to God for our blessings?"

She rolled her eyes. "I know what Thanksgiving is. It's just this year the holiday's kind of caught me by surprise."

He crimped the rim of his hat and settled it back on his head. "I don't expect you to work through the holiday. You probably have long-standing Thanksgiving plans."

Since she'd joined the team at PawPals, her

usual plan had consisted of Juliet strong-arming her into joining the Melbournes for lunch and spending the rest of her day catching up on paperwork.

"I hadn't given Thanksgiving more than a fleeting thought." She'd be welcome at Juliet's. But driving all that way for only one day...

"The boys and Dad would love for you to celebrate with us." He cleared his throat. "*I* would love for you to celebrate with us."

"I'd love that, too." Her gaze locked onto his. "Thank you for inviting me."

"Great." He smiled. "Although, I warn you it's not a traditional Thanksgiving."

"What do you mean?"

"Neither Dad nor I lay claim to any real culinary talent. In the last couple of years, we merely slap a few steaks on the grill." He sighed. "Good thing, I guess, since this year we don't have a stove."

"About that..." She rubbed her mouth. "Brian said to tell you the new oven would be delivered first thing Tuesday."

Nathan and one of Brian's teenage sons had pulled the old, ruined one out from the wall yesterday. Brian had loaded the oven onto his truck and hauled it away.

"Don't worry about the food. Let me cook Thanksgiving dinner for you."

She couldn't believe she'd said that. From Nathan's expression, he appeared just as surprised.

"I didn't invite you to Thanksgiving so you'd cook for us."

She nodded. "I know, but I'd like to." Equally shocking, she discovered she truly wanted to make it a real Thanksgiving for them.

"That's awfully good of you, but your company is more than enough."

"You're sharing your home and family with me. Cooking is the least I can do." She touched his sleeve. "Please let me do this. Turkey and all the fixings." Had she overstepped? "Unless it would bring sad memories."

He looked at her. "Deanna had many wonderful qualities, but traditional she was not. One year, she served Korean barbecue." He shrugged. "Dad and I haven't had a traditional turkey dinner since my mother died. We'd love it. Thank you."

She steepled her hands under her chin. "I can't wait to get started."

"I hope you still feel as enthusiastic four hours into prep. Consider me your sous chef."

She laughed.

"What?"

"Just picturing you in a chef's hat and not a Stetson."

Crossing his arms, he grinned. "I may not be professionally trained like Kara, or Maddie Lovett at the bakery, but I can hold my own."

"Of that I have no doubt."

LATE MONDAY AFTERNOON, Bridger dropped off the boys with take-out bags for dinner. An aroma of French fries wafted through the air.

The boys hadn't been home since the fire. She could tell they were hesitant about what they might find, but the kitchen had been restored to its original state, minus the oven.

"Looks pwetty much the same." Pushing his way past his brother, Kody released a huge sigh of relief. "Let's eat."

Connor tugged at her sweater. "I missed you, Miss Gemma."

Her heart turned over. "I missed you, too, Connor." She hugged him. He smelled of cinnamon spice. And everything nice. Maggie must have been baking.

Nathan ruffled Connor's hair. "What about me and old Granddad? What are we, chopped beef?"

Ike snorted. "Who are you calling old?"

Kody held up the white take-out bag from the Burger Depot. "We bwought the beef."

After dinner, the boys headed out to check on the rabbits.

Finding herself alone with Nathan, she grabbed a pad of paper and a pen from the catch-all drawer next to the refrigerator. "Besides turkey, what says Thanksgiving to you?"

"Pumpkin pie." He leaned his elbow on the counter. "Or pecan. You pick."

The back door squeaked open. Connor and Kody tromped inside.

"Boots!" she and Nathan cried in unison. They smiled at each other.

The boys toed out of their barn boots.

"Watcha doin', Miss Gemma?"

"You've got homework, too, Miss Gemma?"

She tapped the pen against the pad. "I'm taking orders for our Thanksgiving menu."

Kody's eyes got big. "You're gonna be with us on Thanksgiving?"

"If that would be okay with you?"

"Woo-hoo!" Kody fist-pumped the air and did a little dance in his stocking feet around the kitchen island.

Connor didn't say anything, but the smile on his face told her he was also pleased. Unlike his party-waiting-to-happen younger sibling, he was quieter. It was far too easy for most people to overlook Nathan's oldest child. But not on her watch.

She brushed a lock of hair out of his eyes. "What says Thanksgiving to you, honey?"

"Mashed potatoes." His eyes shone. "And gravy. Lots of gravy."

She wrote it down with a flourish. Mashed potatoes she could do, although the gravy would be unexplored territory. She turned toward Kody. "And you, Sir Dances-a-lot?"

He giggled. "Sweet tea."

She wrote it down. "The sweetest."

"And biscuits with butter."

"You got it." She crossed the *t* and dotted the *i*.

He held up his index finger. "One more thing."

Nathan grabbed his youngest and put him in a headlock. "Seriously, Kode? She's not running a cafeteria here."

She waved the pencil. "What else, sweetie?"

Kody freed himself from his father's hold. "Deviled eggs."

Connor snorted. "Deviled eggs for Thanksgiving?"

"Deviled eggs are appropriate for any season, any occasion." She nodded. "Deviled eggs it is."

With Rascal at his heels, Ike ambled into the kitchen. "What's with the hootin' and hollerin'?"

Connor took his grandfather's hand. "Gemma's making Thanksgiving dinner."

Ike grinned. "Is she now?"

"And she's taking pwayer wequests," Kody piped.

Connor planted his hands on his jeans. "Menu requests, Kode. Not prayer requests."

"You pway your way, and I'll pway mine." Kody rubbed his flat little belly. "This is a dweam come true."

Connor snickered. "He's so silly, Miss Gemma."

"The silliest," she agreed.

She and Nathan exchanged a smile.

Ike cleared his throat.

Her cheeks heating, she returned to the matter at hand. "What says Thanksgiving to you, Ike?"

"Cranberry sauce. Green bean casserole." Ike ticked the items off on his fingers. "Sweet potato casserole and apple-cornbread dressing, Nathan's mom's specialty." He cocked his head. "You know what dressing is, don't you?"

She patted his arm. "I may not be from Truelove, but Greensboro is still the South. In coastal,

Piedmont or mountain North Carolina—dressing is served alongside the turkey. Not in it."

Ike gestured toward the cupboard over the coffeemaker. "All Pammie's recipes are in there."

"Dad." Nathan opened his hands. "Let's not overwhelm Gemma."

She opened the cabinet. "The recipes are much appreciated." A small wooden box sat on the top shelf.

Nathan reached up and handed it to her. "You do not have to fix all this food."

"It'll be fun." She took the recipe box from him. "I'll make out my shopping list for ingredients."

He scratched his head. "What says Thanksgiving to you?"

She looked away. "Thanksgiving was never a big deal with my family."

He frowned. "But surely you have a favorite."

Corn pudding—Gemma's mom had made the dish every year for Thanksgiving. Until she died. But corn pudding—like most things associated with her family—was best left in the past. The only legacy they'd passed on was shame.

She forced a smile. "It will give me a great deal of joy to make everyone's favorites."

On Tuesday morning with the boys off for

their final day of school before the holiday, Nathan hung around the house longer than usual to oversee the delivery and installation of the new stove. Sheepish about the trouble he'd put them to, Ike banned himself from any more cooking.

Gemma spent most of the day combing through Pamela Crenshaw's old recipe box. Inside was a treasure trove. A time capsule from the mid-twentieth century. A family legacy of pleasant, shared gatherings.

She thumbed through the contents. "What was with the obsession with gelatin?"

Lime. Cherry. Orange. Side dish or dessert. There was even a banana loaf recipe which called for gelatin. Blue ink faded, the index cards were splotched and fraying. Some of the oft-listed ingredients she'd never heard of before—like oleo?

It was only after she made her grocery list and planned out when everything had to go into the oven the enormity of the task hit her. And only two days to prepare before the main event.

What had she been thinking? Her skills extended beyond boiling water and the microwave, but this was well out of her comfort zone.

She'd never cooked a turkey in her life. She rested her head in her hands. This had the makings of a culinary disaster. She was doomed.

Perhaps she ought to bow out now, make her excuses and order Thanksgiving takeout from the actual cafeteria in Asheville. But she couldn't bear to disappoint the boys. And by boys she meant Ike and Nathan, too. She'd seen the wistful expression on Nathan's face when his father mentioned the apple-cornbread dressing.

This was no time for pride. She called Maggie.

"Hey, Gemma. How's—"

"What in the world is oleo?" She burst into tears.

After Maggie talked her off the ledge, she gave her new friend a rundown of the corner she'd painted herself into.

"No need to panic, Gemma."

"I wanted this to be a perfect Thanksgiving for Ike. And I still don't know what oleo is," she wailed.

"Oleo is what my grandma called margarine. No matter what you do or don't fix, it'll be perfect because Ike, Nathan and the boys will know how much you care about them. We'll work on this together."

"You must have food preparations to make for your own family."

"Bridger's sister is hosting this year in Fayetteville, where her husband is stationed. I'm bringing an already made pie. We'll head there on Thursday morning so tomorrow I'm totally yours."

"Your sons will be home for the holiday and—"

"Bridger and the boys have plans to work with the new puppies. I'm free to help."

She drew her first even breath in an hour. Maybe this wouldn't be so terrible after all. "If you're sure…"

"This is what friends are for, Gemma. I'm touched you trusted me enough to reach out."

She and Maggie quickly made plans to meet at the Hollingsworth house after Gemma made her grocery run Wednesday morning.

"Oh," Maggie threw in. "Bring enough clean dishes so we can put everything together."

Feeling much better than she had before calling, she thanked her friend again before saying goodbye.

Now Gemma needed to let her oldest friend know she wouldn't be spending Thanksgiving with Juliet's family. But how would Jules take the news?

With some trepidation, she sent a text. Immediately, squiggly dots appeared.

Juliet: Everything going well?

Gemma: I'm cooking Thanksgiving dinner for them.

More dots followed. Including wide-eyed-amazement emojis. Breathing a sigh of relief their friendship remained intact, she chuckled.

Juliet: I want the juicy details re. you & Nathan.

She shook her head. Keeping it professional. Nathan & I r friends.

Juliet: Don't believe you. Have fun with your "friend," We'll miss you.

She smiled. Miss you, too. Happy Thanksgiving.

Just because Juliet got her second chance, happily-ever-after didn't mean she wanted one, too.

Yet despite her oft-stated resistance to romance, when she fell asleep that night, Nathan's handsome features were the last image in her mind.

## CHAPTER NINE

THE NEXT MORNING, with so many tasks on her to-do list, Gemma bounded out of bed. Despite the boys being out of school for the holiday— or perhaps because—the morning was unusually hectic.

When Tom Arledge picked up Ike and Rascal for a pre-Thanksgiving ROMEO get-together, she grabbed her purse to run errands.

Driving away from the ranch, she patted her purse with the all-important shopping list on the seat beside her. She couldn't remember the last time she'd looked forward to a holiday as much.

Holidays had brought out the worst in her father. He nursed his anger and a bottle of liquor, and the combination was a toxic brew. Too often, she and her mother had been the collateral damage.

She hadn't been much older than Kody when she learned to stay well out of his reach. Thanksgiving or Christmas were at best days to endure, never to enjoy.

The first year after she went to live with the Spencers, she'd been too shell-shocked to do much more than go through the motions. Later once their grandkids were born, the Spencers took to spending the holidays out of state. Despite their well-intentioned invitations to go with them, every year she politely declined.

Her excuse—she couldn't leave her current dog-in-progress over the holiday. But the truth was, even with only a canine for company, she never felt as alone as when she found herself surrounded by other people's families.

Leaving the ranch, she stopped at a large grocery chain on the highway outside of Truelove to purchase the items she'd need for Thanksgiving dinner. The store was filled with last-minute shoppers. Holiday music played on the intercom.

Consulting her list, she went aisle by aisle until she had all the ingredients for the most wonderful Thanksgiving ever. Including a few items she hadn't intended to buy.

After going through the checkout, she loaded the bags into her car. The wind was brisk coming off the mountain today. Brown leaves swirled on the pavement underneath her feet.

Returning to Truelove, she found herself humming a Christmas carol. Most of the storefronts were shuttered, except for the Jar, which was doing a booming business.

Per Maggie's instructions, she pulled into the Hollingsworths' driveway and steered around to the back of the house.

To her surprise, a bevy of other vehicles were already parked there, including the GMC pickup she recognized as belonging to Nathan's great-aunt, GeorgeAnne. Her anxiety ratcheted.

Had she misunderstood? Had she gotten the time wrong? Was she interrupting a private party?

Stomach knotting, she threw the car in Reverse, but Maggie dashed out of the house. "Gemma, wait."

Heat flooded her cheeks. She'd been spotted. Any hope of making a graceful, unobtrusive withdrawal faded. Cutting the engine, she got halfway out of the car. Best to make her excuses and beat a hasty retreat.

"You're busy," she called. "No worries." Although, how she was going to pull this dinner off alone threatened to bring on another round of tears.

"Where're you going?" Maggie motioned. "Come inside."

A handful of women filed out of the house. With the exception of GeorgeAnne, the rest of them were around her own age. Like Kara. Maggie introduced her to most of them when they came to help the Crenshaws after the fire.

She wrung her hands. "I... I don't want to intrude."

"You're not intruding." Maggie's ponytail whipped in the breeze. "Everyone is here for you."

She frowned. "For me?"

"Many hands make light work." Maggie smiled. "When I told Aunt Georgie what you were trying to do for Ike and his family, she rallied the troops."

"But everyone has their own dinners to prepare."

Kara stepped forward. "The MacKenzie clan is having Thanksgiving with the Ferguson brood. My mom and sisters-in-law insisted I take a vacation from cooking." Her adoptive mom was the undisputed queen of North Carolina barbecue.

Gemma bit her lip. "You're not taking off if you're helping me."

Maggie smiled. "Kara isn't here in a chef capacity, but as a teacher."

GeorgeAnne harrumphed. "My role is supervisory."

Maggie exchanged a wry look with the others. "Of course it is, Aunt Georgie. Supervising is what you do best."

GeorgeAnne pushed her glasses higher on the bridge of her nose. "We wanted to show our appreciation for everything you're doing to make this holiday season special for Ike and the boys."

"It really is my pleasure." She slumped. "I just got in over my head with the cooking."

"We've got you covered," Callie McAbee, ROMEO Nash's daughter, assured her. The Apple Valley orchard was next door to the ranch.

"Fact is," AnnaBeth, Truelove's resident style maven and host of the popular weekly podcast *Heart's Home*, interjected. "In our families, we're the second-string cooks. The heavy lifting is done by the older generation. Our only responsibility is to bring a dish or two."

"Life always comes full circle." GeorgeAnne's thin lips creased. "Your generation's turn will come soon enough. Then it will be your responsibility to carry forward the family traditions you learned from your mothers, aunts and grandmothers."

"We brought ingredients to make our own dishes." Lila Gibson, resident landscape artist at nearby Ashmont College, touched Gemma's arm. "No one wanted to miss the chance to help you, have a good time with friends and learn from the best."

"That would be Kara," Kelsey Summerfield declared.

Everyone laughed.

Recently engaged to Bar None ranch owner Clay McKendry, Kelsey co-owned a wedding venue with the petite blond chef, who had fingers in many culinary business pies in Truelove.

Despite her initial misgivings, Gemma found herself and her bags of groceries hauled into Maggie's kitchen.

True to form, GeorgeAnne soon had the medium-sized kitchen and its young cooks organized. Gemma found herself mixing ingredients for a sweet potato casserole with AnnaBeth. Followed by a green bean casserole with Callie. Once assembled, everyone's dishes were labeled and stored in Maggie's garage fridge to be taken home later and put into the oven the morning of Thanksgiving.

Kara gave detailed instructions on how to thaw, prepare and roast a turkey. Gemma took copious notes. Because gravy could be tricky, under Kara's close supervision, she also learned to make a roux to thicken the sauce.

Usually, she didn't feel at ease with people she didn't know. But somehow—thanks to Maggie's hospitality—in the process of cooking alongside each other, Maggie's friends had become her friends, too. The feeling of belonging was new to her and heartwarming. Filling her with no small sense of gratitude.

"If you have time…" She pulled out the worn recipe card from her purse. "There's one more thing Ike specially requested."

Behind the glasses frames, GeorgeAnne's glacier-blue eyes widened. "Is that Pamela Crenshaw's apple-cornbread dressing recipe? I recognize the handwriting."

"It is. This is the one I want to make sure I get right."

Maggie took the card from her. "This recipe is a family legend."

"I'm delighted you found it." GeorgeAnne put a liver-spotted hand to her throat. "After she died, I feared it was lost for good."

Callie peered over Kara's shoulder. "I wouldn't

mind learning Miss Pamela's recipe, too. After all, apples are kind of a McAbee thing."

Everyone laughed, but declared themselves equally eager to learn.

By two o'clock, Maggie's kitchen smelled amazing. The tantalizing aroma of roasted nuts filled the air. Everyone made short work of helping Maggie put her kitchen to rights.

Her arms full of containers collected from the garage fridge, Kelsey turned to go. "I can't think when I've had so much fun."

"Me, too." Lila was right behind her. "Happy Thanksgiving, everybody."

Callie was next to depart.

"Have you thought about table decor?" On her way out the door, AnnaBeth paused. "Dressing the table is as pleasing to the eye as the food is to the stomach."

"No… I haven't…" She threw Maggie a panicked look.

But it was GeorgeAnne to the rescue. "Deanna kept special holiday decor in the sideboard in the dining room." Nathan's great-aunt tapped her chin. "Knowing my nephew, it's probably right where she left it."

Kara and Maggie insisted on helping Gemma

load her car. Walking out with them, GeorgeAnne supervised, per her nature.

As she gazed at the multitude of dishes, ready to be popped into the oven on Thanksgiving morn, tears pricked Gemma's eyes. "I know what I'll be most thankful for this Thanksgiving." She looked at them. "Friends like you," she rasped.

Maggie hugged her. GeorgeAnne, not a hugger, patted her shoulder.

Kara glanced at her watch. "You can't go yet. Not until—"

A light blue vintage Volkswagen Beetle chugged into the driveway and parked next to Gemma's car.

Kara smiled. "Not until Maddie gets here with the pies. She was running a holiday pie special today. Buy one, get another fifty percent off."

The curly-haired, always effervescent baker launched from her car. "The pies have sold like hot cakes." Eyes twinkling, she retrieved two aluminum-wrapped pie tins from the back seat. "After Kara called in your pie SOS, I saved a pumpkin pie and a pecan pie for you."

Gemma reached for her handbag, but Kara shook her head. "All taken care of. A welcome-to-Truelove gift from the Mason Jar and Madeline's."

She gave Kara and young Maddie a hug. "I can't thank you enough for everything you've done. You've been the true definition of community."

"It's the beginning of my busy season, otherwise I would've been here for the rest of the fun today." Maddie grinned. "But I promise to give you a private pie-making lesson after the holidays."

But the New Year would find Gemma far from Truelove.

She swallowed. "That's kind of you, but I'm only in Truelove temporarily. The agency promised to send another caregiver by January."

"That's a shame." GeorgeAnne cleared her throat. "You'll be missed."

She blinked. *Who was this person and what had they done with the real GeorgeAnne Allen?* The older woman's attitude toward her had seemingly done an about-face. She wasn't sure why, but she was grateful.

Gemma swallowed. "I'll miss all of you, too." And she meant it, even the curmudgeonly Truelove matchmaker.

She headed to the ranch. The reminder of her leave-taking left her feeling empty.

It was a disconcerting sensation—to feel such connection to a place and one family in particular. With the exception of Juliet, she'd made a habit of not getting too attached to humans.

She didn't like the idea of needing anyone. Though she'd certainly needed the combined efforts of Truelove's gracious matrons today.

At the farm, Nathan was on the porch. A sudden lump burned her throat.

She hurried out of the car. "Is everything okay with Ike?" There was no sign of Tom Arledge's truck, though he'd promised to sit with Ike until she returned.

"Everything's fine." Nathan leaned against the railing. "The boys and I finished the chores early so I sent Tom home. Dad and the little guys are working on a puzzle."

A sweet relief washed over her. She opened the trunk and retrieved the box of dishes.

He came over to the car. "Let me take that. It looks heavy."

Taking the box, he sniffed the air appreciably. "Something smells delicious. Sounds like you and the ladies were cooking up a feast."

She cocked her head. "How—"

"Truelove grapevine." He grinned. "Bridger and the twins sought refuge at the ranch for lunch. He told me about the hen party at his house." Nathan trudged up the steps. "I hope you had fun. You work too hard."

Flitting ahead, she held the door for him. "Says the hardest-working man I've ever known."

Inside the kitchen, he set the box on the counter. "I think we both need to make a plan for some fun." He took one of the covered casseroles out of the box and handed it to her.

She put the dish in the fridge. "What does it say about us that we have to plan for fun? How boring am I?"

Nathan handed her another container. "You're the least boring person I know. We're superresponsible people with busy lives who have a lot of people and animals depending on us. I admire the work you do, Gemma. How you've helped us." A warmth lit his face.

Her pulse leaped. Hiding her confusion, she put the dish on the refrigerator shelf. When she felt steady enough to face him, she turned around to find he'd lifted the foil on the pecan pie. Caught out, he reddened. She chuckled.

"Maddie Lovett made the pies." She fiddled

with the gold hoop at her earlobe. "There wasn't time to make them myself."

He snitched a tiny bit of crust and popped it in his mouth. "Love Maddie's pies, but what I'm looking forward to most is spending Thanksgiving together with you."

Connor and Kody trudged into the kitchen. "We're hungry," Kody declared. "When's supper?"

Nathan shook his head. "Bottomless pits." Ike and Rascal soon followed, also wanting dinner.

"Guys!" He threw out his hands. "Gemma's trying to put together Thanksgiving."

"Which is why tonight's dinner is every man for himself." She pointed to the fridge. "Do me a favor and clean out the leftovers Kara brought from the Jar. I need room for the turkey."

With the guys on microwave duty, she got to work thawing the turkey per Kara's safe-practice guidelines. Gemma wasn't bothered with so many people in the kitchen. Despite her usually solitary existence, she liked having the boys underfoot, the noise and the commotion they wrought in their wake.

Once she returned to her apartment in Greensboro, she wasn't sure how she'd ever get used to the quiet again. But for now, she intended to soak up every last morsel of joy, like a biscuit sopping gravy. Which, thanks to Kara, she now knew how to make.

Like Nathan, what she was looking forward to the most was spending time with all of them. Especially the man she admired more than any other in the world. Not only for his commitment to care for his ailing father, his devotion to his sons, but also—and she wasn't too proud to admit it—for how he made her feel.

Seventeen again. With the whole world and a lifetime of possibilities yet before her.

## CHAPTER TEN

THANKSGIVING DAY DAWNED crisp and cold. Overnight, the temperature had plummeted. Snow was forecast over the holiday weekend.

Filled with anticipation, Gemma awoke early to get a jump start on a timetable that would have rivaled D-Day. She didn't bother putting on fancy clothes. She'd change into something more festive later.

Donning jeans and an old gray sweatshirt, she hurried into the darkened kitchen. Getting the turkey into the oven was her first priority.

She hadn't been in the kitchen fifteen minutes before Nathan joined her. Downing a quick cup of coffee, he scanned her to-do list. Padding into the kitchen, Rascal availed himself of the new doggy exit. The little door flapped behind him.

A blast of frigid air followed in his wake.

"Brrrr…" She reached for her coat hanging

on the peg. "I think I left my purse in the car last night."

"I'll get it for you. Stay inside where it's warm. I'm headed outside anyway." Nathan shrugged into his heavy, fleece-lined coat. "I have to chop through the ice so the cattle can drink."

On frosty winter mornings, he was the kind of guy who had probably warmed the car for his wife. A woman would be blessed to have him as her husband. A woman like her?

A ridiculous notion, but she smiled at him. "Thank you. Happy Thanksgiving."

Nathan smiled back. "You're welcome, and happy Thanksgiving to you, too."

Her heart ticked up a notch. *Just because he smiles at you… Stop being such a teenager.*

Nathan put on his work gloves. "I'll be back to help." There was another rush of air as he went outside.

Seconds later, Rascal bounded into the house once more.

Gemma gave him a hug. "Good dog." His fluffy fur was cold against her face. The collie disappeared down the hall to resume his protective watch over Ike.

Wistful for the home she'd always longed for and never known, she took out the odd assortment of items she'd bought on a whim yesterday. She wasn't sure why she'd purchased the ingredients for her mom's corn pudding. Everything else on the menu was a Crenshaw family tradition.

Perhaps she'd merely wanted to bring something of herself—one of the few good things she'd carried from her own dysfunctional childhood.

She'd been angry with her mom for so long—unreasonably so—for failing to fix the toxic atmosphere with Gemma's dad. But most of all, for failing to rescue them until it was far, far too late.

Yet putting together the recipe made her feel close to her mother in a way she hadn't felt since the tragic events of that long-ago day. The ending of her family had been so painful she'd developed the habit of pushing her memories of her mother away. As if her mother had never existed.

But in pushing away the bad, how much of the good had she lost, too?

It made no sense to blame the parent who'd been most wronged for the situation. Yet she had.

Over the months that followed the tragedy,

a host of trauma counselors had cautioned her that until she was ready to find compassion for her mother's all-too-human fragility, and come to terms with the harrowing consequences of her mother's ultimate act of courage, she'd never be free to move forward into her own future.

Frowning, she opened the can of cream-style corn. Why, of all days, was she thinking about this now? But grief never paid a house call when it was convenient. Certainly not when she was in the midst of preparations for Thanksgiving dinner.

On that cold November morning, for the first time in a long time she missed her mom. Really allowed herself to miss her.

It had been her mother who passed on a love for God's creatures. Her mother who taught her to read her Bible and pray. Who encouraged Gemma. Cheered her every endeavor. Who loved her.

Her mother, isolated by her father from friends and relatives, uneducated and with few options for escape, bound to a controlling, abusive narcissist. Finding herself in an impossible situation, her mother had done the best she knew how.

With God's help, wasn't that all anyone

could do? Stifling a sob, Gemma put her hand to her mouth.

Standing over the uncooked corn pudding, with the hindsight of maturity, she found compassion in her heart for what her mother had suffered. For everything they'd suffered together.

Then, amid much silent weeping lest she wake the boys or Ike, she forgave her mother the hardest thing of all—for dying. In sacrificing herself, she'd saved Gemma's life. Yet her death had shattered Gemma. Leaving her to face an unknown future alone.

"Gemma?"

Her head shot up. Concern darkening his features, Nathan stood in the doorway. Such had been her grief, she hadn't heard the telltale squeak of the door.

She felt her cheeks burn crimson.

Why did she have to break down now? And in front of Nathan of all people?

TOEING OUT OF his boots, Nate crossed the room. "What's wrong?" He laid her purse on the island stool.

Frantically, she swiped at the tears coursing across her face. "I'm fine."

Nate peeled off his gloves and stuffed them in

his coat pockets. "You're not fine. What's happened to make you feel sad?"

"Holidays bring reminders of people no longer in my life." Taking a shaky breath, she fluttered her hand as if waving her cares away. "Sorry for being such a downer. I should dice the apples for the dressing."

She tried to move past him, but he stopped her with a gentle touch on her arm. "Believe me, Gemma, I understand all too well."

Her stomach twisted. "You lost your wife. Of course you understand." She dropped her eyes to the floor. "Forgive me for being insensitive."

Capturing her chin between his thumb and index finger, he lifted her gaze to meet his. "Gemma."

Tears like tiny dewdrops clung to the edges of her lashes. Tenderness filled him.

"Dad is fond of saying that pain shared is pain halved. Talk to me." The knot in his belly tightened. "Tell me what you're thinking and feeling."

Her chin quivered. "You should take your own advice."

Nate dropped his hand. "I... I can't." He tugged at the back of his neck. "I'm sorry."

Surprisingly, it was Gemma who comforted

him. She squeezed his hand. "It's taken me a long time to battle through the baggage to the feelings I experienced this morning."

"Which are…?" He shook his head. "Sorry. I've no right to probe."

"Ike is right. It is better to share it with someone." She sighed. "Making her corn pudding, I found myself missing my mom. How's that for crazy?"

"Not crazy." He prayed she wouldn't shut him down. "You never talked about your family. Is your mother still living?"

Gemma stared out the window at the swaths of pink and gold in the sky over the mountains. "Sadly, no."

Shoulder to shoulder with her, he kept his gaze trained on the rolling pastureland beyond the window. Sometimes confidences were easier shared without eye contact.

Gemma sighed. "My mother died the day I got home from camp."

His eyes jerked to hers. He scanned her face. Not what he'd expected. But maybe that explained something about what happened between him and Gemma.

She let go of his hand to tuck a tendril of

hair behind her ear. Immediately, he missed the warmth of her hand in his.

Burnt orange, her ribbon of the day, reminded him of autumn leaves on the nearby Blue Ridge Parkway.

"I'm sorry." Finding her hand again, he laced his fingers through hers. She didn't pull away. "You must've been devastated."

"You would think so, wouldn't you?" She gave a self-deprecating laugh devoid of mirth. "But anger is easier than devastation."

"I get it."

Her eyes darted to him.

"As shields go, there's nothing better than anger to keep from feeling the pain." Or in his case, the guilt. "Anything to keep at bay the grief."

She tilted her head. "You don't seem angry to me."

He hunched his shoulders. "Anger is the fuel driving my workaholism. Which you were right to call me on. I'm trying to change. To do better for the boys and Dad."

"I see how hard you try." Her mouth wobbled. "Your efforts do not go unappreciated by your family. Or me," she whispered.

Bringing her hand to his mouth, he brushed his lips across her fingers. "I'm sorry Thanksgiving recalled tough memories."

Her eyes glistened with tears.

For the past two weeks, it had taken everything in him not to gather her into his arms. The desire to cradle her, to hold her in the circle of his arms, intensified. He fought himself no more.

Nate put his arms around her. He kept his hold loose, letting her decide to break free or not. But turning into him, she put her face against his shoulder. He buried his nose in her hair.

Over the last few weeks, he hadn't allowed himself to get this close to her. For a moment, she let him hold her. She seemed to find comfort in his embrace. But neither of them were the naive teenagers they'd been.

His chest heaved. "Gem—"

A commotion sounded down the hall.

The boys, his dad and the dog stampeded into the kitchen. Wrenching free, she planted herself next to the island and folded her arms around her sweatshirt.

Placing his palms flat on the edge of the

countertop, he leaned over the sink, willing his heartbeat to regulate.

Connor's nose twitched. "Something smells awesome."

"I'm hungry," Kody said.

Slowly, he angled.

Gemma swiped her index finger under her eyes. "You're always hungry."

To his ears, her dry, husky laughter felt a tad hollow. Was she having as hard a time regaining her equilibrium as him?

She handed Kody a cereal bowl. "A light breakfast this morning, if you please, gentlemen. Everyone needs to save their big appetite for all the food I'm cooking."

"We're here to help, right, guys?" He was proud of how even his tone sounded, but his heart continued to drum furiously against his rib cage. "Put us to work."

He might have pulled off normalcy with his sons, but his father gave him a swift, calculating look.

Becoming brisk, she put Nate to work peeling potatoes. When the timer buzzed, he took the turkey out of the oven for her. His dad and the boys were appointed with setting the dining room table.

She'd unearthed harvest decorations, including the large ceramic turkey that had graced every Thanksgiving meal until Deanna died.

While he assembled the deviled eggs, she bustled around, putting the finishing touches on several dishes. His father, the boys and Rascal trouped outside to scavenge for further table decor. They returned with a basket of pine cones and small boughs of cedar. The house filled with the tangy aroma of evergreens and the mouthwatering scent of roasted turkey.

Once the turkey cooled sufficiently to handle, she put him in charge of carving the bird. With organized chaos reigning in the kitchen, he carried the roasting pan and a white platter to the breakfast alcove, where they ate most of their meals.

His dad pulled out the chair next to him. Rascal plopped at his feet. Anointing himself chief taste tester, his father sneaked bits of turkey to Rascal underneath the table.

At the island, she helped the boys roll dough and cut out the biscuits. Kody brandished the rolling pin like a knight of old. Connor and Gemma laughed themselves silly at his silliness.

Flour soon coated most surfaces, but she didn't seem to mind. Smiling, she kissed the dusting of flour on Connor's cheek, which prompted Kody to throw a handful of flour directly into his face. He sputtered. Connor hooted, but Gemma gave Kody a quick peck on his forehead.

His dad chuckled. "She's good with the boys. They really like her."

Nate distrusted the mischievous look in his father's eyes.

Wresting his attention from the hilarity ensuing around him to turkey carving, he concentrated on not slicing off a finger. "It's good they like her since she's helping us over the holidays."

She placed the biscuit tray in the oven and set the timer. "Boys, stand here and watch the biscuits. Make sure they don't get too brown."

Gemma took off her apron. "I'm going to change out of these old work clothes, but if the timer dings before I get back, let your dad take the biscuits out of the oven."

She ambled over to him and his father. "Looks like you have everything under control."

His dad winked at her. "That's because, as the Crenshaw family quality control engineer, I'm keeping a close eye on him." He jerked his thumb in Nate's direction.

Smiling, she disappeared down the hall. Peering through the oven glass, the boys' attention remained riveted on the slowly browning tops of the biscuits.

Leaning closer, his father plucked a morsel of succulent meat off the platter and passed it to Rascal. "The boys aren't the only ones that like her."

Nate raised his eyebrow. "We all like and admire Gemma. She's great."

"My mind may be going, but it isn't gone yet, son. The boys and I interrupted something between you earlier."

"I have no idea what you're talking about, Dad. Gemma and I are just old friends."

His father snorted. "Back in the day, you were head over heels for that little gal. And from the way you look at her when you think no one's looking, you still are."

"I do not look—" He pressed his lips together.

Ecstatic over getting a rise out of him, his father grinned. "'Course I'm not saying she doesn't look at you the same way, too."

"She does?" Clutching the carving knife, he straightened. "I mean…" Sweat peppered his forehead. "I'm sure you must be mistaken."

His father cackled.

The timer dinged.

"Dad!" Kody shouted.

Saved by the timer.

Ending the awkward conversation with his matchmaking father, he hurried to remove the tray from the oven.

"I heard the—" She dashed into the kitchen. "How are the biscuits?"

The breath knocked from his lungs, his eyes widened. *Wow.*

Kody touched the tip of his finger to the hem of the silky, moss green blouse she wore over her jeans. "You look so pwetty, Miss Gemma, doesn't she, Dad?"

The girl had been pretty. The woman was beautiful. His heart lodged in his throat. Something until now he'd believed an anatomical impossibility.

"Uh…" He opened his mouth. Closed it. Opened it again. "Ummm…"

"What my son is trying and failing miserably to say is, 'Yes, you do.'" Getting out of his chair, his father gave Gemma a hug. "You look a right treat, my dear."

Avoiding eye contact with Nate, she blushed. "Thank you, Mr. Ike. And you, too, Sir Kody." Ducking her head, she exclaimed over his sons' first foray into baking.

The boys were ridiculously proud of the biscuits. Somehow the food managed to arrive on the table, steaming hot, all at the same time. The credit was entirely hers.

"If you'd allow me?" His dad smiled at each one seated around the dining room table. "I'd like to say grace, son."

"Of course, Dad." He studied his father's bright gaze. "Go ahead."

His dad's prayer was short but heartfelt. He thanked the Lord for the bounty they would partake of, for the hands that prepared it, for the opportunity to be together and for the blessing of loved ones no longer with them. "Amen."

Opening his eyes, Nate cleared his throat. "Amen." Across the table, Gemma drew his gaze like a magnet.

"Amen," she whispered.

They dug in. He relished the happy faces of his sons and his father. Gemma had made this day a wonderful occasion.

It did his heart good to behold his father's returning confidence and quality of life restored. Gemma and Rascal had done that. The future was unknowable, but today—his vision blurred—if only for today, he had his dad back.

Everyone made much of Gemma's corn pudding.

"Good as dessert," his dad proclaimed.

A warm glow softened her features. "I'm glad you like it."

Kody stabbed a slice of turkey with his fork. "This was a gweat idea."

He cut his eyes at his youngest son. "What is, Kode?"

"Thanksgiving."

"Dude…" Connor threw out his hands. "We do Thanksgiving every year."

"Are you sure?" Kody bunched his eyebrows. "I don't 'member anything like this." The little boy's eyes flicked to the ceramic turkey centerpiece. "Butterball looks familiar, though."

Nate's heart constricted.

Deanna had put out the porcelain turkey every Thanksgiving. He'd suspected Kody might not remember much about his mother. He'd only been three when she died so suddenly.

The confirmation of what he'd feared brought him no small measure of pain. Deanna had loved the boys so much. He needed to do better at keeping her memory alive for her sons.

"Oh, no." Scraping back her chair, Gemma jumped up from the table.

His pulse quickened. "What?" He started to rise.

She waved him into his seat. "I forgot to put together the cranberry gelatin salad from the recipe box." Her face fell. "I'm so sorry, guys."

Connor lanced a green bean. "I like the canned stuff better anyway."

"Me, too," Kody chimed.

Nate was reasonably sure Kody had no recollection of cranberry sauce, either way. But whatever his brother liked, Kody liked, too.

"I agree," Nate rasped. "Who needs the gelatin salad? The nuts get stuck in your teeth."

She flashed him a smile. "I see where Kody gets it from."

"Gets what?"

"The endearing silliness." Her brown eyes gleamed. "Thank you."

"It is I who thank you."

A gentle smile lifted the corners of her lips. "For what?"

"For making this the happiest of Thanksgivings for Dad and the boys." His gaze found hers. "And me."

The clink of silverware and the hum of voices momentarily faded. There was only him and her. And the dawning awareness pulsing between them.

At that moment, Kody upset his water glass. Vaulting out of their seats, everyone else grabbed a handful of napkins in a vain attempt to stem the flow of liquid from reaching the floor. For a few minutes, chaos again reigned.

But he wouldn't have it any other way.

To his surprise, he felt content. An emotion so long foreign to him, he barely recognized it. Happy, even. There could be no question of why.

Nate's gaze drifted around the table to the people he loved most in the world.

His father, enjoying life in a way he'd feared forever lost. His sons, blossoming under Gemma's nurturing presence.

As for Gemma? He took a quick intake of breath. He'd loved the girl.

Was he falling in love with the woman?

# CHAPTER ELEVEN

THE GUYS INSISTED on doing the Thanksgiving cleanup.

Gemma found herself sitting on the sofa in the living room with her feet propped, unsure what to do with such unaccustomed leisure.

From the kitchen came the sound of running water, the clink of silverware deposited in the drawer and the low murmur of conversation. She smiled at the boys' bright chatter.

A few minutes later, Kody ventured into the living room. His feet dragged. He was tired. It had been a full day. He sank onto the couch next to her.

He nestled against her. "Can I tell you a secret, Miss Gemma?"

She tilted her head to get a better look at him. "Of course, sweetie. What is it?"

He sighed. "I don't 'member my mama. Her picture is on my dresser and sometimes I think I see her like when she worked in the garden, but I'm not sure if I'm 'membering, or if it's 'cause Connor told me she liked flowers."

Gemma put her arm around him.

Rubbing his eyes, he laid his head against her shoulder. "Connor says it makes Daddy sad to talk about her so we don't. But I wish I 'membered her."

Gemma's heart pinched.

He yawned. "I'm the only one in my class without a mom. Know what else, Miss Gemma?"

She hugged him closer. "What, sweetie pie?"

"I love you."

A lump settled in her throat. "I love you, too, Kody," she rasped.

His eyelids had closed. Fighting tears, she kissed the top of his hair.

Connor hovered on the other side of the coffee table. "Miss Gemma?"

"Yes, honey?"

He bit his lip. "Is there room on the couch for me?" The yearning on his face just about broke her heart.

She patted the spot on her left. "There's always room for you, Connor."

With a grateful smile, he plopped down beside her. Kody didn't stir. She put her other arm around Connor. They talked for a few minutes about nothing and everything until his eyelids drooped, too.

Blame it on the early morning, the excitement and the tryptophan, but soon both of Nathan's sons were out for the count.

Effectively trapped, she made no move to disturb them. There was no place she'd rather be than with the two dearest little boys in the whole world.

Closing her eyes, she thanked God for her job and dogs like Rascal at PawPals that gave her life purpose. She thanked God for the people He had placed in her life. Juliet and her family. At her lowest point, God had brought the Spencers into her life to give her back her life.

Had God brought her into Kody's and Connor's lives, for even this short time, to do the same?

Overcome with fatigue from a day well spent, she floated in and out of wakefulness.

What was she looking forward to the future?

Her last coherent thought was to wonder if her future would include Nathan.

HIS DAD HAD insisted on washing the dishes. Nate dried, and the boys put the dishes away.

Eventually, he sent the boys off to play, but they headed into the living room to see what Gemma was doing.

He winced. "Not what I meant when I told them to go have fun."

"Can't say I blame them." His father grinned. "Gemma's a lot of fun."

His dad plucked the leash hanging from the peg on the wall. Tail wagging, Rascal rose to his feet. "Think I'll take a stroll to clear the cobwebs from my head."

Nate went in search of his sons. Stepping into the living room, what he found wasn't what he expected. Both boys were asleep, snuggled against Gemma, who was also asleep. The sweet picture stole his breath.

Despite his initial misgivings, she had proved herself unlike the girl who'd callously broken his heart. This Gemma, the one he was gradually getting to know, was kind and generous. Good with dogs, little boys and ailing old men. Quick to laugh.

But it was hard to reconcile the two Gemmas. Which one was real? Was this Gemma too good to be true just like the teenage Gemma had been?

If his family hadn't walked in on them this

morning, would he have kissed her? Part of him had wanted to, but would that have been wise? Doubts warred with the feelings she reawakened inside him.

For his father's sake, he'd opened his home to her. But did he dare open his heart to her? There was so much more at stake. Namely, the hearts of his sons, more precious to him than anything in the world.

They trusted her. Why couldn't he? But the burned child dreads the fire, and he'd already been burned by her once before.

He made a move to backtrack lest he awaken them, but a floorboard squeaked under his foot. Her eyes flew open. The look on her face stopped him cold.

Alarm flared in her expression. As recognition dawned, her gaze cleared. Who or what had taught her to be so hypervigilant?

Her mother died the day she returned from camp. Why wouldn't she tell him what else happened that caused her to end things between him? Why must she be so secretive?

Nate's conscience smote him. *Why can't you talk to her about Deanna?*

"I didn't mean to startle you," he whispered.

The boys didn't stir.

Carefully extricating herself, she placed a cushion under Kody's head and propped Connor against the armrest. Inching to the edge of the sofa, she eased upright.

They tiptoed into the kitchen. She brushed her hair out of her face. "Tell me I wasn't drooling."

"Far from it." His voice gruff, he cleared his throat. "More like Sleeping Beauty."

Her gaze flitted to his and away. "Where's Ike?"

"Gone for his afternoon walk." Leaning against the counter, he crossed his arms over his chest. At his movement, her eyes flickered. "Thank you again for the day you gave my dad and the boys."

A smile softened her lips. "It's me who should thank you for allowing me to share the day with your family."

Her gaze swept over him. His heartbeat stuttered. Swinging around, she opened the refrigerator door. "Are leftovers for dinner okay with you?"

Nate's ribs ached as if he'd run a long, painful distance. "Leftovers are one of the best parts about Thanksgiving." He strived to keep his voice matter-of-fact. "But I hired you to look after Dad, not cook and clean up after us, Gemma."

"I don't mind." She toyed with the end of her braid. "I like looking after you. You and the boys."

He liked the way she looked after him—and the boys—but he mustn't tell her that.

She tucked a strand of hair behind her ear, playing havoc with his nerve endings. "Ike is doing well today. I was concerned he might not be."

He jammed his hands in his jeans. "Why's that?"

"It's usually when patients get overtired that the mental confusion sets in."

He fingered his chin. "Dad seems more like himself than he has been in a long time. I've been trying to take my cues from him. Was that wrong?"

She shook her head. "Allowing him to set the pace within reasonable limits should be fine. We just need to be aware the holidays will tax his mental and physical energy."

Nate sighed. "I can't help wondering if this year will be the last real Christmas he's able to enjoy with us. I want it to be everything he wishes it to be."

She wrapped her hand around his arm. "We'll make sure it's the best Christmas ever for Ike and the boys."

It was amazing how less alone he felt since she returned to his life. A shared burden was truly a halved burden.

The back door squeaked open. His father and Rascal ambled into the kitchen. His dad's cheeks were rosy from the cold, and his eyes shone. His father had always loved the outdoors. Being confined to the house so much was a trial for him. But thanks to Rascal, his dad could still enjoy a measure of independence.

His father eased into a chair. "Where's the boys?" Rascal plopped onto the floor beside his feet.

"They're taking a nap." He grinned. "Thanksgiving wore them out."

"Me, too." His father laughed. "But before I get a little shut-eye, I wanted to make sure we're going to set up the Christmas tree tomorrow as usual."

Nate exchanged a look with Gemma. "If you aren't too tired."

His dad waved his hand. "It's a Crenshaw family tradition to decorate the tree the day after

Thanksgiving. The boys will be disappointed if we don't."

"Let's see how you're feeling tomorrow morning, but if you're still gung ho, we'll head out to the Christmas tree farm."

His father smiled. "Great."

Nate hoped his dad would still be as clear-eyed tomorrow. The boys would be disappointed if the annual Christmas tree expedition didn't happen.

These days, one day at a time was the most Nate could manage. Who was he kidding? What was the use in dreaming?

Anything—much less love—beyond his father's illness felt totally out of reach.

THAT NIGHT, NATHAN warned the boys the Christmas tree hunt would be dependent upon how their grandfather felt the next day.

Friday morning was another beautiful blue-sky, cold winter day. At breakfast, Gemma could see the boys struggling to contain their excitement. They'd rushed out first thing to tend to the animals. But all through toast and oatmeal, they were on tenterhooks waiting for Ike to appear.

*Please, God…* She sent a quick prayer sky-

ward. *Let Ike have another good day for the boys'
sake.* She glanced at their father, His posture
stiff, he stirred brown sugar into his oatmeal.
*For Nathan's, too.*

Rascal was first into the kitchen. Shoulders
bowed, Ike trod heavily behind him. Her heart
sank. Not a good sign.

Spoons halfway to their mouths, the boys
froze. Hope dimmed in their faces. Nathan's
eyes flickered. A line furrowed his brow.

Broadening his chest, Ike grinned. "Anyone
up for Christmas tree hunting this morning?"

Eyebrows arched like a question mark, the
boys' gazes cut to Nathan. She held her breath.

Nathan put down his spoon. "Since the
morning chores are done, I think something
could be arranged." He smiled.

"Yahoo!" Kody fist-pumped the air.

She released the breath she'd been holding.
Connor didn't say anything, but happiness shone
from his face. Catching the general air of excitement, Rascal gave a quick, short bark.

Ike ran his hand across the collie's fur. "A ban-
ner day for us all."

After breakfast, the boys made a mad scramble
to find their coats, hats and mittens. She donned
her puffy black overcoat and wound a woolen

teal scarf around her neck. She tucked her hair into the matching teal knit hat atop her head. Then they were off.

Rascal sat secured between the boys in the rear of the crew cab. With Ike riding shotgun, she took the middle front seat in Nathan's slate gray, six-seater, full-size truck.

"Sorry for the tight fit," he apologized. "The tree farm isn't far. On the other side of the ridge."

Buckling her seat belt, she faced forward. "I'm fine."

At the sign for the Morgan Tree Farm, he veered off the rural road onto a long, graveled driveway. Between standing rows of evergreens, she caught her first glimpse of the Morgan family homestead.

The tin-roofed, two-story white farmhouse with a wraparound porch and a stone chimney crowned the top of a knoll. Behind the house lay a barn and a white outbuilding. Acres of Christmas trees surrounded the entire complex. In the distance, the smoky purple Blue Ridge Mountains undulated like the folds of a fan.

Ike gestured toward the horizon. "Purty parcel of land, isn't it?"

She sniffed. "Nothing beats cattle grazing on

the gently rolling hills of the High Country Ranch, though."

Ike grinned. "A woman with impeccable taste. Surest way to a rancher's heart."

She tilted her head. "What's that?"

"Love me, love my steers." Mischief gleamed from his gaze. "Or at least my son's heart, right, Nate my boy?"

Nathan rolled his eyes.

She chuckled. "For a K-9 trainer, it's love me, love my dog."

"I hope you made a note of that, son. The way to this woman's heart is through a dog."

He shot his father a look. "Dad..."

She nudged his shoulder. "Your father is an incurable romantic."

Nathan shook his head. "He's something, all right."

Following the driveway behind the house, he parked between the barn and the farm store. The parking lot was already three-quarters full. The boys and Ike got out of the truck. Ike unbuckled Rascal, but kept him on a leash. Nathan came around to assist her out of the pickup.

His hand felt warm and strong against her skin. "Thank you." The calluses on his palm bore testimony to his hard work.

For a second, his gaze locked with hers. His eyes went a darker shade of blue. Her stomach somersaulted.

His father coughed gently. "Looks like the Morgan Open House is off to a promising start."

Nathan broke eye contact first.

Pulling on her gloves, she took a deep breath of the tangy, evergreen-scented air. Garlands and wreaths hung on the lattice surrounding the broad porch of the white outbuilding.

A pleasant-faced man a few years younger than her and Nathan came forward with a firm grasp on a blond, towheaded little boy about three years old. "I wasn't sure we'd see you this year, Mr. Ike."

Ike beamed. "Gemma, meet Luke Morgan, our favorite Christmas tree farmer."

"Better known as Jeremiah's dad." The pride in his voice was evident. Luke placed his palm on the little boy's hooded coat. "Nice to meet you, ma'am."

She smiled at the little boy with the big blue eyes.

Kody wiggled his fingers. "Hey, Jeremiah."

Ducking his head, the child smiled.

Ike patted his canine companion. "This here gorgeous creature is my new buddy, Rascal."

Hearing his name, the dog woofed.

Ike planted his hands on his hips. "We're on a mission to find the most perfect Christmas tree ever, isn't that right, boys?"

Luke batted the furry pom attached to Connor's orange-striped knit cap. "You've come to the right place then. Go see my sister, Krista." He motioned toward a young woman with long, curly brown hair handing handsaws to customers. "She'll get you started."

The boys surged forward. Ike and Rascal, too.

"Hang there a minute," Nathan called. "I'll be the one in charge of the saw."

"Guys? Wait for me." As he raced after Nathan's boys, Jeremiah's small legs churned. "This year, I give out de carts."

"That's right, son." Luke winked at Nathan. "Get to work."

"Dibs on the cart," Connor shouted.

"But Dad…" Kody wailed.

"You'll take turns hauling it up the mountain." Nathan flicked an amused glance at Luke. "Got your boy on the payroll already?"

He laughed. "You know how it is with family-owned operations. Put 'em to work young and train 'em right."

Nathan looked around. "Where's your better half?"

"Shayla's manning the storefront. She'll ring up your ticket while I put the tree through the baler. Be sure and introduce Gemma to my sisters and my wife."

Nathan nudged her. "You'll probably recognize Shayla Morgan from television."

"*The* Shayla Morgan?" She gaped at the young Christmas tree farmer. "The country music star whose 'Cradle Lullaby' tops the charts every Christmas is your wife?"

"Hard to believe, isn't it?"

She blushed to the soles of her boots. "I didn't mean—"

"Every time I look at her, I wonder the same." He chuckled. "How I ever came to be blessed with someone as wonderful as her in my life."

She smiled. "I've been a fan since her first recording hit the airwaves."

He clapped a hand to Nathan's back. "Your dad is looking more like his old self."

Nathan rubbed his jaw. "It's amazing what an assistance dog and Gemma can do in two weeks."

At his praise, her cheeks went crimson. "I'm thankful Ike is back to living his best possible life."

"Dad! Miss Gemma!" Returning, Connor and Kody tugged at their arms.

"Quit your jawin' and get over here!" Ike yelled. "Us lumberjacks got Christmas trees to fell."

Nathan took possession of the handsaw. Connor pulled the cart up the incline. Ike and Rascal took point on the tree-hunting expedition.

At the uphill exertion, she puffed, her breath fogging in the cold mountain air. "Didn't realize I was so out of shape," she wheezed.

"Such a flatlander," Nathan teased. "Thin mountain air. You'll get used to it."

For a split second, the idea of searching for the perfect Christmas tree every year over multiple Christmas futures flashed across her vision.

She sneaked a glance in Nathan's direction. A lovely dream, but of course not her future. Good things like that didn't happen to her.

"Miss Gemma!" Kody shrieked. It was his turn at pulling the cart. "Come see the one I found!"

Sucking in a lungful of oxygen, she plunged onward.

Reaching a largely untouched section midway on the hill, the boys dashed about, proclaiming the merits of this tree and that one. Eventually, two top contenders emerged. Ike cast the deciding vote for a perfectly proportioned six-foot Fraser fir.

She removed the red price tag and handed it to Kody for safekeeping. Crouching at the base, Nathan placed the saw against the trunk and commenced cutting.

"Timber!" Kody hollered.

Keeping one hand on Rascal's leash and the other on the tree to keep it from toppling over, Ike chortled. With the cut tree placed atop the cart, they descended to the farm store. More people had arrived. Everyone called out greetings.

It gave her a warm, fuzzy feeling to realize how many people stopped to welcome her, too. She had lived in Greensboro most of her adult life. Yet she didn't know as many people there as she'd met after only two weeks in friendly little Truelove.

Ike chatted up a storm with two of his ROMEO compadres. Rascal sat on his haunches, his brown-eyed gaze fixed in rapt attention on Ike's animated face. The boys played hide-and-seek with a passel of children behind various Christmas trees up and down the hilly terrain.

Her gaze drifted to Nathan, talking to tall, lanky Clay. As if drawn, his eyes lifted to hers and held. A blush rose in her cheeks that had less to do with the frosty morning and more to do with the bond connecting them since one long-ago, unforgettable summer.

Burying her face in the steam rising from her cup, she ventured to the far end of the porch. Nathan joined her. As always, her pulse did a quick staccato whenever she found herself close to him.

"I didn't realize the extent of the Morgan Open House." She pressed her lips against the rim of the cup.

"You can count on Truelove to make any event, large or small, an occasion." Surveying the tree-studded hillside, he gripped the porch railing. "Any excuse to get folks together."

She warmed her hands around the cup. "I like how the town supports one another."

His eyes cut to her and slid away. "What we lack in size, we make up with heart."

And then some. Her heart clanged like sleigh bells against her rib cage.

But abruptly, without warning, he turned away.

## CHAPTER TWELVE

FEELING THE SUDDEN chill between them, Gemma knotted her hands. Perhaps it was only her who harbored these ridiculous feelings from the past.

Nathan motioned toward the bedecked wreaths and garlands. "We should probably get a few decorations for the house."

After picking out two wreaths and a swath of garland for the mantel, she followed him inside the small farm shop to pay for their purchases. She finally met the talented and very sweet Shayla Morgan.

For Gemma, it was a total fan-girl moment, much to Nathan's apparent amusement. Whatever had prompted him to turn away from her appeared to have passed.

With the tree strapped into the bed of the truck, they headed home, singing Christmas carols at the top of their lungs. The rest of the day, they decorated the tree and the farmhouse with ornaments from the boxes Nathan and Ike hauled out of the attic.

That night, long after everyone had gone to bed, she sat in the living room. Except for the glow of the multicolored lights on the Christmas tree, the room was dark.

A lump rose in her throat. It truly was the most perfect tree ever.

The back door creaked. Seconds later, Nathan's broad shoulders filled the doorframe. "Oh, hi."

"Hey." She unfolded from the couch. "I didn't realize anyone was still awake."

"I needed to check on a heifer." He shuffled his stocking feet. "I saw the tree shining through the window and figured Dad must've left on the lights."

She sighed. "I wasn't ready for the day to end."

"It was a fun day." He moved toward the tree. "You're such a good sport about everything Dad and the boys throw at you."

She'd believed Thanksgiving to be the best day ever, but each day spent with Nathan and his family felt better than the last.

"Thank you for staying on through the holidays until we can get a permanent caregiver for Dad."

"You don't have to keep thanking me." The last thing she wanted was his gratitude. "It's been my pleasure entirely."

"Still, we've taken you away from your usual celebrations with family and friends."

"No family." She crossed her arms over her sweater. "I don't do much in the way of decorating my apartment in Greensboro. Seems a lot of trouble with only me to enjoy it."

He frowned. "You don't spend Christmas alone, do you?"

Not meeting his gaze, she shrugged. "I attend a Christmas Eve service with Juliet's family and her mom. Then Rob's aunt and uncle host a small party at their farmhouse. After that, I drive back from Laurel Grove to my apartment."

He stared at her. "But what about Christmas morning?"

She blew out a breath. "Christmas morning is best enjoyed by families unwrapping their gifts without the unnecessary burden to entertain an outsider like me."

"The last two days—the last two weeks—wouldn't have been the same without you." His brow creased. "I hope you don't feel like an outsider with us."

"Actually, I don't."

Not even once. The feeling of belonging was something she hadn't experienced in a long time.

He glanced at something outside the window. "Would you look at that?"

Illuminated by the floodlight on the corner of the house, tiny snowflakes drifted lazily from the darkened night sky.

She rushed to the window for a better look. "Ohhh…"

"The first snowfall." He caught her hand. "Let's go out and enjoy it."

"But it's late."

He cocked his head. "Not too late, I hope."

Was he referring to more than the time of day? Her pulse quickened. Something sweet swelled in her heart. "It's never too late."

He grinned. "Come on then. Grab your coat, and let's get out there."

In the kitchen, she retrieved her coat, scarf and gloves. She stepped into the ankle boots she'd left by the door. He clapped his Stetson onto his head and donned his boots again.

He drew her into the yard. The snow was coming down heavier, covering the ground.

Feeling like a kid, she lifted her face to the sky and closed her eyes.

Arms outstretched, she did a slow three-sixty. The snowflakes skimmed her cheeks with the delicate grace of a butterfly. "Should we wake the boys?"

"Let's not," he rasped.

She opened her eyes. Something unreadable flickered across his features.

"They'll get their fill of snow in the morning." Taking off a glove, he caught the edge of a snowflake, trembling on the end of her eyelashes, with the tip of his forefinger.

"Let this first snowfall be for us." His Adam's apple bobbed in his throat. "You and me." His gaze moved to her mouth.

Her knees melted. Was he going to kiss her? Did she want him to kiss her? Her heart pounded.

"Would it be okay if I kissed you?" He gulped. "I've been wanting to since the day you arrived."

Reason warred against the feelings churning in her gut. This was a bad idea. She was leaving in a month. Why was she even thinking about—

"Yes," she whispered.

His breath felt warm against her cheek. He tilted his head. Her lips parted. He brushed his mouth against hers.

Gemma's innate, well-earned caution blared warnings of danger ahead, but for once she didn't listen.

The press of his lips was the tenderest of touches. Something she'd believed would never happen again with him, her first and only love.

It had been so long since she'd felt happiness of any sort. So what if she was only here another four weeks? Why not seize any happiness by the fistful while she could? Soon enough, she'd return to her usual solitude.

She didn't delude herself anything long-term could ever come from this most unexpected reunion. Too much had happened. Their lives were on different trajectories, but if their paths intersected only for Christmas…why not?

A blast of sudden cold air jolted her back to reality. Nathan had taken a step away. She shivered.

"Gemma?" His voice deepened. "It was okay I kissed you, wasn't it?"

It was better than okay. It was simply everything. The snow continued to fall around them.

He raked his hand over his head. "I shouldn't have kissed you."

And though she'd been thinking the same, it hurt to hear him speak her thoughts aloud.

"There's so much upheaval in my life right now. I'm not in a position to pursue a relationship with anyone."

Gemma took a quick, indrawn breath. "Of course. I understand."

"Sometimes the loneliness gets to me."

"Me, too," she rasped.

"Once upon a time, you and me somehow seemed so…"

She swallowed past the boulder in her throat. "Right?"

He shook his head. "I was thinking *inevitable*, but *unfinished* works, too. Yet now…"

Closure, Ike had called it.

"You don't have to explain, Nathan."

He blew out a breath. "I've been stuck in limbo since Deanna died."

The stark anguish in his eyes pierced Gemma to the core.

"I've been frozen. But with you, I feel…" He threw out his hands. "I don't rightly know how I feel. But it scares the stuffing out of me."

"You mean the dressing?"

A ghost of a smile quirked his mouth. "The last thing I want to do is hurt you, Gemma. Nor get hurt, either."

She wasn't the naive teenage girl he'd once

courted. She was a strong woman. A woman who knew how to protect her heart.

"Nobody dreads getting hurt more than me, but here's what I learned over fifteen painful years. Life is risky."

"I can't make you any promises, Gemma."

"Right back at you." She held up her hands, palms raised. "No expectations here."

He pursed his lips. "We don't want to make a spectacle of ourselves and give the Truelove grapevine more grist for the gossip mill."

She nodded. "Let's just enjoy Christmas."

If in the process, they helped each other heal, to get past their individual roadblocks, so much the better.

She might be helping Nathan move on toward the next love in his life. But the boys needed a mother. He deserved to find love again. Even if it wasn't with her.

What did she want?

To be happy.

If only for this briefest of seasons.

NATE LAY AWAKE half the night pondering every possible disastrous ramification of kissing Gemma. What had he been thinking? It wasn't often—as in never—he threw caution to the wind and just reacted.

Lying on his back staring at the darkened ceiling, he felt a wave of terror engulf him. As if he stood on the brink of a precipice of no return. Beneath his proverbial feet, there lay only a bottomless gorge of fear.

This would not—could not—end well. For either of them.

Ever since she returned to his life, there'd been an intense attraction between them. In the wee hours of the night, he rationalized, maybe it was better to get it out in the open.

First loves were powerful, yet probably only in extremely rare cases were they forever loves. He consoled himself he'd been clear about the likelihood of any future relationship. Boundaries ensured their friendship would survive any brief holiday romance.

"No expectations. No promises," he whispered.

Settling the issue in his mind, he finally drifted off to sleep.

The next day, a cold, brittle sunshine beamed from a blue sky. Snow had transformed the ranch into a winter wonderland. The boys were beyond ecstatic at the prospect of a day spent romping in the snow.

After last night, he felt self-conscious with Gemma. He dragged the sleds out of the barn, and she joined the boys on their downhill runs. His dad and Rascal took a turn, too.

Later that morning, Nate waved them over. "Time to head inside."

"Awww, Dad…" Kody groaned.

Her cheeks bright red from the cold, Gemma had her arm around Connor's shoulder. "You've been out here so long your clothes are wet through."

Kody glowered. "I want to play outside some more."

She tapped the end of Kody's nose with her finger. "Rascal's been out here a long time. His paws are probably freezing."

Connor perked. "Rascal needs snow booties for Christmas."

"I have a gweat idea, guys." Kody bounced up and down. "When we see Santa this afternoon, we could give him Rascal's Christmas wish list."

She cocked her head. "Santa's coming this afternoon?"

"We go see him."

Her gaze pinged between the boys. "You two are heading to the North Pole today?"

Kody giggled.

Smiling, Connor shook his head. "Saturday after Thanksgiving is the Truelove Christmas Parade. We always visit Santa on the Square, don't we, Dad?" His face fell. "Unless Grandpa doesn't feel like going—"

"We always go see Santa. Daddy!" Kody wailed. "Please, please, please…"

He frowned at his son. "Kody, that's enough."

Gemma put her hand on Kody's shoulder. "I'll stay with Ike, Nathan. You take the boys to the—"

"While I appreciate the offer, Gemma—" his father drew himself up "—I can answer for myself, thank you very much."

Nate crossed his arms over his coat. "It's been a busy couple of days. There's no shame in skipping the festival this year, Dad. I wouldn't mind a quiet afternoon at home."

"You stay home and rest then." His father scowled. "I'm not tired."

"There's no point in overdoing things." Nate widened his stance in the snow. "We've had fun over Thanksgiving, but—"

"Don't talk to me like I'm a child," his dad snapped.

"Stop being stubborn," Nate grunted. "I'm trying to look out for you."

"I can look out for myself." His father's voice rose.

"That's just it, Dad." He jabbed his finger in the air between them. "It breaks my heart, but the truth is you can't."

His father became livid. "There's nothing wrong with me that warm clothes and a good, hot lunch won't cure."

"Nathan, please. Ike." Gemma inserted herself between them. "You're scaring the boys."

Connor had gone quiet, too quiet. Kody looked to be on the verge of tears. His sons huddled against Gemma.

Deanna would have known how to defuse the situation before it ever escalated to a shouting match.

Nate slumped. "Fine. Dry clothes. Lunch."

"I won't allow myself to get overtired, I promise." The defiance faded from his dad's gaze. "I'm sorry, son. I hate I've become such a burden to everyone I love."

Nate hugged his father. "You're not a burden, Dad."

His father tugged at Rascal's leash. "I think I'll head in now." His dad and the collie shuffled toward the house.

Ashamed of the example he'd set, Nate

crouched beside his sons. "I'm sorry for raising my voice to Granddad. And to you, too."

Kody's lips trembled. "Does this mean we're going to the parade?"

He pinched the bridge of his nose. "I guess so."

"But before y'all go, I think some quiet time for everyone sounds like a great idea." She patted Kody's knit cap. "How about you and Connor set the table for lunch?"

The boys took off at a run, but with a troubled look, Connor spun around. "Miss Gemma, you're coming with us, aren't you?"

She fingered the fringe on the end of her scarf. "Maybe it would be better if I stayed at the ranch."

"Nooo…" Connor protested. "It won't be as much fun without you."

"He's right." Nate cleared his throat. "It won't be as much fun without you."

She looked at him. "Okay, I'll come."

The usually reticent Connor whooped with joy and took off after his little brother.

"Are you okay?" she asked Nate.

"I forgot how quickly Dad can flare up." He shook his head. "I should've handled it better." They headed across the yard toward the house.

"Traveling this journey alongside a loved one with dementia isn't easy." She linked her arm through the crook of his elbow. "It's not you he's really lashing out at. It's the increasing restrictions on his independence that he resents."

Nate heaved a sigh. "It sure feels like it's me he's angry at."

She hugged his arm. "For that, I'm sorry."

At the foot of the porch, he paused. "If you're tired or need a break from us—" He grimaced. "I could use a break from us sometimes—please don't feel you have to go this afternoon."

She fluttered her lashes at him. "Spending the afternoon with Santa, your father, the boys... and you?"

He heard the smile in her voice.

Taking his hands in hers, she rose onto the tips of her toes. "There's no place I'd rather be." She kissed his cheek.

The warmth of her lips tingled against his skin. He felt the same. There was no one he'd rather spend the afternoon with than her.

SINCE HER LAST VISIT, Gemma was amazed at the holiday transformation the little town had undergone. The Parks and Rec Department had been busy.

Heading toward the square with Rascal leashed at his side, Ike elbowed her. "Wait till you get a gander at the matchmaking trio."

"Oh?"

"They double as elves for the Santa on the Square event." He grinned. "Pointed shoes. Floppy hat. Striped stockings. The works."

Nathan laughed. "Boggles the mind, doesn't it?"

Ike grunted. "Worth the trip to Truelove."

From the loudspeakers mounted at the edges of the square, strains of "Winter Wonderland" provided a festive note. Friends called out greetings to the Crenshaws. Greetings to her as well. It looked as if the entire population had turned out for the annual Christmas parade. And for the free hot chocolate, courtesy of the Mason Jar.

In the middle of the green, Santa—aka the mayor—sat enthroned in the gazebo. Next to the mayor, the diminutive Miss IdaLee, oldest of the matchmaking trio, sat on a chair playing Mrs. Santa.

Gemma snapped a photo of Connor on Santa's

lap first. In their pint-sized Stetsons and boots, both boys were adorable.

Connor asked for various calf-showing accoutrements for next year's 4-H competition at the county fair. Easing Connor off his lap, Santa steered him toward the grandmotherly Erma-Jean on the steps of the gazebo. Her silvery hair tucked into a green felt hat, she resembled a jolly, if somewhat plump, elf. She handed Connor a green-striped candy cane.

As befitted her take-charge demeanor, GeorgeAnne, armed with a clipboard and a whistle, supervised the line of children waiting to talk with Santa. Also in elf attire, she looked more Christmas scarecrow than Santa's helper.

The jolly, Santa look-alike mayor patted Kody's knee. "Have you been a good boy this year?"

An interesting look came over Kody's face. "Well, it's like this, sir." He opened his hands. "I think I've been as good as could be weasonably expected."

Ike chortled. "Lot of personality in that grandson of mine."

Nathan rolled his eyes. "Ain't that the truth."

Gemma hid her smile in her hand.

Santa's blue eyes twinkled. "Tell Santa, young Crenshaw, what you'd like for Christmas?"

"I've given it some thought," the littlest cowboy mused. "I've decided what I want most for Christmas is for Gemma to be my new mommy."

She gasped. GeorgeAnne's eyes behind the frames of her glasses went owllike. IdaLee put her hand to her mouth. "Oh, my."

Oh, my indeed.

"Uhhh, well then…" Santa scratched his neck under the fluffy white collar. "Perhaps your father should field this one?"

Field it he did. Nathan pulled Kody off Santa's lap. His hand clamped onto his son's shoulder. "We're going home."

Kody jutted his jaw. "Santa asked me what I wanted so I told him."

"That is a matter for grown-ups to decide. Not you."

Hands on his hips, Kody glared at his dad. "What's so bad about wanting Gemma to stay with us forever? Connor wants a new mommy, too."

Palms raised, Connor backed away, wanting no part of guilt by association.

The look on Nathan's face... If he hadn't been so mortified, it would have almost been comical.

He towed his son down the gazebo steps. "I don't know what's gotten into you."

"I didn't get a candy cane..." Kody wailed.

"Maybe you should've thought of that before you totally embarrassed Gemma—all of us—in front of everyone." Nathan raked a hand over his head.

His hat fell off. GeorgeAnne picked it up.

Nathan shook his finger at his son. "You and I are going to have a serious talk when we get back to the ranch, about what is and is not appropriate behavior."

GeorgeAnne handed Nathan his hat. "Don't be too hard on him. He was simply expressing his feelings." Her gaze swung to Gemma and back. "Something we should all aspire to do."

ErmaJean thrust a candy cane at Gemma. "For later," she whispered.

The ride to the ranch was accomplished in near silence. Gemma wanted to hug Kody so badly, it hurt like a physical pain.

But squished in the front seat between Ike and Kody's dad, she stared straight ahead through the windshield as the truck ate up the miles between Truelove and the farm.

A day that had begun with such promise… If she'd ever doubted where she stood with him or how he envisioned his future—a future that did not include her—she doubted no more.

He fired a glance in the rearview mirror at his youngest son. "You will go to your room as soon as we get home."

At the house, Ike climbed wearily from the pickup. "Connor, I think Rascal would enjoy meeting the rabbits." They set off. Tears streaking across his face, Kody headed inside.

Nathan stopped her. "Could we talk first?" He sucked in a breath. "I had no idea Kody would say something like that. I'm so sorry."

After the initial shock had worn off, strangely she wasn't. Kody had been honest. Expressing the deepest desire of his heart. And as she was slowly coming to realize, hers, too.

None of that mattered, of course, since Nathan didn't feel the same.

"Please go easy on him." She bit her lip. "He gave you a glimpse of his heart. That kind of bravery is a rare and beautiful gift."

"But—"

She fluttered her hand. "Forget the particulars of me and you. See what he said for what it truly is—a little boy who doesn't have even a memory of a mother. And it's Christmas."

Nathan sagged against the porch railing. "At the diner the other day after you left, Aunt Georgie told me much the same thing." His gaze slid away. "Among other things."

From his expression, she guessed whatever his great-aunt had said about her had probably not been flattering. But the only thing that mattered was helping Nathan see this moment for what it was—an opportunity for healing.

"If you shut Kody down, he may never open up to you again." She lifted her chin. "Trust me when I tell you, that's not the sort of relationship you want with your son."

He studied her. "You're speaking from experience?"

"I am."

"With the father you don't talk about?"

She wrapped her arms around herself. "Yes."

"Is he still living? Is there hope for reconciliation between you?"

"As far as I know, he's still alive." She pursed her lips. "But he's not like you. Reconciliation is not possible."

"That makes me sad."

Her eyes jerked to his.

"Sad for you." He scuffed the toe of his boot against the porch step. "I'm not sure which is harder, forgiving ourselves or those who've hurt us. I'm working on both."

"Have I told you how much I admire the man you've become, Nathan Crenshaw?"

A whisper of something startling, like the wing of a blue jay in flight, flitted across his gaze.

"You make me want to be better." A muscle ticked in his jaw. "To believe there could be more. For the boys." His cheeks beneath the beard stubble reddened. "For myself."

Her heart hammered. Fifteen years ago, Nathan had been crystal clear about his feelings and intentions. Over the last few weeks, however, he'd been the master of mixed signals. Was he implying—

He moved to the steps. "I'd best talk to Kody."

She wasn't sure what he said to Kody. They were in his room a long time. When they emerged, both man and boy looked a little worse for wear. Their eyes appeared red-rimmed, but from the way Kody held on to his father's hand, restoration had occurred.

Kody apologized to her. She hugged the little boy and told him not to worry about it anymore. Ike, Rascal and Connor drifted into the house.

It had been a fun, busy weekend. Too busy. Her emotions felt raw and wrung out.

Tomorrow would be Ike's first foray back to church. But she couldn't help but dread what the notorious Truelove grapevine would have to say about what happened on the square today.

# CHAPTER THIRTEEN

THAT NIGHT, NATE fell asleep almost immediately, but his sleep was interrupted with fragmented, random dreams of the sweet spring Connor was born. He and Deanna had been young and unsure of themselves but so in love with the little boy God had given them. In the confusing way of dreams, one minute he and Deanna were delighting in Connor's first steps and the next, the dream segued to Deanna, getting into her car that final day.

Gasping for breath, pulse jumping wildly, he awoke with an ache so intense in his chest, for a minute he wondered if he was having a heart attack. When his breathing slowed and the strange ache faded, he rolled out of the bed, knowing further sleep was impossible.

Pulling on his work clothes and donning his coat, he slipped out of the house earlier than usual to do his chores. Pushing the dream aside, he took comfort in the taxing physical labor.

Returning to the house, he was surprised to find his father staring out the kitchen window and drinking coffee. Rascal thumped his tail on the floor. Toeing out of his boots, Nate shot a look at the carafe of coffee. He hadn't thought to get it going before he left the house. After what happened with the soup...

His dad raised his mug. "Gemma made the coffee, not me."

Nate's gaze darted, but his father was alone in the kitchen.

"She's getting ready for church. The boys, too."

Nate poured himself a cup of coffee. He sank into a chair.

"Everything all right with you, son?"

"I'm thinking the heifer will calve sometime over the next few weeks." Nate lifted the mug to his lips. "The wind has shifted. Temps are on the rise. The boys will be disappointed to see the snow melt."

"First day of December." His dad's mouth curved. "No need to get in a lather about snow. There'll be more, lots more, before the daffodils bloom in spring. But I wasn't asking about the ranch or the weather. You seem subdued."

He shrugged. "Didn't sleep well last night."

"Something troubling your mind?"

Too much on his mind. None of which he wanted to delve into with his father.

"I'll be fine once I get some caffeine in my system."

His dad set down his coffee cup. "If you're worried about me with Rascal at church today, you and Gemma cleared it with Pastor Bryant this week, right?"

"Pastor Bryant has no issues with Rascal. He was thrilled you'd be able to worship with the church family again."

"Is it just thoughts of me in general keeping you up at night, son?" His father laid his hand over Nate's. "I worry what this disease is doing to you, too."

Nate squeezed his hand. "Last night wasn't about you, Dad. I kept having this dream over and over…"

"About?"

"It was weird. One minute Deanna and I are just married, then Connor is born and the next minute we're both older and she gets into the Jeep…" He turned his face away. "I don't know why all of a sudden I'm dreaming about that again."

His father sat back. "I could hazard a guess."

Nate stiffened. "Not everything is about Gemma, Dad."

"I didn't say it was, but I do wonder if God sent her into our lives not just for me, but also as a catalyst to help you face your loss once and for all."

"It's been two years. I've put all that behind me and got on with my life."

"Have you?" His father looked at him. "Take it from a guy who's been widowed longer than your mother and I were married. Missing someone doesn't ever completely go away. And that's okay. That's the price we pay for loving and being loved in return."

He glared at his father. "I'm not having this conversation with you about Deanna."

"It would do you a world of good to talk about her. If not to me, then someone. Your sons are confused by your silence on the topic of their mother. They need to hear you speak about Deanna almost as much as you need to talk about her. Keeping her locked inside your heart isn't healthy for anyone."

Nate scraped back his chair. Rascal raised his head. "The usual over-easy egg for you, Dad?"

"It's no surprise to me this is cropping up in your dreams. You've never let yourself grieve properly. Often the subconscious will force you to acknowledge in the darkness what the conscious mind refuses to deal with in the daylight."

He scowled at his dad. Why wouldn't his father let this go? "Every time I think about her, much less talk about her, I feel like I'm the one dying." He pinched the bridge of his nose. "Don't you see, Dad? I can't... Once I open the floodgates, I'll drown."

"You're drowning now, son." Sorrow clouded his father's features. "Once you open the flood-gates, I think that is when you'll finally reach the surface."

He stared at his father. Was he right? Instead of hiding from the pain, was the only way forward to face it?

Kody stumbled into the kitchen. "What's for bweakfast?" His son winked sleep from his eyes.

Nate's gaze pinged from his father to his son. His heart lurched. In refusing to talk about their mother, he'd thought to spare his sons. But was it them he was really trying to spare or himself?

His dad dropped his head and Nate realized he was praying. For him.

The whisper of a memory floated through his mind. Of Deanna, her bouncing blond curls, and the love in her sparkling eyes when she looked at her youngest, most rambunctious son, Kody.

And at him.

"How about pancakes, Kode?" He swallowed. "With chocolate chip eyes and a mouth just like Mom used to make you?"

Kody stilled. "Mommy made me chocolate-face pancakes?"

"Every Sunday morning before church." Connor wandered in behind his brother. "Right, Dad?"

He smiled. "That's right."

"I 'member that, Connor." Kody pulled at his brother's arm. "I really 'member."

Kneeling in front of his boys, he gathered his sons in his arms. *God, forgive me. Help me to do better by them and by Deanna.* The boys helped him put together the pancakes. Bellies full, they were sitting around the table later when Gemma hurried into the kitchen.

"Something smells delicious. Am I too late?"

"Not too late." Nate took in the soft glow in

her cheeks and the russet ribbon tied at the end of her single braid. "You're just in time."

In more ways than one?

SOMETHING THIS MORNING felt different about Nathan, but for the life of her, Gemma couldn't quite pinpoint what it was. But she sensed something within him had shifted. He was quiet as ever, but there was a peaceful quality to his gaze that hadn't been there yesterday.

When he'd looked at her in the kitchen this morning…she'd felt… She wasn't sure what she felt.

In the graveled church parking lot, she got out of the truck. Afraid to give voice to the emotions that filled her every time she looked at him, she took in her surroundings instead. Nestled in a glade on the edge of town, the black church steeple brushed a picture-perfect Blue Ridge sky. She followed the Crenshaws over a tiny footbridge, which spanned a small creek. Water trickled over moss-covered stones.

Patches of melted snow dotted the glossy green leaves of the camellia bushes around the entrance. The boys hurried off to children's church in the education wing. Ike and Rascal led the way into the white clapboard church. A slight tension between her shoulder blades, she and Nathan followed him into the sanctuary.

This was the last big hurdle for Rascal in restoring to Ike a semblance of his previously independent and vibrant social life. Pastor Bryant had been so accommodating on the phone. He'd sent out a special church-wide email to members, explaining the protocols that should be observed with an assistance dog on Sunday mornings.

Inside the foyer, Ike strode confidently ahead to a side pew near the back that Reverend Bryant had set aside for him. It had the benefit of being close to the exit should Ike feel the need to a sudden, unobtrusive departure.

She need not have worried about the congregation. Old friends greeted him but left Rascal to do his duty. Ike fairly beamed at the prospect of being back in the Truelove fold once again.

The music from the organ swelled. Nathan gestured for her to take her seat first. She became aware of significant glances thrown her way and Nathan's. That the two of them together represented a topic of great interest did not escape her notice. Not that they were together, of course.

But the service began and she let herself soak in the ambience of the two-hundred-year-old sanctuary. Wide-planked beams soared overhead and prisms of light shone through the stained glass windows onto the gleaming brass cross on the altar.

After a brief, but powerfully reflective sermon, Reverend Bryant said a benediction and everyone dispersed to the fellowship hall for Christmas cookies and hot apple cider.

To her surprise, Shayla made an effort to seek her out. "I was wondering if you'd meet me for coffee sometime this week."

"I would love that. Let me check with Tom to see when the ROMEOs are getting together. The boys will be in school. What about your little guy?"

"Luke's mom is always ready to Jeremiah-sit. I could drop him off at her house and meet you at the Jar."

They made tentative plans to coordinate their schedules. But the next day, Shayla called to beg off due to Jeremiah developing a fussy cold. They rescheduled. But as it turned out, the day they chose was the same day as Connor's winter wonderland production at the elementary school. He had a speaking part, which she rehearsed over and over with him. One line, but he was nervous. He asked her to go and she would as soon miss his performance as cut off her arm. Sitting in the audience between Ike and Nathan, she couldn't have been more proud of him if he were her own.

She was a bit embarrassed canceling on Shayla but the singer insisted they put another date on the calendar closer to Christmas.

Over the next few weeks, there was lots of pre-Christmas fun. Including teaching the boys to decorate sugar cookies. Nathan got into the merriment. Ike got into the eating.

They were the best weeks of her life. A permanent caregiver wasn't set to arrive until after the New Year.

She couldn't wait for Christmas. Yet at the same time, she never wanted this time with Nathan and his family to end.

ABOUT A WEEK before Christmas, Nate was getting an early start on gathering receipts to pay his quarterly taxes in January. Looking troubled, Gemma came into his office. "I'm sorry to interrupt."

"I'm working on taxes." He leaned back. "Please interrupt."

She fingered the red silk ribbon in her braid. A nervous habit, he'd noticed. A habit that never failed to play havoc with his nerve endings. "You've probably already taken care of this, but I noticed there were no presents under the tree for the boys."

He rubbed his chin. "I've been meaning to go shopping. I've ordered a few things online, but haven't gotten around to wrapping them."

"I'd be glad to do that for you, if you'd like."

"Thank you." He sighed. "I'm a complete failure in the dad department, aren't I?"

She shook her head. "Not in any way that actually matters."

"There's still several things I'd hoped to buy the boys and Dad, too, but that would involve a mall." He shuddered. "Which involves heading to Asheville. I'm pretty hopeless at shopping period."

"Greensboro has a mall." She fiddled with the small gold cross at her neck. "I hate to ask for time off, but the Spencers left for Virginia last week and Ma got a message a package had been left on the porch."

"You are doing us a tremendous favor by looking after Dad until New Year's." He leaned his elbows on the desk. "You are due more than a single day off."

"If I leave first thing tomorrow morning, I'll

be back before bedtime. Maggie asked CoraFaye Dolan to sit with him while I'm away."

He smiled. "Cousin CoraFaye is a firecracker. She'll keep him on the straight and narrow." His smile fell. "That's a long way to go—three hours?—to put a package inside a house. Isn't there a neighbor who could—"

"Ma didn't ask. I offered. The Spencers have done so much for me."

He looked at her, willing her to open up to him if only a little.

She took a breath. "After my mother died, I lived with them for several years while I took classes at the community college."

"You lived with them because you and your father are estranged. They adopted you?"

Immediately, her expression closed and he realized he'd pushed too far.

"I'd like to check on my apartment, too. If you give me a list, I'd be happy to do your shopping." She batted her lashes at him. "I'm real good when it comes to spending other people's money."

He wasn't fooled by her deflection, but he let it go. "Not that I don't trust you with my money…" He smiled to take the sting out of his words.

She laughed.

"But six hours of driving is a lot in one day." He steepled his hands under his chin. "I wouldn't mind a minivacation from the ranch myself. What would you think about me tagging along and doing the driving?" He held his breath, certain she'd refuse. She was such a private person.

"If you're sure you can spare the time…?" She gave him a pleased, shy smile. "I'd like that."

He felt like he'd just hung the moon. "Christmas road trip, here we come."

The boys were distraught they had to go to school and miss the fun.

With a knowing look in his eyes, which Nate did his best to ignore, his dad chuckled. "There's kid fun and then there's young-folk fun. I'm sure your dad and Gemma won't get up to much trouble." He winked. Gemma went scarlet. He glared at his father.

Bright and early the next morning, they got into his truck.

She tossed her braid over her shoulder. "My first time riding shotgun in your truck."

He grinned. "How's it feel?"

She waggled her shoulders. "Great."

"You look great."

Her eyes flitted to his. It was true. Riding beside him in the truck, she looked more than great. Beautiful.

They stopped at the bakery for coffee and pastries to go. The time flew by. They laughed and chatted and talked about everything under the sun.

Before he knew it, he was pulling into Laurel Grove. It was a pretty town. "You going to give me the grand tour?"

"Hardly grand." She rolled her eyes. "A ten-cent tour will suffice and you'll have change left over. I forgot you've never been here."

"Juliet and I videoconferenced most of our business regarding Rascal." He drove around the town square. "Reminds me a lot of Truelove."

They rode up and down Main Street. She pointed out the knit shop owned by Juliet's mom.

"Ewe Made Me Luv You." He laughed. "I love it."

She pointed out the PawPals office building. She directed him to a suburban section not far from downtown. When he pulled into the driveway of a small midcentury modern brick house, she hopped out of the truck. She tucked the brown parcel inside the house and clambered back into the truck.

"Where to now, boss lady?"

"Since when did I become the boss lady?"

He grinned. "Since you became my personal shopper."

They headed to Greensboro. They hit the mall first. He was amazed at how easily she secured the items on his list. Found a lot of bargains, too. She even made a few suggestions for gifts he hadn't thought about buying for the boys.

By lunchtime, his Christmas shopping was done for another year. She took him to one of her favorite places for a late lunch, a locally famous Mexican restaurant. They went to her apartment. No photos of family. But a lot of dog paraphernalia. She gave him a tour of Greensboro. Despite the cold, they had ice cream. It was one of the most perfect days he could remember—just spending time with her.

Sitting in his truck, she straightened. "I didn't realize how dark it had gotten. We should probably head back to Truelove."

He shrugged. "Kind of hate for the day to end." He looked at her.

"I hate for the day to end, too." She looked

down and then up at him. "There's one more place I'd like to show you if wouldn't mind another detour. One of my favorite places this time of year in Greensboro, but it is at its best when seen at night."

He cocked his head. "That's intriguing."

She fluttered her hands. "Totally worth the wait, I promise."

Like Gemma herself? His heart thudded.

"There's this neighborhood—Sunset Hills— they started the tradition to collect cans for the food bank, but more and more houses got involved until now…" She smiled. "Well, you'll see. It's better than any theme park or light show. It's magical, especially with snow on the ground."

What was magical was the sweet, childlike look on her face as she described the multi-colored, illuminated Christmas balls the neighbors hung from trees with the aid of a potato launcher. She gave him directions. It was a short drive.

Her description failed to do justice to the spectacle before him.

"Wow," he rasped.

She grinned at him. "I told you."

They drove through the neighborhood for

a while. He pulled over to an empty parking space along the curb, out of the way of the line of cars snaking through the subdivision, also taking in the sights.

"Want to get out and stretch our legs before the long journey home?"

For a second, her eyes watered. He wondered if she might cry, but he had no idea why. "I'd love, that, Nathan." Her voice had gone small. "So much."

Him, too. Anything to prolong their time together. Getting out of the truck, she tucked her hand in the crook of his elbow and they wandered down the block until they found a relatively deserted spot under a gigantic oak, heavy with blue-and-white illuminated Christmas globes. Looking out over the illuminated neighborhood, her eyes shone.

"I wished you could always look as happy as you do now," he rasped.

She turned to him. "I wish that for you, too, Nathan."

With her, suddenly he felt it possible. But what about Deanna? How could he make her understand?

"I wasn't always a great husband to Deanna."

Her posture tensed. "What do you mean?"

"Too often, I was emotionally unavailable. It wasn't fair to her. I have a difficult time expressing my emotions. I prefer to bury them. I've found it less painful."

Her mouth quivered. "How much of that is my fault?"

"Not all of it. It's how I coped when my mother died and after Deanna…" He swallowed. "But it's hard. I want to talk about her with you. I need to talk about her, but I…" His throat closed.

"There's no rush." Her hands cupped his face. "Whenever you're ready."

His heart leaped. *God, this time could they make it work?*

The distance between them had lessened. He had only to bend his head. Their lips were a mere fraction apart. But kissing her again—this, them—was a bad, bad idea. Yet he could no more deny her than he could deny his desperate need to hold her in his arms. If only once more. He drew her closer into the circle of his arms.

Her face upturned to his, her lips parted. "Nathan…"

Nate's heart turned over in his chest. He wrapped a tendril of her hair around his finger, and her hair was as he remembered. Like spun gold.

The pain of the past fell away. The uncertainty of the future didn't exist. All that mattered was that she was in his arms. She felt so good in his arms. So right. Like she'd always belonged. And nothing that had gone before mattered.

She lifted her face to his. He lowered his head. Only a hairbreadth separated them. Their breath mingled in the frosty air.

Gently he brushed his lips across her cheek. Then his mouth drifted to hers. When he would have pulled away, she cradled his face in the palms of her hands and kissed him back.

There was a rightness in her kiss. An undeniable truth. As inexorable as the moon rising over the mountain. Kissing her felt like coming home.

But his doubts, his fears, and his guilt remained an ever-present reminder of why a future with Gemma might never be possible.

# CHAPTER FOURTEEN

IT WAS LATE when they returned to Truelove. Yet in the days that followed, Gemma felt so hopeful. Nathan wasn't the kind of man who would have kissed her like that unless he was falling in love. He was also starting to open up to her about his late wife.

Christmas and the New Year felt bright with possibilities.

On the afternoon of the twenty-third, Gemma left the ranch for her coffee get-together with Shayla.

Nathan practically ushered her out of the house. "No need to hurry back."

Ike waved from the porch. "We've got plenty to keep us occupied."

She propped her hands on her hips. "What are you guys up to?"

Kody dissolved in a fit of giggles. "You're gonna be surprised at what's under the tree."

Connor glared at his little brother. "Hush, Kode. It's supposed to be a secret."

From the tape dispenser and scissors left on the kitchen island, she suspected an afternoon of gift wrapping was about to commence on her behalf.

"I'm sure whatever you do, I'll love it." Smiling, she got into her car. She didn't need presents. Observing their joy when they opened their packages on Christmas morning would be gift enough.

At the Jar, she found Shayla waiting for her. Settling against the blue upholstery of the booth, Shayla smiled and folded her hands in her lap. "Tell me about yourself."

From long practice, it was a question easily dodged. She spent a full five minutes chatting about the Crenshaws and her work at PawPals. A waitress brought their drinks.

Gemma wrapped her hands around the steaming white porcelain mug. "What about you?" A Christmas aroma of cloves and nutmeg filled her nostrils.

As she talked about her son and her husband, Shayla's eyes took on an added luster. The Truelove songbird was refreshingly down-to-earth.

"I feel so honored you made time for coffee with me."

A glimmer of uncertainty flickered across Shayla's gaze. "At the open house…there was something about the way you held yourself that reminded me of… I felt I should get to know you better."

Unsure what to make of that, Gemma changed topics. "Any upcoming platinum selling song of yours I should be on the lookout for?"

Shayla took a sip of her peppermint-spiced concoction. "I've written a new song for the Christmas Eve candlelight service. I hope people will like it."

"Don't tell me *the* Shayla Morgan gets nervous."

"I wasn't always Shayla Morgan." She shrugged. "I come from a run-down trailer park on the other side of the river. My family are locally notorious ne'er-do-wells."

Cup halfway to her lips, Gemma stilled.

Shayla gave her a brittle smile. "When I was a little girl, my mother walked away without a backward look. In and out of prison, my father and brothers specialize in grand theft auto."

Gemma put down her mug. "I had no idea. Seeing you at the tree farm with Luke and Jeremiah—"

"My life is wonderful, but it wasn't always so."

"How did you...?" Gemma stopped.

"How did I overcome the shame of the past and get to where I am now?"

Gemma dropped her gaze to the tabletop. "It's none of my business."

"At first, I made a lot of bad decisions. Trying to outrun my past—which never works—I jumped out of the frying pan into the fire with Jeremiah's abusive, drug-dealing father."

Gemma looked at her.

Shayla fingered the handle on her cup. "In every way that matters, Luke is Jeremiah's dad, but he isn't his biological father."

"I... I didn't realize."

Uncharacteristically, she found herself wanting to share her family background with Shayla. With someone who might actually understand where she was coming from. Who might give her hope beyond the web of shame in which she was entangled.

"Where I'm from—Laurel Grove, a small, rural town—my father is notorious, too." She locked eyes with Shayla to gauge her reaction. "He's serving life without parole for murdering my mother and a law enforcement officer."

Shayla laid her hand on top of Gemma's. "I'm so sorry."

"My childhood…" She bit her lip. "My father was violent. We were constantly on tenterhooks to please him. We never knew what would trigger his rage."

Shayla nodded. "It's a hard way to live. And confusing. Especially for a child."

"I learned early not to trust men. One minute he'd be warm and charming. The next?" She clenched her fists. "He could—and still does—turn on a smile at the drop of a hat. Most of the time, I never saw the hit coming."

"Your mother didn't report him to the police?"

Gemma looked at her. "He was the police. The chief of police."

Shayla put her hand to her throat. "Oh."

"His public image was everything to him. Neither my mother or I ever said a word about what went on within the four walls of our home. Weird, isn't it, how we kept his secrets? A conspiracy of enabling silence."

Shayla shook her head. "My father's abuse took the form of neglect. Though several loving adults in my life tried to intervene on my behalf, I would've died before telling them the truth. Children in our situation are conditioned from birth to protect the dysfunction we know."

"I believed it was normal." Gemma pressed her lips together. "I believed I deserved it. Until recently, I was angry at my mother for refusing to leave him, forcing me to endure it, too. But now I understand how over the years he'd worn her down. To believe she was nothing and powerless. Robbing her of hope."

Shayla squeezed her hand. "That was my greatest challenge—to overcome the worthlessness I felt. It was only when I became pregnant with Jeremiah I found the courage to leave. Because my baby deserved better. How did your family situation go unnoticed?"

"My father is clever and manipulative. The psych eval after the fact diagnosed him as a narcissist with sociopathic tendencies. No excuse, but apparently, his own childhood was less than stellar, too. No one ever suspected the truth until that last, fatal day."

Shayla sighed. "I understand if you don't want to talk about it, but I'm here for you if you do."

"At the time, it was front-page news." She knotted her hands. "Outside Laurel Grove, most people have forgotten, but it's the reason I never

settled there. In an effort to live down his no-
toriety, I changed my last name."

"The Spencers aren't your family?"

Gemma took a deep breath. "On the tiny
Laurel Grove police force, Pa Spencer was second-in-command. He and his wife took me in
after what happened. I think he felt he owed me
for not seeing what was right under his nose.
For not doing something until it was far, far
too late."

Shayla fingered the handle of her mug. "Laurel Grove is near Greensboro?"

Gemma nodded. "There are a group of
older ladies in Laurel Grove—the Knit-Knack
Club—who remind me of the Double Name
Club. They chair every church committee, fun-
draiser or festival. My father demanded community participation to make him look good. He
didn't allow Mom to have friends, but I think
they suspected the truth. Garden of the year.
Quilt shows. Unable to get her to leave him,
they supported her the best way they could—
by making sure she always won."

"What about you?"

"His expectations were impossible to meet,
but I excelled at school sports. I tried to project
the confident, self-assured Gemma on the out-

side I most definitely was not on the inside. I became adept at hiding the real me."

Toying with a sugar packet, she told Shayla about joining the 4-H Club in Laurel Grove.

"I always loved animals. The summer after my junior year, Juliet and I were hired as camp counselors for the regional 4-H camp, located a couple of hours west. Mama knew how badly I wanted to go. Behind my father's back, she helped me fill out the job application. It was understood he would never let me go."

"But you went anyway."

"I'm not sure how she managed it. I never stopped to consider what she must've suffered once I set off with Juliet. The small act of defiance would've cost her dearly. But if only for a summer, I escaped his clutches."

"Camp is where you met Nate?"

Gemma smiled. "It was the most wonderful summer of my life."

"You fell in love?"

"I never fell out." She sighed. "He was so different from my father. Kind, gentle. And good."

"What happened to separate you and Nate?"

"At summer's end, I had to go home, but I'd hoped… I'd hoped…" For a second, she squeezed her eyes shut. "Instead, I walked into the house to find my father waiting. His anger had an entire summer to fester."

Gemma gazed out the window overlooking the Truelove green, grounding herself in the present and away from the life-altering moment she returned to Laurel Grove. "This time his rage had no words. And that was the most terrifying thing of all."

Shayla's mouth quivered.

"He pulled his service revolver. Mama told me to run to my bedroom and lock the door." Her breath came quick, short and uneven. "If only I hadn't left her to face him alone."

Shayla grabbed her hand. "You would've been dead, too."

"I ran. Slammed the door behind me. Locked it. Barricaded it with every piece of furniture I could shove against it. My father, the master of control, lost it. Lost it completely. Mama got between him and my door."

A single tear cascaded down Shayla's cheek. Her lips moved, but no words emerged. Gemma knew she was praying for her. Praying for her to be able to tell the rest of the story.

"He shot Mama." Saying the words made her stomach roil. "He was doing his best to batter down my bedroom door when Pa Spencer and the patrol officer on duty arrived. The officer's wife was expecting their first child. He'd only been on the force a few months. He tried to stop my father. My father killed him, too. While he was distracted, Pa Spencer was able to immobilize him."

"Does Nate know what happened?"

She shook her head. "You know the kind of man he is. The sort of family he comes from. How could I bring my garbage into his life?"

"You weren't to blame for the choices your father made, Gemma."

"But I am to blame for the choices I made. It's because I went to camp my mother died." She opened her hands. "How could I be with Nathan? Knowing my happy life with him cost my mother hers?"

"Because she would've wanted you to be happy." Shayla clutched her arm. "Only God can help you work through the feelings of unworthiness. To answer your question about how I overcame the stigma of my circumstances...?"

Gemma glanced up.

"I made a distinct break from the past. Jeremiah's birth was the catalyst that ended that chapter of my life."

Gemma considered her words. "For me, I

think the catalyst was the therapy dog the Spencers adopted to help me work through the trauma I'd experienced. It was because of the difference the little Cavalier made for me, I became a K-9 trainer."

Shayla nodded. "You stopped being a victim and became an advocate on behalf of others."

"I never looked at it that way, but that's exactly what happened."

"Marking a break with the past doesn't make the past disappear, nor should it." Shayla leaned forward. "The past is a part of you. Your new identity can only take hold if a new path forward emerges from the ashes of the old."

Gemma tilted her head. "Ultimately, the darkness led me to a fulfilling career with Juliet at PawPals."

"For obvious reasons, you find it difficult to share your feelings about what happened. But not talking about challenging emotions serves no purpose other than keeping you stuck in the past." Shayla waved her hands. "An emotional paralysis."

Her thoughts flew to Nathan and his difficulty in talking about Deanna.

"Every time I find the courage to share my story with someone, I work through more of the negative emotions. I am far more than the unloved, neglected child I was or a man's punching bag." Shayla lifted her chin. "I am a musician. A wife. A mother. A lot of people love me. I refuse to remain defined by my family's estimation."

A lot of people loved Gemma, too. Although until now, she hadn't stopped to consider how many. Juliet, her mom—Lesley—the Knit-Knack Club, Ma and Pa Spencer.

"Don't allow your father's warped perspective to hold you forever in its grip." Shayla laid her palms flat on the tabletop. "You can't break the cycle until you accept who you are and what was done to you. No one moves forward until they forgive themselves. If you don't, you condemn yourself to a lifetime of guilt and shame."

Shayla locked eyes with Gemma. "The sad, scared little girl from the trailer park deserves better than that. And so do you, my friend. So do you."

For the first time in her life, Gemma found herself believing it. "You've given me much to think about." She bit her lip. "And pray about, too."

"If you ever need to talk, I'm here for you."

"Thank you, Shayla. For everything." She glanced at the clock on the wall. "I need to get back to the ranch to check on Ike." She eased out of the booth.

Shayla rose. "Secrets take on a life of their own. I came close to losing the beautiful future God had waiting for me with Luke." She gripped Gemma's coat. "No matter how ugly it is, we owe the ones we love the truth. Tell Nate what happened before it's too late."

"I will," she promised.

Driving toward the ranch, she thanked God for Shayla's willingness to be vulnerable with someone she barely knew. Maybe one day, Gemma could do the same for someone else.

How would Nathan react to learning the truth about her past? Once he learned what had happened, would he reject her and the possibility of a future together?

Veering into the long graveled drive of the High Country Ranch, she prayed for courage to speak the truth to him. And most of all, for him to be able to receive it.

Gemma had every intention of finding a quiet moment alone with Nathan to finally explain why she'd ended their relationship, but instead she walked into an unexpected Christmas crisis.

She gaped at Nate. "Ike did what?"

Leaning against the kitchen counter, he folded his arms. "Dad signed us up to participate in the church's Living Nativity tonight."

She shrugged. "Okay…"

Nate shot a dark glance at his father, sitting with Rascal at the kitchen table. "I don't think you fully appreciate the dilemma in which we find ourselves. It's a costumed event."

His dad smiled. "It'll be fun."

Seated on a stool, Connor rested his elbows on the island. "Who are we supposed to be?"

Beside his brother, Kody swung his legs. "I want to be a camel."

"You and Connor are shepherd boys." Nate grimaced. "If Reverend Bryant hadn't called to check on us after we didn't attend the dress rehearsal, the entire pageant would've been ruined when we didn't show up tonight. Why didn't you tell me, Dad?"

A stricken look on his face, his father scratched his head. "I wanted to make a memory as a family. But since I couldn't even remember to tell you about it, I guess I'm not much of a wise man."

"You are a wise man, costume or not. Dementia or not." Lips pursed, she crossed the kitchen to stand behind his dad's chair. "I think it's a wonderful idea. But having missed the dress rehearsal, is this still doable?"

His father nodded. "They use the same costumes every year. No need for special fittings." He hung his head. "I'm sorry, Nate."

She put her hand on his shoulder. "Are there lines to be memorized?"

His dad shook his head. "They play Christmas carols from the loudspeakers. Everybody in the nativity scene just stands there and looks authentic."

She threw Nate a pointed look. "Then I see no reason the Crenshaw family can't give Ike his Christmas wish, do you?"

He scrubbed his face with his hand. "When you put it like that…"

"Yay!" Kody fist-pumped the air. "Can I be the little dwummer boy?"

"No!" Connor and Nate said at the same time.

Kody frowned. "Will there be sheep?"

His father smiled. "One for each of you."

The boys grinned. "Cool!"

She arched her eyebrow. "And what is your role, Nathan?"

He rubbed at the kinks in his neck. "Dad signed me and Tom up to be the other wise men."

"A Stetson-wearing wise man." She smirked. "Are you in charge of the gold, silver or myrrh?"

"Laugh it up." He cocked his head. "But we aren't the only ones making a command performance. You'll be the most dazzling Christmas angel the Truelove Living Nativity has ever seen."

She blinked rapidly. "An angel?"

Nate grinned. "Dad also promised one of the heifers and Rascal, too."

His father chuckled. "What would a stable be without animals?"

AT THE CHURCH that evening, under the supervision of his great-aunt GeorgeAnne, they donned their costumes and took their places.

Like the pinpricks of diamonds on a field of black velvet, stars studded the night sky. Sam and Lila Gibson, with their five-month-old son, Asher, were the principal players in this year's Living Nativity. People from as far away as Boone and Asheville arrived for the cherished Truelove tradition.

However, when he realized he had to stand still and not speak for the duration of their shift, Kody became less enthused. But averting a potential shepherd mutiny, Gemma assured him she knew he could do it and told him how proud she was of him.

His breath fogging in the chilly air, Nate looked with love and pride over the little tableau of his family. As for Gemma?

Dressed in a flowing white costume and bedecked with golden wings, she was positioned on a small balcony overlooking the manger scene below. He hadn't been kidding earlier when he told her she would be the most beautiful Christmas angel Truelove had ever seen.

She was all that and then some.

He'd never seen her hair out of the single braid she favored. But tonight it hung loose and crinkly, waving about her shoulders. She took his breath away. But she'd been doing that since he first laid eyes on her so long ago.

Nate's heart turned over in his chest. She was so lovely, inside and out. Standing under the brilliance of the Christmas balls in Greensboro, it hadn't been easy talking about Deanna. He'd hoped it might spark a reciprocal conversation about why she'd ended things between them.

Yet even after he'd bared his feelings in the aftermath of Deanna's death, Gemma held tightly to her own secrets. Leaving him more confused than ever that pursuing a relationship with her was the right thing. For the boys. For himself.

The Living Nativity ended soon after eight o'clock. Everyone congratulated the boys on their portrayals. Gemma's eyes sparkled. It was all he could do not to take her into his arms and announce his growing feelings for her to the world. But he didn't. He couldn't. Not with secrets between them.

The next day was Christmas Eve. Several times, he sensed Gemma maneuvering to have a private moment together. But beset with his own doubts, he took care to avoid being alone with her.

Late afternoon, he and Connor tromped out to the pasture to check on the heifer about to calve.

"How much longer, Daddy? Maybe a Christmas Eve calf?"

"No sign the cow's in labor yet." He slung his arm around his eldest son's shoulders. "We'll check on her again when we return from the candlelight service tonight. In the meantime, let's roll out hay in case she needs a warm, dry place to lie down."

Later at the church, with dozens of lighted candles in the windows lining the walls of the sanctuary, the service was especially beautiful. When they returned to the ranch, his dad, Gemma and the boys decided to help him check on the heifer. They left Rascal inside the house.

He spotted the black heifer sprawled on her side in the bed of hay he and Connor laid down earlier. By the time they reached her, the heifer was pushing for all she was worth.

"We're just in time." Connor gasped. "I already see the calf's front feet and a nose, Daddy."

"Hang back, guys." He put his hand on Kody to stop him from rushing forward. "Keep your voices down. Let her do her thing."

Gemma stood close to his elbow. "Shouldn't we do something?"

He shook his head. "As long as she isn't having trouble, it's better for her to calve on her own. We'll stand by in case she has difficulty getting up afterward to mother her calf."

"The birthing doesn't take long," his dad assured her.

Immediately after the delivery, the heifer began to lick her calf.

Ike crouched between the boys. "If a calf doesn't get up right away, it runs the risk of death due to cold or dehydration."

Nate smiled at his father, happy to see him in

his true element again, a proud cattle rancher. Within five minutes, the calf was standing.

A sheen of happy tears shone in Gemma's eyes. "God's creation is so amazing and precious."

Like love.

He slipped his hand into hers. Leaning into him, she squeezed his fingers. Tonight, everything in his world felt so right. So perfect. So meant to be.

Something long numb in his heart blazed to life. Gemma got it. She got the ranching life. She got him. He put away his fears for the future to relish the here and now.

It was late by the time they were able to tear the boys away from Mistletoe the calf and his mother. Yet the boys were awake before the crack of dawn, eager to dive into opening the presents under the Christmas tree.

Full of their usual high spirits, they ripped off the paper Gemma had so painstakingly wrapped for them. They oohed and aahed over the gifts she'd helped him select.

Bleary-eyed from lack of sleep, he got as much enjoyment out of watching her animated face as in his sons tearing open their gifts.

She declared herself enchanted with the presents the boys had clumsily wrapped for her. Rascal had gifts, which Kody out of the kindness of his heart offered to open for the collie.

Connor threw his brother an exaggerated eye roll.

There was also a present for Mistletoe. Nate had tucked the gift away in case the calf made an appearance for Christmas. Sir Hops-a-Lot and Hare-i-et were not forgotten, either.

Sipping coffee, he was about to talk to Gemma about what he'd been feeling over the last few days, when his phone—lying on the kitchen table between them—buzzed.

It wasn't a number he immediately recognized. "Hello?"

Just like that, everything changed.

# CHAPTER FIFTEEN

IT WAS THE woman from the agency regarding a permanent caregiver for his dad.

As he clutched the phone to his ear, Nate's gaze cut to Gemma.

Beside him at the kitchen table, she touched his arm. "What is it?" she whispered.

He spoke into the phone. "When?" His eyebrows rose. "That's…that's…" His voice hitched. "That's good news."

But his gut tanked.

"Nathan?"

With a slight shake of his head, he listened as the agency lady gave details about when to expect Mrs. Jewell. His mind racing, he thanked the lady and clicked off. Nate stared at the phone in his hand.

Silence ticked between him and Gemma.

"Tell me."

He laid his cell on the table. "Because of

the urgency of our situation, even though it's Christmas day, the lady at the agency called to let me know a permanent caregiver has become available sooner than expected."

"When?"

"I hoped we'd have until the New Year." He took a breath. "Mrs. Jewell will arrive first thing tomorrow morning."

She went still. Too still. She looked at him. "What does this mean?"

He plowed his hand through his hair. "I don't know what it will mean."

"What do you want it to mean?"

"Things will have to change." He dropped his gaze to the table. "Dad will have to adjust to a new caregiver."

"I meant what do you want it to mean for us?"

Nate scrubbed his hand over his face. "I don't know."

"I think you do know."

He looked at her. "I thought I'd have more time to…"

"To what?"

He heaved a sigh. "To come to terms with the past."

"I should've explained long before now why I ended things between us. I meant to but—"

He walked over to peer out the window over the sink. "How can there be an 'us' when you can't bring yourself to tell me what you were thinking and feeling then, much less now?"

Jumping up, she hurried to his side. "I want to tell you. I need to tell you."

She told him what happened the day she got home from camp. He stared at her in horror at what she'd endured.

"I never suspected…" His throat went tight. "You never said anything that summer about your father."

Tears filled her eyes. "It was hard to talk about. It's still hard to talk about."

He touched her arm. "I'm sorry you lost your mom that way. Why didn't you tell me, Gemma? Why the voicemail?"

"After it happened, I wasn't in a good place. I was a mess. I was consumed with shame and self-loathing."

Placing his hands on her shoulders, he turned her to face him. "Nothing about what happened was your fault."

She took a shuddery breath. "It took a long time to get my head straight. A lot of love to heal from the trauma."

He shook his head. "I would've been there

for you. I wanted nothing more than to be with you. I could have been the one to love you back to recovery."

"For a long time, guilt and my love for you were mixed up in my head." She put her arms around him. "But not anymore."

Guilt and love? He stiffened. *Deanna*...

"Forgive me, Nathan." She pressed her cheek against his shirt. "Forgive me for failing you."

He clamped his jaw tight. "There's nothing to forgive."

"We can move forward from here." She lifted her head. "The time wasn't right then for us, but now..."

Move forward? The ache in his chest intensified, becoming nearly unbearable. Sweat broke out on his brow.

She peered at him. "What are you thinking? Talk to me."

Nate felt at a point of no return. He couldn't do this again. Risk falling into an infinite abyss of hurt with Gemma like the last time.

He pushed her away. She staggered. "I... I can't. There's Dad's illness and the boys to consider. I told you from the beginning I wasn't in a position to pursue a long-term relationship. We agreed there'd be no expectations. No promises."

Nate's head throbbed. His heart hurt. He raised his hand to his forehead only to realize it was shaking. He dropped his hand to his side.

"We don't have to return to the way things were, Nathan. Give us a chance. Please. If this is about my past…"

Once upon a time, she'd been his greatest strength. Now she felt like his greatest weakness. He put the island between them. If he touched her, he'd be lost.

"This has nothing to do with your father."

Her face became stricken. "It wasn't just our past you aren't ready to face. It's Deanna, isn't it?"

Nate gripped the hard, smooth edge of the countertop. "After you broke up with me, she was my light at the end of the tunnel. I was messed up for a long time, too. Even after we got married, I kept her at an emotional arm's length. Now the guilt and love…"

"…are mixed up in your head," she rasped.

He swallowed. "Deanna's shadow will always be between us. A life with you wouldn't be fair to her."

Gemma's nostrils flared. "She's dead, Nathan, but you don't have to be."

His chest heaved. "No matter how hard we

tried, we'd never work. We'd only hurt each other. Hurt the boys." Across the expanse of the granite counter, he threw her a bleak look. "I can't allow them to be hurt any more than they already have been. Don't you see?"

She opened her hands. "What I see is a man so afraid he'll be hurt, he won't allow himself to love again. Take your eyes off the past. I love you, Nathan Crenshaw. Even if you don't feel the same now, could you ever see yourself loving me in the future?"

"The last thing I want to do is hurt you." Unable to bear the anguish in her eyes, he looked away. "But the answer to your question is no. In the future I envision at the ranch, there is no you and me."

She flinched as if he'd struck her.

He clenched his jaw so hard it ached. "I will always be grateful for everything you've done for Dad. For everything you've been to Connor and Kody."

"Be honest with yourself, Nathan, if not with me." Her mouth trembled. "What has this last month been about if not falling in love?"

He forced himself to lock eyes with her. "Finishing the unfinished."

"Closure," she whispered. "Time has run out for us, hasn't it?"

"I'm sorry." He stuffed his hands in his pockets. "First loves aren't meant to be forever loves."

She wrapped her arms around herself. "I need to pack."

He frowned. "It's Christmas Day. You don't need to go now."

"You'll need time and space to prepare your father and the boys for the new caregiver. There's no point in prolonging the inevitable." She winced. "I always believed you and I were inevitable."

Once upon a time—as recently as last night—he'd thought so, too. Shattered at the prospect of her imminent departure, he wasn't sure what he believed. Only there'd be no once-upon-a-time for him and Gemma. No happily-ever-after.

He doubted he'd ever know happiness again. But this last month, he had been. Happy.

"I'll say goodbye to Ike and the boys." She edged around the island. "Then I'll go."

By the time the boys and his father returned, he'd managed to get his emotions under lock and key.

Gemma emerged with her suitcase just as he finished explaining about Mrs. Jewell.

Kody flung himself at her. "I don't want a jewel. I want Gemma."

Blinking rapidly, Connor buried his face into her side. Nate could tell it was all she could do not to burst into tears herself. But she didn't. And he was grateful.

Instead, she hugged them hard and whispered sweet, soothing words of comfort. Sensing something amiss, Rascal rubbed his coat against her leg.

His dad touched his arm. "Just because Mrs. Jewell will be here doesn't mean—"

"It's better this way, Dad," he grunted.

"Better for whom?" his father growled.

His dad drew her into a fierce, hard hug. "Thank you, dear girl. For everything you've done." He threw Nate a sad look. "For all of us."

Almost as soon as Gemma drove away, Nate wished he'd made a different choice. But he hadn't. She was gone from his life almost as quickly as she'd reappeared.

This time, forever.

MRS. JEWELL TURNED out to be a pleasant, motherly sort of woman. She and Rascal took to each other right away. After reviewing the routine Gemma had created for his dad, she declared her intention to stick with it. To his credit, his father vowed to give her a fair chance.

Nate found her friendly, efficient and professional. Per the terms of their agreement, she looked after his dad, did light housekeeping and had supper on the table at the end of the day before she returned to her home near the county seat.

Everything was working out for the best. Although, the boys moped about the farmhouse like the end of the world had come. A week passed. He remained heartsick and miserable. Unable to sleep. Unable to eat.

New Year's Day came and went.

The next day, the boys returned to school. He was in the barn shoveling fresh hay into a stall when he heard the sound of an engine in the drive.

His head down, he kept working. Maybe whoever it was would go away. He wasn't in the mood for company.

A vehicle door slammed. Heavy boots clomped across the compacted snow in the barnyard toward him. He was contemplating a hasty retreat when a tall, skinny scarecrow wearing horn-rimmed glasses blocked the light between him and the door.

Worst-case scenario. Turning his back, he gripped the handle of the shovel. Great-aunt GeorgeAnne.

He was actually surprised she hadn't arrived before now. His mouth twisted. "Come to gloat?"

"I was wrong about Gemma."

He wheeled. "What happened to 'She's not from around here... She doesn't belong.'?"

GeorgeAnne pushed her glasses farther along the bridge of her nose. "Turns out she does."

"You said we weren't a good fit. We weren't a good match."

His aunt sniffed. "After I had the chance to know her, I changed my mind. Gemma would make an excellent rancher's wife. A wonderful mother to those boys of yours."

"Connor and Kody already have a mother," he growled.

She cocked her head. "That's what this fit of yours is truly about, isn't it? This has nothing to do with Gemma and everything to do with your inability to acknowledge the loss of Deanna."

"I don't need your interference in my life." He set his jaw.

She set hers. "Good. Because this isn't me interfering. This is an intervention to make sure you don't ruin your life."

He gaped at her.

"Self-pity is unattractive in anyone, much less a great, big, hulking man like yourself. Not every minute of your marriage was perfect. So what? I don't know many relationships that are. You have regrets? So do I. Congratulations. Welcome to the human race."

His jaw dropped.

"If only you'd look beyond the mistakes to the happiness you shared with Deanna. Recall the joy you gave her." Her eyes watered. "And there was so much happiness, nephew. She loved you so much. No matter how you try to deny it and shield yourself from the pain, you loved her, too. Let yourself remember. Not everyone gets a love like Deanna's. Much less two. Don't waste it. We can learn much from sorrow. I beg you, dear boy. Don't let your suffering be in vain."

"Are you finished?" His voice sounded strangled.

"I've said what I came to say."

"And then some," he muttered.

"Your father and Mrs. Jewell are headed to the Jar for an afternoon with the ROMEOs. After school, the boys are going to Maggie's. You'll have the ranch to yourself until supper."

She touched his cheek. "You really are my favorite nephew, you know."

Glimpsing the compassion in her eyes, he felt his anger fade. Standing in the doorframe of the barn, he watched her drive away.

It was rare he had the farm to himself. He couldn't recall the last time he'd truly been alone for any stretch of time. Not since Gemma came into his life again.

Restless, he wandered into the house. The silence felt oppressive. Or maybe that was merely his emotions, roiling beneath the surface he kept so carefully stoic.

Seeking a distraction, he drifted into the boys' bedroom, only to be confronted with the lone picture of Deanna he'd allowed to remain. Everything else he'd packed away.

As if Deanna and what he'd felt for her could be so easily eradicated.

He picked up the framed photo of his late wife with their sons. He recalled taking the picture on an early-autumn day a few weeks before she died. She and the boys had been standing in front of one of her rose bushes.

She wasn't a pale, golden beauty like Gemma. Everything about Deanna had been bubbly and vibrant. Warm. Generous to a fault. The most loving, forgiving person he'd ever known. Or loved.

Tears sprang to his eyes. Because yes, he'd loved her. Only now could he bear to admit it to himself. He'd loved her. Deeply.

Clutching the photo to his chest, he stumbled out of the house. He found himself at the ruins of the flower garden she'd once so lovingly tended. In an effort to avoid facing the truth of his loss, the garden he'd ripped out.

But there was no bypassing sorrow. No way forward, except to go through it. His knees buckled. He sank onto the ground, paying no heed to the cold seeping through his jeans.

He'd remained dry-eyed through her funeral. Dry-eyed these last, two, bitter, lonely years without her.

One by one, memories unfolded in his mind. How beautiful she'd been on their wedding day. The joy he'd felt as she carried his sons in her belly. There'd been so much fun. So much laughter. How could he have sought to erase it?

To erase the memories would be to erase her. And that was the last thing he wanted.

Sobs overcame him. He cried out in the stillness of that January afternoon with a pain so great he wondered how it could be borne. Yet he had to bear it. Come to grips with it. So he could breathe again. Live again. Love again.

Because that's what Deanna would have wanted for him.

"I think you and Gemma would've liked each other," he whispered to the wind. "Thank you for giving me Connor and Kody. Thank you for putting me on the right path with Dad's illness."

Deanna had been first to perceive something was amiss with her father-in-law. Deanna, who insisted Nate consult a neurologist. After a ton of research, it was Deanna—he choked up—who found PawPals. And Deanna's idea to get his dad a dementia assistance dog.

Life come full circle, Deanna had set him on a path to a reunion with his first love. Deanna, who'd given him another chance at life and love. Twice...

Grief poured out of him. He mourned Deanna as he'd never allowed himself to mourn her before. "I miss you so much."

He always would. And that was as it should be. The cost of love. A price he'd pay all over again for the chance to love Deanna.

Nate turned his face to the brilliant blue of the Carolina sky.

From somewhere on the ridge, a wren was

singing its heart out. His gaze landed upon something tiny and yellow poking bravely through the mantle of snow at his feet.

He brushed aside the snow. A crocus. One of Deanna's favorites. His breath hitched. In the dead of winter, she used to say, a crocus was the first harbinger that spring would come again.

Gemma might represent to him a forever summer, but Deanna would always be an eternal spring.

As a breeze dried the tears on his cheeks, peace filled him. For a second, her presence was with him so strongly he believed he might yet reach out and touch her one last time. Her love lived on in their sons. One day he and Deanna would have a reunion of their own.

But until then... He got off the ground. He loved Gemma. He wanted a life with her. Had he lost her forever? *God, what should I do?*

The glimmers of an idea etched themselves into his mind, but he would need help. He fished his phone out of his pocket. It might already be too late.

GeorgeAnne answered on the first ring as if she'd been waiting for his call. "Come to your senses yet?"

He rubbed at the kinks in his neck. "I can hardly believe I'm saying this—I need the matchmakers' help."

"I can't tell you how pleased I am the Double Name Club's new nonmeddling policy worked out so well for you." The cat-that-swallowed-the-cream glee in her voice would have been galling, if a beggar like him could've afforded to be choosy. "Better than anyone could've anticipated."

By the time his great-aunt got through rewriting history, he and Gemma would go down as yet another matchmaker triumph.

"Gemma and I were supposed to spend Christmas together. I need to make this right with her."

"Not a problem, dear boy. Ever heard of a little thing called 'The Twelve Days of Christmas'? By my reckoning, you've got about four days to fix this and still make your Christmas deadline. What are you thinking?"

"This is going to require a road trip."

GeorgeAnne chuckled. "Might be interesting to see how the flatlanders survive in their concrete jungle."

"It's Laurel Grove, Aunt Georgie. Not a concrete…" He pinched the bridge of his nose. "I'm going to need yards of chicken wire."

"On it. Your cousin Brian will haul over a bunch from the store. Next?"

"A ton of extension cords. Dozens of strands of lights, preferably white and blue."

His aunt was old school. He heard the scratching sound of pencil on paper. "What else?"

"The jeweler is closed until next week."

GeorgeAnne sniffed. "He won't be after I call him."

Suddenly overwhelmed with what it would take to pull this off, he groaned. "Who are we kidding? This will never work. Gemma may take one look at me and kick me to the curb."

"Not going to happen."

"And there's the not-so-small issue of needing a dog, Aunt Georgie."

"What kind of dog?"

He let his head drop into his hand. "What does it matter? I've got about as much chance of winning Gemma back as sprouting wings."

"Focus, nephew. What sort of qualities are you looking for in a dog for Gemma?"

"Something cute. Cuddly. And sweet. A loyal companion."

"Don't worry. Bridger has connections."

"It's going to take a lot of hands to make this happen in four days."

"Never fear, nephew. Truelove is here."

With that ominous statement, she clicked off to rally the troops. Within the hour, vehicles arrived, loaded with enthusiastic helpers and supplies. By nightfall, Nate began to believe Operation Christmas Ball—as his father dubbed it—might stand a chance of succeeding.

After everyone went home, he talked to the boys about what he hoped to do. "Would it be okay with you, guys, if Gemma came to live with us?"

Connor cocked his head. "Forever?"

"The foreverest of forever."

Connor hugged him. "Thank you, Daddy."

He gazed into their earnest little faces. "It's not a done deal, son. Gemma may not say yes."

"Of course she'll say yes, Daddy." Kody rolled his eyes. "She might be a little mad with you, but she still loves us plenty."

His dad grinned. "Out of the mouths of babes."

*Whatever works... God, please. Whatever works.*

Truelove was on board, but Laurel Grove reinforcements would be essential.

It was late. He'd put in a call to Juliet tomorrow. And he prayed she wouldn't hang up on him before hearing him out.

## CHAPTER SIXTEEN

ALONE AND DEVASTATED in her apartment that week, she grieved for what had never been and what would never be with Nathan. Despite her assurances to the contrary, she had totally given in to the hope something long-term could grow between them.

Yet her initial instincts had been correct. Since that long-ago summer, too much had transpired. Their lives had followed different trajectories.

She'd hoped, prayed, that their Christmas reunion might lead to the future she'd always wanted, but she'd deluded herself.

Over the week between Christmas and New Year's, the finality of losing him—although hadn't she lost him long ago?—produced in her an ache so intense, sometimes she found it difficult to draw breath.

That first night, she'd called Juliet to let her

know what had happened. Her next phone call had been to the Spencers.

Ma Spencer had wanted to cut short their Christmas vacation with the grandkids to return immediately. Gemma managed to dissuade her, but the fierce love in Ma's voice on the phone made Gemma rethink her years with them. In a state of shocked numbness following the tragedy, she'd refused to allow herself to belong to the family and home the Spencers offered.

Juliet was relentless in her repeated attempts to console. A much-needed reminder Gemma wasn't alone. Never alone. Fifteen years ago, there'd been Juliet, the Spencers and God. In losing the love of her life, she found it to be much the same now—Juliet, the Spencers and God.

Yet knowing the outcome—that no shining future awaited her in Truelove—would she have done anything different in the last few weeks? Held back her heart? Trained Rascal for someone else?

If given the chance, she wouldn't have traded the opportunity to know Nathan's boys for anything. Or deprived Ike of what Rascal offered—a better quality of life.

As for opening her heart to Nathan?

Spending those precious weeks with him…
She had no regrets for falling in love with the
man he'd become. She loved Nathan. She prayed
God would use their brief time together to help
him move toward a new life and a new love.
The boys needed a mother.

It hurt to imagine someone else mothering
Connor and Kody, but Nathan deserved all the
happiness in the world. It just wouldn't be with
her.

A bitter, bitter truth, but it was time to move
forward into the life God meant for her.

The news of her leave-taking must have
quickly made the rounds of the Truelove grapevine. It meant the world that Maggie, Kara and
Shayla called to check on her.

She also had time to ponder what she wanted
her future to look like. It wouldn't include the
boys and Nathan. But her mother's sacrifice
made sure she still had a life. It was time she
started living it.

On the morning of New Year's Eve, for the
first time in days, she got dressed and braided
her hair. Then she drove to Laurel Grove.

Gemma parked across the street from the
house where her mother died. It no longer resembled the house she'd known. On that late-

December day, colorful, vibrant pansies sat in pots on the front stoop. There was an air of happiness about the home of the current owners.

She wasn't entirely sure how she knew that. But for someone who'd grown up with unhappiness, it was easy to spot its opposite.

Per Shayla's sage advice, she made a deliberate choice to close that painful chapter in her past. Leaving behind her father's legacy of shame, she headed for the town cemetery.

There, she laid a bouquet of flowers at the base of her mother's headstone. She was here to embrace her mother's legacy. She was her mother's most-cherished legacy.

Gemma gazed at the milky sunshine of the cold winter's day. "Thank you, Mama. For everything."

Swiping her eyes, she returned to her car. Driving down Main Street, she steered around the back of PawPals headquarters. The office was closed for New Year's Eve, but her best friend was taking advantage of a few quiet hours to catch up on administrative tasks.

"Hey, stranger." Inside PawPals, Juliet hugged her. "I'm glad to see you out and about."

Gemma smiled, a wobbly one but a smile nonetheless. "About time, right?"

Juliet examined Gemma's features. "Grieving takes as long as it takes."

She nodded. "I've decided to give up my apartment in Greensboro. Would you help me find a new place closer to Laurel Grove?"

"You're sure about this?"

Gemma lifted her chin. "I've made my peace with the past. It's made me who I am and who I am is okay. I want to be closer to the work I love, the friends who love me and a future I've put in God's hands."

Tears sprang into Juliet's eyes.

"Put me on your apartment-hunting schedule." She draped her arm around her friend. "Would it be possible to move up the training for the next assistance dog?"

Juliet opened a file on her computer. "A black Lab. From the Hollingsworth kennel in True-love."

"I vetted Liberty myself. Very adaptable, friendly and trainable. Who's our next client?"

Juliet clicked a few keys on the keypad. "An elderly woman near the coast. Do you want me to contact Bridger about moving up the delivery date?"

She bit her lip. "He'll bring Liberty to us, right? I won't have to—"

"You won't have to return to Truelove." Juliet moved around the desk. "I'll contact the client's family about sending the usual personal items so you can begin scent training." Her friend propped her hands on her hips. "What're your plans for tonight?"

"I plan to enjoy the Laurel Grove fireworks and celebrate the coming of the New Year with your family." Gemma's mouth twitched. "If you'll have me."

She grinned. "You're always welcome at the Melbourne house."

"Great." Gemma made a show of wiping her brow. "Because I already packed an overnight bag."

At Juliet's that night, there was fun and laughter. She got her dog fix with Sophie's sweet golden retriever, Bixby, and funny little Moose, who basically ran his humans like the alpha dog legend he was in his own doggy mind. She also spent a lot of time with baby Tyler.

She didn't know how or when, but someday she wanted children in her life. Whether that meant fostering or adoption or biological. Although, she couldn't imagine ever loving anyone like she loved Nathan. But she put the uncertainty and her hope into the hands of the One who loved her the most and the best.

God would decide if and when. And if His plan was for her to not have children, she would rest knowing He had something else in store for her. A future and a hope better than what she could imagine.

The day after New Year's, she and Juliet met for apartment hunting. They inspected two available apartments within the same complex, but during lunch, she sensed a change come over her PawPals partner.

Juliet found flaws with each of the next three places. Gemma suggested revisiting the first two, but Juliet suddenly found fault with each of them, too.

She frowned at her friend, her dark head bent over her cell phone again. Something was off. Juliet had been distracted ever since getting a phone call. There'd been a flurry of subsequent texts.

"Is everything okay, Juliet?"

Not bothering to look up from the most recent text, Juliet fluttered her hand. "Just working through some unexpected logistics. I should get home."

"I'll follow you to Laurel Grove."

"Um…" Juliet's brow creased. "Maybe you should head to Greensboro."

Gemma blinked.

"You'll need to start packing if you plan on moving out soon, right?"

"I… I guess…" She fingered the strap of her purse. "We're still on for more apartment hunting tomorrow?"

Juliet agreed, but later called and cancelled. Over the next couple of days, her friend continued to fob off Gemma's attempts to reschedule.

More than a little bummed, she reminded herself Juliet had family and business responsibilities. She'd find her own apartment. Then just after six o'clock one evening, her cell rang.

"I think I've managed to finally pull it off," Juliet gushed.

Having not heard from her in several days, Gemma stared at the cell in her hand. "You've found me an apartment?"

"Better than that."

"A house to rent? I hadn't dared hope I could afford— You're sure it's in my budget? Room for me to train the dogs?"

"Totally within your reach, Gem. Room for lots of animals to roam around."

"Oh, Jules." She squeezed her eyes shut

for a second. Juliet had been working this whole time on her behalf. "I can't thank you enough."

"Your happiness is all the thanks I ever need." Something that sounded like tears laced Juliet's voice.

"When can I—"

"First, I need you to pick up your dog."

Not her dog. A dog for their next client. Although once she moved into the house Juliet had found, maybe she'd look into acquiring her own pet.

"Oh. Okay. Sure." She frowned into the phone. "When?"

"Now."

She glanced out the window. It was already dark, and a light snowfall was expected tonight. "You want me to drive to Laurel Grove to pick up the dog now?"

"Meet me at the office. You'll head over right this minute, won't you?"

Gemma grabbed her key fob. "I'll head over this very second, I promise."

"Um…you got dressed today, didn't you?"

On her way to the door, she stopped. "Yes-sssss…"

"Something nice?"

Her gaze flitted to the ceiling. "I guessssss…"

Juliet's tone went brisk. "Tell me what you're wearing."

"What does it matter what I'm wearing, Jules? I'm picking up a dog, not a date."

But Juliet would not let it go until she described in detail her current attire.

"Satisfied?" she huffed. "Didn't realize there was a PawPals dress code."

"You've fixed your hair and you've put on makeup, too?"

"What's going on, Juliet?"

"Nothing."

"You're not setting me up for a blind date, are you?" she growled. "Because I'm not ready for that."

"On my 4-H camp counselor's honor, I promise a blind date is the furthest thing from my mind."

"Then if you and the fashion police are done, I'll be on my way."

"We'll be waiting."

By "we'll," she figured Juliet was counting Liberty the dog, too.

It was almost seven o'clock by the time she turned off the highway and reached Laurel Grove. Main Street storefronts lay dark and shuttered. The sidewalks rolled up at the close of the business day. She veered around the Paw-Pals building to the employee parking lot, but there was no sign of Juliet's car.

Doing a U-turn in the empty lot, she steered into a space in front of PawPals, usually reserved for clients. No lights shone from within. Her pulse ratcheted. Where was Juliet? What was going on?

She spotted a piece of paper taped to the glass door. Switching off the engine, she retrieved the note.

Waiting on the square.

Perhaps Liberty had gotten restless and Juliet had taken her for a short walk. But in the dark?

Gemma pivoted at the same moment the square blazed to life. Whoa. At the sudden brilliance of the festive display, she threw up her hand to shield her eyes.

Similar to the larger, annual Christmas event in nearby Greensboro, dozens of blue-and-white illuminated balls hung from the bare canopy of trees dotting the square. What was with the Christmas—

Gemma checked her phone. It was January 6.

Old Christmas. In some cultures celebrated as the Feast of the Three Kings. In others, Epiphany.

She'd never known Laurel Grove to celebrate Old Christmas before, but maybe it was a new tradition.

However, she didn't relish venturing into the deserted square alone. What was Juliet thinking? More than a little irritated, she sent off a quick text to her friend. There was no reply, but a pair of headlights swept across the sidewalk.

A lone vehicle pulled in beside her car. Tensing, she had her finger poised over the alarm button on her key fob when she caught sight of the man behind the wheel.

She stepped closer. "Pa?"

Getting out of the sedan she also now recognized, he drew her into a hug. "Happy Christmas, darlin'."

Her gaze darted to the lighted balls across the street. "I didn't realize Laurel Grove celebrated Twelfth Night. Is there an event planned for later?"

He chuckled. "You could say that."

Not getting the joke, she shrugged. "I didn't expect to see you for another few days."

"Juliet called. We came home early to meet your new dog."

"You drove from Virginia to meet my latest K-9?"

He grinned. "Ma thought you might need a little last-minute reassurance so she sent me over to encourage you."

"I don't understand."

He put his arm around her shoulder. "To tell you how proud your mother would be of the young woman you've become."

Tears stung her eyes. "Whatever I've become is because you and Ma made me feel safe enough to follow my dreams."

"And now you have another dream to follow." Releasing her, he gestured in the direction of the square. "You better head over before we're frozen."

She bit her lip. "You'll go with me?"

"Not this time, darlin'." He leaned against his car. "But I'll be here when you come back. Like always."

Her gaze cut to the illuminated globes across the street.

"Go on now." Pa Spencer gave her a little push. "You've waited long enough."

She looked at him.

"Don't be afraid." He smiled. "All will come right in the end. At long last, just like I told you."

Once upon a terrible, terrible day, he'd made her that promise.

Gentle snowflakes floated down around them. Reminding her of a first snowfall under the dark Truelove sky with Nathan. And his kiss. A memory, no matter how things turned out, she would cherish forever.

She crossed the street. The snow crunched under her boots. It was only after she stepped into the grove of trees it occurred to her to wonder how Pa knew Juliet's note had told her to meet in the square. But by then, it was too late to turn around and ask.

The glittering panorama of Christmas balls enveloped her. It was as if everything outside the square had ceased to exist. She found herself in a world of its own. A beautiful world.

No sign of Juliet, but on the path leading to the center of the square sat a small wicker basket. Something wiggled underneath the warm, fuzzy blue blanket lining the basket.

There was a whimper. She put her hand to her throat. A tiny black nose peeked out from the blanket. Two round black eyes like buttons peered out at her. The fluffy, white, powder-puff Maltese puppy cocked his head at her and barked.

Relaxing, she smiled. "Hello, you." Crouching, she let the dog smell her hand. "Have you gotten yourself lost?"

The puppy licked her fingers.

Unable to resist, she plucked the dog from the basket and cuddled him—it was a him—close to her coat. "Where's your human, sweet little pup?"

There was a tag on the Maltese's collar. Winston. Only Jules had known Gemma's favorite dog name. Her breath caught. And Nathan.

A note was attached to his collar. "Will you keep me forever?"

Jules and her little jokes. Whoever this dog belonged to, it wasn't her. The adorable puppy wasn't the black Labrador she was expecting from Bridger, either. But Winston would make someone a wonderful companion pet.

Finding a leash coiled in the basket, she clipped it onto Winston's collar. Best not to get too attached. She'd said the same when she went to Truelove. And look how well that turned out.

Maybe Juliet had also taken it upon herself to gift Gemma with a pet of her own. She set Winston on his feet. His nose twitching, he yanked Gemma forward. A small dog but mighty in heart. His paws scrabbling in the fresh-fallen snow, he uncovered something and promptly ate it.

"Winston! No. Don't eat—"

He yanked her forward. He pounced again, but this time she beat him to it. Someone had left a trail of dog treats for Winston to follow. What further surprises lay in store?

Smiling, she decided to play along. What a lovely gesture. Jules's latest effort to lift her spirits. What a good best friend she was.

For such a little dog, Winston set a fast pace. She emerged in the center of the square fully expecting to find her best friend and possibly Sophie, Tyler and Rob.

But what she discovered was better. So much better. Encircled by an enormous heart of rose petals, crimson against the snow, stood Nathan, handsome in his Sunday Stetson, a suit and a tie.

She ground to an immediate halt. "What are you doing here?" she whispered, hardly able to believe her eyes. "Has something happened to the boys? To Ike?"

"Everyone is fine." He cleared his throat. "Except for me."

She scooped Winston into her arms. "What's wrong?"

"Nothing's been the same since you left." He

scrubbed his hand over his face. "Many, many people have taken care to point out my stubborn pigheadedness."

"Comparing yourself to a pig…that seems terribly unfair." She cut her eyes at him. "To the pig."

His mouth twitched. "I can't begin to tell you how much I've missed you, Gemma Spencer."

She tilted her head. "Try."

"Why don't you step into the heart with me and I'll try to explain?"

She narrowed her eyes at him. "I can hear you fine from here. Why don't you start by explaining what you're doing in Laurel Grove."

"You leave me no choice, except to use every tool at my disposal."

He whipped out a squeaky rubber duck. Winston lunged. Trying to maintain her grip on the small dog, she stumbled into the petal-strewed heart.

"No fair, Nathan Crenshaw." She glowered at him. "Using the dog against me."

Seizing the duck between his jaws, the Maltese shook his head from side to side, chomping down. Rolling her eyes, she set Winston on his feet, but kept a tight hold on the leash and her wildly careening emotions.

"That's better." Nathan smiled. "I'm here to

apologize for the things I said. I also believed it high time you had a dog of your own."

Her mouth opened. "Winston's for me?"

"You told Dad the way to your heart was through a dog."

Her eyes widened. "All of this…" She motioned. "It's about giving me a pet?"

"All of this took the combined efforts of a lot of people who care about you. I've had half of Truelove making Christmas balls to my exact specifications. And half of Laurel Grove, including the Spencers, Juliet and the Knit-Knack Club working this end on your behalf."

She shook her head. "It's kind of you to think of me—"

"I haven't been able to stop thinking about you, Gemma," he grunted.

Her lips trembled. "First loves are never meant to be forever loves. Isn't that what you said? Is Winston supposed to be a consolation prize?"

"This isn't going the way I…" He pinched the bridge of his nose. "When you asked me if I could ever see my way to loving you—"

"You said you couldn't."

"I lied." His Adam's apple bobbed in his throat. "But I promise I'll never lie to you again." His gaze bored into hers. "You're all I see. I can't imagine a future without you. Loving Connor and Kody. Loving me," he rasped. "Unless..." He looked away.

"Unless what?"

His gaze found hers. "Unless you don't love me anymore. I wouldn't blame you if you didn't."

The aching vulnerability on his face nearly buckled her knees.

"I do love you." She shut her eyes and opened them. "I always have."

"Then ask me your question again." He took her hands in his. Tingles from the always-something-between-them flew up her arm. She could tell from the wry twist of his lips he felt it, too.

"Sparks have never been our problem," she whispered. "That summer—"

"This is so not about a long-ago summer." He locked eyes with her. "Please, Gemma. Ask me again how I feel about you."

"What about Deanna?"

"There will always be a place in my heart that belongs to her. She's the mother of my sons." A muscle throbbed in his cheek. "But tonight, there's no one here but you and me."

"And Winston."

Nathan smiled at the Maltese sitting at their feet.

Pa Spencer had been right. She'd waited long enough for the man standing in front of her. She would wait no more.

"Do you love me, Nathan?"

His face gentled. "From the moment you stepped out of the shadow of the barn your first day at the ranch… One glance and you had my heart. Again. I love you, Gemma. I doubted seventeen-year-olds could experience true love. In our case, it turns out they can."

She made no effort to stem the flow of tears down her cheeks. He pulled a ring from his coat pocket and dropped to his knee.

Gasping, she put her hand to her mouth. Was this really happening? Or merely a dream?

But at the warm touch of his strong hand taking hers, she knew it was for real. God's plan for her. The future she'd longed for.

"Will you share all my tomorrows?" His voice went husky. "Will you marry me?"

"Yes." She quivered. "I will."

With a whoop, he jumped to his feet and pressed his mouth against hers. Clasped in his arms, he swung her around.

In a frenzy of doggy delirium, Winston raced back and forth across the rose-encircled heart, scattering crimson petals to the wind.

Cradling his face between her hands, she smiled against his lips. "We've got Winston's approval."

He grinned. "Rascal can't wait for the pup to join the High Country Ranch on a permanent basis."

She cocked her head. "Rascal's met Winston?"

"The boys, too. Who do you think scent-trained him to follow the treats?"

"Your dad is okay about us?"

"Sweetheart..." Nathan shook his head. "Dad's been after me to pop the question since the week you arrived."

"It takes some people a little longer than others to clue in, I guess," she teased.

His arms tightened around her. "I got here eventually. Where I was always meant to be."

"Me, too." She brushed her mouth across the rough stubble on his jaw. "All's well that ends well."

Closure. Life come to its full, glorious circle. Happily-ever-after.

"There's plenty of room at your new home for K-9 training."

Home. She smiled, thinking of Juliet's phone call. Room for all kinds of animals, she'd said.

*Thank You, God. And thank you, Juliet, for putting the pieces of this magical night together.*

"When will you make me the happiest man on earth?"

She laced her fingers around the nape of his neck. "As soon as we're reunited with the family."

Her own family to love and cherish.

Nathan cocked his head. "The boys and Dad are at Juliet's. 'Scared to death,' to quote Kody, I'll mess this up for him."

She pressed her forehead against his. "I don't need anything fancy. Just you. And the boys."

Barking, Winston continued to race around them.

Nathan lifted his head. "Can somebody come get this dog and give us a moment?" he hollered.

"Who are you talking—"

A sheepish grin lightening his rugged features, Bridger sauntered out of the trees. Securing the leash, he touched his hand to his forehead in a brief salute before heading off again.

"We've had witnesses?"

"The half of Truelove I mentioned before? Yeah. The matchmakers, too."

She gaped at him.

"At a discreet distance, I assure you. Reinforcements in the event of dire disaster. Like you throwing the ring in my face."

"Marry me tomorrow," she breathed.

Through the opening in his coat, she felt his heartbeat kick up a notch. "I'm yours forever, Gemma Spencer, but how do you aim to pull this off tomorrow?"

"Laurel Grove's got churches." She smiled. "When the Double Name Club of Truelove combines forces with the Knit-Knack Club of Laurel Grove, there's not much those ladies can't accomplish."

"Possibly even world domination," he joked.

First loves could be forever loves. The best of loves. They'd waited long enough for their happily-ever-after.

His eyes shone. "The best is yet to be, sweetheart."

"Kiss me," she whispered.

Sweeping her off her feet, he did.

★ ★ ★ ★ ★

# Bonding With The Cowboy's Daughter

Lisa Jordan

# MILLS & BOON

Heart, home and faith have always been important to **Lisa Jordan**, so writing stories with those elements comes naturally. Happily married for over thirty years to her real-life hero, she and her husband have two grown sons and two rascal rescue dogs. In her free time, Lisa enjoys quality family time, reading and being creative with friends. Learn more about her by visiting www.lisajordanbooks.com.

Visit the Author Profile page
at millsandboon.com.au for more titles.

The Lord is nigh unto them that are of a broken heart; and saveth such as be of a contrite spirit.
—*Psalm* 34:18

# DEDICATION

Bill and Lynn, it wasn't the year we wanted or even expected, but through it all, God is always good.
I'm so glad we faced it together.
You're the best siblings on the planet. I love you.

# ACKNOWLEDGMENTS

Lord, may my words glorify You.

My family—Patrick, Scott and Mitchell.
You are the best. I love you forever.

Thank you to Nola Perrin and Nola Santiago
of Nola's Angels & Horse Rescue for allowing me
to visit and ask so many questions.
All mistakes are mine.

Thanks to Jeanne Takenaka, Dana R. Lynn,
Christina Miller, Dalyn Weller, Wendy Galinetti,
Heidi McCahan, Linda Jo Reed, Kathy Hurst and
Susan Anderson for your prayers, brainstorming,
encouragement, sprinting and answering
so many questions.

Thanks to Cynthia Ruchti, my awesome agent,
and Melissa Endlich, my exceptional editor,
for your support, grace and patience.
And to the Love Inspired team, who works hard
to bring my books to print.

# CHAPTER ONE

WHAT SHOULD'VE BEEN one of the happiest days of her life now brought Callie Morgan nothing but heartache.

Instead of exchanging vows with the man who'd promised to love and cherish her, she'd dumped the cheating jerk, cashed in the honeymoon tickets to Hawaii she'd purchased, and escaped to southwestern Colorado for a fresh start.

Needing to get away and clear her head, she'd gifted herself an early birthday present and rented a yurt at the Stone River Guest Ranch in Aspen Ridge for a week.

Maybe she'd have the serenity she needed to decide if she should reopen her grandmother's artisan gift shop or sell the cottage that had been Callie's sanctuary since childhood.

Instead of donning the gorgeous wedding dress she should've been wearing that morning, she'd pulled on a pair of faded jeans, her favorite purple T-shirt, a pair of flip-flops, and faced the day with determination despite the state of her heart.

But that resolve took a nosedive when she ended up stranded on the side of an unfamiliar Colorado road with sketchy cell service.

She turned the key in the ignition once more, but this time, the dash lights didn't even come on.

"Now what?" Her words floated away in the light breeze that brushed across her face.

At least she was on Stone River property, if the map she'd downloaded to her phone was anything to go by.

Callie popped the hood on the ten-year-old blue VW Bug she'd inherited from her grandmother. Hand on her hip, she stared at the foreign-looking parts under the hood.

Why hadn't she paid attention when her dad had offered to give her a basic course in car maintenance?

She pulled her cell phone out of her back pocket once again and checked for any sign of service.

Still nothing.

Early June sunshine warmed the top of her head as she turned and leaned a hip against the car's fender. Folding her arms over her chest, she gazed at the snow-tipped mountains shouldering a sapphire sky and towering over fenced green pastures where pink, purple and yellow wild-flowers swayed in the breeze. Cattle and horses in the distance lifted their heads, then returned to their grazing.

She could see for miles—or at least that was how it seemed—yet there wasn't a person in sight. Well, standing on the side of the road wouldn't solve her problems.

Callie slammed the hood shut, then opened the trunk. She retrieved her roller bag and her black art case. After slipping her favorite navy ball cap on her head and pulling her dark pony-tail through the back, she pocketed her phone and keys. She grabbed her water bottle, locked the door and headed for the dirt road that would lead her to the tranquil retreat promised on the Stone River Ranch website.

Hopefully.

Ten minutes later, she rolled her shoulders, wiped the sweat from her forehead, then drained the rest of her water. Even though it wasn't even noon, the sun heated her skin. She shoved the empty bottle in the top of her bulging suitcase.

As she wheeled it again in front of her, one

of the corners banged against a rock. The case lurched forward, then fell sideways. Callie stumbled but caught herself from face-planting in the dirt. A small black wheel lay on its side next to her purple bag.

"Perfect."

Heaving a sigh, Callie shoved the broken wheel in her pocket, then maneuvered the bag, pulling it behind her.

At the sound of an approaching vehicle, she moved to the edge of the road. Instead of driving past her, a black Ford Explorer pulled ahead and stopped.

Callie's fingers tightened on the handle.

The door opened, and a tall man climbed out and strode over to her, wearing aviator sunglasses and a backwards baseball hat covering short dark brown hair. His navy T-shirt emphasized his broad chest and muscled arms. Faded jeans clung to muscular thighs. And his dusty boots weren't for show.

She was definitely in cowboy country.

"Hey, there. You the owner of the blue Volkswagen back there?" Half turning, he jerked a thumb over his shoulder.

Pulling her suitcase in front of her, she nodded. "My car stalled out on my way to the

Stone River Guest Ranch. I'm renting a yurt for the week."

"Well, then, it looks like I came along at the right time." He pulled off his sunglasses, revealing blue eyes, and hooked the arm over the collar of his T-shirt. He held out a calloused hand. "Wyatt Stone. My parents own this spread."

Wyatt Stone.

Her secret crush from her early high school years.

As a teenager, she'd held on to hope he'd see her as more than Ada Morgan's city-girl granddaughter who visited Aspen Ridge during the summer and holidays.

But he'd had eyes only for Linnea Douglas, whose parents owned the animal shelter next to Gram's cottage.

"Hey, Wyatt." She reached for his hand, then jerked hers back and wiped her grimy fingers on the leg of her jeans. "Sorry, my hand's a bit grubby from messing under the hood." Then she pulled off her own sunglasses. "It's me, Callie. Ada's granddaughter."

"Callie Morgan. Good to see you again." He smiled wide, deepening tiny lines bracketing his mouth, and nodded. His eyes softened. "I'm sorry I couldn't do more than express my condolences at your grandma's funeral."

"No worries. There was a line out the door." She dropped her gaze to her feet, then looked up at him again. "Good to see you too. How are you doing?"

"A little better than you, it seems. Know much about cars?" He shot her another grin.

She tightened her hands on the handle of her suitcase once again. "I can pump my own gas and check the tire pressure. That's about it."

"Let me give you a lift, and I'll see what I can do." He reached for her suitcase.

"I really appreciate it. I promise—you won't hear a peep from me for the rest of my stay."

"No need for that. We want everyone to feel welcomed. Once the rest of our guests arrive tomorrow, we'll have plenty of activities for you to enjoy."

"What I need most is solitude. I have some tough decisions to make. Gram left me the cottage that housed her gift shop. I have to decide if I'm going to keep it or sell it."

"Ada was quite a lady. Her death left a big hole in the community She'd been friends with my family for a long time. My mom loved her stained glass classes." Wyatt opened the lift gate and set her suitcase in the back.

She handed him the art case. "She mentioned you guys a lot."

He closed the lift gate, then rounded the passenger side of his SUV and opened the door. "Hop in, and we'll see what's going on with your car."

Callie eyed the black SUV. "Isn't there an unwritten rule or something that cowboys are required to drive pickup trucks?"

"Nah, those are just guidelines." He flashed her another lopsided grin. "Actually, the SUV belonged to my wife, and it's easier for my daughter to climb in and out of. I use the ranch truck when necessary." He nodded to the small child buckled in a car seat in the middle of the back seat. "Callie, this is my daughter, Mia. Mia, say hi to Callie. She's Miss Ada's granddaughter."

"Hi." The little girl lifted a small hand, then buried her face in the pink elephant clutched in her arms.

"Hi, Mia." Callie slid onto the seat, then faced Wyatt's daughter. The little girl wore pink plastic sunglasses, and her blond hair had been pulled back into two ponytails. "I like your elephant. What's her name?"

"Ella. Today's my birthday. I'm three." She held up three pudgy fingers.

"Ella the Elephant. I love that. And happy birthday. Three is a fun age."

"You know about being three?"

Callie smiled. "A long time ago."

Wyatt slid behind the wheel and closed the door. "Three going on thirteen. Sweet as frosting and stubborn as a bull."

Callie laughed. "You and your wife must have your hands full."

"We… I mean, I'm…my wife passed away." The rich timbre of his voice lowered to nearly a whisper as his neck reddened.

The look on his face had her wishing she could snatch back her words.

"Come to think of it, Gram did mention your loss. With everything happening the last few months, it slipped my mind. I'm so sorry." She dropped her gaze to her hands and rubbed dirt off her index finger as heat warmed her cheeks.

"Thanks." He started the engine and pulled onto the road. As they drove back to the car, her rescuer remained quiet after she'd mentioned his late wife.

The familiar-looking Bug came into view.

She'd barely gotten it on the side of the road before it shut down.

Wyatt glanced at her. "Wait—is that your grandma's car?"

"I inherited the car along with her cottage. Didn't make sense to keep two cars, so I sold mine. Maybe I got rid of the wrong one."

"I thought the Bug looked familiar. If so, then no need for me to look under the hood. The alternator needs to be replaced. Ada wouldn't let me fix it for her. Stubborn. Then she got sick… So, what happened before it broke down?"

Callie lifted a shoulder. "I'd just headed through the gate when the dashboard lights came on, blinked off, then the car quit. I barely had enough power to get it to the side of the road."

"Yep, sounds like the alternator." Wyatt pulled alongside the pasture fence, parked, and reached for his door handle. "Let's see if I'm right." Then he turned to Mia. "Stay put, Peanut. I'll be right back."

"Okay, Daddy."

Callie climbed out of the SUV and followed Wyatt to her car.

He lifted the hood, jiggled something, then peered at her. "Try and start it."

Callie slid behind the wheel and turned the key. The engine caught for a second then died. She tried again, but this time, the engine didn't even turn over.

Wyatt closed the hood and wiped his hands on his jeans. Then he rested an arm on Callie's open, driver's-side door. "Just as I figured, the alternator's shot. I'll load up the rest of your stuff and give you a lift to your yurt. Then I'll give Gavin Copeland a call and get it towed to his garage in town."

"I don't want to be a bother. I can take care of it."

"It's no bother at all."

She slid her sunglasses back in place. "Good thing I don't have plans to do much more than work at the cottage or start a new painting this week. Or maybe take that trail ride."

"Right—you're an artist like your grandma. I'd forgotten that."

She unlocked the trunk, and he reached for another small suitcase the same time she did. His fingers covered hers, then he jerked his hand back. "Sorry." He shot her a grin. "So, you like to ride?"

"Like to?" She shrugged, then laughed. "I've spent most of my life living near cities. I've ridden a time or two with some assistance, but I'm certainly no pro. When I came to Aspen Ridge to care for Gram after her stroke, I didn't have much time to leave town, let alone get on a horse. Now that I've moved here, I need to find a job as soon as possible so any horse riding will be limited to what the guest ranch offers this upcoming week."

"You moved to Aspen Ridge?" He set her suitcase next to the other one in the back of his SUV, then leaned against the rear quarter panel, crossed his ankles, and folded his arms over his chest. "What kind of job are you looking for?"

She diverted her eyes from the way the T-shirt material stretched over his shoulders. "Anything that pays a decent wage. I have degrees in art history and elementary education, but I'm not looking to head back to the classroom anytime soon."

"Have any management experience?"

She squinted against the sun reflecting off the back window and shielded her eyes. "Spent my college summers being a counselor and organizing activities for a kids' camp. Does that count?"

"It does to me. Interested in a job?"

Her eyes widened. "Seriously?"

"My oldest sister planned to oversee our family's guest ranch, but she just had a baby. So I took over for her as director, but I have a lot on my plate as well. I'll supervise everything, but I'd like to have a manager to help with the day-to-day. That way, Macey can devote her time to her family. The job's yours if you want it. Unless you're looking for something closer to the city."

"I moved to Aspen Ridge for a fresh start. I need open spaces and plenty of sunshine." She cocked her head. "But why would you offer a job to someone you picked up on the side of the road? I could be a serial killer for all you know."

He laughed, a deep sound that rumbled low in his chest. "Picked up? You're not some kind of empty bottle someone tossed out the window."

After her ex's infidelity, she felt tossed aside.

"We used to hang out when we were younger, and the Callie I once knew wasn't much of a serial killer."

"I'm not much of anything these days. Gram's death has been…tough." Her throat thickened as her vision blurred. Again. Grateful for her sunglasses shielding her eyes, she rolled them upward to prevent unexpected tears from spilling out her pain. "Thanks for the offer. I'll take it."

"Listen. I know what it's like to lose someone you love." Wyatt's voice lowered and held compassion that threatened to break the hold on her emotions. He held out his large hand. "Give me your phone, and I'll add my number. You can relax tonight, then we can work out the details in the next day or so."

"Sounds good." She pulled her phone and handed it to him. "Thanks for stopping. I couldn't get a cell signal and wasn't sure what to do."

"Depending on your provider, service can be spotty on the ranch. We do have Wi-Fi for guests, so you can connect to that. I have your information packet and keys at the lodge. I'll grab those, then you can get settled."

*Settled.*

She hadn't felt that in months. Not since the call after Christmas about Gram's stroke that landed her in the hospital, and then learning her fiancé had cheated on her while she'd taken a short leave to care for Gram.

She'd resigned from her teaching position, closed up her apartment, and left the city to start over in a newish town.

And she'd never felt more alone.

Hopefully, this was just what she needed to make the right decision about Gram's shop. She promised to reopen, but in order to do so, the place needed some renovations. And that took money she didn't have.

As her parents continually reminded her—*God will provide.*

Perhaps working for the Stone family for the summer was just what her heart needed. Then she could focus on where to go from there.

Had God answered her prayers by allowing her car to break down?

Only one way to find out.

THE ANNIVERSARY OF his wife's death always hit Wyatt Stone in the gut. Three years later, it was no exception.

Maybe that was why he'd stumbled over his marital status when Callie mentioned his wife. Why was it still an issue?

Because he didn't want to believe it was true. To be reminded of what he'd lost. He and Mia. But instead of dwelling on that, he needed to focus on what he'd gained.

His eyes shifted to the rearview mirror where his daughter sat in her car seat with Ella tucked in her tiny arms and her eyes watching Callie.

With today also being Mia's birthday, she deserved to be celebrated even if he wanted nothing more than to forget about the date on the calendar. With everything going on, he didn't have time to dwell on his pain.

Midmorning sunshine glinted off the silvery, snow-capped peaks of the San Juan Mountains towering over the valley of his family's cattle ranch as he passed the horseshoe drive lined with tall, green-leafed aspens in front of his parents' stone-and-timber ranch house.

At the fork, he took the left road and pulled into the small gravel lot next to the log-sided lodge with an evergreen metal roof.

Adirondack chairs sat on a stained wrap-around deck and faced the water. A short trail took guests to the four yurts—cylindrical, tent-like structures on platforms—nestled in their private groves of aspens and pines.

After cutting the engine, he unbuckled Mia from her car seat. She scrambled down and raced for the front door, her blond ponytails bouncing against her shoulders.

"Nana! Papa! I'm here. Can we have my party now?"

Laughing softly, Wyatt rounded the front to open Callie's door, but she beat him to it.

He jerked his head toward the lodge. "Come in and say hi to my folks. I'll grab your paperwork then show you to your yurt."

"Thanks, but I don't mind waiting out here. I don't want to intrude."

Following Mia, he grabbed the front door before it slammed shut and held it open. "You won't be, and they'll want to see you."

They stepped into the expansive room with a gleaming floor. Sunshine spilled through arched windows and highlighted the polished wood planks with darkened knots lining the walls. Three deep brown overstuffed leather couches formed a boxy U in front of a floor-to-ceiling stone fireplace.

To the left, half a dozen round tables with chairs dotted the dining area. A large kitchen showed stainless appliances and a deep farm-house-style sink. A timber-planked staircase opened into a loft that overlooked the first floor.

Soft music and quiet laughter came from the open kitchen where his parents stood at the sink on either side of Mia, who had pulled up a stool to help.

Callie removed her sunglasses, glanced at the exposed beam ceiling, then looked at him. "This is gorgeous."

"Thanks. My brother-in-law's crew finished it last month. The wood used on the walls and floor was planed from downed trees on Stone

River property." He nodded toward the kitchen. "Let's say hi."

A light breeze blew through the open window above the sink and stirred the blue-and-white striped curtains.

His dad stood with his back to them as he helped Mia wash red and yellow bell peppers under the running water.

"Hey, Dad. What's going on?" Wyatt moved behind Mia.

Dad glanced at him. "Hey, Wy. Prepping for tomorrow night's welcome dinner. With Mia's party this afternoon, church tomorrow morning, and then preparing for everyone's arrival, there won't be much time later."

"Hey, Mom." Wyatt dropped a kiss on his mother's cheek, then turned to Callie. "You guys remember Callie Morgan?"

"Hi, honey." Mom wiped her hands on the blue dish towel hanging from the oven door and moved around him. She pulled Callie into a hug. "It's good to see you again, Callie."

"You too, Mrs. Stone."

"Please call me Nora. You remember my husband, Deacon?" She handed the towel to Dad, and he dried his hands.

"Of course. Good morning."

"Morning, Callie." His father extended a hand, and she took it. "Heard you rented one of the yurts. How about a cup of coffee?"

Callie glanced at Wyatt.

Holding the stool as Mia climbed down, he lifted a shoulder. "Unless you're in a hurry to get unpacked, you're welcome to hang out for a few minutes."

She nodded to his dad. "Okay, then. Sure, thanks."

Wyatt pulled two coffee cups out of the oak cabinet and filled them from the full pot next to the stove. Inhaling the scent of the dark roast, he handed one to Callie.

"Thanks." Smiling, she took it and added creamer that Dad slid closer to her.

"Callie, how about if Mia and I give you a tour of the lodge?" Mom reached for Mia's hand.

"Mind if I bring my coffee?" Callie lifted her cup.

"Not at all."

Once they were out of earshot, Wyatt palmed his mug and moved next to his dad. "I had a talk with my in-laws this morning when I picked up Mia."

"Yeah? What's going on? Everything okay with Ray and Irene?" Dad unrolled the sleeves on his red plaid Western shirt, then snapped the cuffs closed. "Let's head outside and get the wood split for tomorrow night's campfire."

Wyatt dropped his gaze to his mug, swirled the black coffee to break up his reflection, then drained his cup. He set it on the counter, then followed his dad out the back door. "I heard a rumor their horse rescue was in danger of being shut down due to lack of funds. I offered to partner with them to keep it going."

"I hadn't heard that about the horse rescue." Rounding the back of the lodge, his dad pulled keys from his front pocket and unlocked a small work shed. He threw both doors open, turned on the lights, and nodded to the black-and-yellow machine against the wall. "Give me a hand, will you?"

They wheeled the portable wood splitter outside next to a pile of cut-up logs. Dad pulled the cord, and the machine rumbled to life.

Wyatt grabbed two pairs of work gloves off one of the shelves and tossed a pair to his dad, who caught them in one hand. He set a log on the tray.

Dad moved the lever forward as the blade divided the wood in two. "You've mentioned wanting to take it over should it become too much for Ray to do on his own."

"I asked them about it. Ray was his usual crusty self and said I had no business listening to rumors. But Irene confirmed it was true. Ray resists the idea of monthly sponsors. Their donors haven't been as giving as in the past." Wyatt stacked the split wood on a low pile by the shed and added another log to the tray. "She said if something doesn't change soon, they may have to sell. Today's hard enough with the anniversary of Linnea's death. I don't want them stressing about this too."

"Their ranch has been in the Douglas family for as long as Stone River's been a part of ours." Dad added another log to the tray and split it. "What can we do to help?"

That was so like Dad—quick to step in and lend a hand.

"Talk to Ray. He listens to you. Show him how a partnership with Stone River—if you'd be willing—could benefit all of us. Linnea always wanted to turn the rescue into a horse sanctuary. With Mia being their only granddaughter, I don't want her to lose her mother's legacy."

"We don't want that either." Dad cut the

power and leveled Wyatt with a compassionate look. "You doing okay today? We loved Linnea too, you know."

Despite the sudden thickening in his throat and pressure behind his eyes, Wyatt blinked several times and nodded. "I have to be. No time for anything else."

"No one would blame you if you weren't."

"Thanks. I'm good." Wyatt stacked the remaining wood on the pile.

"You sure taking on the horse rescue won't be too much? You just took over the guest ranch. Between that, helping Bear and me with chores, leading the single fathers support group and caring for Mia, you don't want to spread yourself too thin."

Yeah, that had crossed his mind too, but he didn't dare voice it. He didn't need his parents or anyone else worrying about him needlessly.

"I'll handle it. I won't let any of you down. I promise."

Dad dropped a hand on Wyatt's shoulder and squeezed. "You're not alone, son. We're all here to help. Ray's always been like a brother to me. I'll talk to him and see what he thinks about a partnership with us."

"Thanks, Dad. I appreciate it. I don't want to

add more work for you or Bear, especially since he's trying to get his rehabilitation ranch up and running. If we do partner with the rescue, then we could consider using the horses for the riding program we've been wanting to start. I can use some of Linnea's life insurance money to buy into the rescue."

Dad pulled off his gloves and slapped them against his thigh. "You know Ray won't go for that. It's earmarked for Mia's future."

"And turning the rescue into a sanctuary would be part of that future. I know it's what Linnea would want."

Dad lifted the end of the splitter and pulled it back into the shed. "If we use the horses for the riding program, they'll need to be retrained first. Many of them have been abandoned or abused and have serious trust issues."

Wyatt removed his gloves, then wiped his sweaty face with the hem of his T-shirt. He followed his dad inside the shed and grabbed a rake off the wall. "Yes, but they'll also be protected from future kill lots and have a renewed purpose again."

Something he'd desperately been searching for himself since losing the love of his life.

"Troy Branson, one of the guys in my single

fathers' group, is a horse trainer looking to expand his business. We could send some work his way." Wyatt headed outside and raked a small pile of shavings toward the woodpile.

"Pray about it, son. See where God's leading you. Taking on the rescue is a big responsibility, but we'll back you up. You know that. Let's head back inside the lodge. I need to finish cutting the peppers for tomorrow night's welcome dinner."

Yes, he knew he had his family behind him. Having their support was the only way he could've left the Marine Corps after losing his wife tragically during childbirth. The way they'd stepped in to help care for Mia when he could barely care for himself had put him in their debt.

One he hoped to repay someday.

"Thanks, Dad. I appreciate it." Wyatt followed him back up the deck and into the lodge kitchen.

The front door opened, sending a stream of sunshine across the floor along with female laughter.

Mom, Callie and Mia stepped inside followed by his older sister, Macey, who slid her sunglasses to the top of her head as she snuggled her newborn son against her chest. Wrapped in a receiving blanket covered in horseshoes, the baby was barely visible. Wyatt could see only his nephew's dark hair.

Wyatt washed his hands, then left the kitchen and crossed the room. He reached for the newborn. "Come see your favorite uncle, little guy." He glanced at his sister as he cradled the baby against his chest. "My first day on the job and you're already checking up on me?"

Macey laughed and gave him a playful shove. "Hardly. I'm heading into town to meet up with Cole. He took Lexi to the doctor for a checkup. Then we're meeting Piper and Everly for lunch. I wanted to double-check with Mom to see if things had changed and she could join us." She glanced at Callie. "Cole's my husband, Piper is Bear's wife, and Everly is our baby sister."

Callie nodded.

Their mother chimed in. "Wish I could, honey, but I promised your Aunt Lynetta I'd help at the diner this afternoon. One of her servers quit last week, and she hasn't found someone to replace her yet."

Callie moved next to him, smelling of fresh air and sunshine. She pulled back the blanket and caressed the baby's cheek. "He's precious. What's his name?"

His sister's eyes softened. "Thanks. We adore him. Deacon Cole, or DC as his papa started calling him." She shot a look at Dad. "He's only a couple of weeks old."

Callie glanced at Wyatt. "Mind if I hold him?"

"Not at all." He released his nephew into her arms.

She embraced the baby and swayed gently from side to side.

Macey nudged Wyatt's shoulder. "Callie said you hired her to manage the guest ranch."

He glanced at Callie, who shifted Baby Deacon to her shoulder and rubbed his back. "She needed a job, and I needed an assistant, so it seemed like a good idea. Plus, it saves me the hassle of finding people to interview."

Wyatt looked at Callie. "Sorry. I meant for this to be a quick stop."

She grinned. "Don't worry about me. Holding this baby is the most fun I've had in a while."

Wyatt cleared his throat. "If you'd like, I can give you a tour and talk about our expectations for the guest ranch."

"The tour sounds good too, but I don't want

to keep you from your family, especially since today is Mia's birthday." She rubbed her cheek over the baby's head.

"You took a lot off my plate by agreeing to be the manager for the summer. By the way, Mia will be going with us as well."

"Sounds good. She's adorable." She returned the baby back to Macey, then jerked her head toward the front door. "If you direct me to where I'll be staying, I'll change into something more suitable for walking."

Callie looked so natural with his nephew in her arms. She'd make a great mom someday.

Wyatt's chest tightened as he ran his thumb over the back of his platinum wedding band. He and Linnea had wanted a handful of kids, but her sudden death had wrecked that dream.

He wouldn't find another woman like her, so why bother looking?

He couldn't change things, no matter how much he wanted to. So he'd power through the day as he'd been doing every day for the past three years.

Besides, when would he have time for romance with his busy schedule? Someday, maybe, he'd change his mind about falling in love again. But that was doubtful. He couldn't risk losing someone else he loved. He didn't know if he could recover a second time.

For now, he'd focus on making the summer season at the guest ranch a success. He hoped hiring Callie was the first of many good decisions. Only time would tell, but he had a feeling this was going to be a memorable summer. For all of them.

# CHAPTER TWO

IF HE WANTED his dad to seriously consider partnering with the Douglas ranch, then Wyatt needed to prove himself more than ever and show his family he was capable of managing his responsibilities.

All of them.

The last thing he wanted was to cost his daughter her legacy.

But he couldn't dwell on that right now. He needed to give Callie a tour to confirm he'd made the right choice in hiring her.

His job offer had been off the cuff, and her acceptance had surprised him. At least he'd have much-needed help to ensure their first summer at the guest ranch was a success.

No way was he about to let that venture fall apart, especially after the time and money his family had invested in getting it up and running.

He traded his SUV for the utility vehicle his

parents had driven to the guest ranch, which would be easier for taking Callie on the tour.

Outside her yurt, he braked and hopped out. He released Mia's seat belt and helped her down.

The sun caught him in the eye, and he patted the collar of his T-shirt for his sunglasses. He slipped them on his face and adjusted the brim of his cowboy hat.

Mia tugged on his hand. "Can we go see Uncle Bear?"

"We'll drive by his place, sweetheart, but we won't be able to stop. Uncle Bear, Aunt Piper and Avery went away for the day."

Still clutching her pink elephant in the crook of her elbow, Mia cocked her head, tapped her chin, then nodded. "Will they be at my party?"

"Yes, they'll be there tonight."

"Yay!"

The door to the yurt opened, and Callie stepped out wearing the same purple T-shirt and faded jeans that hugged her curves, but she'd exchanged her flip-flops for gray sneakers. Her navy ball cap covered her dark hair, giving him only a glimpse of the ponytail brushing her shoulders. She wore the same dark sunglasses she'd had on earlier. At the lodge, he'd seen her eyes were the same dark brown as he remembered.

He lifted a hand, then reached for Mia's. They headed toward her. "Hello, again."

"Hey." Her eyes shifted from him to Mia. "Hi, Mia."

"Hi." Her little voice chirped, then she buried her face in Wyatt's leg.

Wyatt nodded toward the Gator. "I figured we'd drive around different parts of the ranch so you could get a feel of what's here."

"Sounds good to me." Callie rounded the front and climbed in the passenger seat.

Mia climbed in behind the driver's seat, and Wyatt helped her with the seat belt buckle. Then he slid behind the wheel and did a U-turn in the middle of the dirt road. He glanced at Callie. "What do you know about our ranch?"

She grabbed the frame as they bounced over a rut in the road. "Just what I've read online and learned from my grandma."

"I'll give you a refresher. Feel free to ask questions." At her nod, he continued. "My great-grandparents started the ranch, then it was handed down to my dad's parents. They were killed by a drunk driver just over ten years ago, so Dad took over the ranch with all of us helping out. Macey and Cole got married not quite a year ago and were a bit surprised to learn they were going to have a baby so soon. Cole also has an adorable daughter from his first marriage. Bear and Piper got married a few months ago, and Bear is raising Piper's daughter, Avery, as his own."

"Your family's grown so quickly over the last year or so. I met Cole and Piper at Gram's funeral." Callie's fingers tightened on the frame as they hit through another rut in the road.

"Daddy, this road is bouncy." Mia's laughter from the back seat warmed his heart.

He turned and grinned. "Hold on tight, Peanut. But don't worry—Daddy will keep you safe."

He looked at Callie. "Sorry about that. The recent spring rains made a mess of the roads, and we haven't had time to fill in the holes."

"No worries. I saw Everly at Gram's funeral as well, but you have another sister, right?"

"Yes, Mallory. She's in the navy, currently stationed in Virginia. She has a six-year-old son, Tanner. She's scheduled to be discharged at the end of the summer. Everly teaches second grade at Aspen Ridge Elementary and helps Mom with cleaning the yurts and preparing meals for our guests."

"Your family has a lot going on."

"One of the reasons I took over the guest ranch. Dad had a terrible bout of pneumonia little over a year ago, and I'm not so sure he ever fully recovered. I don't want him or my mom overdoing it."

"It's great the way you watch over each other."

"That's what our family does. They were there for me when my wife died, and I had an infant with no clue how to care for her." Wyatt lifted a shoulder. "Your family seems pretty close too."

"We are, but being so far apart these days, we stay connected by video chatting every week. My younger brothers, who are fraternal twins, will start med school in Denver in the fall."

"Wesley and Trevor, right?"

"Good memory. I don't know if you remember or not, but my parents are missionaries in South America." Callie clasped her hands and blew out a breath. "I'm the one who's a bit at loose ends these days. The life I'd planned isn't living up to my expectations."

He wanted to ask more about the life she'd planned, but he didn't want to pry.

But he got it—his life hadn't gone the way he'd expected either.

Wyatt swung down the road leading to his brother's cabin. "This road isn't marked, and we discourage our guests from walking this way. It's Bear's property, and we need to respect his and Piper's privacy."

The trees gave away to a clearing that show-cased a wood-sided cabin topped with a dark green metal roof and matching shutters.

"Wow, that's gorgeous."

"Yeah, it's a pretty sweet place. Bear built it from his rodeo earnings, but now he's retired from bull riding. He and Piper are transform-ing their property into a small rehab ranch for cowboys with traumatic brain injuries in mem-ory of Piper's late husband, who was also Bear's best friend."

"What an incredible thing to do."

"They're pretty incredible people." Wyatt turned the Gator around and headed back to-ward the ranch. "If you're not bored yet, Mia and I will take you to Stone River, my family's working ranch."

"Bored? Not likely. This place is perfect." Callie turned in her seat. "Thanks for allowing me to come along, Mia."

Wyatt smiled at the way Callie tried to include his daughter.

"Want to meet the horses?"

Callie's eyes widened as she clasped her hands together. Her knuckles whitened. "Horses?"

"Yes, those large animals we ride in these parts."

She shot him a mock glare. "I know what a horse is…"

"They make you nervous?"

She didn't respond for a moment, then glanced at him. "They're just so big."

They passed the ranch house, the hoop barn, and stopped between the arena and the horse barn.

"Big, yes. But also gentle." Wyatt climbed out from behind the wheel, then released Mia's seat belt. "Okay, gang. Everybody out."

Callie stepped out but kept her hand tightened around the frame of the Gator.

Wyatt motioned toward the barn. "Let's head inside, and I'll introduce you. We don't have a barn built near the guest ranch yet. For now, we tack them up here and transport them to the guest ranch when we have rides scheduled."

Her steps slowed, but he'd wait. She wasn't the first guest to be nervous around the animals.

They stepped inside the barn, and Wyatt flipped on the light.

"How many horses do you have?" Callie stood next to the tack room, her arms hugging her stomach.

Scents of hay mingled with warm animals. Flies buzzed as the horses nickered upon their arrival.

"Eight, but we have room for ten in this barn. We're hoping to expand, but that depends on how the summer goes."

"Why's that?" Then she scrunched her face. "Sorry. None of my business."

He laughed. "You're fine. I'm trying to convince my father-in-law to allow me to partner with his horse rescue. I'd love to turn it into a sanctuary, then retrain the horses for a riding program we'd like to set up here at Stone River."

Callie took another step into the barn. "You Stones trying to corner the market on admirable endeavors?"

He grinned again. "Just obeying God's call for our ranch and resources." He reached into a bucket for a handful of treats, then knelt in front of Mia and put a few in the palm of her hand. "Show Callie how well Patience takes her treats."

She hurried over to his mother's mare's stall and called for the chestnut-colored horse. Patience lowered her muzzle and nudged the top of Mia's head.

Mia giggled and patted the horse's nose, then held a treat in her hand. Patience took it, causing Mia to laugh again as she wiped her hands on her denim shorts. "That tickles, Daddy."

As they passed each horse, Wyatt named them and gave them a treat. They greeted him by nudging him with their muzzles. He rubbed their foreheads as they swished flies away with their tails.

"I thought horses spent most of their time outside."

"Generally, yes. Depends on the weather too. This week is calling for some pretty high temps, especially for this early in the summer, so we bring them in each morning and feed them. They hang out in the barn during the day to avoid the flies and the heat. Then we feed them and let them out for the night when it's cooler and the flies aren't biting. While they're in the pasture, we clean their stalls and put down fresh bedding."

He handed her a small apple then held his palm flat. "Hold your hand like this and let Ranger take it from you."

Callie's eyes widened. Did she take a step back? She hadn't said much once they entered the barn. Her tense shoulders and tight jaw showed she wasn't as relaxed around horses as she maybe wanted him to think. She kept a cautious distance from the stalls, particularly when the horses extended their heads over the top of the stall doors. "You sure it's okay?"

"Ranger's a big boy, but he has a gentle heart. He's been my horse since I was in high school. He won't bite you, I promise."

Her fingers curled around the apple as she remained rooted where she stood in the middle of the aisle. She eyed Ranger, then glanced at Wyatt. "You guys stay pretty busy, don't you?"

He pressed a shoulder against Ranger's stall door. "There's always something that needs to be done on the ranch."

"You have cattle, too? I think I read that on your website."

"We have about a hundred head. We had more, but sold some off to keep the ranch afloat a year or so ago when we hit a rough patch. The livestock barn is on the other side of this one. Mom has chickens too. Plus, we acquired a few sheep and a couple of small goats this past spring." Wyatt rubbed Ranger's forehead once more and gestured for Callie to come closer. "He won't bite you. I promise."

"Ranger is nice, Callie. He won't hurt you." Mia tugged on Callie's hand and tried to pull her closer to the horse.

Callie glanced at his daughter, smiled tightly, then blew out a breath and took a step forward. She held out her hand as Wyatt directed, and Ranger took the fruit gently.

"Good boy." Wyatt patted the side of the black stallion's neck.

"That wasn't so bad."

Was she talking to him…or herself?

Callie took a step back, wiped her hand on her jeans and turned to him, an overly bright smile in place. "So, what will my responsibilities be?"

He bit back a smile, pulled a folded sheet of paper out of his back pocket and handed it to Callie. "As I mentioned, tomorrow is our first official opening for the summer season. This past spring, we had a family or two as well as some outdoor enthusiasts who traveled to the area to fish and hunt. This is the overview that we created."

She read it over, then looked at him. "So you'll want me available from eight in the morning until six in the evening?"

Wyatt reached for Ranger's water bucket and refilled it. "We want to be present for part of the day, but you'll have time for yourself. When new guests arrive each week, we'll greet them and provide them with registration packets that outline our policies and procedures and a list of activities for the week. Tomorrow night, we'll have a campfire, introduce everyone, and answer any questions. I'd love for you to be available for that."

"Yes, of course. How do you do the meals?"

"Family-style breakfast is offered each morning at eight in the lodge, with lunch at noon, and dinner at six. Guests can participate or do their own cooking in their yurts. You're welcome to eat with the guests, the staff, or even my family. We'll end each day with a campfire and s'mores. Throughout the day, we offer organized activities such as trail riding, kayaking and other water sports, archery and fishing. Dad will give tours of the ranch, including a petting zoo for the kids. Macey will be offering photography walks. Bear and I will oversee the trail riding and water sports. Everly planned some family-friendly activities that we've included, such as geocaching, hiking and craft projects. My parents handle the finances."

"You all pitch in."

"We do, but we still need someone to manage the day-to-day details and ensure people are where they're supposed to be. Does this sound like something you're still interested in doing?"

"Yes, I think so as long as you don't mind me being in town during my free time. I want to do as much as I can in Gram's shop."

"Not at all. Your time is your own." Wyatt motioned for them to follow him outside. "You're not planning to return to teaching in the fall?"

"Not if I can help it." She lowered her eyes, but not before he caught the shadow that passed over them. "I love children, and my time as a teacher taught me a lot, but it's not my passion."

"What is?"

"My art. Being creative in a self-expressive way, not teaching to a curriculum. I'd love to teach the kinds of art classes Gram and I always talked about doing together—pottery, stained glass, watercolors. That kind of thing."

Outside, he slid his sunglasses back on his face. "If you love art so much, how'd you end up in the classroom?"

"My parents wanted me to have a reliable job to support myself. They didn't want me to be a starving artist."

"I can appreciate that." He ran a hand over the back of his neck. "You're seriously overqualified for this position. Are you sure it's something you want to do?"

"It's exactly what I need right now. No long-term commitments. Plus, it's a step outside my comfort zone. Hopefully, by the end of summer, I'll have the gift shop open and can move onto the next phase of keeping my promise to my grandmother."

"Okay, then. Welcome to the ranch." Wyatt stuck out his hand, and she shook it, her skin soft against his calloused fingers.

Mia pressed her head against Wyatt's leg. "Daddy, I'm tired."

He lifted her in his arms and pressed a kiss against her forehead. "Okay, Peanut. Let's get you down for a nap." He looked at Callie. "Mind if we head back? That way, you can relax and have a peaceful afternoon."

She shook her head. "Not at all. I've enjoyed the tour. Thank you."

They climbed back into the utility vehicle and headed back to the guest ranch.

As Wyatt stopped in front of Callie's yurt, his phone vibrated in his front pocket. He dug it out, and his mother-in-law's number appeared on the screen.

"Who is it, Daddy?"

"It's Grammy, sweetie." He showed her the screen, then tapped the accept button. "Mama D, what's up?"

"Wyatt, I'm in the ER with Ray. He took a nasty fall and hurt his leg." Her words came out in a rush.

Eyeing Mia, who stared at him, Wyatt forced a calm tone. His fingers tightened around the phone. "How bad is it?"

"They're talking surgery. We're still in the emergency department at Aspen Ridge General, but they're talking about life-flighting him to Durango. I hate to ask, especially today, but could you pick me up so I can get my car? I rode over in the ambulance." The catch in her voice tugged at Wyatt's chest.

"Mom and Dad aren't home. Let me see who's available to care for Mia, then I'll be in."

"Thank you so much, Wyatt. You have no idea how much this means to me."

"Anything for you, Mama D. You know that." He ended the call and gripped the phone. Then he turned to Callie. "Sorry to cut this short, but I need to head into town."

"Everything okay?"

Wyatt's jaw tightened as he turned. Certain Mia couldn't see him, he gave a brief shake of his head. "I need to stop by the ranch and see if one of my sisters is around to watch Mia. My in-laws need me at the hospital."

"I'm sorry." Callie's eyes softened as they drifted toward his daughter. "I can do it."

"You can do what?"

"I can care for Mia until you get back."

"Thanks, I appreciate it. Problem is, I don't know when that will be."

She lifted a shoulder. "No worries. I don't have plans anyway."

"But you're on vacation."

"A vacation that ends tomorrow afternoon, remember? Besides, it sounds like you need to leave right away."

"I do, but you just met Mia this morning. I don't want her to be too much or anything."

"Wyatt, listen. I understand your hesitation,

but I do have state clearances. Plus, I've spent the last six years teaching art classes to elementary students. If I can handle a group of twenty kids at a time, then I'm sure one little girl will be just fine."

While he believed her words, his heart had a hard time catching up with his head. But he was wasting time wrestling with his indecision. "As long as you're sure. I'll give Mom a call and ask her to pick Mia up when she returns to the ranch. That way you're not tied down for the rest of the day."

Callie pressed a hand against his arm. "Relax, okay? I can handle this."

Wyatt stared at her narrow fingers with unpolished, trimmed nails. Her gentle touch warmed his skin. He blew out a breath and nodded. Then he knelt in front of his daughter and touched her face. "Hey, Peanut. I have to go into town and help Grammy with something. Would you like to stay with Callie until Nana can pick you up?"

"What about my birthday party? I wanna go see Grammy too."

"Sorry, sweetie. Not right now. You'll see her very soon. And we will have your party as soon as I get back. I promise."

Her lip drooped as she pressed her head against his chest. "Okay."

"You sure you don't mind?" He glanced at Callie over the top of Mia's head.

"Not at all. With the way you helped me out this morning, I'm more than happy to return the favor."

He hadn't left his daughter with anyone other than family since she was born. He didn't doubt Callie's character. And the brief times he'd spent with her had left him with positive impressions.

He struggled with what it meant to lean on someone outside the family.

But he had no choice right now. Time to take a leap and put his trust—and his daughter—in Callie's capable hands.

CALLIE MIGHT HAVE overestimated her skills.

While it was true she didn't have much experience with three-year-olds, she'd been counting on her years as an elementary school art teacher to keep Mia occupied while Wyatt headed into town.

She hadn't expected the little girl to burst into tears as soon as her father walked out the door.

For the past fifteen minutes, she'd rocked her

and sung silly songs until the tears subsided, hoping the tired child would fall asleep.

Callie adjusted Mia in her arms and tried to find a more comfortable position on the coffee-colored microfiber couch that faced the window overlooking the lake.

Mia's chest rose and fell with each shallow shudder she breathed.

Maybe she should've suggested they hang out at Wyatt's place, so Mia would've been in a familiar setting. But she didn't want to intrude on his personal space since she was about to become his employee. And he'd seemed to be in a big hurry to leave.

She'd gotten the sense Wyatt wasn't too thrilled about leaving his daughter in her care, but it sounded like he didn't have many options.

Now she needed something to interest Mia until her dad returned.

Callie spied her open art case on the island in the small kitchen area. What could she pull out to make the little girl smile? She brushed Mia's damp hair away from her face. "Mia, do you like to paint?"

Chin tucked down, the child nodded, her cheek scraping against Callie's T-shirt.

"Would you like to paint a picture for your daddy?"

Again, Mia nodded but remained quiet.

"Let's sit at the counter, and I'll get you some paint, okay?"

Another nod, but this time Mia stood and headed for the high-backed chairs pushed against the kitchen island.

Callie helped her onto the seat, then pulled out tubes of acrylic paint in blue, yellow and red, and squirted a quarter-size drop of each color on a paper plate.

Then she grabbed the nearly empty roll of paper towels, removed the remaining sheets and cut the roll into three-inch chunks. She folded two of the pieces into a triangle and a square, then left the other one circular. She found a small pad of mixed media paper and removed a sheet.

She sat next to Mia and put the paint in front of her. "You can dip these pieces into the paint and make shapes on your paper. How's that?"

Giving her a shy smile, Mia grabbed the square and plopped it in the middle of the red paint, then she pounced it on the paper. Then she reached for the circle and added blue paint to her paper.

Callie grabbed her hobby knife and trimmed a sheet of heavyweight, cold-pressed watercolor paper off the pad and set it on the island in front of her own chair.

She lightly sketched a little of what she'd seen on their tour—the mountains, the ranch house and a horse standing by the river. She retrieved her roll of brushes and tin of watercolors from her bag. Grabbing a spray bottle, she flipped open the lid to her paints and misted the pigments to hydrate them.

She glanced at Mia. "How you doing, kiddo?"

Mia held up her paper covered with splotchy shapes and splatters. "I made purple. It matches your shirt."

"You're right." Callie slid off the stool and moved to the sink. She filled her paint cup with water, then returned to her seat. She loaded her brush with water and applied it to the paper until it shone. "Can you tell me what colors make purple?"

Mia scrunched her face and looked at her paper. Then she shook her head.

Callie tapped the area where a red circle and

a blue square overlapped. "Your red and blue mixed together to make purple."

"Yay. I want to do it again." Mia reached for another cardboard shape and mashed it into the muddied colors. "May I have more paint, please?"

"Nice manners. Of course you can." Callie reached for her acrylic paints and squeezed three more blobs on the plate.

Within minutes, Mia had her paper covered in colorful shapes. Not to mention her fingers and a couple of spots on her yellow T-shirt. Hopefully, the paint washed out.

Someone knocked on the screen door of the yurt, startling Callie. She whirled around and found Nora Stone standing on the deck. She wore a yellow Netta's Diner T-shirt with dark wash jeans. Her silvery-blond hair had been pulled up into a messy bun.

"Nana!" Mia scrambled off the chair, nearly falling to her knees. She rushed to the door then came to a stop. "Where's Daddy? Is it party time?"

Nora opened the door and peeked her head inside. "Mind if I come in?"

Callie waved her inside. "Not at all."

Opening the door wider, Nora stepped inside. Mia wrapped her arms around her grand-mother's legs, and the woman lifted her into her arms and pressed a kiss against her cheek. "Hey, Birthday Girl." Then she turned her attention to Callie. "Thanks for helping out with Mia."

"I was glad to help. There were a few tears after Wyatt left, but I tried to distract her with some shape painting. She did very well." Callie lifted Mia's colorful paper off the counter and held it out to Nora. "It's still damp."

Nora smiled at Mia. "This is beautiful. Can I hang it on my fridge?"

Mia shook her head and pointed to Callie. "It's for her."

Callie pressed a hand against her chest. "Me? Thank you, Mia. I'll hang it on my fridge."

Nora handed the paper back to Callie. "Looks like you received your gift of teaching from your grandma. I loved her stained glass classes. She was a very kind and patient teacher. They were therapeutic as I grieved the loss of my in-laws. I'm happy to hear you're reopening her shop."

"It needs a lot of work. Gram always encour-aged my love of art. I'm so sorry for your loss. I remember Gram talking about your in-laws."

"Thank you. And I'm sorry you're having to learn how to live without her. If you need to

talk, give me a call or stop by the ranch house."
Nora turned to Mia. "How about if we leave
and let Callie get on with the rest of her day?"

Callie crouched in front of Mia and moved
her hair away from her face. "Thanks for spending time with me, Mia. I hope we can do it
again soon. Have a wonderful birthday party."
Then she looked at Nora. "Thank you for the
offer. It's very kind. I may take you up on it one
of these days."

Callie held the door and watched them head
to Nora's gold-colored sedan. After they left,
Callie tossed Mia's plate in the trash, wiped paint
off the counter where she'd had been sitting,
then washed her hands. Returning to her stool,
she reached for her brush. The water wash had
dried, so she applied another light layer.

Her phone rang. She dried her hands on her
jeans and reached for her cell. Wyatt's name
showed on her screen.

"Hello?"

"Hey, Callie. It's Wyatt. Wanted to let you
know I got ahold of Mom, and she'll be picking up Mia shortly."

"They just left, actually." She glanced toward
the door, then set the phone on the counter and
put it on speaker.

He exhaled. "Sorry. I meant to call sooner. I've been a little distracted."

"I hope everything's okay."

Wyatt didn't say anything for a moment. "My father-in-law broke his leg in two places. They were able to do X-rays here, but they need an orthopedic surgeon in Durango to do the surgery. Our small hospital isn't equipped for something like that."

Callie's hand stilled. "I'm sorry to hear that. Is there anything I can do to help in any way?"

"Caring for Mia was a great help. Thanks for offering, though it was last-minute."

"It wasn't a problem. I enjoyed spending time with her." He didn't need to know about his daughter's tears. "What can I do to help you?"

He didn't respond for a moment. "What do you mean?"

"With everything on your plate, how can I ease some of your burden? I don't know much about horses, but I'm a fast learner. I can help with feeding or brushing, or whatever else needs to be done."

As soon as the words left her mouth, she wanted to snatch back her offer. Too late.

She'd get used to their size, wouldn't she?

"Once I get a feel for the different activities

at the guest ranch, I can lend more of a hand there as well. Or even with Mia, who is precious, by the way. I know you have your family and everything, but they seem busy too." Callie rehydrated the pans of color, loaded her brush with blue pigment, then applied it to her paper.

"Yeah, we're all busy. That's part of the problem."

"Then please let me help."

Again, another pause.

"Why would you do that? We're not your problems."

Callie rinsed her brush and let it sit on the edge of the cup. She moved off the chair and pushed through the screen door. She stepped onto the deck and pressed her back against the railing. "Because we're friends. Plus, my grandma would've been first in line to help her friends. Ray and Irene were so helpful when my grandma was sick. Now it's my turn to help them…and you. From what I've seen, you're pretty great at giving help but not so great at receiving it."

"How can I turn down such an offer? Tell you what—you mentioned needing renovations done on your gram's shop. I'll help you when I can, and I'll accept your help with the guest ranch, the horse rescue, or even with my daughter. How's that sound?"

"Sounds good to me. One more question."

"Shoot."

"How are you doing?" She lifted her face toward the early evening sun.

"I'm fine." His words came out in a rush.

"Are you?"

"I have to be. My in-laws need me."

"But what about what *you* need?"

"To be honest, Callie, I don't get asked that very often." He exhaled. "They're about to load Ray into the chopper, then I need to take Irene home. I'll touch base with you soon." He ended the call before she could say goodbye.

Callie stared at the screen and shook her head.

What was she doing? Acting so eager to step in and fix Wyatt's problems? Maybe because she couldn't manage her own chaos, it was easier to focus on someone else?

She didn't need any more complications right now. But she couldn't take it back. Instead, she'd work at being the kind of friend Wyatt needed.

And nothing more.

## CHAPTER THREE

CALLIE HADN'T EXPECTED to spend the last morning of her very brief vacation heading into Aspen Ridge and stepping foot inside her gram's cottage.

It had been her favorite place as a child. And now, only memories kept her company.

Early morning sunshine filtered through the dusty stained glass window, throwing a prism of color across the dull wooden floor that needed a good polish to restore the shine.

Callie trailed a finger through the dust blanketing the empty display tables and high counter that held the register and doubled as Gram's desk. She pinched a cobweb strung from corner to corner of a wrought iron stand that used to hold handmade jewelry.

Music had always played in the background of the small shop that featured handmade products from local artists. Now only the sounds of

Callie's flip-flops against the wooden floor disturbed the quiet.

As she scanned the walls that needed to be scrubbed and refreshed with a bright coat of paint, Callie's eyes landed on a photo behind the cash register. She headed around the counter and lifted the frame off the sun-bleached wall, leaving behind a darker rectangle.

She traced a finger over the picture of Gram with her arm draped over Callie's shoulders. They held up ribbons they'd won at the art show they'd entered together—Callie with her first watercolor painting at the age of nine and Gram with her intricate and beautiful stained glass.

That was the moment Callie had realized she wanted to be an artist, and Gram had encouraged that dream until the day she died.

Her phone rang, signaling a video call. Callie pulled it out of her pocket and answered. "Hey, Mom."

"Hi, sweetheart. I tried to call last night, but you didn't answer. Figured you were busy getting settled at the guest ranch." Mom's phone bounced as she walked through what appeared to be some sort of outdoor market. Sunglasses shaded her eyes and her hair—the same dark color as Callie's—had been pulled back into a ponytail, highlighting her high cheekbones.

At fifty-two, her mother looked more like her older sister. A compliment that always pleased her.

Callie brushed off a wooden bench by the front door and sat. "Yeah, sorry about that—I had a busy day and went to bed earlier than expected. I'm in Aspen Ridge right now."

"Doing what? You're supposed to be relaxing."

"I was. In fact, I started a new watercolor yesterday and plan to explore the area a little this afternoon. Now I'm checking out Gram's shop." Callie turned the phone and gave her a quick scan of the room, then turned it back to face her.

"I'm sure that's not easy." Mom cocked her head.

"Not really, but I can't put it off if I'm going to reopen the shop."

"Are you sure that's the best choice? Teaching is a much more stable profession, you know. You could always sell the cottage and use the money to pay off your student loans. Or use it for something more practical, like a down payment on a house."

Practical was her mother's middle name.

"I promised Gram, remember? She left me the shop for a reason, and I can't walk away without even trying. You and Dad taught me that. It's your fault for instilling a sense of integrity in the boys and me."

Mom sighed. A little too loudly. "Yes, we did. But what will you do for product?"

"I'll contact the artists who used to sell here and see if they're interested once I bring the shop back to its former glory."

"You have a long way to go before that could happen."

"I'm aware." The to-do list growing in her head pressed on her shoulders. "But I have the whole summer to move in the right direction. I'll figure out how to come up with the money and make it happen."

She needed to be sure her move to Aspen Ridge wasn't going to cost her more than she could afford. Both in her wallet and in her already wounded heart.

"Since you won't take money from your dad and me, you could consider a short-term business loan so you can get the repairs done sooner. Then you can see if the shop is worth reopening or selling."

"That's an option." But not one she really

wanted to take if she could help it. Her student loans were enough debt right now.

"Have you read the letter yet?"

Callie bit her lower lip and shook her head. "I can't."

Aaron Brewster, Gram's attorney, had given her family members letters Gram had written before she passed. Callie still had hers tucked away in Gram's bookcase upstairs. Unopened.

"You will when you're ready. Okay, I won't take up any more of your time. I'm walking into church, but I wanted to see how you're doing. Love you, sweetie." Mom pressed two fingers to her own lips, then touched them to her screen.

"Thanks for calling, Mom. Love you too. Give Dad a hug. I'll check in soon." Callie ended the call and blew out a breath.

Her mother meant well and wanted only the best for Callie and her brothers, but a little encouragement would go a long way.

She was tired of living her life according to others' expectations. So, yes, Callie needed to get the shop reopened.

Somehow.

She headed for the back stairs that led to Gram's small apartment, where Callie would be living once her time at the guest ranch came to an end.

But as she put her foot on the bottom step, she lost all energy to keep climbing.

She wasn't ready to go upstairs where Gram's scent lingered. When her family was there after the funeral, Mom wanted to box up Gram's things, but Callie had talked her out of it.

It felt too soon to get rid of the neatly made bed, the knitted afghan thrown over the back of the couch, or even the translucent blue cup Gram used every morning for her first cup of tea.

She wasn't able to do it today either.

But eventually she'd have to find the strength to dive in so she could keep her promise.

As she moved off the bottom stair, she stepped on something. She bent down and pulled out a white piece of glass wedged under the wood.

But it wasn't just glass.

She retrieved a small stained glass dove with a sprig in its mouth.

Covered in dirt, the tiny bird appeared abandoned. Discarded. Unwanted.

She could relate.

Callie rubbed the smudges off the bird's wings. She'd take the bird back to the cabin, search the cataloged remaining inventory on her computer and try to find the rightful owner.

Releasing a deep sigh, she pulled her sunglasses off the top of her head, slid them onto her face and left the shop, locking the door behind her.

She lifted her face to the sunshine and pulled in a lungful of air.

Next door to Gram's cottage, barking echoed from inside the Aspen Ridge Animal Shelter, which was owned by Ray and Irene Douglas, Wyatt's in-laws. Painted barn red with black shutters, the shelter was a part of the Douglases' horse farm. Very few cars drove down the unlined road, which was on the outskirts of town.

Other than the barking, the only sounds were the wind chimes hanging from the Douglases' front porch and blowing in the light breeze that brought up scents from the pasture.

The back door to the animal shelter opened. Wyatt stepped outside and closed the door behind him.

Dressed in tan slacks, a light blue button-down shirt open at the throat that highlighted his tanned skin, shined boots, and the same sunglasses he had on yesterday, Wyatt smiled. "Hey, Callie. I'm surprised to find you in town."

"Gavin Copeland came out last night and got me so I'd have my car. I was surprised he'd fixed it so quickly, but he was able to find a new alternator and get it installed yesterday afternoon. Said he didn't want to leave me stranded. This morning, I decided to head into town for breakfast, passed Gram's cottage and made an impromptu decision to check out the shop."

"Gavin's a good guy." He nodded toward the worn blue cottage. "How'd your visit go?"

Her fingers tightened around the stained glass dove. "Bittersweet."

"I get it. Been there. Sorry you have to go through that." His voice softened, and the tender tone nearly undid her.

She swallowed and cleared her throat. "What are you up to?"

Wyatt jerked his head toward the shelter. "I stopped by to feed the animals. Ray had his surgery last night, and Irene spent the night in Durango with him, but she'll be back this afternoon."

"How's he doing?"

"He's in a little pain and tired. Didn't sleep much. His limited mobility is making him cranky. I talked with Irene, and I'll be handling the horse rescue."

"My offer to help still stands. Gram and Irene were good friends. I believe Gram bought her cottage from them after my grandfather passed away."

"Right—it used to belong to Irene's mother. Irene was pretty broken up over Ada's death. So, you're definitely reopening her shop?"

Callie dragged a hand through her hair. "When I stopped in, I planned to make a list of what needed to be done. But now I just don't know."

"Know about what?"

"It was tough walking inside this morning. Everything needs to be scrubbed down and re-painted. The front porch needs fixing. Gram kept putting it off, then she had her stroke. I need to be able to stay longer than ten minutes if I'm going to get it reopened."

"Grief is tough. You can't rush it. Just walk through it." He removed his sunglasses and slid them into his front pocket. "Elbow grease is free, and I could give you a hand with paint-ing. I know some guys who will fix the porch for you."

Callie settled a hand on her hip. "You're so kind to offer, but when will you have time?

Your plate is nearly overflowing with responsibilities already."

He lifted a shoulder. "I like to keep busy. To help out where I can. To give back."

"That's sweet, but you don't owe me anything. There's nothing to give back. If anything, I owe you for yesterday. Not to mention all the help you gave Gram. She appreciated your family very much."

"If it weren't for your grandmother, I wouldn't have asked Linnea to marry me." He twisted his wedding band.

"I didn't know that. Gram never mentioned it."

"I had just enlisted and was heading off to boot camp. Linnea and I had talked about our futures since she was going off to college. And we ended up in a fight. I'd gone to the diner and found your grandma sitting there. She asked why I looked so sad and I spilled my guts."

"Gram had that effect on people."

"She was a great listener. After I told her what was going on, she looked at me and said, 'Wyatt, if you want to hold on to that girl, marry her.' I wasn't expecting to get engaged at eighteen, but Linnea and I had been together since ninth grade and I knew she was the one for me."

"So, you proposed?"

"Well, it wasn't quite that easy. I had to go through her dad first and he was a tough nut to crack. We talked and decided it would be best for me to get through boot camp, and then when I took leave before my next duty station, we'd see where we were in our relationship. If we could handle three months apart with limited communication, then maybe we could handle the tough stuff too. But enough about me." His eyes drifted to her hand and his eyebrows knitted together. "What do you have there?"

"Oh, this." She lifted it to show him. "As I was leaving the shop, I found it wedged under the corner of the staircase. I pulled it out and was surprised to see it was intact. I decided to take it to the yurt and try to find the owner."

He moved closer and took it gently from her. "When I graduated from boot camp, your grandma gave me one just like it. Apparently, she'd taught a class on making them, so it's probably hers. Several ladies, including my mom and Irene, made them. It's probably kind of silly that a grown man would keep something like that, but she told me it symbolized hope. When things weren't going well, or I was getting deployed, I kept it around, I guess, as a reminder to hold on to hope."

Fresh tears filled Callie's eyes. She really needed to get a grip on her emotions. She swallowed hard, then nodded. "Gram was great for holding on to hope."

Wyatt rubbed the back of his head. "Hey, not to change the subject, but I planned to stop by the guest ranch and run something by you. Since you're here, do you have a minute?"

She glanced at his clothes. "You look dressed for church. Sure you have time?"

"Actually, I hit the early service, then ducked out. Everly is teaching children's church today and promised to care for Mia so I could take care of things at the shelter for Ray and Irene."

The man was practically perfect.

If she were looking, he'd be the right kind of guy for her. But she wasn't looking. Love didn't last and led only to heartbreak. No, thank you.

"I probably should've gone. I thought about it, but I haven't been there since Gram's funeral." Arms folded over her chest, she turned and faced the road. The tip of the white steeple could be seen against the horizon. She faced Wyatt. "I'm not mad at God or anything like it. It's just…"

"You still see her sitting in that middle pew, don't you?"

Her head jerked up. "How'd you know?"

He shoved a hand in his front pocket and kicked a toe against the weathered railing. "When I came back home, it took me a while to sit in the same sanctuary where I got married."

She shook her head. "Grief is weird."

"Definitely." He held out a closed fist.

She bumped her knuckles against his. "What did you want to run by me?"

He handed the dove back to her. "You're welcome to stay in the yurt since you paid for it already. But if you'd like to spend this coming week training with Macey and me, then we're willing to refund your rental fee. You could move into the staff suites upstairs in the lodge." He nodded at the cottage. "Or stay here, if you wanted to commute. Our guests are scheduled to arrive this afternoon, so we'd have to move you soon."

She worked out the numbers quickly in her head. Putting the money back into her dwindling bank account would help.

She nodded. "Last night in the yurt was fun, but I could use the extra funds toward repairing the shop. Staff housing would be better.

Gram's apartment isn't ready for me to move into just yet."

Neither was her heart.

One side of his mouth lifted in a lazy, Sunday morning way. "Not a problem at all. I'm sure you saw the suites when Mom gave you a tour of the lodge yesterday. You're our first staff member outside of family, but we built it hoping for continued growth. I need to head back to my place and change, so how about if I catch up with you in an hour or so?"

"Sounds good. See you then." She waved.

As Wyatt opened the door to his SUV, Callie fingered the textured milky glass one more time, then looked back at the cottage in need of a fresh coat of paint.

Maybe she needed to hold on to hope just a little longer and see where it took her.

ONE THING AT a time.

Wyatt repeated his father's favorite mantra as he pulled into the graveled parking space in front of Callie's yurt.

Now that he'd taken care of things at the animal shelter for Ray and Irene, he could focus on getting Callie settled, then get ready for the arrival of their guests.

Then he could relax.

Right. Until something else—or someone else—needed his attention. But he wasn't about to begrudge the busyness.

It kept his mind occupied and didn't leave a lot of time for thinking, for longing, for missing what he should've had but didn't.

As he cut the engine, he spied someone sitting in one of the chairs at the end of the dock.

Callie.

He strode down the path that led to the water.

She twisted in her chair and waved. She set some sort of tray on the floor of the dock, then stood and faced him. "Hi, again."

He strode down the dock, his worn boots thudding against the new wood. "Hope I'm not intruding."

Shaking her head, she pushed her sunglasses on top of her head. "Not at all."

She wore the same green T-shirt and a pair of denim shorts from when he'd seen her in town. And bare feet. Her flip-flops had been kicked to the side. Her dark brown hair had been gathered in the same sort of messy knot that his sisters favored.

And the sight of her made his heart thump wildly in his chest.

What was *that* about?

At the end of the dock, he stretched out his arms and inhaled, breathing in the scents of the lake.

The sun hovered over the treetops, spilling liquid gold over the darkened water. A family of ducks flapped and landed on the glassy surface and sent ripples toward the shore.

"It's easy to get lost in the beauty, isn't it?" Callie's words came out in nearly a whisper as if she were afraid to disturb the tranquility.

"Best place on earth, in my opinion."

"I can see why." She lifted a large sheet of paper off the tray and held it out to him. "Paint can't capture the essence, but I've been trying."

He took it and found splashes of color gliding across the thick paper as the landscape in front of him came to life in a watercolor haze. He shook his head, then looked at her. "Callie, this is incredible. You're underestimating yourself."

She shrugged and reached for it. "First time I painted since Gram died. Started it yesterday while caring for Mia. When I returned from town, the water beckoned so I decided to paint for a while."

"Until I interrupted."

She shook her head and shot him a smile. "I'm glad you did."

Spoken quietly, the four words quickened his pulse.

What was his problem?

"Ready to get moved into the lodge, or would you rather do more painting?"

"I can paint later. I didn't do much unpacking, so moving my things won't take much time." She reached for a tray that held a metal rectangular tin, a few brushes, a worn towel with splashes of color, and a disposable cup of murky water.

"Here, I'll take that." He took the tray from her as she reached for her pad of paper and the loose sheet she'd been painting.

As they headed back, she sidestepped an exposed tree root, and her shoulder brushed his.

At the yurt, he reached for the door, then followed her inside. He set the tray on the island. She gathered brushes, paints and a pad of paper off the counter and tucked them in her black, zippered case.

She moved to the fridge and retrieved a paper covered in paint, then handed it to him. "Mia painted this yesterday while I cared for her."

He took it and smiled. "Cute. She talked

about you all night and wanted to know when she could paint with 'that lady' again. Feel free to add any art activities to the daily schedule."

"I'd like that." Callie wheeled her suitcase across the floor, flung her art case over her shoulder and picked up her purse off the table by the door. "All set. I'll drop my things off at the lodge, then come back and clean up."

"No need. Everly will go through it after church. We have a couple of families on our waiting list, so we'll see if they're still interested in renting it this week."

"But it's my mess. She's not responsible for cleaning up after me. She's busy enough. I don't mind."

"If you're sure, then I'll let her know. Macey plans to meet with you after lunch, if you have time, to review what will happen this afternoon."

She spread out her arms, her grin just as wide. "All I have right now is time. I do plan to make another quick trip into town before the guests arrive and make an actual to-do list of what needs to be done at the shop. I kind of rushed through it this morning."

"If you want to go after we move your things into the lodge, I'll be free for a couple of hours."

He reached for the handle of her suitcase and wheeled it onto the deck.

Callie followed and closed the door behind them. "That's a luxury for you. Don't waste it going through dusty rooms. Take time for yourself."

"I'm not sure how to do that anymore."

"Exactly. Sounds like you need to learn."

Wyatt dug out his keys, found the one for the lodge, then unlocked the main door. He pushed it open, then stepped back for Callie to pass.

As she moved into the expansive room, a light citrus scent floated past him.

Scents of wood and lemon oil mingled with the pork roasting in the slow cookers that Mom had filled before leaving for church.

He nodded toward the stairs. "I'll show you to your room."

Upstairs, Wyatt stopped in the middle of the loft and waved his hand toward several closed doors. "You have your choice of suites. They're all pretty much the same—queen beds, love seat and desk, private bathroom and a kitchenette. You're welcome to join us for all meals, but if you need a break, you can bring food up here or make something yourself."

Callie moved past him and turned in a semicircle. She headed toward the room that faced the water, turned the handle and stepped inside.

Shards of light sprawled across the bed covered with a quilt done in blues, purples and reds. A wooden rocker sat in one corner. In the opposite corner, a love seat and a small workstation took up the space. A four-drawer dresser stood against the wall across from the bed. Next to it, a microwave sat on a stand with a dorm fridge tucked in underneath.

"It's lovely."

"I'm glad you like it." He wheeled her suitcase in front of the closed bathroom door. "I'll leave you alone so you can unpack. The offer still stands if you'd like help when you head into town."

She pulled out her phone and glanced at the screen. "I can unpack later. I'll take advantage of the time I have now and head back into town."

"I can drive, if you'd like. Or would you like to take two vehicles?"

She eyed him a moment then shook her head. "Wyatt, you're so kind to offer, but I get the sense you don't have a lot of downtime."

He shrugged. "There's always something to be done or someone who needs help."

"Exactly. And I don't want to add to your incredibly long to-do list, even though I truly appreciate your offer. Besides, you're my employer now. How would it look?"

"Look? To whom? I'm simply a guy helping a friend. Nothing more."

It would stay that way. Keeping his distance was best for the both of them.

"Besides, didn't you offer to help me out too? It's an exchange of services."

She paused a moment, then nodded, although her shoulders remained tense as she brushed past him and headed down the stairs.

Five minutes later, they headed into town with the windows down and radio turned up to hear over the wind.

Callie settled into the passenger seat, her fingers drumming to the beat against her knee. Maybe now she'd relax a little.

He pulled into the driveway between the cottage and the animal shelter and cut the engine.

Callie didn't wait for him to open her door. She scrambled out and headed for the small back porch. She unlocked the back door and stepped inside the cottage.

And stopped so quickly he nearly ran into her. He grabbed her arms to keep from plowing her over. "You okay?"

She nodded but didn't turn around. "Her scent gets me every time. It's everywhere."

He understood all too well. Unfortunately.

He released her arms and scrubbed a hand over his face. "After my wife died, Mia and I slept on a buddy's couch for a month because I couldn't stand to be in our apartment. He took my keys, went to my place and packed enough things for Mia and me so I didn't have to deal with it."

She turned and looked at him, her eyes large and glistening. She lifted a hand toward his face, then dropped it before she made contact. "Thank you for sharing that. I'm so sorry you had to suffer such a loss."

She dropped her purse on a small table inside the door, took two steps forward, then wrapped her arms around her stomach, facing him once again. "How am I going to get the shop fixed up if walking inside is such a big deal?"

"The same way I did—one day at a time. Some days will be easier than others."

She nodded and took a few more steps into the room. She squared her shoulders then strode behind the counter. She ducked down then stood with a yellow legal pad and a pen in her hand. "Enough dillydallying, as Gram would say. It's time to make a plan."

Despite the shimmering in her eyes, her smile showed she wouldn't let her grief defeat her.

He rubbed his hands together and joined her at the counter. "Okay, what's first?"

Tapping the pen against her chin, she moved around him and stood in the middle of the room, slowly turning in a circle as if appraising everything. "Everything needs to be removed from this room. The walls need scrubbed and repainted. Windows need to be washed and new shades or coverings put up. The floor needs refinishing. I think that will be a good start."

"I agree." He jerked a thumb over his shoulder. "I'll head next door and see if Irene has boxes that haven't been broken down for recycling yet. We can begin taking things off the walls and clearing the room today."

"That sounds great. Thanks." She shot him another smile that caused his gut to tighten.

Behind them, someone rapped on the back door.

He turned and found his mother-in-law standing on the back porch, a foil-covered plate in her hands.

He crossed the room and opened the door. "Hey, Mama D. When did you get back?"

"About an hour ago. Ray's napping. I saw your SUV but you weren't in the house. Then I saw the lights on in the cottage and figured Callie was here."

"Yes, she is. I came to give her a hand before we have to head back to the ranch. Come in."

He stepped aside and held the door open. "Callie, you have a visitor. Remember my mother-in-law, Irene Douglas?"

Irene's kind blue eyes softened as Callie approached with her arms outstretched. "Of course. It's great to see you again, Irene."

"Hi, Callie. It's good to see you again too. Ada was a dear friend, and I miss her every day."

Callie nodded, understanding that feeling well.

Irene thrust a plate at her. "I just made a batch of brownies and wanted to share."

Callie took the plate and peeled back a corner of the foil, releasing the scent of sugar and chocolate. "Thanks, they smell great. Sorry to hear about Ray's fall and surgery. Please let me know if there's anything I can do to help."

Irene's eyes lowered, then she gave Callie a small smile. "Thanks. Right now, we're trusting the Lord for his healing. So prayers would be greatly appreciated."

"Of course."

Irene reached for the door handle. "I'll get out of your hair. Wyatt, got a minute?"

He followed Irene outside and down the steps. She paused at the driveway and faced him, a wide smile across her face. "Callie's a great girl. Ada adored her, you know."

Nodding, he stuffed his hands in his pockets, sensing he wasn't about to like what she said next. "Don't you think it's time to get back on the horse, as they say?"

He didn't know who *they* were, but he wasn't interested in what they had to say.

He slung an arm over the woman's shoulders and steered her toward her own back porch. "Mama D, I appreciate the advice, but I'm not interested in dating. I'll never find someone like Linnea."

"Oh, honey." She turned and pressed a hand against his cheek. "I know that more than anyone. My daughter was one of a kind. But don't look for her clone. Find someone who makes you happy. That's what she'd want for you. She wouldn't want you to spend the rest of your life alone. And Mia needs a mother."

He wrapped his fingers around her small hand and gave it a gentle squeeze. "I am happy. Besides, Mia has you, my mom and my sisters. She's not lacking for strong role models. She's one blessed little girl."

"Don't allow the pain of your past to dictate your future. That's all I'm saying."

Despite her words, that wouldn't be the last thing she said on the subject. She'd been hinting for a while that it was time for him to move on.

While Wyatt appreciated his mother-in-law's advice—and anyone else with an opinion about his future—she didn't get it.

She understood grief and the pain of losing a child, which no parent should have to endure, but she hadn't lost the love of her life.

Opening his heart again meant exposing himself to future heartache, and he definitely wasn't going to do that again.

No matter what anyone said.

# CHAPTER FOUR

CALLIE JUST NEEDED to get through the next hour.

She didn't need to learn everything about managing the guest ranch in one day. Macey had promised to be by her side all week long and answer any questions she had.

Would one week be enough?

While they moved everything out of Gram's shop and took everything off the walls, Wyatt had asked if she was ready for the challenge of managing the guest ranch.

She'd said yes, hoping her voice was stronger than her nervous stomach.

Had she taken on more than she could handle? She never second-guessed herself like this, even when she was doing student teaching or finding her way through her first year.

But she'd figure it out, like she always did when faced with new situations. She didn't want to let Wyatt down and have him regret hiring her due to her lack of experience.

She needed to get a grip, or it was going to be a very long summer.

In the last hour, two different families had arrived in minivans as well as a young couple who showed up in a vintage bright yellow VW Beetle that her grandma would've loved.

The serenity of the guest ranch had been shattered by slamming doors, laughing children and adult voices.

And the Stone family took it in stride.

To them, registration meant all hands on deck.

Wyatt's older brother, Bear, and Macey's husband, Cole, helped outside while Piper, Bear's wife, stayed in the lodge with Callie and Macey and directed the families to their correct yurts.

Everly kept the younger children engaged with bubbles and sidewalk chalk while their parents unloaded their vehicles.

Deacon and Nora worked in the kitchen, preparing a welcome dinner of pulled pork, baked beans, potato salad, tossed salad and several kinds of pies.

The scents wafting throughout the lodge made Callie's stomach growl even louder. She pressed a hand against her abdomen, hoping no one else heard. She hadn't eaten anything other than coffee and one of Irene's brownies.

Maybe some water would help.

She searched for her bottle, but it wasn't on the registration table. She must've left it on one of the picnic tables outside.

She turned to Macey, who kept her cool through the very busy hour. "I'm going to grab my water. I'll be right back."

"No problem." Macey smiled at her as the baby napped in her arms.

As Callie left the air-conditioned lodge, the sticky heat smacked her in the face. Humidity hung in the air as dark clouds rolled across the sky. A storm was coming. Hopefully, it would hold off until everyone had gotten settled in their yurts for the night.

She found her now-warm water bottle sitting where she'd left it on the picnic table. As she turned to return to the lodge, something fluffy and white streaked past her and raced for the water.

"Fewix, come back." A boy, a little younger than Mia maybe, ran between the two yurts on Callie's left side and toddled after the dog.

Callie waited a second for an adult to emerge,

but no one appeared. Everly had gone inside right before Callie left, but where were the guys?

The dog stopped at the end of the dock next to one of the Adirondack chairs and barked, its tail wagging. The little boy with dark curls ran toward it with chubby, outstretched arms.

Oh, that wasn't going to end well.

Callie ran down the path, praying she'd reach him before he could fall in. As she reached the dock, someone stepped off the path that wound along the water.

They collided and something smacked against the ground. Dressed in black, the person wasn't much taller than she was. A teen maybe? Not taking the time to stop and check, Callie called over her shoulder. "Sorry!"

"Hey, you broke my…" The person's words carried in the wind as Callie's feet pounded against the wood.

The little boy tried to grab the dog, but it spun quickly. Its backside hit the child's legs, buckling his knees. The child pitched forward headfirst into the water.

"Nooo!" The words, ripped from Callie's throat, echoed across the lake. Dropping her water bottle, she dove into the water. She surfaced, pushed the hair out of her eyes and searched frantically for the little boy.

He flailed just a few feet in front of her, crying and choking. Then he went under again.

Callie's blood turned to ice. She dove back under and made out the hazy red of his shorts in the murky lake water stirred up from the activity. She caught him around the waist and hauled him to her chest. She kicked hard and pushed to the surface.

Choking, the little boy sobbed and clung to Callie's neck so tightly she struggled to fill her burning lungs with air. She tried to loosen the tight grip he had on her throat.

Footsteps thundered down the dock. A large splash on the other side of her threw water in their faces. Treading water, Callie turned and held the little boy against her chest, using her shoulder to protect him against the blast.

She wiped her face again and found Wyatt swimming toward her. He dragged a hand across his face. "Hey, you okay?"

She nodded, her teeth starting to chatter.

"Callie, give him to me."

She turned and found Bear kneeling at the end of the dock with his arms stretched out.

Another man with his face twisted in anguish knelt beside him.

With her own arms feeling like icicles, she lifted the child up with as much strength as she could.

Bear reached for him, but as he grabbed him, Callie's hands slipped off the little boy's wet skin.

Losing her balance, she fell forward and grazed the top of her head on the edge of the dock. She went back under, water shooting up her nose.

Wyatt wrapped a strong arm around her and pulled her against him. She surfaced once again, coughing.

Teeth chattering, she shivered as the adrenaline drained from her body. She clung to Wyatt as she caught her breath.

"Think you can climb back onto the dock?"

Suddenly aware of just how close he was and how tightly she'd been holding on to him, she nodded.

With her forehead burning, head aching, and body turning to jelly, she forced herself to move out of his strong arms. She swam a few strokes to the ladder attached to the side of the dock and pulled herself out of the water.

She wanted nothing more than to collapse on the wood.

Clapping ricocheted across the lake, jerking her attention to the crowd gathered on the dock.

Heat seared her face.

The man who had knelt next to Bear hugged the little boy close. A woman raced toward them and wrapped a blanket around them.

Turning to Callie and with tears streaking her makeup, she threw her arms around her. "Thank you for saving my son. I tried to get Teddy into the yurt and didn't realize our dog Felix had run outside. I'm so sorry for the trouble we've caused, but I'm so thankful you were there."

Trying not to shiver, Callie shook her head. "I'm just grateful he's okay. You should get him checked out to be sure there are no injuries."

With a nod, the woman returned to the man holding the soaked little boy and they headed back up the dock.

As she wrapped her arms over her chest and rubbed her skin to generate some warmth, Callie's eyes drifted to Deacon and Nora talking to a man who didn't look pleased standing next to the person in black, who Callie could now see was a male teen.

The kid turned and pointed at her.

Macey rushed past them and wrapped a fleece blanket around Callie. "Take this so you can warm up."

Callie burrowed in it and tucked her fists under her jaw as she tried to calm her chattering teeth. "Who's that kid?"

"The son of one of our guests. Apparently, he was searching for a signal for his phone and claims you pushed him. His phone fell against a rock and shattered the screen."

"I didn't push him on purpose. I was running for the dock and ran into him. I'll pay to have his phone fixed." She did a mental calculation, knowing the cost was going to take money from her dwindling savings.

Macey slid an arm around Callie's shoulders. "The only thing you're going to do is take a shower. Then we're going to the clinic to get your head checked out."

Callie had forgotten about her injury. She touched her forehead. She couldn't tell if the moisture was lake water or blood. "It's fine. Just a graze."

Macey eyed her. "I'd feel better knowing you didn't have a mild concussion."

"I appreciate it, Macey, but other than a scrape

and maybe a bruise, I'll be fine. Truly. If I have a headache or anything, I'll let you know."

She walked barefoot across the warm wood. Her flip-flops must be floating in the lake since they hadn't stayed on her feet after she dove in to save Teddy.

Someone called her name. She closed her eyes and paused. She turned and found Wyatt jogging toward her, soaked and in socked feet. He must've kicked off his boots before plunging into the water. His gray T-shirt clung to his brawny chest like a second skin.

He caught up to them and framed her face in his cold hands. His eyebrows scrunched together as he touched her wound gently. Then he glanced at his sister. "Can you take her in to get this checked?"

"That's what I was trying to talk her into doing. She claims she's fine." Macey raised an eyebrow. "Sounds like someone else I know."

Wyatt laughed, and the timbre of his voice warmed Callie's numb insides. Then he looked at Callie with a more serious expression. "Other than your forehead, are you sure you're okay?"

She nodded, not wanting him to release her.

He flashed her a smile and wrapped his arm around her shoulders, giving her a quick squeeze. "Good. Can't lose my best employee on her first day."

"You're not firing me?"

He released her and scowled. "Fire you? Why would I do that?"

She nodded to the teenager still standing on the dock with the man and Wyatt's parents. "Apparently, I broke that kid's phone."

Wyatt scoffed. "Phones can be replaced. If it weren't for you, we would've had a tragedy on our hands. Your quick thinking saved Teddy. You're a hero."

Callie's face heated under his watchful eyes and generous words. She shook her head. "Thank you. I just did what anyone else would've done."

"But you were the one who did it." He placed his hands on her blanket-covered shoulders, then rubbed her upper arms. "Get warmed up and into dry clothes. I really want you to get your head checked." Releasing her once again, he walked backward while pulling his keys from his sodden jeans pocket. "When I get back, we'll have dinner, then I need to head to Ray and Irene's to feed the animals."

Macey gave Callie's shoulder a squeeze. "You heard the boss. Get warm, and I'll take you to the clinic. On the way, I'll share what we have planned for the week. I promise not every day will be this adventurous."

As Callie entered the air-conditioned lodge and climbed the steps with rubbery legs, Macey's words echoed in her head.

Wyatt's sister was wrong.

To Callie, the adventure had just begun.

Working alongside Wyatt was going to test her in every way possible. She had a feeling he was going to be a distraction she didn't need. Was she up to the challenge of managing the guest ranch alongside him?

Only one way to find out.

WHAT A WAY to kick off their new summer season.

Wyatt didn't even want to think about what would've happened if Callie hadn't acted so quickly.

After he returned to the guest ranch in dry clothes, he, Dad, Bear and Cole had a quick discussion about adding a gate and fence in front of the dock. While it may ruin the aesthetic, they needed to prevent another situation like this afternoon's mishap and protect their youngest guests.

At least Callie had agreed to get her head checked and allowed Macey to take her.

When Mia overheard him tell his parents that Ray had been released from the hospital, she begged to go with him so she could visit Grammy and Pappy and give him a kiss so he would get better.

How could he say no to that?

After a quick call to Irene, he now stood on their back porch, holding Mia's hand. He needed to leave her with Irene so he could get the animals fed and turned out.

Wyatt rapped two knuckles on the side door that led into Ray and Irene's kitchen. Then he opened it and stepped inside. "Mama D? You here?"

"Come on in, Wyatt. I'll be down in a minute."

Releasing his hand, Mia ran into the kitchen, then stopped. She cupped her small hands around her mouth. "Pappy, where are you? I wanna give you a kiss to make you better."

"In here, Peanut." Wyatt's father-in-law called from the living room, his deep voice threaded with fatigue.

Mia raced through the dining room and the open French doors that led into the living room.

From his spot by the sink, Wyatt watched as

she hurried to the couch where Ray lay reclined, his left leg in a cast and propped on pillows.

Mia knelt beside him, kissed his cheek and pressed her hand against the older man's forehead. He wrapped an arm around her and hauled her to his chest.

Turning away to give them privacy, Wyatt faced the window over the sink that gave a gorgeous view of the horse rescue.

A pair of recently rescued, underfed palominos grazed in the grass. They swished away flies with their tails that needed a good brushing, as the evening sun turned their gold coats nearly white.

They should've been brought in and fed a while ago. Wyatt should've gotten there sooner, but with the chaos at the guest ranch, things had taken longer than he'd expected.

He scanned the fence line and noticed a sagging post. That would need to be shored up so horses didn't find an escape route.

The weight of his new responsibilities pressed on him, but he'd find his rhythm and get a schedule worked out so he could manage his responsibilities.

He had to.

"Okay, sorry about that. I was getting bedding from the upstairs linen closet to make a bed for Ray in the guest room. He won't be able to climb stairs for a while." Irene came into the kitchen carrying a loaded laundry basket. Her hair had been pulled back into a low ponytail and she wore a white T-shirt and jean shorts. Dark circles shadowed her eyes. Apparently, she didn't get much sleep either.

"Let me get that for you." He took the basket and carried it into the guest room on the other side of the dining room. Seeing the queen-size mattress covered in only a pad, he made quick work of making up the bed. Instinct had him folding down the top sheet and blanket and tucking the edges tightly under the mattress.

He wasn't in the Marine Corps any longer, and no one would be inspecting his rack. He pulled the blanket out and smoothed out the sides.

As he returned to the kitchen, Mia streaked past him and climbed onto her booster seat attached to one of the wooden chairs that stayed at the table. "Grammy, do you have any brownies left?"

"Did someone say brownies?" Ray hobbled

slowly into the kitchen, a little unsteady with the crutches. "Wyatt. How's it going?"

Dressed in his usual plaid Western shirt and a pair of shorts that exposed very pale legs, he appeared to be the same ole Ray Douglas Wyatt had known most of his life.

Except for the paleness beneath his tan and the deep lines fanning out from reddened eyes darkened with circles.

Ray gripped the back of Mia's chair as he lowered himself onto the seat next to her. With hunched shoulders as if carrying the weight of the world, Ray appeared a decade older than fifty-eight.

"How are you doing, Ray?" Wyatt clamped a hand on his shoulder.

Ray glared at him, then raised an eyebrow. "About like a guy who just had his leg cut open."

"I'm sorry."

Ray waved away his words and rested his crutches against the table, but one toppled over and knocked to the floor. He muttered something under his breath and stretched out an arm for it.

"I got it." Wyatt picked it up and set it back against the table within Ray's reach. "Hey, I wanted to run something by you."

"What's on your mind, son?"

"I talked with Dad yesterday and wondered if you had a minute to talk? It can wait until after I do the feeding."

Ray lifted a hand and dropped it at his side. "Sure. I have at least six weeks of doing nothing. Plenty of time to talk. What's weighing you down?"

That was a loaded question.

Wyatt's gaze shifted between his in-laws. As if reading his mind, Irene unbuckled Mia's booster seat. "Mia, let's go check on the kitties and make sure they have enough water before they go night-night."

Always excited to visit the animals in the shelter, Mia smiled and clapped her hands. "Okay, Grammy." She reached for Irene's hand.

Once the kitchen door closed behind them, Wyatt pulled out a chair and sat. He folded his arms on the table in front of him. "Yesterday, I offered to buy in as a partner. I could use—"

"What'd I tell you about that rumor?" Ray cut him off, his voice thundering in the quiet room.

Amazing how quickly the man could turn from doting Pappy to a crusty cowboy.

"I know money's tight right now, so don't

even try to deny it. Partner with me, and you'll retain the ranch for good. You're out of commission until your leg heals anyway, and you need someone to look after things."

"I'll manage." Ray scrubbed a hand over his unshaven face.

Wyatt shook his head. "Trying to manage everything by yourself is what got you hurt in the first place. You're too stubborn to ask for help."

"Fine. I'll accept a hand for the time being as long as I can trust you to not to mess up what my family has worked so hard to establish. Happy?"

"You can trust me. You also know how much Linnea loved the horses. If I buy it, then I'll turn it into a sanctuary so they're protected."

"That takes too much time and work. Not to mention money. And constant monitoring of the kill lots to find the right horses. We can't save them all."

"I get that. I wish we could." He stood, moved to the sink and filled a glass with water. "You once said you try to get them healthy, so they can be adopted by good families. And those fees help fund the rescue. But if we turned the rescue into a sanctuary, then we could apply for nonprofit status and receive grants to cover costs. Plus, we could retrain those horses for a renewed purpose."

"Adopting a horse isn't as easy as picking out a cat or a dog." Ray jerked a thumb toward the barn. "Right now, I have ten malnourished or abused horses that need more love and care. They won't be eligible for adoption for a long time."

"Then let's consider monthly sponsorships—people who are willing to donate time and money for their care and feeding. In return, they can provide affection and gentle riding so the horses can get used to riders again."

"Son, your heart is in the right place, and I appreciate that, but my mind's made up."

Wyatt folded his arms over his chest and schooled his tone. "A month ago, there was a big write-up in one of the magazines I read online about horses being sold for slaughter. As a sanctuary, we could stop that and offer them so much more."

"You don't give up, do you? If I become a nonprofit, then I need to create a board, and I don't need other people telling me how to run my own ranch." He waved his hand toward the property. "I'm one guy, and I'd like to keep it that way."

His set jaw and raised brow told Wyatt he wasn't about to budge, and that Wyatt was wasting his breath trying.

He drained his water, then he lifted both hands, palms facing Ray. "All right. Fine. Just know the offer's still there. I'm heading to the barn. Once I'm done, I'll swing back for Mia. If you feel up to it, we can talk about what needs to be done this week, and I'll fit it into my schedule."

Ray straightened in his chair and puffed out his chest. "Of course I'll feel up to it. All I'm asking is for a hand. Think you can do that?"

Wyatt wouldn't let Ray's gruff tone get under his skin. He stuck out his hand. "Sure, Ray. Not a problem."

"Good. And stop carrying the world on your shoulders, Wy. Give those burdens over to the Lord, and let Him carry them for you."

Easier said than done.

As he headed to the barn, Wyatt longed to head back to the ranch. Maybe stretch out in front of the campfire that would be starting soon and relax for the night.

But that wasn't about to happen. Too much still needed to be done. Maybe if he could prove himself to Ray, then the older man would allow him to partner with the rescue and help ease some of his burden.

Didn't at least one of them deserve a break?

# CHAPTER FIVE

What had Callie gotten herself into?

Why had she even offered to help with the horse rescue when the large animals intimidated her?

Because Wyatt was willing to give up his valuable time to help her at the shop. She wanted to do what she could to help him out in return…and to convince him he hadn't made a mistake in hiring her.

But could she do this? Really?

She'd have to. She'd given her word.

When Wyatt mentioned skipping tonight's campfire to head to Ray and Irene's to feed the horses before his meeting, she'd offered to lend a hand since she planned to wash walls in the shop anyway. She wanted to start painting tomorrow.

With the first part of the week having been so busy, she hadn't been in town since Macey took her to the clinic to get her head checked.

Inside the barn, the air swirled with dust motes riding on bits of hay from bales being thrown down from upstairs. Wyatt jogged down the wooden steps and strode to the middle of the first floor where several bales toppled over one another.

"The hay separates into flakes, and each horse gets two flakes. We're not fancy around here, so it gets dropped into their stalls." He pitched hay over the stall door, then turned to her and waved a hand down the remaining stalls. "Do what I just did—break it apart and drop it in their stalls. While they're eating that, I'll mix their grain. We'll pour it into their feeders, rinse out their water buckets, refill them, then they'll be good to go."

He pushed to his feet and brushed dust and hay off his jeans. "When I return from my meeting and get Mia from Irene and Ray's, I'll turn them out and clean their stalls."

Mia twirled next to him, her sandaled feet making tracks in the dirt. "Daddy, can I feed the horsies too?"

"Sure thing, squirt. You can scoop the grain into the buckets, okay?"

Mia nodded and danced in a circle.

Oh, to have that kind of enthusiasm.

Callie broke apart the flakes as Wyatt had done, then eyed the stalls that came up to her shoulders.

The horses with their long muzzles and dark eyes watched her.

How was she supposed to get the hay in the stalls with them in the way?

Wyatt just dropped it in, but he'd been around the animals his whole life.

And these horses seemed more on edge than the calmer ones at Stone River.

On the way to the Douglas ranch, Wyatt had shared some of the conditions the horses had been in before Ray rescued them. Callie had to fight back tears against the inhumanity. Even now, some of them were still nothing more than skin and bones.

"What's the matter, Callie? You scared?"

Callie jumped at the sound of Mia's voice behind her.

Leave it to her to be so skittish that a child startled her.

Still holding an arm full of hay, Callie turned. "I'm not used to horses like you. How long have you been riding?"

Mia threw her arms out wide and rolled her eyes at Callie. "Like my whole life."

Callie bit her lip.

Right. Schooled by a three-year-old.

"The horsies just want some love. Right, Daddy?"

"Right, sweetheart." He carried a bucket and set it in front of the stalls. Then he looked at Callie. "You okay?"

What could she say? That she was too afraid to throw hay into the stall?

Instead, she nodded and tossed the hay over the stall door as Wyatt had a moment ago. Except, she tossed it in the same stall. "Oops, sorry."

He grinned as he patted the brown horse's neck "No worries. Pearl won't mind. She can use the extra forage. She's being kept inside until her wounds heal."

Callie didn't even want to ask where they came from. Instead, she grabbed more flakes and carried them to the stall next to Pearl. A smaller whitish horse named Charlie nudged her arm.

"Daddy, can I pet Charlie?"

Wyatt lifted Mia in his arms and carried her to the horse's stall. He held on to the horse's harness while Mia rubbed her small hand over the black spot on the horse's head. "Charlie's a pony, and he's blind. We found him at a k-i-l-l lot a year ago. He's as gentle as can be and loves the attention. Mia adores him because of his size."

"How do you handle it?"

Wyatt didn't pretend not to understand her question. He lifted a shoulder. "Through the grace of God, I guess. What we see when we rescue these fine animals is enough to get the kindest, most patient person fired up."

Callie dropped the flakes over the pony's stall. As she reached out to rub Charlie's muzzle, he nudged her arm. She tried to move out of his way, and he nipped the tender flesh above her elbow.

"Ow!" She jumped back and twisted her arm.

Wyatt set Mia down and reached for Callie's elbow. "Did he nip you?"

"I think so. It doesn't really hurt. Just surprised me more than anything."

"Silly pony. Charlie, Callie's not food." Mia stood in front of the stall with her hands on her hips. "He doesn't know the difference between a nip and a nuzzle."

Wyatt ran a rough finger over the reddened spot. "I'm sorry. He doesn't usually do that. Maybe he thought you were sweet and wanted a taste."

Callie's eyes flew to Wyatt's face and found

him grinning at her. But there was something else in his eyes. Something she couldn't quite decipher. Did she even want to try?

"Let me kiss it." Mia pulled on Callie's arm. "Grammy says kisses make everything better."

Callie crouched in front of the child and offered her arm. Mia brushed a light kiss across her skin. "There, how's that?"

Callie hugged Mia. "Thank you for making me feel better."

"You're welcome." She pressed a hand against Callie's cheek. "I like you."

Her heart nearly melting, Callie twirled one of Mia's pigtails around her finger. "I like you too, Mia."

"Can I help you throw the hay to the horsies?"

Callie glanced at Wyatt, and he nodded. "Mia, I'll pick you up. Callie will give you the hay, and you can throw it over the door. How's that?"

"Good idea, Daddy."

Wyatt scooped his daughter up, and Callie broke off more flakes for Mia. Since they all worked together, they were done in just a few minutes. Wyatt added grain to their feeders and refilled their water.

The horses shuffled their feet and lifted their

heads when he approached their stalls. But when Mia came near them, they settled down.

"Mia's a little horse whisperer like you." Callie rested a shoulder against one of the empty stalls as she listened to Mia talking to Charlie again.

"I believe they sense her innocence and gentleness." Wyatt rested a hand against the stall above her head and searched her face. "I wish you'd told me the horses still made you nervous. I would've fed them."

His quiet words and lack of judgment still caused her face to warm. "I didn't want to go back on my word. You've been helping me so much this week, I wanted to return the favor. And I didn't want you to think you'd made a mistake in hiring me."

"Callie, no one's keeping score. You're more of a help than you know. Hiring you was one of the best decisions I've made in a while. You've been a pro this week. We'll work on getting you more comfortable with the horses, but no pressure." He shot her a smile that tripped her pulse, then looked at his watch. "I need to take Mia into the farmhouse, then get to my meeting. I'll see you back at the guest ranch?"

"Thanks." His words brought her more comfort than she was willing to confess. "I'm heading to the shop for a while. I want to get the walls washed down, then I'll call it a night."

"If you're still planning to paint tomorrow, I'll give you a hand."

Not trusting her voice at the moment, she nodded and followed him outside. Mia ran across the grass and disappeared into her grandparents' house. Callie cut across to the shop.

As she unlocked the back door, she replayed Mia's reactions to the animals. Callie longed to have that kind of confidence and peace.

And Wyatt's reassuring words did more than dispel her fears. They reminded her of her priorities—her job and getting the shop reopened.

She couldn't get sidetracked by anything else, including a very handsome cowboy and his adorable daughter.

WYATT WAS LATE to his own meeting, but he had no one to blame but himself.

He'd spent too much time with Callie, then ended up talking with Ray longer than expected when he dropped Mia off with her grandparents.

The time with Callie had him wishing he didn't have to leave. He didn't like the way they'd left things. He felt like a jerk for not seeing her nervousness around the horses. The last thing he wanted was to make her uncomfortable anywhere on the ranch.

If only she'd gone with him a different night. Part of him wished he could cancel the support group, but that wasn't possible since he was the leader of the motley crew of fathers.

Usually, he looked forward to seeing the guys who'd become like family. They understood each other's struggles, and it was a safe place to vent, when necessary.

At the church, he parked his SUV and stepped out into the muggy evening air. Even though the sun was lower in the sky, the heat hadn't leveled off yet.

Sweat slicked his forehead by the time he reached the back door. He took the carpeted stairs two at a time down to the basement where a dozen single fathers waited to discuss their dating and parenting struggles in one of the adult Sunday school rooms.

The rich scent of freshly brewed coffee floated up the steps, reminding him he'd forgotten to stop at the diner for whatever weekly treat Lynetta liked to send to spoil the men.

He'd been too focused on meeting Callie at the ranch. More like just too focused on Callie.

As he passed the open door that led to the pastor's office, a familiar laugh stopped him in his tracks.

Callie?

What was she doing there?

As he tried to peek discreetly around the corner, she turned and caught him. Her eyes widened as she cocked her head. "Wyatt? What are you doing here?"

Busted.

He jerked a thumb over his shoulder toward the lit room across the hall. "My meeting is here. I oversee a support group for single fathers. What about you?"

She shook her head and reached behind him, tugging on the back of his T-shirt.

"What's wrong?"

"Nothing. Just checking to see where you keep your cape. You're like some sort of Superman. Is there anything you can't do?"

He laughed softly and shook his head as heat crawled up his neck. "There's a lot I can't do. Thankfully, I have people in my corner like you who pick up the slack. What are you doing here?"

"I found a couple of books in Gram's things that belonged to the church. I called Pastor Miles and learned he was staying late, so I brought them over. I'm getting ready to head back to the guest ranch now." She turned back to the older pastor and extended her hand. "Thanks for meeting me, Pastor."

"Of course, Callie. We loved Ada. You're welcome here anytime."

"Thanks. I appreciate that."

As she started to slide past Wyatt, thundering footsteps sounded down the steps.

"Ezra. Andrew. Get back here. Remember what I said about running." A deep voiced echoed in the stairwell.

Two little blond-headed boys raced past them, their laughter bouncing off the walls in the well-lit hallway.

"I said stop!" Troy Branson, the boys' father, rounded the corner. His blond hair was still cut military short. Like Wyatt, he'd left active service to care for his boys. But unlike Wyatt's situation, Troy's ex had abandoned her family, leaving Troy bitter and hurting.

Seeing Wyatt and Callie, he stopped and his shoulders slumped. He held out a hand, but his eyes strayed to Callie. "Hey, Wyatt."

"Hey, Troy. What's going on?" Wyatt clasped

his hand and wanted to squeeze it to get the man's focus back on him.

Troy rubbed the back of his neck. "My mom couldn't keep the boys, so I brought them with me, hoping they'd settle down for the meeting. Guess that's not happening. They've been a handful today. I'll load them back up, head home and catch you guys next week."

Wyatt held up a hand. "Hold up. Maybe we can figure something out." He turned to Pastor Miles. "Are you sticking around for a while?"

Pastor Miles clapped Troy on the shoulder. "I'd love to help, but I'm actually on my way to another meeting."

"No worries, Pastor. Thanks, though." Troy jerked his head toward the laughter coming from the room down the hall. "I'll grab the boys and see you next week."

Wyatt stuck out an arm and blocked him. "Stay. Between the group of us, we can manage a couple of boys."

Callie turned to Wyatt. "How long's your meeting?"

"An hour."

She looked at Troy. "I'll watch them while you're at your meeting."

Troy's eyes bounced between Wyatt and Callie. "And you are?"

Wyatt stepped forward. "Callie Morgan, meet Troy Branson. Troy, this is Callie, Ada Morgan's granddaughter."

Trent extended his hand. "That's right. I thought you looked familiar. I was at Ada's funeral. I'm sorry for your loss. She was a nice lady. Made chocolate chip cookies for my boys' birthdays."

"That sounds like Gram."

A crash sounded down the hall. Callie turned to Pastor Miles. "Would it be okay if I kept an eye on them in there?"

Pastor Miles waved his hand toward the room. "By all means. That's the children's room they ran into—the one where they attend Sunday school each week."

"Great, thank you." Callie returned her attention back to Wyatt and Tory and jerked her head toward the noise. "You guys have your meeting, and I'll take care of those little rascals."

"You sure?"

"I can handle two little boys."

"Yeah, I thought so too when my wife left. Boy, they challenge me every day, though. Let me try to get them in line so you don't pull out your hair." Troy headed down the hall.

Callie started to follow, but then Wyatt reached for her elbow. "Thanks for doing this. Troy needs this time, but are you sure we're not keeping you from anything important?"

Callie covered his hand with her own. "This is what's important right now. We'll be fine. If I run into any trouble, you're all just down the hall."

She flashed him a smile that shot him right in the gut.

What was that about?

Standing in the doorway, he watched her walk away. Then he stepped into the adult Sunday school room where the guys were hanging out in groups, clutching cups of coffee.

Wyatt headed for the coffee maker and filled a to-go cup nearly to the top for himself.

A moment later, Troy returned to the room, looking calmer than he did five minutes ago.

He strode over to Wyatt and lowered his voice. "I don't know where you found her, but don't let her go. She got those rowdy boys settled down in less than a minute. If I hadn't given up on women, I'd marry her tomorrow."

Wyatt's gut tightened.

Let her go?

He wasn't bitter toward women like Troy, but he wasn't in a rush to head to the altar either. His buddy's declaration gave him an uneasy feeling in the pit of his stomach, and he wasn't sure why.

He had no claim to Callie, but he just couldn't make sense of why Troy's words tensed him up.

He needed to shake it off and focus on this week's meeting.

And not on Callie.

Though, if he was being honest, she was beginning to take up more time in his thoughts. And he wasn't sure how he felt about that.

He needed to concentrate on his responsibilities and not the friend from his childhood. He was her boss and her friend. But nothing else.

And he needed to keep it that way.

# CHAPTER SIX

IF WYATT SAID he was fine one more time, Callie was going to flick paint on him.

From the moment she'd seen him at breakfast this morning, he seemed distant. When she tried to review next week's schedule with him, he put her off. Yet, he had time to chill at the picnic table with his brother for half an hour talking about the rodeo.

Whatever.

To be honest, she hadn't expected him to show up and paint as they'd talked about the night before. But he did. And Mia was with him, which made Callie smile.

She pushed her roller in the paint tray, covering it with the lemony yellow color she'd purchased a few days ago from the local hardware store. She applied paint to the wall and moved the roller as high as she could on her tiptoes.

Mia had taken her stool and sat on it while she

applied paint with a small paintbrush. She had as much paint on her hands and legs as she did on the wall. At least she'd arrived in old clothes. Or so Wyatt had said when Callie expressed concern about ruining her shirt and shorts.

Wyatt stood on a ladder and applied white paint on the dingy ceiling with an extended roller. He worked silently. Even when he was busy around the guest ranch, he still managed to engage her in conversation. But today? Nada.

Something was definitely going on with him. She didn't know what to make of his mood. And she didn't dare ask what was wrong. No doubt she'd get the same answer—he was fine.

She struggled to keep her attention on the wall. Instead, her eyes drifted toward Wyatt, watching his back as he stretched and moved.

Oh, boy.

She was in trouble.

"Thanks for letting me paint, Callie. I like it." Mia's voice pulled her attention away from the man distracting her from her job.

Callie smiled at the little girl. "You're welcome, sweetheart. I couldn't have asked for a better helper."

"What about Daddy? Is he a good helper?"

"Yes, Daddy's a good helper too."

Wyatt made a noise, and Callie shot him a look. "What was that? Do you have something to add?"

He shook his head. "Nope. Just trying to get things done."

"Do you have somewhere you need to be?"

He didn't say anything. Then he climbed down the ladder and strode over to the paint tray and layered more paint onto his roller. Without a word, he headed back to the ladder.

Callie jumped to her feet and blocked his way. "Hey, what's going on with you? You're quiet today."

"I'm busy."

"You're always busy. That doesn't stop you from having a conversation."

He planted a hand on his hip and glared at her. "Do you want to talk or work?"

Callie gritted her teeth, backed out of his way, then waved her hand toward the ladder. "Work, by all means. Don't let me stop you, Cranky Pants."

"Daddy, did you wear cranky pants today?"

"Callie's silly, sweetheart. I'm fine." Despite the smile he flashed at his daughter, his jaw tightened.

There it was—those two words that set Callie's teeth on edge. She snatched Mia's brush out of her hand and brushed a slash of paint on Wyatt's muscled forearm.

He looked at her with wide eyes. "You put paint on me."

"Yes, I did. What are you going to do about it?"

He looked at her with an expression Callie couldn't decipher. Then he nodded slowly. "I see how it is. Two can play this game." He caught Callie's arm and encircled her wrist between his thumb and forefinger. Very gently, he removed the paintbrush from her fingers.

Heart already pounding from his closeness, she turned her face as she braced herself for what was to come.

Wyatt grinned for the first time since arriving an hour ago and took a step closer. He waved the paintbrush in front of her. "Let's see how you like it."

She squeezed her eyes shut and tried to pull her hand free. She threw her other hand up to shield him from getting any closer.

Wyatt laughed softly, a sound that rippled through her. Then he captured her other wrist in the same large hand.

Callie could almost smell the paint before the cold, sticky liquid coated her nose. She tried to shield her face, but he kept her hands pinned. She turned her face into her shoulder just as a swash of paint tickled her cheek.

"Wyatt Stone, you don't play fair."

"Oh, I play to win." Wyatt tugged her closer. She opened her eyes and found him smiling down at her. "Give up?"

Part of her wanted to say no so she could still feel his touch on her skin.

Knowing her words wouldn't be coherent, she simply nodded.

"Good. Now hold still." He pulled a red bandanna out of his back pocket, released her hands and reached for the water bottle sitting on the floor by the ladder. After dabbing water onto the cloth, he cupped her chin and gently wiped the paint off her face. "Don't start something you can't finish."

"Daddy, I wanna play too."

"Play? You think we're playing? Mia, my girl, we are doing serious work here." Still holding the brush in one hand, Wyatt scooped Mia up with his free hand and cupped her in his arm. Then he took the paint brush and dotted her nose.

"Daddy!" Her giggles echoed in the empty room.

Wyatt's phone chimed. He set Mia down and pulled it out of his back pocket. He scrolled up the screen. Then he laughed quietly and shook his head. He looked at Callie, smile still in place. "Sorry to leave, but I gotta run. Seems a skunk has decided to take up residence under the deck of one of the yurts. How about if I come back in an hour or so?"

Callie shook her head. "Don't worry about it. I'll clean up here and head back to the guest ranch. I'll come back and paint tomorrow. Thank you for your help."

"Any time."

Callie walked Wyatt and Mia to the door, then closed it behind them.

He may have said 'any time' but she couldn't take advantage of his kindness. She needed to do something to show her appreciation. Maybe bake him some cookies or something.

Hadn't Macey mentioned something about chocolate chip being her brother's favorite?

Callie returned to the shop and poured the

paint from the tray back into the gallon can. She should probably take advantage of the time to get more done, but suddenly, she wanted to head back to the guest ranch.

Even though a radio played softly, she missed Mia's giggles and Wyatt's deep voice.

Watching Wyatt playing with Mia filled Callie with longing. In order to have the family she always wanted, she needed to risk her heart.

But it couldn't be with Wyatt. He was completely off limits.

Now she just needed to keep reminding herself of that so she didn't do something silly like falling for her boss and risk losing her job, no matter how much her teenage crush wanted to revive those old feelings.

WYATT'S EVENING WASN'T going as planned. He'd arrived at Ada's cottage ready to paint, just as he'd offered.

But the moment Callie opened the door to the shop, Troy's comment from the other night floated around in his head. And he still didn't know what to make of it. So he'd quietly gone to work. And apparently, that made Callie think he was upset.

How could he tell her what was wrong when he couldn't figure it out himself?

Then, when she slapped paint on his arm... well, he couldn't let that go.

Maybe he'd been out of line to retaliate. All he knew was something was stirring within him that he hadn't felt in a very long time.

His sister Everly's phone call had come at a good time. She'd been preparing the yurts for the incoming guests and complained about the smell.

Since he was the director of the guest ranch, she'd determined he was the best person to take care of the problem.

If it'd happened on any other place on the ranch, he would've ignored the skunk. But he didn't want anything to create a nuisance for their guests. Or risk one of them getting sprayed.

Wyatt knelt on the ground and shined a flashlight under the wooden platform. Sure enough, the beam illuminated a black-and-white hide.

Hopefully, it was a loner. He didn't want a family of skunks living under one of the decks.

Wyatt pushed to his feet and headed for the ranch truck. He retrieved the wire live trap and a peanut butter sandwich he'd made back at his parents' place when he dropped off Mia before heading to the guest ranch.

He carried the trap to the yurt and set it on the ground where the skunk had dug under the lattice. He placed one slice of bread covered in peanut butter inside the trap past the trigger plate.

Since the skunk wouldn't venture out of its new den until dusk, Wyatt pushed to his feet and headed back to the truck. He'd check the trap first thing in the morning.

As he reached for the door handle, metal clinked behind him. He turned and found the skunk inside the trap.

That was fast.

The scent of peanut butter must've been too good to resist.

Wyatt pulled a tarp from the back seat to protect himself from getting sprayed as he hauled the trap to the bed of the truck.

Callie's car barreled down the dusty dirt road toward him. He moved to the middle of the road to stop her.

As she braked, music blared through her open windows. She lowered the volume as he headed to her car.

"Hey, mind waiting here a couple of minutes?

The skunk is trapped and I need to get him to the back of the truck without getting sprayed."

"Not at all." She reached for the door handle. "Need any help?"

He raised an eyebrow and shook his head. "And risk you getting sprayed? I don't think so."

"How big is it?"

"About a pound. It's a Western spotted skunk. The ranch has a permit to relocate animals, so I'm moving it to a safer place."

She drummed her fingers on the steering wheel. "I'll stay put until you're done."

With a nod, Wyatt moved away from the car, unfolded the tarp so the skunk couldn't see him. He moved closer to the trap, one quiet step at a time so he didn't spook the skittish creature who'd lifted its tail already.

His booted foot caught on the edge. He stumbled and reached out to steady himself, dropping the plastic material. Wyatt took a step back, crouched and tried to pull the tarp toward himself, but he ended up dropping it again. The rustling sound caught the skunk's attention. It raised its tail again, this time fanning out as the creature stomped its front feet.

Wyatt froze. His heart pounded against his ribs as his chest rose and fell.

The mammal was about to get serious if he didn't cool it.

As he forced his breathing to slow, his phone rang in his pocket, the ringtone piercing the nearly silent air.

The skunk's head whipped around as it shuffled backward and raised its back end like it was trying to do a handstand.

Before Wyatt could move, the skunk's spray hit him, the putrid odor soaking his side as he turned and tried to use the tarp as a shield.

Having grown up on the ranch and spent a lot of time in barns, Wyatt wasn't a stranger to strong smells, but the skunk spray had him gagging and nearly getting sick in the grass.

He needed to wash off the skunk stench. Now.

Behind him, a door slammed.

Chest tight and his breathing more of a wheeze, Wyatt whirled around and held up a hand. "Callie, don't come any closer."

"Is there anything I can do?" Callie yanked the collar of her shirt over her nose and backed toward her car, but not before a giggle escaped.

Was she laughing?

If this had happened to one of his brothers, he'd be busting a gut. But now that he was the one caught in the line of fire and could barely breathe because of the smell, he didn't find it the least bit funny.

Wyatt pointed to the lodge. "Head inside. I need to call wildlife control and have them remove the critter. Then get this stink off me."

She saluted, then climbed back inside her car and started the engine.

An hour later, he knocked on the door to Callie's suite, his skin still tingling from scrubbing hard to get rid of the smell.

She opened it, then wrinkled her nose and took a slight step back. "Wyatt. Hi."

Apparently, the dish soap and baking soda weren't enough to neutralize the smell.

He stepped away from her door, heat scalding his neck. "You can still smell it, can't you?"

She bit the corner of her lip but it didn't stop a grin from spreading across her face. "There is a lingering scent…"

He groaned. "Great. I'll have to figure out something else to get rid of the odor. I wanted to talk to you for a minute, but maybe I should wait?"

Callie waved toward the water. "Let's sit on the dock. I'll have you sit down wind."

"Laugh it up. At least wildlife control was in

the area already and picked up the skunk. Now no one else will get hit like I did."

Leaving the lodge, they walked down the dirt road toward the dock and settled in the Adirondack chairs.

Kicking off her shoes, Callie closed her eyes and lifted her face to the sunshine. The evening rays burnished her hair to a rich gold. She'd changed out of the jeans she'd worn earlier and into a light blue T-shirt with a sloth curled around a branch, and a white skirt with light blue flowers that brushed against her knees.

He rested his head against the back of the chair and focused on the San Juan Mountains against the cloudless blue sky behind her. "Let's talk, then I'll head back to my place and see what I can do to get rid of the odor."

"We can talk another time, if you'd prefer."

Wyatt laughed. "I've been rejected before, but never because of how I smell."

Callie's cheeks turned a light shade of pink. "I'm not rejecting you. I just don't want you to feel uncomfortable."

"I'll be fine."

"Ugh. That word again."

"Right, the word that brings you to fits of paint rage."

"You just didn't seem like yourself. I wanted to get you out of whatever mood you were in."

"Yeah, about that. It wasn't you. Troy had said something that got under my skin. That's all."

"Okay, I was worried I was adding to your stress by making you paint."

He raised an eyebrow. "Callie, please. I could've said no if I didn't want to be there."

"Like you'd tell anyone no."

"Not anyone I care about." As soon as he spoke the words, he cringed. What if she got the wrong idea?

Her head jerked up.

Wyatt pushed to his feet before he said anything to embarrass himself. "I need to pick up Mia and get her ready for bed. Then search the internet for a way to take care of this lingering scent, as you called it."

She laughed, shoved her feet back into her sandals, and stood.

They headed up the dock and Callie broke away to the path that led to the lodge. "Have a good night, Wyatt. See you tomorrow."

Wyatt waved and strode toward the ranch truck, feeling a bit lighter than he had earlier.

Talking with Callie had been so easy, just

as she had been when they were kids. Which seemed like a lifetime ago now.

If he'd had even a slim desire to date again, Callie was the kind of woman he'd choose for an evening out. But she was his employee now.

And he wasn't about to do something stupid and risk everything by falling for her.

# CHAPTER SEVEN

CALLIE SIMPLY WANTED to show her appreciation to Wyatt for helping with the painting. So, baking his favorite chocolate chip cookies were just a thank-you.

Nothing more. Nothing less.

At least that was what she kept telling herself as she snagged a pot holder off the counter. She opened the oven and pulled out the last tray of chocolate chip cookies. She set the cookie sheet on the stove, then grabbed a spatula and moved them onto the cooling rack.

Scents of melted chocolate, rich butter and brown sugar floated in the air.

Callie ran back upstairs, slid her feet into her new flip-flops, grabbed her purse, then headed back downstairs. In the kitchen, she washed her hands and filled a plastic container with still warm cookies.

Once she cleaned the kitchen, she gathered her things and headed outside.

As she backed onto the road that took her toward the ranch, she nearly braked and turned the car around.

Would Wyatt see the cookies as something more than a thank-you? She didn't want to give him the wrong idea.

She turned down the road that led to his cabin and parked next to his SUV. She pressed a hand against her anxious stomach, then picked up the cookie container before she lost her nerve, and stepped out of her car.

She climbed the steps to the full-length covered porch and knocked on Wyatt's cabin door. She took in the black rocking chair and matching child-size chair sitting near the door. A wooden swing hung at the end of the porch.

The door opened, and Wyatt filled the doorway dressed in a black T-shirt with gold USMC letters across the chest and a pair of gray shorts.

"Callie, this is a surprise."

She thrust the plastic container at him. "Macey said you liked chocolate chip cookies, so I made you some to say thank you for helping with the painting at the shop."

His eyes widened as he took the container and lifted the corner.

"Who is it, Daddy?" The door opened, and Mia peered around his legs. Spying Callie, she pushed through and bounced onto the porch. "Hi, Callie. Wanna come in and see my playroom?"

Before Callie could respond, Mia tugged on her hand and pulled her toward the door.

Wyatt took a step back. "Yes, come in."

"I don't want to intrude."

"You're not intruding, especially when you bring my favorite cookies." He pulled out a cookie and took a bite. Then he closed his eyes and groaned. "Oh, man, these are awesome."

His reaction was exactly what she'd hoped for. "My gram's recipe."

Callie stepped into the open living room with exposed log walls. A rust-colored couch and chair sat in front of a stone fireplace that touched the ceiling. Puzzle pieces lay scattered on a navy-and-rust braided rug. A large flatscreen TV was mounted on the wall above the mantel.

A framed picture of Wyatt wearing his Marine Corps dress blues with his arms wrapped around his wife caught Callie's attention. The top of Linnea's head brushed his shoulders. Her dark hair had been pulled into a pile of curls on top of her head secured by a tiara with a veil trailing down her back. Her strapless white gown with the sweetheart neckline and lacy skirt accentuated her tiny waist. A string of pearls lay against her collarbone.

On the other side of the fireplace, another image in a matching frame showed Wyatt holding Mia as an infant. He smiled in the picture, but the light in his eyes had dimmed.

Even though the photograph was taken only a few years ago, she could see how life events had changed him.

The boyish, almost cocky, glint in his eyes had been chased away by grief. She couldn't even imagine the pain he must have gone through.

She forced her attention away from the man in the pictures to the same one standing next to her. "Very nice."

"Thanks. After I returned to Colorado, we lived at the ranch for a while, then I decided Mia and I needed our own place. This used to be the foreman's cabin. Dad, Bear and I fixed it up for Mia and me to call home."

"You guys did a great job."

Mia tugged on Callie's hand again. "Callie, come and see my playroom."

Callie glanced at Wyatt.

He waved a hand, then bit into another cookie. "Sure, go ahead. I'll be out here eating cookies."

Callie laughed as Mia led her to a small room off the living room. She stood on a stool and turned on the light, revealing walls painted soft pink.

A bright pink child's chair sat in the corner next to a white bookcase overflowing with books. A molded plastic playhouse sat on top of a small square table, the people and furnishings scattered on the floor. Stuffed animals tumbled out of a hammock strung between two windows that cast light across a floral rug that covered most of the wooden floor.

"Mia, what a fun room." Callie knelt on the rug and picked up one of the people for the playhouse.

Mia moved to the play kitchen and handed Callie a pink cup. "Would you like some tea?"

"Absolutely. Thank you." She took a pretend drink. "That was the best tea I've had all day."

The little girl beamed. "I'm glad you liked it."

"Sorry to break up this party, but can I talk

to Callie for a minute, Mia?" Wyatt stood in the doorway, his hands braced on the frame.

Mia nodded. "You can play in my room anytime you want, Callie."

"Thank you, Mia. I'd like that." Callie pushed to her feet and followed Wyatt out of the playroom.

He stopped in the living room and faced her. "I'm taking Mia into town to spend the night with Ray and Irene. I'll check on the horses, then I'm heading back to the ranch. Would you like to take a ride with me before dinner?"

She tensed, but tried to keep her expression neutral. "Ride?"

He shrugged. "If you feel comfortable enough. I know they intimidate you, but if you give them a chance, you'll see just how gentle the horses can be."

She thought back to the way Mia engaged with the rescue horses, and Callie found herself nodding. "Actually, that would be a good idea. The more I'm around them, the better that will be for the guest ranch."

"Just the guest ranch?"

Callie shrugged. "After the summer, you won't need me."

Wyatt scowled. "What makes you think I won't need you?"

Her head shot up. "Well…"

"Unless you're planning to look for another place to work, our guest ranch runs year-round."

She raised her eyebrows. "I didn't realize that."

"Didn't I say that when I offered you the job?"

"You may have. To be honest, I was assuming it was a summer gig. I figured you'd shut down at the end of the season."

Wyatt laughed softly. "Even though this summer was the start to our season, we will be accepting reservations through the year, with plenty of activities for every season."

Wyatt turned and touched Callie's chin. "We'd love to have you for as long as you'd like to stay. If you feel the need to look for different employment, I understand. I just ask for a short notice so we aren't left hanging."

"Absolutely. I wouldn't do that to you all."

He jerked his head toward her car. "What do you say we meet back up at the guest ranch in an hour or so and take that ride?"

Callie nodded and fell in step as he walked her to the front door.

On her way back to the lodge, the same question tumbled through her head—was she making a mistake?

The more time she spent with Wyatt, the harder it was going to be to protect herself from any future hurts. Wyatt was her employer, and she needed to remember that.

No matter that her heart longed for more.

AFTER HIS DEBACLE the other day with the skunk, Wyatt couldn't have made a worse impression with Callie.

Besides, it wasn't like the invitation to go horseback riding was a date or anything. Wyatt wanted Callie to get used to the horses and being in the saddle so she'd be more comfortable around them, especially if she planned to stick around the ranch. What better way than to take her riding?

So why couldn't he stop thinking about her? And what was up with the knot in his gut?

The past few days he'd been hustling Mia out the door so he could get to the guest ranch and see her before their busy days began.

Wyatt parked the ranch truck, then led his black stallion Dante and his mother's mare Patience out of the horse trailer.

He put his sunglasses on, adjusted the brim of

his cowboy hat and led the horses to the paddock so they could graze while he waited for Callie.

She walked toward him wearing a light purple button-down shirt with the sleeves rolled to her elbows, faded jeans and cowboy boots. Add a hat, and she'd look like she'd walked off the pages of one of the horse magazines he read online.

He lifted a hand. "Hi, again."

"Hey." She waved back.

Wyatt jerked his head toward the horses. "Ready to ride?"

Something flashed in Callie's eyes. She clasped her hands together in front of her until her knuckles whitened. Then she shrugged. "Ready as I'll ever be, I guess."

"If you're not comfortable, we don't need to do this. I don't want you to be scared."

She shook her head. Her ponytail threaded through her ball cap bounced against her shoulders. "I'm nervous, but let's do this."

He admired her courage.

"Thatta girl. You'll be riding my mom's horse. Patience is as gentle as they come. Plus, we'll go slow. Any time you feel nervous or uncomfortable, we'll stop and walk the horses for a bit. Sound good?" At her nod, he continued.

"How much do you remember about getting on the horse?"

Wyatt opened the gate and stepped inside. He gathered Patience's reins and led her to the dirt road.

Callie eyed the mare, then shifted her attention to Wyatt. "It's been so long. Someone held onto the horse the last time I rode. I remember putting my left foot into the stirrup and lifting my right leg over, then settling into the saddle."

"Good memory. I'll hold on to Patience and guide you."

She shot him a wry grin. "Too bad you saddled the horses already. I won't be able to show off my amazing tack skills."

"Next time." He winked at her.

Shaking her head, she grimaced and held up a hand. "No rush. Really."

He laughed. "Like I said, Patience is very gentle. She loves being talked to. Offer your hand so she can sniff you."

She did as he instructed, and Patience touched her nose to Callie's palm.

"She wants you to pet her." Wyatt laid his hand against Patience's neck.

Callie followed his movements and talked softly to the horse.

Wyatt moved in front of Callie and reached for Patience's harness. He lifted the reins over her head and allowed them to rest on her neck. "Hold on to the reins and grab a handful of Patience's mane."

"Won't that hurt?"

"Not as much as pulling on her mouth does. Put your left foot in the stirrup. Lift your other leg over her back and sit carefully in the seat. Try to remain relaxed so she doesn't pick up any anxiety you may have."

Callie did as instructed. The leather creaked as she made herself comfortable. She clasped the reins in both hands.

"Good job." Wyatt reached up and tapped her left hand. "Hold the reins in your left hand. Sit straight but make sure your weight is distributed evenly in the center. Keep your back and arms relaxed, and move with Patience."

Once he felt confident Callie wasn't about to slide off Patience's back or anything, he returned to the paddock for Dante.

His black stallion eyed him, and Wyatt rested a hand against the horse's strong muzzle. "Hey, boy. Let's go for a ride."

He led the horse outside, then slipped his foot

in the stirrup and threw his other leg over the strong animal's back.

Dante nickered, and Wyatt leaned forward and stroked the animal's neck. He gathered the reins and nodded toward the dirt trail in front of them. "Ready?"

Callie nodded, but the look in her eyes had him wondering if her heart matched her head.

He clicked his tongue and nudged Dante with his inner knee. Callie did the same.

He rode down the middle of the trail with Callie to his right along the fence line. She sat straight in the saddle, her arms pinned tightly to her sides, and her jaw clenched. He reached over and touched her arm, her skin smooth and soft against his calloused fingers. "Remember to relax and move with Patience."

As they continued down the path, Callie relaxed a little. While she still sat straight, her arms loosened.

Ahead of them, the late afternoon sun cast a glow across the pasture, spotlighting the rich green grass and turning it to gold.

A light breeze cooled his heated skin and caused purple flowers in the fields to sway. Black and red Angus cows grazed in the fenced pastures. Gray mountain ranges peaked against a cobalt blue sky. The horses' steady clomping set a rhythmic pace and prevented a need to fill the tranquil silence.

Perfect day to forget about his worries.

If only it were that easy.

"Feeling okay?"

She nodded and shot him a tight smile.

The grass stirred beside Patience. A quail flew away suddenly, flapping its wings in front of the mare.

Patience danced back, jerking her head up. Her ears flickered back and forth. Her eyes widened and nostrils flared as she snorted.

Callie shot him a panicked look and pulled on the reins, yanking Patience's head up.

Wyatt brought Dante to a stop, then dismounted quickly. He moved slowly to the mare. Careful to not to get kicked, he reached for one of the reins. He pulled it toward his foot and brought her to a stop. Once she calmed, he pressed a gentle hand on her forehead. "Easy, girl. It's okay. Just a bird."

He glanced at Callie, whose eyes were as wide as Patience's. Her knuckles whitened against the other rein wrapped around her hand. He covered her hands and squeezed gently. "Hey, it's okay. Relax. Breathe. You're safe."

Callie lifted a shaky hand and ran it over her face. "That was…unexpected."

"Yeah. Patience is used to riding the trails, so I'm not sure why the bird spooked her. Are you sure you're okay?"

Callie nodded, but he wasn't convinced. He didn't want her to feel skittish around the horses, especially since she was going to spend much of her summer being exposed to them.

Wyatt lifted his hat and swiped his forearm across his brow as his own heartbeat returned to a steady rhythm.

"Maybe going down the trail was a mistake. Perhaps we should've ridden around the arena at the ranch until you're more familiar with being in the saddle again."

She shook her head. "No, I'm good. I promise. Let's keep riding."

"You sure?"

She expelled a deep breath, then rolled her shoulders. Gathering the reins in her left hand again, she nodded.

Wyatt mounted Dante, then turned the horse until he faced her. "The horse rescue is up ahead. I can feed and water the horses quickly. Or we can return to the guest ranch."

"I'll give you a hand."

He shot her a smile. "We'll make it a quick trip, I promise."

As they rode toward the back gate, Callie's arms and shoulders relaxed.

"You appear less tense on Patience, considering the way she spooked a few minutes ago."

She laughed. "I'm a great pretender. She is a gentle horse, but that was a little scary for a moment. Hopefully nothing else distracts her again."

"Yeah, that was a little weird for her to react that way, but we handled it."

"We? More like you. I tried not to panic."

"Not panicking is a huge part of it."

The trail widened, and he dropped back alongside Callie rather than walking in front of her. "The back gate is around this next bend. We'll ride through the pasture and head to the barn."

Ahead of them, the trail forked. The right path led them to his in-laws' horse farm.

A couple of chestnut Morgan geldings grazed along the fence line. They lifted their heads. Seeing Wyatt and Callie, they bolted across the pasture.

Callie sucked in a breath.

"You okay?" Wyatt turned to her.

She pointed toward the skittish horses galloping away from them. "I'll never get used to seeing their ribs."

Wyatt's jaw tightened as he nodded. "Ray rescued them from a kill lot a couple of months ago. They were malnourished and abused. They won't let him near them, but they are coming into the barn now, so that's a plus. Another reason why what Ray's doing is so important—protecting these beautiful animals and giving them peace."

"I really admire what you guys're doing."

"Thanks. We can't do it alone, but it can begin with just one."

Wyatt led the way into the barn, then dismounted. He held on to Patience while Callie practically jumped off her back. He hid a grin as she winced and put her hands on her thighs.

She was going to be sore tomorrow.

Wyatt showed her where the grain was kept and how to add it to each feeder attached to the stalls. While she did that, he headed upstairs and dropped bales of hay through the floor door. When he returned to the first floor, she'd filled the final feeder.

He pulled apart one of the bales and dropped flakes of hay in each of the stalls. Then Wyatt showed her how to rinse the buckets and refill them with fresh water.

Charlie, the blind pony, nickered as Callie approached his stall. Callie talked to him in a soothing voice as she had earlier to Patience. The horse's ears perked as he lifted his nose and nuzzled her palm.

"You're much calmer than the last time you visited Charlie. That's what he needs."

She turned to him, her eyes filled with sadness. "I can't stop thinking about the visible ribs on those other two horses."

"It gets me too." He waved a hand across the stalls. "The good news is that all ten of the horses Ray's brought to the rescue are beginning to thrive. We're done with feeding, so let's head back to the guest ranch. Dinner will be served soon, then we'll have a campfire. Planning to stick around?"

She nodded, but kept her eyes on the pony. Then she fell in step with him as they headed to the door. "I just don't get it."

"Get what?"

"How people can mistreat animals like that."

"I hear you. If I can help make a difference with at least one, then that's one horse who will have a new purpose."

"Is there anything else that can be done?"

Wyatt laughed low in his throat. "There's always plenty that needs to be done. Problem is, Ray's stubborn and won't let me do much. I did manage to talk him into offering monthly sponsorships. So now the sponsors come on a weekly basis to care for their horses and help with the grooming, but there's always something that needs to be done."

"I'm sure every bit helps." He held on to Patience while Callie mounted her, with a little more confidence this time. "What about you? Your time is maxed out too."

Wyatt's fingers curled around the saddle horn. "I'm fine."

"Right." Her raised eyebrow showed she didn't believe a word he said.

He settled himself in the seat and guided Dante through the pasture. "I still hope I can talk Ray into agreeing to turning this place into a sanctuary."

"What's holding him back?" Callie moved alongside him.

"Asking for help was tough for Ray, and I don't think he's ready to relinquish control just yet. I'd love to be a partner and keep him invested without having to carry the burden."

"You'd carry it for him. That's what you do."

Wyatt lifted a shoulder. "I'm fine."

"There's that word again. When was the last time you weren't fine?"

Wyatt squinted against the sun and swallowed several times as a memory of Linnea's funeral surfaced—one he rarely allowed himself to see. "The night my wife died."

Callie leaned over and laid a hand on his shoulder. "Of course. I'm sorry. I shouldn't have been so callous."

He drew up the reins and brought Dante to a stop. He looked at her, then focused on the field next to him. "When I was a kid, my mom and I were in an accident. She hit her head pretty hard and needed to be taken to the hospital by ambulance. I was terrified and maybe even crying, I think. She tried to reach for me and comfort me, but one of the police officers pulled me back. He was a gruff old-timer who knew my grandparents. He said I needed to be strong and brave and hold it together for my mom's sake. She was upset enough and couldn't worry about me too. At the hospital, everyone praised how brave I was being. So ever since, that's what I do—I keep it together for everyone else so they don't worry about me."

"Oh, Wyatt. That cop was so wrong. It's not up to you to carry everyone else's emotions."

He dismounted and reached for Patience's harness. "After Linnea died, I left the Marine Corps instead of re-upping and came back to the ranch because I wasn't strong enough for my daughter. I kind of fell apart, and it wasn't fair to her."

Callie climbed down and faced him. Her eyes shimmered as she pressed a hand against his cheek. "You'd lost your wife. Your response was expected and even necessary. How many times have I said grief is tricky? Just when you think you're fine, those waves of emotion crash over you, threatening to drown you. You're strong, but not because of your muscles or how you hold it together for everyone else." Her hand moved slowly to his chest and she palmed the area around his heart. "You're strong because of your faith that feeds your strength and empowers you to keep going. You don't have to be fine around me. Be you, no matter how you feel."

Wyatt sucked in a breath as her words swirled around in his head. Other than family, no one had worried about him since Linnea. He missed having that special someone in his corner.

What would it be like to have someone to

lean on again? Someone to see him and still support him when he was feeling weak? Someone to hold his hand without telling him to suck it up?

Someone like Callie.

Without taking time to think it through, he covered Callie's hand, then slid his fingers into hers. He drew her closer and cradled her other cheek.

Her breath caught and her eyes widened.

He lowered his head and kissed her gently. She released his hand and slid her arms around his neck as he tightened his embrace, breathing in the scents of sunshine, fresh air and the barn.

A moment later, he reluctantly dragged his mouth away from hers and released his hold but didn't let her go. She pressed her cheek on his chest and he rested his chin on top of her head, trying to get a handle on his ragged breathing.

Until this moment, he'd kissed only one woman in his life, but she was gone.

What would it be like to put the past where it belonged and focus on his present…and perhaps his future?

Falling in love meant risking his heart once again. He wasn't ready to do that. Or was he?

What about Callie? She had her own pain to work through.

Would she want to take the risk too?

# CHAPTER EIGHT

CALLIE WASN'T SPEECHLESS very often, but that unexpected kiss had stolen her breath…and her words.

She wanted nothing more than to stay in Wyatt's arms forever, but they needed to get back to the guest ranch.

She closed her eyes as she listened to the steady rhythm of his heart in her ear. She needed to say something, but she was afraid to lose this moment.

What had he been thinking kissing her like that? And what did that mean moving forward? Did she dare ask him? What if she didn't like his answer?

"You're quiet."

"I'm not sure what to say."

"I hope I didn't upset you."

Her head jerked up, nearly connecting with his chin. "Upset me? How?"

"By kissing you."

She shook her head, a little more forcefully than necessary. "No. Not at all."

"So you wouldn't be upset if I did it again?"

"You want to kiss me again?"

A slow smile spread across his face as his hands slid down her arms.

She soaked in the feel of his embrace, a place she'd dreamed of for years as a teenager.

But they weren't kids anymore, and this couldn't be a summer fling. At least not to her.

Wyatt tipped up her chin. "What are you thinking, Callie?"

"That I've wanted to do that since I was fourteen."

He laughed softly and drew her against him once again.

"But I also want to be sure this is happening for the right reasons," she said.

"What would those right reasons be?"

Ignoring the voices in her head screaming not to, she stepped back from him. She gazed at Dante and Patience grazing close by. Wrapping her arms around her waist so she wouldn't reach for him again, she looked at him. "The day I came to Stone River was supposed to have been my wedding day."

His eyes widened. "Are you serious? You never said anything."

She shrugged. "I didn't want to talk about it. Instead of walking down the aisle on what should've been one of the happiest days of my life, I holed up at an unfamiliar guest ranch, cried myself to sleep, then woke and decided to figure out what was next for my life."

"What happened? With the wedding, I mean. Although, if you don't want to share, that's fine. I get it."

She shook her head. "It's okay. Shawn and I had a difference of opinions."

"Every couple has differing opinions."

"True, but I believed I should have been the only woman in his life. He believed that he could cheat on me with a coworker and everything would still be okay."

"What a jerk."

"I could have forgiven him and worked it out through counseling, but then I learned she was pregnant. With the three of us teaching at the same elementary school outside of Denver, it would've been so awkward." Callie glanced at her bare hand where the carat diamond used to be. "I taught art while he taught Phys Ed and coached high school track. My parents were in

Chile, and my brothers were in college. When Gram had her stroke after Christmas, I decided to take a leave of absence to care for her. I'd call Shawn nearly every day to stay connected, but he'd talk only a few minutes, claiming to be busy. He gave me some excuse as to why he couldn't come to Gram's funeral. I decided to head back to Denver without letting him know so I could surprise him. When I went to his apartment, he wasn't home, but his girlfriend was. And it was apparent she'd been there for a while. I went to the track at the high school where he was coaching, gave him back the ring, and told him to have a nice life."

"Wow, Callie, I'm so sorry. That stinks."

Tears clouded her vision as the humiliation surfaced all over again. "Gram tried to tell me Shawn wasn't the right guy for me, but I wouldn't listen."

"Love is blind for a reason."

"I don't know. I mean, I'm not even sure if I truly loved him. I think I loved the idea of being with him and starting a family someday. Once my parents left for South America, I was so lonely and he filled that void." She blew out a breath and faced him. "So, I guess those right reasons would be you kissed me because you wanted to kiss *me*. Not because you're lonely or the circumstances felt right."

Wyatt laughed softly as his mouth slid into another slow half grin. He reached for her hand and drew her closer. He traced his thumb over the curve of her cheek. "Until today, I've kissed only one woman in my life. And she's gone. I can't change that. What I can change is my future. Since I saw you on the side of the road that day, I haven't been able to stop thinking about you. I kissed you because I wanted to. I find myself thinking about you even when I'm busy with very little time for anything else."

Standing on her tiptoes, Callie brushed a light kiss on his lips. "Thank you."

"For what?"

"For being honest."

Wyatt pressed his forehead against hers. "Honesty creates some complications."

"Such as?"

"Well, technically, I'm your boss."

Callie's stomach tightened as her gaze dropped to the toes of her boots. "I'd forgotten about that. Does this mean I need to quit? Find a teaching job?"

"Only if that's what you want. Personally, I love being around you."

"It may not be that simple."

"Why not?"

"While I love working at the ranch, teaching offers benefits such as insurance and retirement."

"Again—is that what you truly want to do?"

"No, but I may need to settle. Especially if Gram's shop proves to be more work than it's worth."

He tipped her head until he captured her eyes with his and framed her face with his hands. "Callie, listen to me. Never settle. Not with me or anyone else. Not with doing what you love. God gave you a talent, and He will show you the way it's to be used."

She mulled on his words. Being with him wouldn't be settling. Definitely not. But she couldn't say that. Not now. And maybe not ever.

FOR THE FIRST time in three and a half years, Wyatt didn't want to be sitting in the basement of his church, surrounded by the dozen or so single fathers who'd become like brothers to him.

He'd started the single father support group when Mia was only six months old, and the weekly get-togethers had helped him through the trials and challenges of single parenting.

Sure, he'd had his family helping out, and he'd truly appreciated them. After losing his wife and trying to be both mother and father to his daughter, he'd needed to be with guys who understood. Guys who walked the same road. Guys who could rally around one another and help them get through life.

Tonight, he realized he'd rather be back at the guest ranch, seeing Callie as she managed the daily activities, played with the kids, picked flowers with his daughter and smiled at him.

At least she was only a few doors down caring for Troy's two boys. When she learned Troy's mom couldn't watch the boys any longer, she'd offered to care for them so he could attend the support group.

One more reason why he couldn't stop thinking about her. In fact, it took everything in his power to remain in the room.

He looked around at the guys who sat on beige armchairs and half a dozen folding chairs in a semicircle, holding ceramic mugs of strong coffee and eating blueberry muffins he'd picked up from his aunt's diner.

Wyatt headed to the coffee maker and topped off his cup. Then he took one of the empty armchairs near the front of the room. He placed his mug on the side table, leaned forward with his elbows resting on his knees, and clasped his hands. "Okay, guys. How about if we get started? Who wants to lead the prayer?"

Troy raised his hand. Once the rest of the guys found places to sit, he opened in prayer.

Amens echoed around the circle.

Scanning the room, Wyatt rubbed his hands together. "How's it going?"

Several of the guys bobbed their heads, but no one spoke immediately.

Ryan, one of the newer members of the group, set his cup on the floor, and then braced his forehead in his hand. "Well, I went on my first date since my marriage ended two years ago. Paid through the nose for a sitter. Got dressed up. Met her at a nice restaurant in Durango."

Wyatt raised an eyebrow. "How'd that go?"

Ryan shook his head. "Disaster, man. Absolute disaster. This whole online dating thing is not for me, I guess. She didn't like the food. She talked about reality TV shows. I think I only said three words the entire night. We definitely weren't a match." He imitated holding a phone and swiping. "I'd like to meet a nice girl at church. Not some phony who shows up looking nothing like her profile pic."

A couple of the guys burst out laughing and nodded. "Yep, been there, dude."

"At least you tried, man." Troy, sitting in the chair next to Wyatt, lifted his chin toward Ryan. Then he glanced at Wyatt. "When should we start dating again? My wife left two years ago as well."

Wyatt rubbed his hands on his thighs, then reached for his coffee. "I don't have that answer, man. It's different for everyone. You feeling ready?"

He shrugged. "I don't know. Who has the time? After working all day, I have to pick up the boys from day care, feed them, bathe them, spend time with them, and then it's bedtime. Plus, there's dishes, laundry. How do you find the time to even look for someone to date?"

"I hear you. I'm right there with you. You guys all know what it's like to manage a busy schedule."

Troy jerked a thumb toward the back of the church where children's laughter could be heard. "At least you have it easy."

Wyatt scowled. "Easy? How do you figure that?"

He grinned. "Callie. Your new guest ranch manager."

Wyatt's stomach tightened as he straightened

in his chair and seared Troy with a direct look. "Yeah. What about her?"

"Just sayin', man. You're spending all that time together. You trying to say nothing's going on between you two?"

Wyatt clenched his teeth as he tamped down on the words choking his throat. Needing to get a grip, he leaned back in the chair and tried to look relaxed. "Callie and I are just friends. I've known her since we were kids. I told you that."

"Just friends, huh?"

"That's what I said."

Troy's eyes narrowed as he shot Wyatt a wolfish grin. "So, you'd be okay with me asking her out?"

Wyatt fisted his fingers. "I wouldn't suggest it."

"Why not?"

"Because then I'd have to deck you, and I don't want to mess with the group dynamic like that."

Troy let out a howl and slapped his leg. He thrust a finger at Wyatt. "I knew it, man. I've seen the way you watched her. What's going on?"

"I told you—we're just friends."

"Aww, come on, Wyatt." Troy circled a finger

around the group. "We're tight, right? What's said here stays here."

Wyatt scanned the group of men who'd experienced similar types of loss and dragged a hand over his face. He stood, moved to the door and closed it, shutting out the laughter from down the hall. His hand tightened on the knob. "Callie and I are just friends."

"You keep saying that." Troy leaned forward. "But…"

Wyatt held out a hand. "A gentleman doesn't kiss and tell."

As soon as he'd said the words, he wished he'd kept his mouth shut. Especially when whoops, hoots and claps erupted around the room. Heat climbed up his neck.

What a bunch of jerks.

Troy shot him another grin, looking very pleased with himself. "You kissed her."

It wasn't a question but a statement.

One that Wyatt couldn't refute. And he didn't want to. He'd thoroughly enjoyed that kiss. And hopefully, he could do it again.

But he wasn't about to share those intimate details with a bunch of guys. Or with anyone else, for that matter. That was private between him and Callie.

But he could share what was in his heart, especially if it gave the other guys the hope they needed to move forward in finding a second chance. Wasn't that why they were there—to support each other in all areas of their life?

Wyatt settled back in the chair and took a sip of coffee. "I've known Callie for years. Growing up, she used to visit Ada during summers and holidays, and we'd hang out. She recently moved to Aspen Ridge and needed a job, so I offered her one. I had no intentions of getting involved with her or anyone else. While I'll always love my wife, I'm beginning to realize I do not have to live the rest of my life alone. I'm not in a rush to get married, but let's just say I'm a little more open than I was even a month ago."

He palmed his cup with his left hand, and his ring clicked against the ceramic. He looked down at the platinum wedding band. He set the mug on the table. Taking a deep breath, he wiggled the ring, very slowly, from side to side and slid it off his finger.

Releasing his breath, he held up the band that he had worn for nearly a decade. "Linnea and I married so young. Never in a million years did I expect to lose her giving birth to our daughter. Celebrating Mia meant remembering what we'd lost that day over and over and over again.

The other night, Callie and I went riding. And we talked. The kiss wasn't planned, but it happened, and I don't regret it."

He paused, swallowed past the lump in his throat and tightened his fingers around the wedding band. He glanced at his left hand, where only a pale line remained. "I'm ready to move on. But, to be honest, I really have no idea how to do it."

He reached for his coffee cup again and his fingers trembled slightly. Instead of forcing the band back onto his finger, he stretched out a leg and slid the ring into his front pocket. Then he wrapped both hands around his cold cup before he could yank it back out of his pocket.

A slow clap sounded, then escalated.

Wyatt's head jerked up. Troy stood and placed a hand on his shoulder. "That took guts, man."

Wyatt glanced at him. "The kiss?"

Troy shook his head. "No, bro. The ring. You really are ready to move on."

He stared into his mug. "Thanks, man."

He pushed to his feet and walked to the coffee maker to refill his cup. Taking a sip, he turned back to see the guys still watching him. "I think many of us are ready to move on. Maybe the best way to do it is to take that first step. Meet the girl. It's not going to be easy. I've watched Macey and Bear muddle through their relationships. But now they have their families. And I want that, too."

Troy planted a fist on his hip. "I can't speak for anyone else, but fear is a great motivator to stay single. My wife was the girl next door. Or so I thought. I didn't realize she was living a secret life as an alcoholic. How could I have been so blind? Now, part of me is afraid to take a chance because how can I trust my own instincts when I screwed up so badly the first time?"

Murmurs rumbled through the room as heads nodded. Several of the guys had gone through a divorce. A couple, like Wyatt, were widowers. And a couple had become single fathers out of wedlock.

"I don't know what to tell you, Troy. You can't paint everyone with the same brush. And I think that goes for the women we meet and decide to date." Wyatt removed one of the Bibles off the bookshelf behind him and held it up. "We need to stay true to God's Word. Give your fears and frustrations over to Him. Ask for His wisdom and guidance as we step into the dating pool once again. He'll connect us with the right women. When He's leading the way, and we're walking in step with Him, then we won't go wrong. We'll find those relationships that will, hopefully, last a lifetime."

Before anyone could comment, a cry sounded from down the hall. A moment later, someone knocked on the door.

Troy crossed behind Wyatt's chair and opened it. Callie stood in the doorway, holding one of his sons in her arms. Three-year-old Ezra had a red mark on his cheek and tears running down his face. "I'm sorry for interrupting, but Ez fell off his chair and smacked his cheek on a toy. He wants his daddy."

Troy took his son from Callie and gathered him in his arms. "Hey, buddy. What's going on?"

"I fell. I hurt my cheek."

Troy kissed his son's cheek, then used the hem of his T-shirt to dry the little boy's face.

"I'm sorry that hurt. Daddy's in a meeting. Will you be okay with Miss Callie for a couple more minutes?"

He nodded and wiggled out of Troy's arms.

Wyatt's eyes connected with Callie's. She mouthed, "Sorry."

Wyatt shook his head and waved away her apology.

She lifted the little boy in her arms, pressed

a kiss on his red cheek, then guided his head to her shoulder. She gave the group a wave. "Sorry, guys."

Troy closed the door and pressed his hand against the frame. Then he turned and locked eyes with Wyatt, his face serious. "Wyatt, I'm going to give it to you straight, man. Let go of your fear, and take a chance on that woman. Because if you don't, someone else is going to snatch her up very quickly. She's the kind of girl that we're all looking for."

Wyatt nodded, digesting his friend's words.

Troy was right.

Callie was the kind of woman he could see being a part of his life.

Even though he was now a little more open to the idea of having a relationship, was he ready for a real date?

He couldn't answer that. He needed to take his own advice—ask God for wisdom because he didn't have much faith in his own.

# CHAPTER NINE

CALLIE COULDN'T BE more pleased with the way the shop was shaping up.

And that was partly thanks to Wyatt and his willingness to help.

Even though the walls were now refreshed with a lemony yellow paint that made the main room seem so much bigger and brighter, Callie couldn't keep ignoring the upstairs if she wanted to stay on schedule with the new reopening.

Fatigue settled in her bones, and her muscles ached from moving different pieces of furniture back in place. She decided against refinishing the floors, choosing to scrub them by hand and oil them to bring out the shine.

Now she wanted nothing more than to turn off the cottage lights and head back to the guest ranch and get some sleep.

No campfire for her tonight. She needed to

carry the boxes upstairs to be sorted later. Then she could collapse into bed.

Only to do most of it all over again tomorrow.

Cradling a box of stained glass supplies against her stomach, Callie headed for the back steps. Her foot paused. And she sighed.

This was ridiculous. She needed to go up sooner or later. She couldn't avoid it forever.

Closing her eyes, she exhaled, then opened them and forced herself to climb the dimly lit staircase.

She turned the knob that led to Gram's apartment for the first time since the funeral, pushed it open and nearly tumbled back down the steps at the rank, musty smell.

She dropped the box on the floor beside the small table inside the door and winced at the sound of breaking glass.

Callie hurried through the small four-room apartment, trying to find the source of the odor.

The smell worsened the closer she came to the bedroom with the attached master bath. Forcing her attention away from Gram's neatly made bed, Callie pivoted toward the bathroom door and opened it.

The stench had her stumbling away from the doorway.

She pulled the neck of her T-shirt up over her nose as she fought to gain control of her gag reflex.

Black mold spotted the lavender rug in front of the sink. Brownish water stains rippled across the dated linoleum. The bottom edge of the vanity doors bulged.

Breathing through her mouth, Callie flung open the door and groaned.

Greenish-brown rust corroded the drain-pipe under the sink, causing a hole where water trickled down the side.

Callie checked the plastic knobs, but they were off.

So where was the water coming from? Why couldn't she smell it downstairs?

After the funeral, she'd convinced her parents to keep the utilities turned on because she expected to spend a lot more time at the shop than she had.

Callie grabbed the corner of the throw rug and held it at arm's length. She carried it into the small kitchen and tossed it into the bagless trash can. She'd deal with that later.

She returned to the bathroom and grabbed a handful of towels out of the narrow linen closet next to the shower. She knelt in front of the vanity, folded several and piled them around the leaking pipe. They were soaked with water within seconds.

What was she going to do? Maybe her dad would know.

She grabbed the top of the vanity with her wet hand and started to stand. Her fingers slipped. As she tried to catch her balance, her foot slid out from under her on the wet floor. She slammed her right arm and shoulder against the tub and dropped her weight on her wrist.

A pop sounded and fire shot up her arm. She grabbed her arm and cradled it against her body as she tried to stand again. Again, her foot failed to gain traction.

Tears filled her eyes as the pain rippled across every nerve. Her head pounded as her stomach churned. Using her left hand, she pushed away from the vanity and scooted across the floor until she reached the doorway. She stretched, grabbed onto the doorknob and pulled herself into a standing position.

Bile clawed at her throat as her head swirled. She blinked several times and stumbled to her grandmother's bed.

With shaking fingers, she pulled out her phone and then paused.

Who could she call?

The lights were off next door, so she knew that Ray and Irene weren't home.

Exhaling, she called up Wyatt's number on her phone and pressed the speakerphone button.

After three rings, he answered, "Hey, Callie."

"Wyatt, I need you."

"What's wrong?"

"I'm at the shop." Her heart raced as tears blurred her vision. "There's a water leak. And I fell. I can't move my arm or shoulder. I don't know what to do." Her voice cracked. She dropped her head in her hand and pressed her thumb and middle finger against her soggy eyes.

"It's okay, Callie. I'm coming. I'll be there in fifteen minutes. Okay?"

"Okay."

He ended the call.

Pushing off the bed, she clutched the phone and made her way through the apartment and down the stairs. She found her purse on the counter next to the register and lifted it over her head and across her body.

Then she sat on the wooden bench and waited.

She clutched her upper arm and sucked in a sharp breath as another realization hit.

Without her teaching job, she no longer had medical insurance. And very little money left in her savings. How was she going to afford a trip to the ER?

Moving to Aspen Ridge had drained her. In more ways than one.

If she had a broken arm or wrist, how was the injury going to affect her job? And the work that needed to be done at Gram's shop?

What if she needed surgery like Ray?

Her heart raced as the what-ifs seared her brain. Sweat broke out on her forehead as the heaviness tightened in her chest.

The back door flew open. "Callie?"

"In here." Her voice came out as a squeak.

Wyatt strode through the shop and knelt in front of her.

The sight of him sent a wave of relief through her and she burst into tears.

He pulled her against his chest and gently wrapped his arms around. "Hey, it's going to be okay. I'm here."

As much as she wanted to believe him, he couldn't be more wrong.

Despite his assurances, it wasn't going to be okay, and Callie had no idea how she was going manage to open the shop now.

AFTER RETURNING FROM the emergency department with an emotionally wrung-out Callie, Wyatt had tossed and turned most of the night.

The heaviness in his chest beat away any hopes of sleep.

Somehow, though, he'd managed to drift in the early hours. And he must've hit snooze or turned the alarm off altogether because he woke up to a cute little girl sitting in his bed with Ella the Elephant and her favorite book.

She giggled when he threw back the covers that landed on her head and hurried out of bed. But he wasn't in a playful kind of mood.

He had a team to lead.

But first, he needed coffee if he was going to function today.

"Wyatt, you in there?" His mother's voice sounded muffled as she knocked on his front door.

Wearing only his jeans and T-shirt, he hurried out of the kitchen and to the living room in his bare feet. His big toe hit the edge of the door as he opened it. He groaned loudly in pain.

He yanked the door open. "Hey, Mom."

"You okay? You missed breakfast. And your dad said you didn't show up for chores this morning."

Wyatt dragged the edge of the towel over his face. "Yeah, sorry about that. I overslept."

Mom crossed her arms over her chest and shot him a pointed look. "You never oversleep."

"Yeah, well, I did today." He cringed at the growl in his voice.

Stepping inside, she shot him the same mom look he'd gotten many times as a teen when he'd gotten mouthy. "I was afraid of this—you're overdoing it. What's going on?"

The way her voice softened and held compassion took him back to the years when he could crawl into her lap and she'd make everything better.

He forced a smile. "Nothing, Mom. I'm fine."

She folded her arms over her chest. "When you were younger, you got in trouble for lying to me."

"What are you going to do? Ground me?"

"Oh, honey, if only it were that simple." Mom's forehead creased as she pressed a hand against his unshaven cheek. "I worry about you."

Wyatt brushed a kiss across her knuckles. "No need. I'm good. I'll grab some socks and boots and meet you at the guest ranch."

"If Mia's ready to go, I'll take her back to the ranch with me to save you some time."

"Thanks, Mom." He kissed her cheek, hoping to smooth out the lines creasing her forehead. "I'm fine—I promise."

Fifteen minutes later, with a steaming to-go mug of coffee in hand, Wyatt stepped out of his SUV. He headed across the grass where three families gathered around picnic tables enjoying the buffet his mom and Everly had made.

Morning sunshine streamed through the trees, striping the ground in gray and gold. A breeze blew through the leaves. A boy around five or six chased after a wayward napkin.

Callie sat in the shade by the lodge along with two girls who had to be around nine or ten. She'd laid her right arm—which was in a wrist splint—on the picnic table. Colored pieces of glass lay on a tray between them. Sunlight glinted off the shards, sending a spectrum of colors across the table.

As he moved closer, his shadow stretched across the table. "Morning."

Callie looked up and shielded her eyes. "Good morning."

"Sorry for being late. I overslept. How's it going?"

"Good. We're making faux stained glass suncatchers. Want to join us?"

"Suncatchers? Like what your grandma used to make? Is that safe?"

"These are faux suncatchers. We're using acetate and Sharpie markers to color in our designs. They're outlined with black glue to mimic the soldering. Perfectly safe."

He looked at the girls who were using permanent markers to color in their designs. One had made a heart while the other had created a rainbow.

He shook his head. "No, thanks. I have to get the horses ready for the trail ride."

"Bear and your dad left already."

"What do you mean they left already?"

"The trail ride started half an hour ago. When you weren't here, Bear called your dad. They both took the guests for this morning's ride."

"I wish you'd called me."

Callie's lips thinned. "Check your phone."

Setting his mug on the end of the table, Wyatt dug out his phone. Three missed calls. And a text from Callie—Hey, sleepyhead, get out of bed. There's work to do.

He'd never heard the phone ring. In his haste to get out the door, he hadn't bothered checking his messages either.

"Well, that's just perfect."

"Sit with us and relax a minute. It's okay to take a break."

"I said I don't have time." His words came out so sharply that both girls' heads shot up. They looked at each other with widened eyes, then ducked down to focus on their designs. Callie's cheeks turned as bright as the hot pink marker in her left hand.

He dragged a hand over his face. "I'm sorry."

She nodded but kept her attention on the piece of half-colored plastic in front of her.

He touched her shoulder. "Hey, you got a minute?"

She looked up and he jerked his head to the open doors that led into the lodge.

Her lips thinned again, but she nodded. "Sure." She looked at the girls. "I'll be right back."

They nodded as their eyes darted between Callie and Wyatt.

*Great first impression, idiot.*

Wyatt followed Callie into the lodge where the scents of coffee and bacon lingered. His stomach grumbled, reminding him of his lack of breakfast.

That wasn't all he lacked.

Moving so she could still see outside, Callie

cradled her right arm against her chest, raised an eyebrow and waited.

Yeah, he deserved that.

"Look—I'm sorry for snapping at you. I didn't mean it. I've been kicking myself for oversleeping and worrying my mom. I'm sorry for taking my frustration out on you." He touched her splint. "How's your wrist?"

"Painful. Sleeping last night wasn't fun. I'm trying not to do much. Which is tough, since I'm right-handed."

"Anything I can do to help?"

She raised an eyebrow. "You don't have time, remember?"

"I deserved that." He rubbed a hand over his jaw.

"Why is it okay for you to worry about others but no one's allowed to worry about you? You're taking care of everyone else, but who's taking care of you?"

"I'm fine."

"Right. And that's why you overslept. Your body is protesting your lack of sleep. Wyatt, I'm worried about you."

He held up a hand. "Don't. You have no reason to."

"That's right. You're fine. My mistake." She

dropped her arms to her side, then winced. Cradling her right arm against her stomach, she pushed past him.

He reached for her elbow. "Callie, wait."

She stopped but didn't turn.

He dropped his hand and blew out a breath. "I'm sorry. I know you're just being a good friend. I'm just not used to people worrying about me."

She whirled around, her eyes full of fire. "Then you're blind. If you'd take half a second to look around you, then you'd see how much your family worries. I've seen how your parents watch you. Everyone wants to be sure you're okay."

"That's just it—they have enough to worry about without adding me to their problems. I'm fine."

"If I had a dollar for every time you said you were fine, I wouldn't need to worry about money to renovate Gram's shop."

His jaw tightened. "I just don't want anyone to worry about me."

"Stop saying that! Why not?"

"Because it leads to heartbreak." The unexpected words felt like they'd been yanked from his chest, leaving a gaping hole exposing all of his vulnerabilities.

Needing some air, he tightened his grip on his nearly empty coffee mug and strode through the doorway. As he headed for his SUV, he kicked himself about a thousand times.

Hiring Callie was a mistake.

Not because she couldn't do the job, but because she was a distraction.

Problem was, he couldn't exactly let her go.

Somehow, he needed to figure out a way of working with her without letting his guard down.

Even though he'd said he was more open to letting someone in his life, actually doing it was a different matter.

Maybe he was kidding himself. Maybe he wasn't ready after all.

# CHAPTER TEN

WHY DID CALLIE allow Wyatt's mood to get under her skin, especially since she was the reason for his late night?

If she hadn't called for help after getting hurt, then he could've been home and gotten the sleep he needed. Spending five hours in the emergency room wasn't fun for anyone, but he'd insisted on staying even after she said she could drive back to the guest ranch.

She just needed to put him out of her mind and focus on the rest of her day. After all, the guy was entitled to an off day, just like anyone else.

Problem was, he wasn't just anyone else.

At least to her.

And that really bugged her because she couldn't be falling for someone so soon after her breakup. Didn't matter that she'd known

Wyatt for years. A month ago, she'd been about to get married.

She needed to get a hold of herself and focus on doing her job.

Now that the guest ranch families were either kayaking with Bear and Piper or hiking with Deacon and Nora, Callie needed to figure out a plan for the mess at the shop.

During breakfast, she'd asked Deacon and Nora for recommendations for plumbers and she called the first name they'd given her. Thankfully, the guy on the phone offered to meet with her that afternoon once she explained the situation, including her injured wrist.

She pulled into the empty space behind Gram's shop and parked next to the Pullman's Plumbing truck. Stepping out into the sunshine, she shielded her eyes as a tall man waited for her on Gram's back porch.

Wayne Pullman.

The man who was going to give her good news or ruin the rest of her day.

Removing his stained ball cap and revealing dark hair streaked with silver, he nodded to her. "Hey, there, Ms. Morgan."

"Mr. Pullman. Call me Callie. Please." Cradling her right arm, she stuck out her left hand.

He took it, giving her a firm shake. "Callie. Sorry to hear about your wrist."

"Thanks. I can deal with a fracture. I'm glad it wasn't worse."

If she had to guess, she'd say he was in his fifties. Or at least closer to her parents' ages rather than hers. Deep lines grooved his tanned face.

He nodded toward the door. "Let's head inside and see what the problem is."

She unlocked the door and stepped into the same room she'd visited several times over the past few weeks. Gram's faint scent still lingered despite the windows Callie had opened to air out the rooms.

Wayne gestured toward the second floor. "You said it was the upstairs bathroom, right?"

Nodding, Callie led the way up to the empty apartment.

Forcing herself to keep focus on the problem at hand and not the memories begging for her attention, she showed Wayne the way to the small bathroom and flicked on the light.

The door to the vanity hung open, revealing the same corroded pipes and base spotted with mold. She stepped back and gave him room to inspect the damage.

Wayne lay on the floor, pulled a small flashlight out of his shirt pocket and shined it against the underside of the sink basin. He made a few comments to himself, then slid out from under it and pushed to his feet.

"Yeah, as I expected, the seal around the water valve gave out." Wayne did a little bounce in front of the vanity. "Feel that spongy floor?"

She followed his movements, then nodded. "What about it?"

"Because the leak wasn't caught for a while, stagnant water soaked into the floor. A drip or two may not seem like a big deal, but when it goes unnoticed, it can create a lot of damage."

"I kind of expected that when the mat in front of the sink was wet and covered in mold. Pretty gross."

He crouched in front of the vanity and pulled up a lifted corner of one of the linoleum blocks. "With this much damage, the subflooring and joists may need to be replaced. Maybe even the walls, depending on how much the water damage has spread."

Callie's shoulders sagged as she leaned against the doorframe. "What about the shower and toilet?"

"Because of their age, I'd recommend replacing them as well so you don't have problems in the future, but it also depends again on the damage to the floor."

She glanced at the heavy porcelain tub and matching toilet that had been in Gram's apartment for as long as she could remember. "Hopefully it's minimal. I'd like to hold off replacing them until I take care of higher priorities."

Wayne headed out the door and waved her to follow. "Let's head downstairs and see if there's damage to the ceiling in the room below."

Again, she followed, her stomach tightening with every step.

Wayne disappeared into the small studio located behind the stairs where Gram held her classes. Hands on his hips, he stood in the middle of the room and looked up at the giant brown stain on the popcorn ceiling. "The ceiling needs to be replaced. But until we tear it out, we won't know the extent of the damage. We'll have to replace the insulation and all that. I'm concerned about the wiring as well. This house is pretty old, so I suspect it could be knob and tube."

"So, you're saying there may be an electrical issue in addition to plumbing repairs?"

"Honestly, we won't know until you get a qualified electrician to check it out. But if I were to speculate, then, yeah. Sorry. I know that's the news you don't want to hear." Wayne pulled a pen and small notepad out of his back pocket. He made several notes, then tore off the sheet and handed it to her. "I've been in this business for over thirty years. I won't have an exact cost until I can get back to the office, but here is a ballpark figure of what I'm estimating for repairs. In the meantime, I'll shut off the main water valve so the leaking stops."

Callie took the paper and scanned the scrawled numbers while Wayne shut off the valve. As she reached the total, her stomach clenched and she sucked in a breath. The estimate was way more than she had expected.

How was she going to afford this?

They talked for another minute, then turned off the lights and headed back outside. Callie locked the door.

She remained on the back porch while Wayne got into his truck and drove away.

Needing to get back to the ranch, she climbed into her car. She pressed a thumb and forefinger to her tired eyes. "Sorry, Gram, I don't know if I can afford to keep my promise."

As she backed down the drive, she remembered the Help Wanted sign in the animal shelter window she'd seen when she arrived in town.

Maybe Irene still needed help?

Could she manage another job while working at the guest ranch and trying to find time to get Gram's place ready?

She braked and headed for the front door to see if the sign was still in the window.

It was gone.

Maybe Wyatt's aunt Lynetta needed help at the diner. She wasn't sure when she'd have time, but she'd find it to earn the money needed for the water damage. Besides, it didn't hurt to ask.

Callie parked in front of the yellow-sided corner restaurant. Purple and yellow pansies spilled out of the window boxes attached to the front wall. White rockers sat on the newly added covered porch that spanned the front of the building.

She headed inside, the bell on the door signaling her arrival, and breathed in the rich scents of coffee, french fries and baked goods.

"Hi, Callie."

Callie turned in the direction of her name and found Mia standing in the booth next to her dad, waving her arm.

Callie moved toward their table. "Hey, Miss Mia. How're you doing?"

"Good. I went to the dentist. He counted my teeth." She gave Callie a toothy grin, then held out a limp fry covered in ketchup. "Want a french fry?"

"Thanks." Callie took it, careful not to drip ketchup on her gray T-shirt.

"Hey, Callie. Have a seat." Wyatt gestured to the empty space across from him.

She raised an eyebrow. "You sure?"

"Yeah, sure. Sit. Tired of ranch food?"

"No, actually, I stopped to see if Lynetta needed help at the diner." She set the soggy fry on the napkin Wyatt pushed toward her.

He eyed her a moment, then leaned back against the booth. He slung one arm over the top of the vinyl seat, then reached for his coffee. "You quitting on me? Because of this morning?"

"Nothing like that." She pulled the notebook paper from the plumber out of her purse and slid it across the table to Wyatt. "I need money to pay for renovations. The water damage I discovered last night at Gram's house comes with a hefty price tag. Managing the guest ranch is great. But it's not enough to pay for repairs, much less renovations. Even if I drain the rest

of my savings." She held up her splinted wrist.
"Especially when those medical bills come rolling in."

Wyatt scanned the numbers, then he whis-
tled quietly. "Man, I hope Wayne's not pulling
a fast one on you."

"Is it too high?"

"Not for a guy who runs his own business,
but it may break your budget."

"I don't have a budget. Just a pipe dream. I
want to make good on my promise, but the
shop may be nothing more than a money pit."
She didn't expect the sudden rush of tears and
blinked rapidly to keep it together.

She was so tired.

"Don't rush into a decision based on frustration and emotions. A couple of the guys in my
support group may be able to tackle this project at half the cost. Let me make some calls and
get back to you."

She slumped against the back of the booth.
"That would be great, Wyatt. Thank you. I appreciate it."

"Don't sweat it. They're a good bunch of guys
who don't mind helping out."

"Even for someone they don't know?"

"They know me, and they knew Ada. And

they've seen what you've done to help Troy. That's enough." He winked, causing her heart to skid against her ribs.

Once again, Wyatt had come to her rescue. Somehow, she needed to repay him without losing her heart in the process.

WYATT WAS RIGHT—CALLIE shouldn't settle. Not in her relationships. Or with her desire to live her life the way she wanted. And she planned to share that information with her father who was bound to ask about her future plans.

Callie had exactly seven minutes to find the courage to let her parents know she hadn't applied for local teaching jobs like they'd been hoping.

The microwave beeped, and Callie removed her mug. She unwrapped a chai tea bag and dropped it into the hot water. Then she set the mug on the table next to the love seat and reached for her laptop.

She crossed her legs and winced. Even a week after her ride with Wyatt, she still couldn't move without her body aching. Who knew it took so many muscles to ride a horse?

But she needed to get used to it if she planned to stick around.

After that kiss, she wasn't in a hurry to leave. The guest ranch or even Aspen Ridge. Ever.

Her phone chimed, signaling an incoming video call. Instead of answering, she opened up her laptop and clicked on the join call button.

Three other boxes popped up as her brothers and parents appeared on the screen.

She smiled and waved. "Hey, guys. How's it going?"

Both brothers had dark hair and green eyes like their parents, but Wesley looked more like their dad while Trevor favored their mother's side of the family. Both boys towered over her and used her head as an armrest every chance they had. Which wasn't too often these days.

Dad's thinning hair had more gray than the last time she'd seen him several months ago. Both of her parents had a look of peace that shone in their eyes.

Callie reached for her tea and settled into a more comfortable position as her brothers took turns talking about their summer jobs at the hospital near their campus. Then her parents gave an update on what was happening with their newly planted church.

Wesley, her youngest brother, folded his arms

and leaned back in his gaming chair. "You've been quiet, sis. What's going on with you?"

Callie shrugged, then winced. She rubbed the muscle in her upper arm. "Keeping busy at the guest ranch and working on the shop in my spare time, which isn't a whole lot."

Dad leaned forward and tilted their computer so they showed up better on the video. "Shouldn't you be applying for teaching positions?"

And there it was.

Callie's fingers tightened on her mug. "I'm not going back to the classroom, Dad."

"Callista, are you sure that's the best choice?"

Her father was the only person who used her full first name, especially when he was annoyed and didn't want to show it.

"It's the best choice for me. At least, right now. I gave Grandma my word. I'd think you'd want to see her legacy continued."

Mom laid a hand on Dad's arm. "Honey, she struggled to keep that shop afloat. We don't want you to have to struggle like that."

"Part of Grandma's struggle was not understanding technology. She did things the old-fashioned way. Once I reopen, I'll have a website set up along with social media accounts for advertising. I'll manage inventory and billing on my laptop."

"What about the building itself?"

"It needs some work." Not wanting a lecture, she didn't share the recent water issue with them.

Dad rubbed his jaw, then drummed his fingers on the table, shaking the laptop. "All right, then. If you're serious about this, we can help. Mom left us a little money too."

She shook her head. "No way. She left that for your church plant."

Someone knocked on her door.

"Hang on a minute. I'll be right back." She set her laptop on the cushion and hurried to the door.

She opened it and found Wyatt leaning against the doorframe. Her heart picked up speed. "Hey, Wyatt. What's up?"

He gave her a long, lazy look as a slow smile spread across his face. "I missed you. Busy?"

She ran a hand over her hair, cleared her throat and waved a hand toward the love seat. "I'm, uh, on a video call with my family."

He pushed away from the doorway, straightened, then took a step back. "Sorry for interrupting. I won't keep you. I'm heading to the rescue in a bit to tend to the horses if you want to give me a hand."

Alone time with Wyatt? Yes, please.

She glanced over her shoulder once again, then back at him and nodded. "I'd love to help. I'll give you a call when I'm done talking with my family."

"Sounds good." He winked as he walked backward toward the steps.

How was she supposed to return to her family after that?

She closed the door and then returned to her computer. "Sorry about that."

Mom raised an eyebrow. "Was that Wyatt Stone?"

"Yes, I'm going to go help him feed and turn out horses in a bit."

"He's cute. And single."

"Don't, Mom. I don't need someone else managing my love life. Falling in love only leads to heartbreak."

Dad wrapped an arm around Mom's shoulders and pulled her close. "Not always, honey. Give yourself time and you'll find the right man. Just make sure he treats you right."

Shawn had said all the right things in the beginning of their relationship, and look how that turned out.

But Wyatt was nothing like Shawn.

She shook her head. "I'm not sure Wyatt's ready to move on yet. He still loves his late wife. I won't compete with someone else again. Learned my lesson with Shawn."

"Shawn was unfaithful. Wyatt is a widower. There's a big difference."

"I don't have time to fall in love if I'm going to get Gram's shop reopened."

Trevor scooted closer to his computer. "Hey, sis. I'm sure you don't want to hear this, but I'd rather you heard it from us."

Callie had a feeling she knew what her brother was going to say, but she needed to hear it anyway. "Spill it."

"Shawn got married."

Just as she expected.

"When?"

"Last weekend."

"Last weekend?! A month after we were supposed to walk down the aisle? That's beautiful. Well, I wish him all the happiness in the world."

"Do you?" Wesley raised an eyebrow.

"What do you think, Wes?"

"I think he's a jerk, and you deserved better."

"Thanks, buddy."

After another couple of minutes, they said their goodbyes and ended the call.

Callie closed her laptop and pushed it onto the other cushion, then buried her face in her left hand.

A burst of laughter echoed from outside.

Callie glanced at her watch. Probably too late to call Wyatt now. He would've left for the rescue by now since he hoped to be back in time for the campfire.

She slipped her shoes on and headed for the door. Maybe a s'more would lighten the heaviness in her chest.

She hurried down the steps and headed out to the fire ring near the lake.

Wyatt's family and several of the guests had gathered in chairs around the crackling fire. Smoke spiraled toward the sky.

"Callie."

The sound of Wyatt's voice spiked her pulse as her heart slammed against her ribs.

She turned as Wyatt walked up to her. "You didn't call, so I figured you changed your mind."

"Actually, I just hung up with my family. Did you go to the rescue yet?"

He shook his head. "Want to join me?"

"Yes, but I meant to bring down a sweat-shirt. I'll run back upstairs, grab one and meet you down here."

"Mind if I walk up with you?" That same slow smile from earlier that turned her stomach to jelly creased his face.

"I don't mind. But won't your family miss you at the campfire?"

He glanced over his shoulder, and then looked back at her. "They're fine. They won't even know I'm gone." He frowned and tipped her chin. "You okay?"

She clasped her hands and dropped her gaze to her feet. "I'm fine."

"Who's the fibber now?"

"So you do admit you're not always fine."

"This isn't about me. You okay?"

She lifted her hands, then dropped them at her sides. "Yes. No. Maybe."

"Glad you clarified that. I love a woman who knows her mind."

Did he just say *love*?

*Don't be ridiculous.*

It was a joke. Nothing more.

"So, what's going on?"

The sincerity in his voice brought her head up and she locked her eyes with his.

"My ex got married last weekend. Can you believe that?" She scoffed and yanked on the door with a little more force than necessary.

Wyatt palmed the door over her head and held it for her to pass through. "And that upsets you."

"I don't know how I feel. I'm certainly not in love with him anymore. He's a jerk. I just… I don't know. We dated for four years before he even proposed. And then, it wasn't even a solid proposal. More like a suggestion. But with her, it was a matter of months." Callie's flip-flops slapped against the steps as she stomped up the stairs.

"So, if you're not upset, then…" His voice trailed off.

Callie whirled around so quickly she nearly slipped off the step. Wyatt caught her and steadied her. "I was thinking what you said during our ride."

"What's that?"

"That I shouldn't settle. With him I would've settled. I'm glad we're no longer together. I just wish…" She sighed and shoved her fingers through her hair.

She didn't even know what she wished for.

She turned and ran up the rest of the stairs.

At her door, Wyatt took a step toward her

and reached for her hands. "Maybe you're wishing for what could've been. Or maybe what should've been. Your breakup with him does not mean you have to spend the rest of your life alone."

Again, the warmth in his tone nearly undid her. She blinked back unexpected tears. "That means learning to trust and risk my heart all over again. What if another guy breaks it?"

Wyatt's eyes darkened as he ran his knuckles over her cheek. "Then he'd be an idiot."

She reached for his hand and squeezed. "Thanks. I don't know, maybe it's time I moved on too."

"What do you mean by moving on? You mean like with this job? With your life?"

"Not the job. I love it here. It's exactly what I needed when I arrived back in town. So thank you for that."

He tipped his hat at her. "Why, certainly, ma'am."

She laughed at his terrible Western drawl.

She opened the door to her suite and flipped on the light.

At least she'd made her bed today and tidied up before she left for breakfast.

Wyatt leaned against the doorframe while she grabbed a hoodie out of the closet.

She pulled it over her head and gathered her hair back into a quick ponytail.

"Okay, I'm ready."

But he wasn't looking at her.

In fact, he was looking at something over her shoulder.

She turned and groaned.

The watercolor she'd been working on lay on the small table.

He took a step toward the table. "May I?"

She wanted to grab it and toss it under the bed. Instead she shrugged and stiffened, waiting for some generic comment.

Wyatt lifted the paper and studied the watercolor she'd begun the morning after arriving at the guest ranch. His brows furrowed as his lips thinned.

He hated it.

"Callie." His voice came out as a whisper.

She fought back a shiver as she braced herself and lifted her chin.

But she didn't see disgust in his eyes. Instead, she saw something like...wonder, maybe?

The lines disappeared on his forehead and

around his mouth as he shook his head and waved a hand over the pad. "This is incredible."

Her cheeks warmed as she dropped her eyes to her toes. "Thank you."

He took two steps toward her and tipped her chin up to meet his eyes, his face serious. "I mean it. This is really, really good. There was a flyer hanging at the diner advertising an art show in Durango. You should submit this."

"What? No way." She reached for the painting. "It's not good enough. I think I told you already—it's the first time I'd picked up a brush since Gram died. It's far from my best work."

He let out a laugh. "If that's not good enough, then I can only imagine what your best looks like."

She glanced at the landscape depicting the ranch complete with a black horse like Dante, added after their ride, drinking from the river running through the property. "You really like it?"

"No."

She knew it.

He laughed. "No, I love it. I love the way that you captured Stone River and the ranch. And Dante."

She picked up an archival ink pen and scrawled her name and date in the corner. She held it out to him. "You can have it."

His eyes widened as he reached for the painting. "Are you serious?"

She hated how vulnerable she felt at the moment. "Sure, but don't be showing it around. It's not that great."

"You are severely underestimating your talent. Anyone who looks at this could see that." Still holding onto the paper, he cupped her cheek and ran a thumb over her jawline. Then he kissed her. "I've been waiting to do that for a week."

Callie's hands tightened on his arms. "What was stopping you?"

"I didn't want to rush you. You're going through a difficult time right now and I didn't want to take advantage of that."

"I appreciate that, but my feelings for my ex died the moment his girlfriend opened the door. His betrayal and the humiliation over my stupidity hurt more than losing him."

"Maybe it's time we both took a chance."

"What are you suggesting?"

The downstairs door slammed open. "Wyatt, you in here? Ray called—you're not answering your phone. Wants to know if you're planning to feed the horses."

Hearing his brother's voice, Wyatt sighed and touched his forehead to hers. "Can we pause this conversation for the time being?"

Callie nodded, not quite sure her voice was strong enough to answer anyway.

Just what *was* Wyatt suggesting?

She didn't want to jump to conclusions and end up humiliated again, but if he was thinking what she was hoping, then she was all in.

Because being with Wyatt certainly wasn't settling.

And she'd simply have to trust that he wouldn't break her heart.

## CHAPTER ELEVEN

WYATT REFUSED TO let Ray's gruffness get to him. If the man needed someone to blast, better it be him than Irene.

He could take it. And ignore it.

He'd arrived at the rescue to feed and turn out the horses and found Ray sitting in the barn. He mentioned something about getting into an argument with Irene about his physical therapy sessions and needing some air.

Ray leaned on the walker he had graduated to using over the crutches. "I'm worried about her."

Wyatt didn't need to ask who. "She's a strong woman, Ray."

"Even strong women have their breaking points, Wyatt. I don't want my health to take a toll on her."

"Yes, they do, sir." Wyatt dug the pitchfork into the hay and removed soiled bedding. He dumped it into the wheelbarrow, then poked the fork into the hay. "Go apologize for being… well, your grumpy and stubborn self. She'll forgive you. She always does. Then focus on healing instead of fighting her about doing your therapy exercises."

Ray closed his eyes and rubbed his forehead.

Wyatt returned to mucking the stall, tossing clean bedding against the wall.

"I want you to have the rescue."

Wyatt's head shot up. "Excuse me?"

Ray opened his eyes and sighed. "You heard me."

Wyatt's fingers tightened around the handle of the pitchfork. "You want me to have the rescue?"

Ray shifted and sat on the walker seat. He braced his elbows on the handles and clasped his hands in front of him. "Irene and I talked last night, and we're in agreement—we want you to have the rescue and turn it into the sanctuary Linnea always wanted."

"But—"

Ray scowled and jabbed a finger in Wyatt's direction. "Son, you've been pestering me for weeks now to buy the horse rescue. Now that I'm giving it to you, you're arguing with me? Make up your mind."

Wyatt exited the stall and leaned the fork against the wall. He moved in front of Ray and held up a hand. "I'm not arguing. I guess I'm not understanding why now."

Ray lifted his hands and then dropped him back in his lap. "What's not to understand?"

Wyatt blew out a breath and forced a patient tone into his voice. "Why do you want to give me the rescue?"

"I just told you…to turn it into the sanctuary that Linnea always wanted."

"I get that. But why now?"

"I'm not able to get around like I used to. Time to face facts."

"Come on, Ray. Don't talk like that. Once your cast is off, you'll regain strength in your leg and be back at it in no time."

"I'm not being a pessimist, but a realist. Take the rescue and begin the proceedings to turn it into a sanctuary so you can qualify for those grants you talked about. That way Mia will have a legacy of her mama. But there are a couple of conditions."

"Such as?"

"Irene and I will keep the house and the animal shelter, but you can use the barn and the ranch as you see fit. I promise not to question or argue."

"I don't know what to say."

"Thank you will suffice."

"Thank you."

Ray reached over and gripped Wyatt's wrist. "You're the son I never had. After Linnea was born, we learned Irene couldn't have more children. She cried because she couldn't give me the son she thought I wanted. But I was more than thrilled with my baby girl. Unfortunately, I didn't have her long enough to let her know how much she meant to me." The older man's voice cracked.

Wyatt rested a hand on the man's shoulder. "She knew. She loved you guys with everything that she had."

Ray swallowed several times and nodded. He closed his eyes, but not before tears drifted down his cheek. "Irene and I have been talking about you."

Wyatt could handle Ray's grumpiness and brush it off. But this…this display of raw emotion that was so seldom seen…well, that was a little harder to come to grips with.

Wyatt worked his jaw. "That's what I've been hearing."

"You could've turned your back on us after Linnea passed, but you stuck around. Made sure we have plenty of time with Mia. You will always be our son. Mia is our granddaughter, of course. Just want you to know your future wife and any other children you have will be family too."

"I appreciate that, sir, but I just don't know if that's going to happen anytime soon. I could buy the rescue as a partner. You don't have to give it to me."

"Nope, it's a gift. If you ask to buy it one more time, then the deal's off and I'll sell it to someone else."

Once all the stalls had been cleaned, Wyatt returned to Stone River. Instead of turning down the dirt road that led to his cabin, he headed for the guest ranch.

His head swirled with his conversation with his father-in-law. Callie was the first person he wanted to share the news with.

He parked and looked around the guest ranch, but no one appeared to be in sight. He headed into the lodge, climbed the steps to her room and knocked on the door.

She opened it, a towel around her shoulders as she dried her damp hair. "Wyatt. This is a surprise."

"Disappointed?"

She shook her head as a slow smile sent his

pulse racing. "Not at all. I just came back from kayaking with the Pollens. Bear and Piper took the Lairds fly-fishing down the river while the Herricks took their granddaughters into town for ice cream. What's up?"

He pressed his hands against the doorframe and blew out a breath. "Mind if we go for a walk?"

The light dimmed in Callie's eyes, but she nodded. "Sure. Just give me a minute to finish drying my hair. How about I meet you downstairs?"

"Sounds good." He pushed away from her door and headed down the steps.

His sister Everly came out of the kitchen carrying a tray of graham crackers, marshmallows, peanut butter cups and chocolate bars.

"Hey, Wy. When did you get back? How's Ray?"

"Just now. Ray's doing okay so far. Thanks for watching Mia for me." He glanced around the room. "Where is she, by the way?"

"Mom had to run into town, so Mia went with her. They'll be back in a bit. You sticking around for s'mores tonight?"

"Sounds good."

Wyatt turned and sucked in a breath. Callie had changed into a pair of jeans and a red, short-sleeved, button-down shirt. But it was the cowboy hat that nearly did him in.

"Look at you, city girl. Fitting in with the locals."

She posed and gave him a saucy look. "When in Rome, right?"

"I don't know about Rome, but you definitely fit in at the ranch." Wyatt took her hand and held it up as she twirled.

"You look great, Callie. Love the hat."

Callie's eyes widened as if she realized, for the first time, that they weren't alone. "Thanks, Ev. I found it at my grandma's."

"I'll see you guys later." She shot Wyatt a pointed look.

Wyatt placed a hand on Callie's lower back and ushered her outside. "Let's walk the trail where we rode a couple of weeks ago, if you don't mind?"

"The one that leads to your in-laws' rescue?"

"Yes, and that's what I wanted to talk to you about anyway."

"Okay." Uncertainty filled her voice. "Is something wrong?"

"Just the opposite, actually."

As they walked, Wyatt slid his hand into Callie's and told her about his conversation with Ray. He tried—and failed—to keep his excitement contained. All the way back to the ranch, his mind had buzzed with ideas for improvements.

"That's nice." She smiled tightly. Callie released his hand and slid her fingers in her front pockets. "I'm happy for you."

Wyatt gave her a puzzled look. He bumped his shoulder against hers. "Nice? That's all you have to say?"

She stopped and faced him. Even though her sunglasses shaded her eyes, she wouldn't meet his gaze. "Yes, it's nice. I'm very happy for you. This is what you've wanted for a long time."

"Callie." He touched her arm. "What's going on?"

Hands still in her pockets, Callie straightened her arms and shook her head. "Nothing."

He really hated when people said nothing and there was definitely something.

"You sure?"

She shot him a bright smile. "Yes, I'm positive. I'm very happy for you, Wyatt. This is something you wanted to do for a long time and it relieves a lot of stress for Ray and Irene. They wouldn't give it to you if they didn't think you could handle it. They really love you and trust you."

While the words sounded sincere, Callie's eyes had lost their spark.

Had he done something to cause the change?

CALLIE WOULD NEVER call Wyatt a liar, but was he really being truthful with himself?

He'd mentioned he was ready to move forward, but his excitement over the horse rescue made her wonder if he truly believed it.

She *was* happy for him. And for Mia. She deserved to have a reminder of her mother.

While walking with Wyatt, she'd given him a noncommittal answer when he asked if she was going to the campfire.

Technically, she was on her own time. So, instead of going to the lake, she chickened out, snuck out the back door and headed into town.

Callie exhaled and brushed the back of her hand across her forehead. She should've been up-front with him instead of being a coward.

The men in Wyatt's support group had fixed the plumbing under the upstairs bathroom sink, replaced the damaged floor and ceiling on the first floor. She couldn't thank them enough, especially when they refused payment for their labor. Thankfully, the materials didn't wipe out the rest of her savings like she'd expected from Wayne's estimate.

She needed to finish painting the trim work and the windows, then she'd feel a real sense of accomplishment.

She grabbed the can of white paint off the counter and set it on the drop cloth on the floor. As she reached for the metal opener, someone knocked on the back door.

Wyatt.

She wiped her fingers on a towel, then headed to the door and opened it.

Instead of Wyatt, Jacie Brewster, her new friend from church who owned a bridal shop in town, stood on the back porch. She wore a cropped denim jacket over a cute sundress covered in yellow sunflowers. Her blond hair was piled on top of her head and her makeup was perfect. Next to her, Callie felt like a grungy mess.

Callie opened the door wider. "Jacie, come in. I'm surprised to see you."

Jacie waved a hand toward the animal shelter. "I needed to drop something off to Irene for our women's ministry event coming up and saw your lights on, so I figured I'd stop by and say hi."

She reached out to give Callie a hug, but Callie put her hands up before the woman could get too close. "I'm a mess."

Jacie hugged her anyway. "You're never a mess, Callie."

"I'd offer you something to drink but I'm not really living here at the moment."

Jacie smiled. "No worries. I can't stay long anyway. Aaron and I are going out for dinner, but I wanted to talk to you about something. I know we just met at church, and you don't know me well. I adored your grandma, and I miss her very much."

"Me too."

"She used to brag on you all the time. She shared the watercolor cards you sent her. Anyway, I wanted to let you know my brother just bought an art gallery. He's looking for an art director, and I told him about you. He asked me to give you his number if you're interested. You should call and talk to him about it. The job offers good pay and solid benefits. I know you mentioned wanting to get your grandmother's shop reopened so you don't have to return to the classroom, but give this some thought." Jacie pulled a card out of her pocket and held it out to Callie.

She took it and ran her thumb over the embossed logo. "Where's his gallery?"

Jacie scrunched up her face. "Well, that's the thing… It's in the Springs."

"Colorado Springs? That's like five or six hours from here, isn't it?"

"Yeah, something like that."

She tapped the card against her palm. "Thank you. I'll think about it."

"I hope you don't think I'm out of line by telling you about it."

"No, not at all. I'm flattered you'd think of me, but there's a lot to consider. For one, I'm not sure I'm qualified." She waved her hand around the shop. "Plus I promised Gram I'd reopen the shop, and I hate to go back on my word."

"I totally understand. Brian—that's my brother—is willing to talk if that's what you decide. Even if it's only to learn more about the position." Jacie looked at her smartwatch. "Hey, I have to run. Let's get together soon, okay?"

"Sounds good." Callie walked her to the door.

After Jacie left, the desire to finish painting waned, but Callie needed to make the most of the little time she did have. She dipped her roller into the paint and applied it to the wall.

The art director position was so tempting. She did have her degree in art history, but she had no gallery management experience. Would helping at the guest ranch count? Probably not.

Not everyone offered jobs as easily as Wyatt.

The idea of decent money and benefits was appealing, but were they enough to move again?

She loved Aspen Ridge. If she did leave, she'd have to start all over again. Not to mention she'd have to sell the shop and forgo her promise to her grandmother.

She needed to consider Wyatt and Mia too… and whatever it was she had with them.

Callie just didn't know what to do. Her mom would tell her to pray about it.

But what if she didn't like God's answer?

# CHAPTER TWELVE

BEAR WAS GETTING on Wyatt's last nerve.

"Did you hear me?" Bear raised his ax and split the pine log in half.

"I heard you. Trying to decide if I want to answer you or not."

"It's a simple question. What's going on between you and Callie?"

Had Bear asked yesterday, Wyatt would've had a different response. But right now, he had no idea.

Shrugging, he grabbed the wood and piled them on the stack for the next campfire. Turning his back to Bear, he stared at the lake. "We're friends."

"Right. Friends. Nothing more? Why don't I believe you?"

"That's on you, man."

The late afternoon heat sent a trail of sweat running down his back. He wiped his face with the hem of his T-shirt and reached for his water bottle.

"I see how you look at her. You haven't shown interest like that in any woman since Linnea."

Having been awake since 4 a.m., Wyatt was feeling the effects of his very long day. And his patience was about shot.

He arched his back, then straightened and glared at his brother. "Like I said, I don't know what's going on with Callie and me, okay? I thought things were good. Then I told her about Ray giving me the horse rescue and... I don't know. Her attitude changed. She congratulated me, but her body language didn't match her words. Then she skipped out on last night's campfire. I feel like she's been avoiding me."

"What do you think that's all about?"

"I don't know, man. Your guess is as good as mine. Being married was so much easier than the single life."

"Amen, brother." Bear held out a gloved fist, and Wyatt bumped it. Then his brother waggled his eyebrows. "But then, I do have the best wife."

Wyatt laughed. "I think Dad might disagree with you. And Cole. And probably every other decent man on the planet. A good husband thinks his wife is the best."

"You're probably right. At least any man who is strong enough to treat his wife with the respect she deserves." Bear pulled off his gloves and drained the rest of his water. He wiped his mouth with the back of his hand, scattering wood shavings stuck to his skin. "How's the search coming for an assistant trail guide?"

"I've been too busy to look. I took Callie riding. Once she's more used to being in the saddle, I'll see if she can help out when you're busy. You have a lot going with getting the rehabilitation ranch up and running. Not to mention needing time with Piper and Avery."

"Brother, I am always here for you. You know that." Bear grabbed him around the neck.

Wyatt clapped his brother on the back. "I do, and I appreciate it. I plan to ask Callie about staying on as manager after the summer season ends."

"What about her shop?"

Wyatt shrugged. "Only she can answer that. I just know I like having her around."

Bear grinned. "I knew it."

"Yeah, well, don't get cocky. And keep it to yourself."

"No worries. Speaking of Callie…" Bear jerked his head toward the guest ranch. "Doesn't look like she's avoiding you any longer."

Wyatt glanced over his shoulder and found Callie walking toward them.

Pulling off his gloves, Wyatt turned around. He couldn't stop the smile at seeing her even if he wanted to…which he didn't. "Hey, Callie. What's going on?"

She jerked a thumb over her shoulder. "Things are quiet at the guest ranch. Everly and your mom are helping the kids make cookies in the lodge while the Yaegles went on a hike. I'm going to head into town for a bit and do some more painting at the shop."

Wyatt checked the time. "I need to pick up Mia from Ray and Irene's. Mind if I go in with you?"

Callie shook her head. "Do you want to take one vehicle or drive separately? I'm only going to be gone a couple of hours. Then I'll be back for tonight's evening trail ride."

"You're planning to ride with us?" He tried to keep the eagerness out of his voice.

"If there's enough room. Families have first option, of course, but I'd love to go back out and give Patience another chance."

"I'm glad her getting spooked didn't scare you away for good. Since I have to pick up Mia, and she needs her booster seat, how about if I drive?"

"As long as you have me back in time. My boss is a stickler."

Happy to see the Callie he'd come to know, Wyatt bumped her shoulder. "Don't worry about your boss. I know how to handle him."

"Give me a minute to grab my bag."

He nodded toward his SUV parked next to her car. "I'll meet you there."

"Sounds good."

After she walked away, Wyatt turned back to his brother. "Sorry, man. I'm ditching you."

Bear held out his hands, palms up, and lifted them as if they were scales. "Chopping wood with your brother or hanging out with the pretty girl." He tossed a balled glove at him. "Pretty girl wins. Get out of here."

Wyatt grabbed his work gloves and slapped them against his thigh. He fished out his keys and headed to his SUV.

Callie met him at the passenger side, and he opened her door. "After you."

"Thank you."

Wyatt started the engine and headed toward Aspen Ridge. At the red light, he stopped and turned to Callie. "Hey, I have something to ask you."

"What's up?"

"Are things okay between us?"

"What do you mean?"

The light turned green and Wyatt headed through the intersection. "Your tone and body language changed after I told you about the horse rescue."

"I was being an idiot. I'm sorry, Wyatt. That was me. Not you. I guess I'm still trying to process some things."

"Like what?"

"My ex marrying so soon after our breakup kind of threw me. I know you wanted this horse rescue for a while. And it's always been your dream to turn it into a sanctuary in your wife's memory. And I think that's beautiful."

"But?" He glanced at Callie.

"Don't forget about me being the idiot part." She ran a thumb over her fingernails. "I just wonder if there's room…"

"Room for what?"

"For me." She exhaled as if she had been holding her breath.

Wyatt pulled the SUV over to the side of the road and shifted into Park. Then he turned, resting his left arm over the steering wheel, and reached for Callie's hand. "I'm not going to lie, Callie. I loved Linnea very much, and I always will. We had a solid marriage. We were so excited about expecting Mia and growing our family. When she died, that dream died with her. Her death nearly broke me." He released her hand and pressed his against his chest. "She will always hold a place in my heart. But I believe there's room for more."

Then he lifted his left hand that still felt a little naked. "Notice anything?"

Callie lifted her face, her eyes tangling with his. Her cheeks reddened. "You are so brave. I'm sorry for sounding so jealous. Especially over someone who isn't even here."

"Jealous, huh? That must mean that you like me."

Callie blinked a couple of times, then looked out her passenger-side window. Then she faced him again and squeezed his hand. "Wyatt, I've liked you for a very long time. And I think you want to like me, but…man, could I sound any more like a fourth grader?"

Again, he couldn't stop the smile that spread across his face. "I'm so glad to hear that." He traced the line of her jaw with his hand. "You are so beautiful, Callie. You are sweet and kind and Ada would be so proud. My family and I had a conversation about you the other night."

"Me? Good, I hope."

"The best. We're all in agreement. We really admire everything you've done at the guest ranch, especially since this hasn't been an easy time for you. You've really made your mark. Some of our success is due to your friendly attitude and the way that you took control of the program. I know you are so overqualified, but would you consider moving from temporary manager into being our permanent one? We're looking into an employee benefits package and hope to offer you more money soon."

Her eyes widened. "Seriously?"

"I wouldn't joke about this."

"I don't think you'd lie about anything. Can I think about it?"

That wasn't the answer he'd hoped to hear, but he realized Callie was a processor and needed to think through her decisions.

"To be honest, I didn't mean to spring this on you in my SUV. I meant to talk about it over the dinner we haven't had yet. Take all the time you need. We still have another month of summer, so let me know if I need to start looking again for someone else." Then Wyatt released his seat belt and shifted closer to her. "While you're considering that, there's something else I'd like you to consider."

"What's that?"

"Would you consider going out with a widower who has a super cute daughter?"

Callie laughed. "Well, that daughter sure is a strong draw."

Wyatt tapped her on the nose. "Sure, hang out with me for the sake of my kid."

Callie rested her cheek against his chest. "I think it's a package deal. And yes, I would love to. And you invited me to dinner already."

"I wasn't sure if you were still interested." Wyatt cradled Callie's face and brushed a kiss across her lips.

"Can I ask you something, Wyatt?"

"Sure thing."

"When I first came to town, you weren't ready to date."

"How do you know that?"

Callie's cheeks brightened again. "Your siblings may have mentioned it a time or two... or three."

"Of course. When you came into town, I wasn't interested."

"So, what changed?"

"You."

"I haven't changed."

Wyatt shook his head. "No, I mean being around you has changed me. You've given me hope." He nodded at the rearview mirror. "Remember that?"

She reached for the small stained glass dove like the one she found on her first day back at the shop. "I didn't even notice it hanging there. You found Gram's dove."

"After our conversation, I dug it out and decided to hang it where I would see it often. To remind me to hold on to hope." Wyatt buckled his seat belt in place.

He'd pulled back onto the road when his phone rang. Irene's number flashed on the screen. He accepted the call.

"Hey, Mama D. You're on speakerphone in my SUV. Callie's here. What's going on?"

She sniffed. "Wyatt, I'm so sorry to keep calling you. But it's Ray again."

Wyatt fingers tightened on the steering wheel. "What's going on?"

"He's having trouble breathing, so I called 911. They're on their way, but I have Mia."

"I'll be there in two minutes."

He ended the call and pressed down the gas. His fingers tightened on the steering wheel. "I'm sorry to ask this of you again, but would you mind watching Mia for me? You're welcome to take her to the lodge or to the ranch. I'll leave you my SUV and take Ray's truck to the hospital."

"Yes, of course. Promise you'll keep me posted?"

"Yes." He reached for her hand and squeezed. "Thank you, Callie. Once again, you're a lifesaver. In ways you'll never know."

CALLIE SHOULD'VE TOLD Wyatt about the job opportunity in Colorado Springs when he offered her the full-time position at the guest ranch. But things were going so well and she didn't want to ruin anything.

Her conversation with Brian from that morning still played in her head. He'd told her about his gallery and his vision, and had outlined the job responsibilities. Then he'd dangled a very generous salary and benefits package that kind of took away her breath.

She did need a job with a little more money and benefits.

Then her talk with Wyatt on the way into

town and now caring for Mia stirred up a lot of conflicted emotions.

She'd been in Aspen Ridge only a short time, but the little girl had already wriggled her way into Callie's heart.

How could she leave Wyatt and Mia?

Working at the guest ranch filled her heart with the peace and serenity she had been craving since receiving that phone call about her grandma's stroke.

The guest ranch was part of her healing journey, and she'd always appreciate that, no matter what she decided.

But what if it didn't work out with Wyatt? Would she have to leave Aspen Ridge?

While Mia played tag with the Herricks' granddaughters, Callie finished setting out items for the leaf printing she planned to do with Avery and Lexi, Wyatt's nieces, and the children visiting the guest ranch.

The Stone River Ranch truck pulled in next to Callie's car. Nora rounded the front, holding a floral arrangement, and headed toward Callie.

"Hey, Nora."

"Hi, Callie" She reached the table and set the arrangement in front of Callie. "These were just delivered to the ranch house, but they're for you."

"For me?" Callie fingered one of the satiny petals. Zinnias, hydrangeas and roses in different shades of pink and assorted ferns and greenery were arranged in a clear glass vase.

Callie pulled the small white card out of the bouquet and read it.

*Please say yes.*

Although there was no signature, the flowers had to have been from Brian, Jacie Brewster's brother, who wanted her to be the director for his art gallery.

Had this opportunity come a month or so ago, she might have been all over it.

But that was before Wyatt. And Mia.

"Thanks for bringing them by, Nora."

Nora sat on the picnic table bench next to Callie and slid an arm around her shoulders. "You're welcome. Thank you for everything you've done for my family, Callie. And I don't mean as manager of this place." She waved a hand over the property. "You've given my son something I haven't seen in a long time."

"What's that?"

"Hope."

Callie's fingers tightened around the envelope.

Hope.

She nodded, then bit her bottom lip. "He did the same to me. I wasn't in a good place when I arrived in Aspen Ridge."

"We love having you here, you know."

Callie nodded. "Wyatt told me earlier. Thank you for that."

"Like my son, I'm not one to dig into other people's business, but I think you should know that Jacie Brewster's mom and I are good friends."

Callie's head jerked up. "So you know."

Nora nodded. "I know Brian offered you the gallery director position." She reached for Callie's arm. "And if that's where you feel God is leading you, then go with our blessing. But I ask that you talk with my son first, please. As his mother, I don't want to see him get his heart broken."

Callie swallowed against the lump in her throat and tried not to let Nora's words stir up guilt. "The last thing I want to do is hurt Wyatt. Or Mia. I'm crazy about both of them. That's the problem. The gallery director job would be great, but I'm not the same person I was a couple of months ago. And I have Gram's shop to consider."

"Your grandma would want you to follow God's leading as well, even if it meant selling and relocating."

"That's just it—I don't know where He's leading me. If it were up to me, I'd stay right here. But shouldn't I at least consider this other opportunity?"

"You're the only one who can answer that. Give it up to God, sweetie, and ask Him to align your heart with His will. That way, you won't go wrong with making the right choice. His plan for you is perfect, no matter if it's here in Aspen Ridge or in the Springs. Or even some other place in the world."

Callie reached over and hugged the woman. "Thanks, Nora. I appreciate you. Can we please keep this conversation between us?"

"Absolutely."

As Nora headed into the lodge, Callie rounded up the kids and directed them to the table. As she showed them how to press their ferns onto their paper and spray with the watered-down paint she'd mixed, Nora's advice tumbled over in her head.

She valued the loyalty of keeping her word,

but the gallery promised financial security that she needed right now.

She had no idea what to do.

But she was going to figure it out somehow.

# CHAPTER THIRTEEN

WYATT PULLED INTO the empty parking space by the lodge. The nightly campfire glowed down by the lake. Laughter drifted toward the treetops.

As he exited his SUV, he noticed Callie's light on in her suite. He headed into the lodge and took the stairs two at a time.

The door to her room was open about six inches, and he started to knock, but then he heard her talking. He took a step back, not wanting to interrupt.

Then she laughed. "Yes, Brian. The flowers did arrive. They're beautiful. I appreciate them." She paused, then spoke again. "The gallery director position would be perfect, but like I told Jacie, there's a lot to consider. I promise to have an answer for you soon."

Wyatt's heart slammed against his rib cage so hard he nearly winced in pain.

Was she talking to Brian Watkins? Didn't he have an art gallery in Colorado Springs?

At least that was what Aaron Brewster, Brian's brother-in-law and the Stones' attorney, had told Wyatt when he ran into him at the diner a month or so ago. Aaron, Jacie and their son were heading to the Springs for a mini vacation to check out the new gallery.

No wonder Callie needed to think about accepting the full-time guest ranch management position.

If it weren't for Callie caring for Mia, Wyatt would've left without making his presence known. But he couldn't leave without his daughter.

Blowing out a breath, he braced the frame with one hand and rapped on the open door with the other.

Still on the phone, Callie opened it wider, and her eyes grew large. She waved him inside, then turned her back to him. "Listen, I have to go. I'll call you in a couple of days. Thank you. Bye."

Then she turned him. "Hi, Wyatt. How's Ray?"

"Daddy!" Mia scrambled off the little love seat where she had been coloring and ran over to him. She wrapped her arms around his legs.

"Callie and I made a picture for you and one for Pappy too."

He took the papers she waved at him and barely glanced at them. "Thank you, sweetie."

As he lifted her in his arms and slung her backpack over his shoulder, he caught sight of the flowers on Callie's small table. A white card poked out of the colorful bouquet.

*Please say yes.*

Three little words that jammed a spike in his chest.

Callie reached for Ella the Elephant on the love seat and handed the stuffed animal to Wyatt. "Are you staying for the campfire?"

Was she really going to pretend he didn't overhear her conversation?

He handed the elephant to his daughter. "No, I need to get Mia home. It's past her bedtime."

"Daddy, I wanna go back to the campfire." Mia rubbed her eye as she leaned against Wyatt's leg.

"Not tonight, honey. A different day."

One when Callie wouldn't be there.

"Are you still on for field volleyball tomorrow?" Callie folded her arms in front of her. "Cole and Bear set up the nets after dinner."

"I can't think about that now. My family needs me."

"How's Ray doing?" She rested a hand on his arm.

"He has pneumonia." Wyatt forced himself not to shake her hand off. He reached down and hooked Mia's sandals around his fingers.

"I'm sorry to hear that. Is there anything I can do?"

"You've done enough with looking after Mia. Thank you." Each word snapped like a bite, but he didn't care.

Callie's head shot up. "What's with the snappy tone?"

Wyatt dragged a hand over his face. Then he jerked his head toward the flowers. "Nice bouquet. Are you planning on taking the gallery director position? If so, at least give me a two weeks' notice so I can fill your position without burdening my family."

Callie's mouth opened, then closed again. "How much did you hear?"

Fatigue robbed him of his manners. "Enough. I have to get Mia home."

"Wyatt." She reached for him once again.

This time, he shook off her arm. "What about

all that talk about reopening your grandmother's shop?"

"If you'd listen for two minutes, then I could tell you that I was offered the job, but I haven't made a decision yet. There are too many other things to factor in."

"When were you going to tell me? You must've had a good laugh at my full-time offer."

"That's not fair. And I'd never laugh at you." The hurt in her eyes had him softening his tone.

"What's not fair is that you couldn't trust me with this information. When did you learn about the position?"

"A couple of days ago."

"A couple of days." He nodded, grinding his jaw.

"I planned to talk to you about it today, but then you got the call about Ray. I wasn't going to keep this from you. I just needed a little time to process everything."

"Well, don't let me keep you. I'll give you all the time you need. Thank you for caring for Mia." Wyatt all but slammed the door behind them.

He was such an idiot.

How could he have risked his heart with someone who planned to leave?

WYATT DIDN'T HAVE to worry about sleeping through his alarm in the morning when he'd tossed and turned all night long. His conversation with Callie had played on a loop in his head until the sun peeked above the mountains.

He'd risked putting himself out there only to learn she might not stick around. They hadn't gone on a real date yet, and he definitely wasn't in love with her.

Like he'd told his family weeks ago—he didn't have time for romance. He needed to focus on his responsibilities, namely his daughter, the ranch, and now the horse rescue.

Then why did his heart feel like it had been squeezed out like an old sponge?

With his head throbbing and his eyes filled with grit, Wyatt headed to the kitchen and filled a to-go mug with black coffee.

"Come on, Mia. Let's go," he called to his daughter.

"Coming, Daddy. What are we doing today?" She skipped out of her room wearing pink polka dotted shorts and a pink shirt he'd laid out for her last night after her bath. Ella the Elephant was tucked in the crook of her arm.

"You're hanging out with Nana while Uncle Bear and I take the guests on a trail ride."

Mia clapped her hands and twirled in a circle. "Yay. Will I see Callie too?"

He shook his head. "Probably not. She's pretty busy."

Mia's face fell as her bottom lip popped out. "Okay."

He didn't have only himself to consider. He needed to protect his daughter from getting hurt too. If that meant keeping her away from Callie while she was still in Aspen Ridge, then that was what he needed to do.

Ten minutes later, he dropped Mia off at the ranch house, ignoring his mother's fussing about the circles under his eyes, and headed for the barn. He needed to tack up the horses and load them into the trailer.

Staying busy would keep his mind off last night's disaster.

As he came out of the tack room carrying Dante's saddle and pad, Bear rounded the corner with his horse Ranger's halter in his hand. He stopped and gave Wyatt the once-over. "Man, you look rough. Bad night?"

Wyatt pushed past him. "Something like that."

"Wanna talk about it?"

"Nope." Wyatt set Dante's saddle on the rack, then headed for his stall.

"Does this have anything to do with Callie?"

Wyatt rested his arm on the stall door, then glared at his brother. "What part of 'nope' confuses you?"

Bear strode over to him and crossed his arms over his chest. "Maybe the part that has me questioning if you're up for this ride today."

"I have to. The guests are expecting it."

"Yes, and they are expecting someone to keep them safe as well. If your focus isn't where it needs to be, then tell me now."

Shaking his head, Wyatt waved away his brother's words and unlatched the stall door. "Don't go all big brother on me. I've seen you do your fair share of moping before you and Piper got together."

"Right, and that's why I can tell that something's off with you."

"I said I was fine."

"Whatever, man. Just make sure your head's on straight."

Grabbing onto his harness, Wyatt led Dante out into the aisle and hooked him to the crossties. He dug through the grooming bucket and found the hoof pick. One by one, Wyatt lifted Dante's legs and picked the stones and debris out of his hooves. He dropped the pick in the bucket and grabbed the brush. He ran it across the stallion's coat, removing bits of straw.

An ache began to throb behind Wyatt's eyes. Still holding onto the brush, he rested his forehead against Dante's neck.

He needed just a minute.

But no matter how tired he was, he had a job to do, with no time to mess around.

Wyatt put away the grooming tools, then reached for Dante's saddle pad. He positioned it, then lifted the saddle on the horse's back. Once everything was cinched and secured, he slid the bridle in place, unclipped Dante and led the horse out to the trailer.

Bear followed and loaded Ranger. Working together but silently, they loaded the other two tacked horses, then headed to the guest ranch.

Bear parked the ranch truck alongside the paddock. As Wyatt stepped out of the truck, Callie came out of the lodge. She spotted him and paused. Then she turned around and went back inside.

He didn't have the time, nor the inclination to go after her. He slid his sunglasses in place and adjusted his hat.

As he rounded the back of the trailer, Bear

caught his arm. "Tell me now if you can't ride, and I'll get Dad to cover you."

Wyatt shook off his brother's arm. "I told you I'm fine."

"You better be because here come our riders now." Bear jerked his head toward the yurt closest to the road.

Clark and Francine, an older couple from Ohio, stepped onto the deck dressed in creased jeans, shined boots and matching black-and-white plaid Western-cut shirts with pearl snaps. Their cowboy hats appeared to be brand new.

"Morning." Clark tipped his hat, then clutched his shiny belt buckle.

Wyatt bit back a smile. "Good morning. Ready to ride?"

"Yes, sir."

"Good. Clark, you'll be riding Storm. Francine, you'll be riding Cheyenne. Both are gentle Quarter horses who are used to our trail rides."

Clark rubbed his hands together. "Can't wait to tell the boys back home about our ranching adventures."

Francine hugged her husband's arm. "Don't worry, Clark. I'll take plenty of pictures so you can show them off."

Wyatt unlatched the trailer and led Cheyenne

out first. He held onto the horse's harness and motioned for Francine to come toward them. "I'll guide you with mounting Chey."

As he instructed each step, Francine listened intently. She put her left foot in the stirrup and started to swing her right leg over the horse's back. The saddle shifted sideways. She let out a scream as she lost her balance, pinwheeled backward and landed hard on the ground.

Cheyenne nickered and stepped back, flicking her head.

Everything happened so quickly, yet it played out in slow motion.

"Francine!" Clark knelt next to his wife. "Are you hurt?"

Bear pushed past Wyatt and sent him a searing look. "I thought you tacked up the horses."

"I did." Wyatt fisted his hands.

"Not very well." Bear growled at him.

Several of the guests who had been eating breakfast or hanging out on their decks rushed over to Francine.

Heat scorched his neck and face as he stared at the saddle still resting sideways on Cheyenne.

He'd been around horses all his life, and he'd never messed up like that. Not only had he put Francine in danger, but it wasn't safe for Cheyenne either. Macey would have his head if he hurt her horse.

Clark helped Francine to her feet.

Wyatt moved past him and touched her arm. "I'm so very sorry, Mrs. Masters. Are you hurt? Can I get you anything? I'll fix the saddle so you can still ride."

Francine rubbed her lower back, then held up a hand and shook her head. "No, thank you. I changed my mind about riding."

Her husband glared at him. "Me, too. Come on, dear. Let's head inside to get you some ice."

As Clark helped Francine back to their yurt, Wyatt ground his teeth.

Maybe they weren't the type to handle a trail ride anyway. But that was still no excuse for his negligence. The guest ranch's number one concern was guest safety, and he'd blown that.

Bear nearly shoved him out of the way as he attended to Cheyenne.

Wyatt dragged a hand over his face and strode toward the lodge. Inside, he headed for the kitchen and filled a glass with water. His hands shook as he downed the liquid and peered out the window at the lake.

The main door slammed open. Wyatt didn't need to turn to know his brother had followed him inside. Bear's heavy footsteps announced his presence.

Still holding the glass, Wyatt turned.

Bear thrust a hand toward the yurts. "What was that?"

"I messed up. I thought I tightened the cinch."

"You should've double-checked before she tried to get on. We always double-check before allowing riders on our horses. Now she's hurt."

Wyatt set the glass on the counter and pressed his back against the sink. He scrubbed both hands over his face, then dropped them at his sides. "I know. I feel terrible."

"And you should. I told you, man, if your head wasn't on straight then you needed to let me handle it."

"And I said I thought I was fine."

"Well, we saw just how fine you are. Whatever is going on between you and Callie, fix it. Ask her out or do whatever you need to make it right."

Wyatt ran a thumb and finger over his gritty eyes. "There's no point."

"Why not?"

"Brian Watkins offered her an art director position at his new gallery in the Springs."

"She's leaving?"

Wyatt shrugged and held up his hands.

"So, you don't even know if she's taking the job?"

Wyatt lifted his head. "No."

"Dude, step up and fight for her. Show her that you want her to stick around. That is what you want, isn't it?"

"Who am I to stand in her way if this is what she wants?"

"You're the guy who's in love with her."

"I never said I was in love with her."

"You don't have to say it. It's written all over your face. I haven't seen you like this since you were mooning over Linnea. Listen, I get it. I've been there. I know what it's like to lose someone close to you."

"My situation is different."

"How so?"

"Imagine if you lost Piper and had to raise Avery on your own. How would you feel?"

"I hope I never have to find out. And I'm sorry that you did. But Linnea is gone and you can't live in the past. Callie is here now. Fight for her, man. Have the life that you've always wanted." Bear turned on his heel and strode out of the lodge, slamming the door behind him.

Wyatt chewed on his brother's words.

Was he giving up without a fight? Would Callie consider staying if he shared how he truly felt? Was she even ready for another relationship? The only way he'd know was if he manned up and did as his brother suggested.

It was time to fight for the woman he loved.

Yes, loved. He'd finally admitted the truth. Now he needed to tell Callie how he felt and hoped she wanted to stay.

CALLIE SHOULD'VE MADE her presence known, but when her name was mentioned, she moved away from the steps as the brothers argued, unaware of how their voices carried through the open space.

She held her breath, waiting for Wyatt to agree with his brother. But his silence crumbled her heart.

He didn't care if she stayed or left?

She had hoped to make a home in Aspen Ridge, but how could she stay now? She'd end up running into Wyatt and Mia and be reminded constantly of what she'd lost. Again.

Maybe it was time to call Brian and accept the job. At least she hadn't fully unpacked, so moving wouldn't be too difficult. At least physically.

But there was the shop to consider. How could she go back on her word?

Was Nora right? Would it be okay to sell if that was what God was leading her to do?

Problem was, she didn't know. And that was part of her struggle.

Whatever she decided, it didn't need to happen this minute. She needed to get back outside and pretend she heard nothing. Pretend her heart wasn't shattered into a million pieces inside her chest. Pretend she wasn't humiliated by the chance she'd taken with Wyatt.

The door slammed a second time, then silence reigned. Callie gripped the banister and headed downstairs. She let out a deep breath, forced a smile in place and headed for the door.

She reached for the doorknob as her phone vibrated in her pocket.

She pulled it out, not recognizing the unidentified number scrolling across her screen, but she answered anyway. "Hello?"

"Hi, this is Susan Hurst, the coordinator of the Durango Local Artists Exhibition. I'm looking for Callie Morgan."

"This is she." Why would an art show coordinator be calling her?

"Callie, I am pleased to inform you that your

entry is one of our top three finalists in the watercolor category."

Callie frowned. "My entry?"

"Yes, ma'am, the watercolor landscape entitled Hope."

"Oh, yes…" Callie's voice trailed off as ice slid through her veins.

"I know this is short notice, but our awards dinner is this weekend. If you'll confirm your email, then we'll share details with you. You're welcome to bring a significant other or guests, if you'd like. All we request is an RSVP within the next twenty-four hours."

Significant other? That certainly wouldn't be happening. And her family was too far away to make a last-minute trip.

She was on her own in a place she could no longer call home now.

Especially after what he'd done.

The call ended, and Callie clutched her phone. Her chest heaved as tears scalded her eyes.

She threw the door open so hard it smacked against the wall. She spied Wyatt heading to the ranch truck.

With her hands curled into fists and adrenaline rushing through her, she rushed across the grass, nearly running to catch him before he could get away.

Wyatt opened the truck door.

Chest heaving, she reached above him and slammed it shut. He whirled around. "Callie, what are you doing?"

"What am *I* doing? You have some nerve." She poked her phone into his chest.

His brows furrowed. "What are you talking about?"

She waved her phone in front of him. "I just got a call from the Durango Local Artists Exhibition. Apparently, my entry finaled in the top three."

His eyes widened, and then he smiled. "Hey, that's fantastic. Congratulations."

"You have got to be joking. It's not fantastic. You went behind my back and entered my piece after I specifically said it wasn't my best work. And now it's out there for everyone to see. How could you betray me like that?"

His mouth flopped open like a caught trout. He lifted his hands and then dropped them at his sides. He tucked his chin to his chest and shook his head. "I'm sorry."

"Sorry isn't good enough." She started to walk away, then turned back to him. Her vision blurred and a tear trickled down her cheek. "I heard your conversation with your brother. Even if you weren't too much of a chicken to ask me out, I'd say no now. I can't be with someone who I can't trust. Find yourself another manager because I'm done."

Callie had never walked off a job before, and she truly hated leaving the Stones in the lurch right now, but there was no way she could stay.

To someone else, what Wyatt had done may not seem like that big of a deal. But after her experience with Shawn, she needed someone she could trust, even with the little things.

And Wyatt Stone had just proved he was not that man.

## CHAPTER FOURTEEN

WYATT WASN'T ABOUT to let Callie walk away without hearing him out.

He looked at Bear. "Take over for me. I got to take care of this."

"Yeah, you do."

"Callie!" Wyatt jogged across the road and hurried to catch up to her.

She wrenched the door open. "I have nothing to say to you."

He followed her inside the lodge. "That's just fine. I have plenty to say. Now it's my turn to talk, and you need to listen to me."

"I don't need to do anything except leave."

"Callie, wait. Please." He hated the plea in his voice, but the weight of what had happened with the horse and now this just about did him in. He couldn't force her to listen but he hoped she would.

Her steps slowed. Even though she didn't turn around, she did stop. "What?"

He moved behind her and lifted a hand, then dropped it. If he touched her, he'd want to pull her into his arms, and that wouldn't solve anything. It would probably make matters worse.

He dragged a hand over his face. "I'm sorry. I truly am. I really loved the painting. You are so incredibly talented. You said your ex was dismissive of your talent. I just wanted to support your gift and show my appreciation."

She whirled around. Her reddened eyes shimmering with unshed tears sparked as she pounded the air with a clenched fist. "By going behind my back? You could've been more open and honest instead of being secretive. Now I have to deal with the fact that my art is out there. I confided in you and trusted you with the first thing I painted since losing my grandma. I even gave it to you as a gift, not to be put on display." Her voice broke as a tear slipped on her cheek.

He gentled his tone and took a step closer. "Callie, don't you see? That's what made the painting so beautiful. You brought the landscape to life with your vulnerability."

She shook her head. "It wasn't your decision to make. You should've been more open with me."

"You keep saying that, but you weren't being open with me. You didn't tell me about Brian's job offer."

"Because you got called away."

"You said you had known about it for a couple of days."

"And I was trying to process things so I could discuss it with you. But then with everything that happened with Ray, it wasn't the best time to talk about it."

"It's a great job, so I could see why you'd want to."

She dropped her chin to her chest, then lifted her head and looked at him, shaking her head. "If you think it's about the job, then you're an idiot, and you don't see anything at all. In fact, you're a hypocrite."

"What?" Wyatt scowled.

"You heard me. You stretch yourself so thin trying to keep everyone happy. You keep a mask in place so people don't see how you really feel. That's not being open and honest."

He flung his arms out. "People depend on

me, Callie. I can't fall apart at every bad thing that happens."

"I get that, but when was the last time you allowed yourself to truly feel? When was the last time you were vulnerable, feeling like you were exposed for the whole world to see? Hmm?"

"I told you—the day my wife died. The day I realized I was twenty-five and had a newborn to care for. A newborn who would never know her mother. But I had to keep it together, I had to be strong for my daughter. Then I came home and found that my family's ranch was in trouble. My dad was sick. My siblings were going through their own struggles. They didn't need someone else to fall apart on them. I did what I had to. And if you can't understand that..."

She waved a finger in front of him. "I understand how you could go through a fog for so many months and come out and not remember much of anything. I understand how you can laugh and talk about a person in one breath, and then cry in the next. I understand the pain of losing someone you love. But I also understand that you have to allow yourself to work through those emotions so you can move toward healing. Have you done that, Wyatt? Because until you do, until you stop being strong for everyone else and allow yourself to have those moments of vulnerability, then there's no place for me in your life. I accept that you were married and will always love your wife. Now you have a beautiful daughter who does need you, but I also think that you haven't allowed yourself to fully grieve your heart-crushing loss." She looked up at him, tears coursing down her face. The brokenness in her eyes wrecked his chest.

Then she brushed the tears away with the back of her hand and reached in her pocket. She pulled out the keys he'd given her when she moved into the lodge. She pressed them into his hand and curled his fingers around the metal. "Goodbye, Wyatt."

She walked up the stairs to her suite while he remained rooted inside the door trying to breathe through the pain in his chest.

He'd fallen in love for the second time in his life. And for the second time, he'd lost that love.

Bear was right. Wyatt was a fool.

CALLIE HAD SNUCK out of the lodge like a coward, not even saying goodbye to Macey, Nora or any of the others who had been so kind to her.

Instead, she wrote a note and left it on the counter in the lodge kitchen. Hopefully they'd understand.

Leaving the lodge and the guest ranch…it shredded her. Even more so than when she had discovered that her ex-fiancé had a girlfriend.

At least she could crash in Gram's apartment until she figured out what to do next.

She dragged her suitcase up the steps and dropped it in the middle of the small living room. Then she reached for the knitted afghan, wrapped it around her shoulders even though it was about eighty degrees inside, and curled up on the love seat. She buried her face in the fibers and sobbed.

She had risked her heart only to have it broken again. Somehow, she needed to figure out how to put it back together.

Her phone rang, signaling a video call from her mother. Callie didn't want to talk, but she didn't want her mother to worry either.

She wiped her eyes with the back of her hand, but that didn't stop the tears from rolling down her face. She accepted the call. "Mom…"

"Callie, honey, what's going on? What's wrong?"

She could only shake her head until she regained her composure long enough to share what had happened with Wyatt.

"Oh, my sweet girl. I'm so sorry that you're hurting and I can't be there to comfort you."

"I don't know what to do, Mom."

"What's your heart telling you?"

Callie scoffed. "Are you kidding? My heart can't be trusted right now. I arrived at Stone River on what should've been my wedding day and fell for another guy who ended up betraying me. Even though he didn't cheat on me, he still went behind my back."

"Callie, I know what he did hurt you, and I'm not trying to diminish that. But, knowing Wyatt Stone as I do…well, as I used to when he was younger, I can't imagine that he did it with evil intentions. Sounds like he truly cares for you and wanted to show how much he believes in you."

"If he cared for me, then he should've been open and honest with me."

"You've said that several times, but what does that mean to you? He encouraged you to enter the show, and you told him no."

"It wasn't ready, Mom. I know you and Dad don't get my art, but it wasn't my best work."

"You shared your passion for art with your

grandmother, but I do understand what it means to have a passion for something you love. Your dad and I gave up full-time careers in the States and moved away from our children to another part of the globe because God called us to minister to people in South America. Others might not understand that, but we did what we had to do. So, only you know your own heart. But you have to remember that your value isn't tied to your art or your family or even the shop. You are God's child, and He values you above all else. Do you still have Gram's letter?"

Callie nodded as her eyes drifted across the room to the small bookcase where she had set her letter. She hadn't been ready to read it when Aaron Brewster had given it to her, or even after she had returned to Aspen Ridge.

"Maybe you need to take time and read it."

They talked for a couple more minutes and then hung up, but not before Callie promised to call her mother again the next day.

She ran her fingers through the tangled mess of her hair and tossed her phone on the cushion. She stood and walked to the bookcase. She pulled out one of Gram's sketch journals and slid the letter out from between the pages.

Returning to the love seat, she pulled the knitted blanket over her legs and pressed the envelope to her nose. She inhaled the familiar scent that filled her mind with memories. Then she ran her finger under the seal and pulled out the envelope.

With trembling fingers, she unfolded the page and read.

Dear Callie,

I'm so blessed to have you as my granddaughter and grateful for every moment we spent together. I'm so thankful you shared my love of art, even if our family didn't quite get us.

I bought the blue cottage to give local artists an outlet for their creativity. Now I'm leaving it to you. It needs a bit of work, but I left a little money with Aaron for some of the repairs.

If it's a burden, or if God is calling you in a different direction, then I release you from your promise to reopen and give my blessing to sell. It's all good as long as you're following the Lord's leading.

Love and prayers,

Gram

Callie rested her head against the back of the love seat as a trail of tears slid down her face. She'd been released from her promise, but what was God really calling her to do?

Maybe she needed to take time and listen to her heart.

# CHAPTER FIFTEEN

AT LEAST SOMETHING was going right for someone.

Wyatt pulled his SUV up to the front door
of Aspen Ridge General and shifted the engine
into Park. He exited and rounded the front to
open the passenger side as the nurse wheeled
Ray outside.

"Good to see you, Ray. You look a lot better than you did the last time I saw you. Think
you can try to stay out of hospitals for a while?"

"I feel it too." He maneuvered his crutches,
thanked the nurse, then hauled himself into the
passenger seat. "Sorry to pull you away to come
get me, but they wanted to kick me out, and
Irene was busy with handling an adoption at the
animal shelter."

"Not a problem." Once Ray was secure,
Wyatt shut the door and moved back behind

the wheel. "Need to go to the pharmacy or any other place while we're out?"

Ray shook his head and patted the plastic bag on his lap. "Let's head home. Doc gave me enough meds until my prescriptions are ready. The pharmacy will deliver them later today. I just want to get home and rest. Can't sleep for anything in those hospitals."

"You got that right." Wyatt drove through the parking lot and headed back to Ray and Irene's.

"What's going on with you?"

Wyatt glanced at Ray while he waited for his turn at the intersection. "What are you talking about?"

"Not very chatty."

"And that's a bad thing?"

"Usually, you're asking me all sorts of questions. Now you've clammed up."

Wyatt kept his eyes on the road. "Sorry, don't feel like talking, I guess."

"Why not?"

Wyatt worked his jaw as he considered his next words. He opened his mouth and found himself spilling everything that happened in the past day or so with Callie.

"Pull over."

Wyatt jerked his eyes toward Ray. "You okay? Are you going to be sick?"

The older man scowled. "No, nothing like that. I want to talk some sense into you, and I don't wanna do it while you're driving. So, pull over."

Wyatt rolled his eyes at his father-in-law's gruff tone, but he found a safe spot, pulled off the road and shifted into Park but left the engine idling.

Resting an arm over the steering wheel, he turned in his seat. "Okay, let me have it. You won't be the first, and I'm sure you won't be the last."

"Son, you are not responsible for making others happy, especially at the expense of your own mental health. You can't shut down how you feel for the sake of someone else. They are responsible for their own emotions and reactions. You're responsible for your own choices and your own actions."

"I have to be strong for my family."

"What does that even mean? You're one of the strongest young men I've known. Otherwise, I wouldn't have let you within ten feet of my daughter. I know Marines are tough and all that, but your strength doesn't lie in not showing your emotions. Your strength comes from who you are and how you use your faith to glorify God. It's not about denying yourself in order to keep others happy."

Wyatt puffed out his cheeks. "My faith isn't as strong as you think it is."

"What if it's not as weak as you think it is?"

Wyatt hadn't expected him to twist the question, and he didn't know how to respond.

"I'm a gruff cowboy. I was born in this town, and I'm going to die in this town. I don't travel much, and I'm fine with that. Everything I want is here. Except for more time with my daughter. But the Lord didn't see fit to give that to me. When I first injured my leg, I threw myself a big ole pity party. I shut Irene, Mia and you out because I didn't know how to express my own feelings. And for that, I'm sorry. This bout of pneumonia was a wake-up call. I'm done feeling sorry for myself. This cast is temporary, then I'll be back doing what I love."

Wyatt grinned. "I'm glad to hear that."

Ray lifted his chin. "I meant what I said. Guys have been taught for generations that emotions are signs of weakness. But you can mourn and be sad and still be strong. It's time to open your heart to your future, whatever that may be." Ray rubbed a hand across his whiskered chin. "Oh, and yeah, I'm taking back the horse rescue."

"What? Why would you do that?"

"I've been taking advantage of you lately, and that's got to stop."

"That's ridiculous. I'm family. You're not taking advantage of anything."

He raised an eyebrow and shot Wyatt with a direct look. "Okay, then. Maybe you're the one who's been taking advantage of me. You're saying yes and burying yourself in all kinds of work and projects. Now it's affecting other parts of your life. Maybe you're worried if you stop for any length of time, then you just might have to feel something."

"What's wrong with that?"

Ray rested a hand on Wyatt's shoulder and gave it a gentle squeeze. "If you don't move through your grief, then you can't heal the pain."

"Why does everyone keep saying that? I'm fine."

"Are you?"

"What do you want me to say, Ray?" Hot tears flooded Wyatt's eyes. To his horror, they leaked out and slid down the side of his nose. "Okay, maybe I'm not fine. Maybe I'm angry.

What should've been one of the happiest days of my life is also one of the most heartbreaking. I lost my wife on the day I gained my daughter. I can't celebrate Mia without remembering what was taken from her. From me. And I'm angry at God for taking her. She was only twenty-four-years old. Why did she have to die?"

Ray's chin trembled as he swallowed several times. "I don't have an answer because I've asked that question many times. I had to learn to stop asking God why and instead ask Him what He wants me to learn through this. Irene reminds me that God allows things to happen so He can write our stories the way they need to be told." He ran a hand under his nose. "Look at what you've done since you've moved back to Aspen Ridge. For the last three years, you've guided a group of men into learning how to become strong single fathers. You couldn't have done that without losing your wife."

Wyatt dried his eyes with the heel of his hands. "I'd rather have my wife."

"I'd rather have my daughter too, but that wasn't God's plan. And it's okay to be mad at God. He can handle it. The more you allow Him to work in your life and through your grief, the more He can use you to tell the next part of your story."

Wyatt rested his head against the seat and closed his eyes. "How did you and Irene do it? How did you move through your grief?"

Ray sighed. "Not very well at first. For the first month after Linnea died, Irene refused to get out of bed until Ada paid her a visit and said Linnea wouldn't want her to live like that. Ada reminded her what it meant to hold on to hope. And that our time on earth was only temporary compared to eternity in Heaven. And I think knowing that she would see her little girl some-day motivated Irene to live a life that honored her daughter here on earth. We will always miss our daughter until we're reunited in Heaven. We sought counseling and attended a grief sup-port group at church. We keep Linnea's memory alive by sharing stories. We had to learn how to live a new kind of normal without her, but we are overjoyed to have Mia and you."

"Ada Morgan was quite a lady."

"Yes, she was. And so is her granddaughter."

Wyatt held up a hand. "Don't even go there."

"Why not?"

"Because things between Callie and me are over before they could really get started."

"Only if you let it, son."

"Callie made it clear she wants nothing to do with me. I'm sure she'll be leaving Aspen Ridge soon, anyway."

"Then change her mind. Fight for her. Show her that you're the kind of man she needs in her life. Because I'm telling you right now, she's the kind of woman you need, and she'll make an exceptional mother for Mia. I've watched the two of them together. Mia adores her too."

Wyatt nodded. "Yes, and that's what worries me. Mia getting attached and then getting her heart broken."

"If that happens, she'll survive because Mia is strong like her daddy and has her mother's blood in her. But this doesn't have to be the end of the story for you and Callie. You have to decide where you want to go from here—live in the past or fight for your future."

With his father-in-law's words echoing inside his head, Wyatt turned back to the steering wheel and shifted the engine into Drive as he headed back to Ray's ranch.

Was Ray right? Only one way to find out.

Now, if only he could get Callie to give him a second chance…

LAST MINUTE WAS better than not at all.

Callie didn't want to attend the awards reception, but Gram's comment in her letter about pursuing her passion sparked Callie to RSVP for a party of one.

Maybe that was part of the problem—she didn't want to show up alone.

Truth was, she missed the guest ranch. She missed Mia. But most of all, she missed Wyatt.

For the past couple of days, she'd waffled about how to approach him, how to apologize for her outburst. Now that she had time to think about it, she saw the tenderness behind his intentions. He believed in her, believed in her talent in a way that no one else other than Gram ever had. He wanted only the best for her.

But her best didn't come with awards or ribbons. Her best came from being around him. And she'd blown it.

So she planned to show up, accept her ribbon and leave.

Simple as that.

The reception invitation hadn't specified a dress code. How did one dress for an art exhibition?

Callie hoped her three-quarter-sleeved coral wrap dress with the geometric design and taupe slingback sandals were enough. She'd twisted her hair into a French knot and secured it with a couple of Gram's combs. She'd also found an ivory beaded handbag in Gram's closet.

She headed inside the gallery and gave her name at the reception table. The tall woman behind the table was dressed in a black-and-white striped cocktail dress with hot pink pumps.

She handed Callie a program, a name tag, and her table number.

She didn't plan on staying long enough to eat, but the program showed that dinner would be served first, then the awards ceremony. She had to sit at a table with a bunch of strangers. Or worse yet—by herself. Her only other option was to leave. That was tempting.

She bypassed a waiter carrying a tray of appetizers and entered the gallery where different art pieces sat on display. Tucking her handbag under her arm, she perused the pen-and-ink drawings, acrylics, oils and, finally, the watercolors.

On the back wall, three framed watercolors hung in a row under spotlights hanging from the ceiling. Callie stood in front of her painting and tried to see what Wyatt saw.

She had gotten up early that first morning after arriving at the guest ranch and taken a walk. Sunlight hovered over the horizon and cast the glow across the lake. In the distance, the ranch house sat quietly nestled against the mountains. The image had taken her breath away and she couldn't wait to capture it with color. She had taken a picture with her phone, but it didn't do it justice.

And neither did her painting.

As she stepped closer, she realized a ribbon hung from the bottom of the frame. She turned it around and gasped.

She had taken first place.

She couldn't believe it. And there was no one to celebrate with.

"Beautiful workmanship." A deep, male voice spoke behind her.

That voice sounded too familiar...

Callie turned discreetly and tried to look over her shoulder without appearing obvious.

Then she gasped out loud.

"Dad!" She threw her arms around the older man standing behind her as tears clouded her vision. "What are you doing here?"

He gripped her arms, then kissed her forehead. "I've never missed an art show, and I wasn't about to start now."

Callie rested her cheek against his chest, not caring if it messed up her updo, and wrapped her arms around his waist. "I'm so glad you're here."

Dad wrapped his arms around her and then turned her toward her table. "Not just me. Your mom and brothers are here too."

Callie peered around him. "Are you serious?"

"Absolutely. After your mom hung up with you the other day, she called me and we booked tickets. We've decided to take a short break but we'll be here for as long as you need us."

"But what about your ministry?"

"We left it in good hands. They understand family emergencies, especially when we said our daughter needed us."

Callie bit her bottom lip, trying to hold back the emotion that filled her chest. "Thank you, Dad."

"No thanks necessary, sweetheart. I wish you had been more up-front about some of the struggles you've been facing."

Callie shrugged. "Can't run to my daddy every time there's a problem."

Her father lifted her chin and looked her squarely in the eye. "Actually, that's exactly what you're supposed to do. Your Heavenly Father wants to know about every struggle. Even if I can't be here, He is always here with you."

"Thanks for the reminder. Too often, I think I need to handle things on my own."

"How's that working out for you?"

"These days, not very well."

They reached the table where Callie thought she'd be sitting alone. Instead, her mother sat with Wesley and Trevor. Callie flew into her mother's arms, having not seen her since a week after Gram's funeral. Although, she appreciated the face-to-face connection, video chatting just wasn't the same. Then she hugged her brothers. "I can't believe you guys are here."

Then she noticed three other chairs had been taken. Maybe the committee had put them with another family.

Sitting next to her mom, Callie felt more settled than she had since her blowup with Wyatt. In the middle of talking about her most recent project in Chile, Mom paused and looked above Callie's head.

Callie turned to see what had caught her mother's attention, and her breath caught for like the hundredth time that day.

She stood slowly. "Wyatt, what are you doing here?"

Wyatt stood behind her, dressed in charcoal-colored dress pants and a light blue button-down shirt with sleeves rolled up, revealing his tanned forearms. He held his cowboy hat in his hand, running his fingers around the brim.

"Congratulations, Callie. I saw your painting had taken first place. I knew it was a winner from the moment I saw it, no matter what the judges had decided. But I see they saw the same value in your talent as I did."

"Thank you."

He took her hand, running a thumb over her knuckles, and gave her fingers a gentle squeeze. He looked at her with pleading in his beautiful blue eyes. "Please hear me when I say how sorry I am for going behind your back."

She looked down at his strong hands and long fingers. Hands that worked hard, tamed horses and wiped his daughter's tears. Then she lifted her gaze to meet his eyes and she smiled. "Thank you, Wyatt. I appreciate that. Now it's my turn."

He frowned. "Turn for what?"

"To apologize. After I left the guest ranch without giving you notice, I realized your motives weren't to betray me but to support me and my passion. I couldn't see past my own insecurities, and I overreacted. I'm sorry for what I said and for walking away."

He shook his head. "I shouldn't have entered

your piece without your consent. You asked me to be more honest with what I'm feeling. I'll do that now. I love you, Callie. I will protect you, fight for you, and trust you every day. More than anything, I'd love for you to stay in Aspen Ridge. I'll help you get Ada's shop restored and reopened, and you can help me run the horse rescue. We'll be busy all the time, and you may have regrets, but we can face them together. However, if you want to take the art director position at the gallery, then I hope you wouldn't mind if a weary cowboy and his adorable daughter joined you."

"You'd do that—give up your dreams—for me?"

"If it means we'll be together, then yes."

"There's something I need to tell you."

"What's that?"

Smiling, she cupped his cheek. "I won't be taking the job at the gallery. I'm not leaving Aspen Ridge."

"What made you change your mind?"

"Well, I hadn't actually made up my mind to take it. I had to consider everything I was giving up, and it wasn't worth the cost."

"Your gram's shop?"

She shook her head. "I've been released from

that promise. I love Gram's cottage, and it will always hold wonderful memories. I was referring to you. And Mia. I can't move away from the man I love. Or his adorable little girl."

Wyatt cradled her face in his hands. He brushed a kiss across her lips. Then he gathered her in his embrace. "I've missed you. It's only been two days but it feels like it's been two weeks."

"Get used to having me around, because I'm not going anywhere."

He kissed her again. "I like the sound of that."

# EPILOGUE

HAD IT BEEN only nine months since she'd returned to Aspen Ridge, ready to keep her promise to her grandma? Nine months since Wyatt had rescued her from the side of the road? Nine months since her planned life had taken an unexpected turn?

And now, nine months later, she was about to walk down the aisle to exchange vows with the man who'd helped her to hold on to hope.

Callie stood in front of the full-length mirror in her former suite at the lodge. She ran her hands over the V-neck lace gown with the beaded appliques at the shoulders and a sweeping train. Her hair had been twisted in a low knot at the base of her head. She'd secured the mid-length veil with the jeweled combs that Gram had worn on her own wedding day so many years ago.

Macey, Everly and Mallory had gone into one

of the other nearby suites to get ready so Callie had a few minutes to herself before the wedding ceremony began.

When Wyatt had proposed at Thanksgiving, letting her know how grateful he was to her for showing up in his life, they decided they didn't want a long engagement. No matter how clichéd it was, they'd chosen February to pledge their love. Since they came together because of the guest ranch, Callie wanted to have a small ceremony there with only family and close friends in attendance. Wyatt was more than happy to give her what she wanted.

Just then, someone knocked on her door.

"Come in."

Irene peeked inside. "Mind if I come in a minute?"

Callie turned away from the mirror and waved her in. "Not at all."

Irene stepped into the room, looking gorgeous in an emerald green dress, and brought her hand to her mouth. "You look beautiful. Wyatt won't be able to focus on what Pastor Miles is saying. He'll have eyes only for you."

"Thank you, Irene." Callie pressed a hand against her stomach. "I don't know why I'm so nervous. I have no doubts about marrying Wyatt and being a mother to Mia."

"Every bride is nervous on her wedding day. It's normal. But the moment you see Wyatt, those nerves will disappear. I brought you something." She reached into her purse and pulled out a white velvet pouch. She withdrew a delicate silver bracelet and laid it across the palm of her hand. "Your grandma gave this to me on the first birthday I celebrated without my daughter. Linnea wore Ada's pearls on her wedding day, so I thought I would offer this and see if you'd like to wear it."

Callie smiled as she ran her finger over the charm of a dove holding a heart in its mouth with the word *HOPE* engraved on it. She looked at Irene and smiled. "It's beautiful. I'd be honored to wear it. Thank you for thinking of me."

She held out her wrist, and Irene fastened the bracelet. She kissed Callie's cheek, then pulled her in for a hug. "Absolutely, my dear. Ray and I are so pleased with how you and Wyatt have come together. We couldn't have asked for a more special person to be a part of his and Mia's lives."

"I'm the one who's blessed. I'm excited to start our lives together as a family."

Irene hugged her again. "I'll scoot out of here so you can finish getting ready."

When the door closed, Callie sat on the end of the bed and slid her feet into the beaded ballet slippers. The fourteen-year-old girl inside her couldn't believe she was about to walk down the aisle any minute and marry Wyatt Stone.

A knock sounded on her door again. This time, Callie stood and opened it.

Her father stood in the doorway looking handsome in his dark gray suit. "Callista, you look beautiful."

Callie glanced down at her gown, then back at him. "Thanks, Dad."

"You ready?"

She nodded and grabbed her bouquet of roses, miniature carnations and ranunculus in shades of navy, pink and blush.

As she stepped out of the room and closed the door behind her, Mia, dressed in her dusty pink flower girl dress, ran over to her and stopped. Her eyes grew wide "You look like a princess, Callie."

Callie leaned over and kissed Mia. "Thank you. I feel like a princess. You look beautiful."

Mia twirled. "Thank you."

The music changed, and Macey herded everyone into position. Macey, Mallory, Everly and Piper, all wearing gowns in shades of blue, descended the stairs ahead of her, then Tanner walked with Mia as she tossed rose petals on the blush-pink runner.

Callie took a step down and caught Wyatt's eyes on her. Her knees nearly buckled at the sight of him standing in front of the stone fireplace in his gray suit with Bear, Cole, Trevor and Wesley next to him.

For the next ten minutes she listened to Pastor Miles talk about God's love and hope.

"The bride and groom have chosen to write their own vows." Pastor Miles nodded to Callie.

"Wyatt, when you saved me from the side of the road last June, I didn't realize how much my life would change. You are the kindest, most generous man I've known. I don't doubt your love or your support of what I do. I look forward to a lifetime of trusting you to keep my secrets, drying my tears, laughing and raising our family together. I give you my heart and all my love." She slid the band on Wyatt's finger and squeezed his hands.

"Callie, I accept the responsibility that comes with accepting the gift of your heart and love. I promise to love, protect, cherish and support you every day that we are given to be together. I'm truly blessed to have been given a second chance at happiness, and I'll never take it for granted." Wyatt paused a moment then looked at her lovingly. "You showed me what it means to be strong and how to continually hold on to hope. Through all the ups and downs that we'll face, I'm so thankful we'll face them together as partners and as friends. My love for you grows daily, and I'm excited to begin our life together as a family." Wyatt's voice caught on the last word as his eyes sparkled. He slid the ring on her finger, then lifted her hand and pressed his lips against her knuckles.

A tear slid down Callie's cheek, and Wyatt brushed it away gently with his finger as Pastor Miles blessed their union. Then he looked at Wyatt, "You may kiss the bride."

"About time." Wyatt wrapped an arm around Callie's waist and drew her against him. Then he kissed her.

Family and friends clapped, and gathered around them to share their congratulations.

For the next couple of hours, they ate, danced and laughed with the people they loved.

Callie sat on the arm of one of the couches, talking with Jacie. Wyatt rested his hands on her shoulders and whispered by her ear. "Can I steal you away for a moment?"

She turned to him. "Of course." After excusing herself away from Jacie, Callie took Wyatt's hand as he led her to the family table where Deacon and Nora sat.

As they approached, Deacon and Nora stood. Deacon retrieved an envelope from his inside suit pocket and held it out to them. "Wyatt and Callie, we are so thankful God has given both of you a second chance for happiness as Wyatt said in his vows. We love you both, and we are excited to see how God uses you. Hopefully, this will help."

Wyatt pulled out a letter and what appeared to be a check from the envelope. He wrapped an arm around Callie's waist, and they read it together.

Callie looked at Wyatt, then at her new in-laws. "Are you serious?"

"We don't mess around when it comes to our children's futures."

Wyatt looked at his parents. "I don't know what to say except thank you."

"That's all you need to say. When your brother and sister got married, they each received portions of Stone River. As the letter states, we are giving you the cabin and the land around it, but your share of the land is smaller. Now that Ray and Irene have given you the horse rescue, which you've turned into the sanctuary, we know how much that means to you. We decided partnering with Linnea's Hope is a better investment."

Wyatt blinked several times and swallowed hard. "Thank you. It's perfect."

Nora looked at them. "We are so proud of the both of you and know God has great things in store for your shop too, Callie."

After exchanging more hugs, Nora pulled a protesting Deacon onto the dance floor.

Callie turned to Wyatt and framed his face with her hands. "I love you, Mr. Stone."

His arms slid around her waist. "And I love you, Mrs. Stone. For the rest of my life."

"Hey, what about me?"

Callie and Wyatt broke apart to find Mia tugging on Wyatt's pant leg with Ella in her arms.

Wyatt lifted her in his arms. "What about you?"

Mia wrapped an arm around Wyatt and one around Callie. "I want to be a part of the hug."

Wyatt laughed and shifted her between them. "You're always a part of our hugs, Peanut."

Mia rested her head on Callie's shoulder. "I love you, Callie."

"I love you too, sweetheart."

"Lexi said when her daddy married Aunt Macey, she could call her Mommy. You married my daddy. Can I call you Mommy?"

Callie bit her lip and nodded. "I would love that, sweet girl."

Nine months ago, she'd arrived at Stone River brokenhearted, with her life in shambles.

But two people with no desire to fall in love again had held on to hope and come together to create their own happily-ever-after.

And she couldn't be more excited to build a life in Aspen Ridge with her handsome cowboy and his daughter.

★ ★ ★ ★ ★

# A NOTE TO ALL READERS

From October releases Mills & Boon will be making some changes to the series formats and pricing.

### What will be different about the series books?

In response to recent reader feedback, we are increasing the size of our paperbacks to bigger books with better quality paper, making for a better reading experience.

### What will be the new price of Mills & Boon?

Over the past four years we have seen significant increases in the cost of producing our books. As a result, in order to continue to provide customers with a quality reading experience, the price of our books will increase to RRP $10.99 for Modern singles and RRP $19.99 for 2-in-1s from Medical, Intrigue, Romantic Suspense, Historical and Western.

For futher information regarding format changes and pricing, please visit our website millsandboon.com.au.

# WESTERN

*Rugged men looking for love...*

## Available Next Month

**The Maverick's Christmas Kiss** Joanna Sims
**A Proposal For Her Cowboy** Cari Lynn Webb

........................................................

**A Fortune Thanksgiving** Michelle Lindo-Rice
**The Rodeo Star's Reunion** Melinda Curtis

........................................................

 LOVE INSPIRED

**The Cowboy's Forgotten Love** Tina Radcliffe
**The Cowboy's Inheritance** Julia Ruth

Keep reading for an excerpt of a new title
from the Intrigue series,
COLORADO KIDNAPPING by Cindi Myers

# *Chapter One*

The little girl squealed with delight as she ran across the playground, blond hair flying out behind her. When she stumbled and fell she popped up immediately, still laughing, and resumed her race with her companions. Sheriff's deputy Ryker Vernon, standing just on the other side of the playground fence, swallowed past the catch in his throat and marveled at his daughter's—Charlotte's—sunny disposition. Where did she get that from? Not from her mother. Kim had a decidedly darker outlook on life, one that had led her to eventually leave him and her daughter behind.

Charlotte didn't get her happy personality from Ryker, either. Five years as a law enforcement officer had shown him too much of the bad side of people to make him inclined toward lightheartedness. Yet here was Charlotte, bubbly personality intact despite her mother's desertion and their recent relocation back to his hometown of Eagle Mountain, Colorado.

Charlotte reached the apple tree that apparently marked the finish line of the race and stopped, puffing for breath, her round cheeks bright pink, deep dimples on either side of her smiling lips. She turned and caught sight of Ryker and all but jumped for joy. "Daddy!" she shouted, and took off toward him.

Her teacher, Sheila Lindstrom, caught up with her just as Charlotte raced past the boundary of the fence and, also spotting Ryker, accompanied the child to meet him. He was glad to see the teacher was so diligent. "Hello, Deputy Vernon," Sheila said as Charlotte threw her arms around Ryker's legs. "I didn't know you were picking up Charlotte this afternoon." She tucked a strand of hair a shade paler than Charlotte's behind one ear and smiled up at him in a way that reminded him he was a single man in a small town where the dating pool might be thought of as limited.

He didn't return the smile, and took a step back, hoping to give the impression that he wasn't interested. Not that Sheila wasn't a perfectly nice woman, but he was juggling enough right now, with a new job, a new home and a little girl to raise. He didn't need the complications that came with a relationship. "Charlotte's grandmother will be picking her up, as usual," he said. "I just started my shift and since Charlotte will be in bed by the time I'm back home, I swung by to say hello." He rested his hand on the little girl's head as she beamed up at him.

"That's so sweet," Sheila said, and tilted her head to one side, blue eyes still fixed on him as if he was some delectable treat.

"Ryker! What are you doing here? Is everything all right?"

He and Sheila and Charlotte all turned to see Ryker's mother, Wanda Vernon, hurrying up the sidewalk toward them. Slender and athletic, with dark curls past her shoulders, Wanda Vernon looked younger than her fifty years, but right now worry lines creased her normally smooth forehead.

"Nothing's wrong, Mom," Ryker reassured her. "I just stopped by to say hello to Charlotte."

"Grammie, I found a horny toad at recess this morning, but teacher made me put it back," Charlotte announced.

"You know our wild friends are happier remaining in the wild," Sheila said.

"I know," Charlotte said. "But he was so pretty. He had gold eyes and a gold and brown body with bumps on it. Amy thought he was icky, but I thought he was beautiful."

Ryker hid his smile behind his hand. That was his daughter. She had never met an insect or amphibian or item from nature that frightened or repelled her.

"Horned toads are very interesting," Wanda said. "But it's always best to just look at them, and not touch. You wouldn't want to accidentally hurt one."

"Oh, I would never do that!" Charlotte looked offended at the idea.

Ryker's shoulder-mounted radio crackled, and the dispatcher's voice came through clearly. "Unit five, report to Dixon Pass, mile marker 97, to assist at accident site. EMS and SAR on the way."

Ryker keyed the mike, aware that everyone within earshot had turned to stare. "Unit five responding. I'm on my way." He squatted down until he was eye level with his daughter. "I have to go now, honey," he said. "Can I have a kiss goodbye?"

She responded by throwing her arms around him and kissing his cheek. "Be careful, Daddy," she said.

"I always am, sweetheart. You be a good girl for Grammie and Grandpa."

"I always am!" she echoed.

"Be careful," his mother and Sheila said in unison as he nodded goodbye, then jogged toward his sheriff's department SUV.

He turned the vehicle toward the highway and switched

on lights and sirens to cut a clear path toward the accident. As he passed the preschool he caught a glimpse of Charlotte with his mother on the sidewalk. The little girl was smiling and waving. Some of the heaviness in his heart lifted, as it always did when he was with her. Through all the upheaval in her young life, Charlotte was resilient.

Ryker was trying to follow her example, to roll with the punches life threw at him, or at least do a better job of hiding his bruises.

"IT LOOKS LIKE the vehicle rolled several times before it came to land on that ledge." Eagle Mountain Search and Rescue Captain Danny Irwin stood with the cluster of volunteers on the side of the highway as they peered over the side at the battered silver sedan wedged between a boulder and the cliff approximately one hundred yards below. "You can see pieces of the car that broke off every time the car bounced."

Harper Stanick, a search and rescue rookie, winced as she took in the trail of debris and the battered vehicle. It looked like this was going to be her first body recovery. She had been warned this was part of search and rescue and told herself she was prepared, but still. What would a person look like after enduring that kind of trauma?

"I saw movement!" Paramedic Hannah Richards, who had arrived with the ambulance but joined her fellow SAR volunteers in surveying the scene, pointed at the vehicle. "There's someone alive in there!"

Her exclamation prodded them into action. Danny directed volunteers Eldon Ramsey and Tony Meissner to rig ropes for a rappel onto the ledge beside the car. Harper joined fellow trainees Grace Wilcox, Anna Trent and veteran Christine Mercer in gathering helmets, harnesses, a litter and other gear they would need to stabilize the injured survivor and get them to safety above. Danny radioed to have a medical helicopter land two miles away at the soccer fields in town to meet the ambulance and transport the injured person or persons to the hospital in Junction.

"What can I do to help?"

At the sound of the man's voice, deep and slightly hoarse, Harper fumbled the safety helmets she had been charged with, and had to juggle to keep from losing one. "Careful," Christine said.

"Close the highway, if you haven't already," Danny said. "Clear space on the side of the highway for us to go down and keep everyone back from the edge. We don't want anyone else falling in, or kicking rocks down on top of us as we work."

Harper turned to see who Danny was talking to and this time she did drop the helmets. Seven years since she had laid eyes on Ryker Vernon and she might have thought she was hallucinating him now, except that it made perfect sense for him to be here. Ryker was from Eagle Mountain, just like her. The first thing she had done when she moved back was to snoop around, long enough to determine he had left town, but apparently he had returned. Just like her.

What didn't make sense was that Ryker was now apparently a cop. No mistaking that khaki uniform or the gun on his hip. Ryker, a cop? The motorcycle-riding bad boy who had practically sent her mother into a faint the first time he showed up at their house to pick Harper up for a date was a law enforcement officer?

And damned if he didn't look just as good in that uniform as he had in his motorcycle leathers all those years ago. Better even, his chest a little broader, his jaw firmer. The Ryker she had known had been barely eighteen, still with a bit of the boy about him. This version of him was harder. A man.

"Hey, earth to Harper. Are you okay?" Christine followed Harper's gaze toward the officer who stood with Danny and she grinned. "I take it this is your first encounter with the newest addition to the sheriff's department," she said. "He's pretty easy on the eyes, isn't he?" She nudged Harper with her elbow. "I hear he's a single dad. Maybe when we're done here you can introduce yourself."

The bottom dropped out of Harper's stomach at the word *dad*. Ryker was a father? When? Who?

"Pull your eyes back in your head and focus on the job," Christine said, her voice firm. "You can chase after the cop later."

Harper turned her back on Ryker. "I'm not going to chase after him," she said. "I was just surprised. He reminds me of someone I used to know."

"Must have been a pretty special someone," Christine said. "The way you were staring at him. Like one of those cartoons, where the air fills with hearts."

"Not like that at all," Harper said, and gathered up the helmets she had dropped. Maybe at one time she was that gaga about Ryker Vernon, but those days were long past.

DESPITE HOW FAR the vehicle had rolled and the shape the car was in, three people emerged alive. Ryker watched from a distance as search and rescue volunteers descended on ropes to the ledge and worked to stabilize the vehicle, then cut most of the rest of the car away to reach the passengers trapped inside.

First up was an infant, a living testament to the effectiveness of child safety seats, as he sustained nothing more than a minor cut on his forehead from broken glass. Volunteer Eldon Ramsey carried the baby, still secured in his seat, up to the road, where the paramedics pronounced him perfectly okay then reluctantly turned him over to the Victim Services volunteer, who was tasked with locating a relative or temporary foster parent to care for him until his parents were released from the hospital.

Said parents also both survived, with several broken bones between them. They were brought up one at a time strapped into litters. The technical aspects of the maneuvers required to bring them to safety fascinated Ryker, who would admit to being nervous about heights.

"That was amazing," he said to SAR Captain Danny Irwin after the injured had been transported to the waiting helicopter and the road had been reopened. Accident investigators from Colorado State Patrol had arrived on the scene and were taking photographs and measuring skid marks for their reports, so Ryker had turned to helping the search and rescue volunteers with their gear.

"We're always looking for more volunteers," Danny said. "Deputy Jake Gwynn is on the team."

"Yeah, I hear he loves it," Ryker said. "Unfortunately, I can't commit that much time. I need to be with my daughter when I have time off."

"How old is she?" Danny asked.

"Four. It's just the two of us. And my parents. They're a big help."

Danny nodded. "My fiancée has two kids. They're a little older but I get what you mean about wanting to be there for them. They won't be little forever."

"Hey there! I heard you were back in town." Ryker turned to find Hannah Richards grinning up at him. The two of them had been in the same grade at Eagle Mountain High School way back when.

"Hi, Hannah. It's good to see you. I've only been back a couple of weeks. I'm still getting settled."

"Jake told me you signed on with the sheriff's department," she said. She held up one hand to reveal a modest diamond. "He's my fiancé, in case you haven't heard."

"He's mentioned the amazing woman he's engaged to, but I had no idea that was you."

She punched his shoulder and he pretended to recoil in pain, both of them laughing. "Hey, there's someone else here you need to see," Hannah said. She turned and waved. "Harper. Come over and see who the cat dragged in."

The name itself was enough to set Ryker's heart hammering, but seeing the woman herself made his world tilt for a moment. If anything, she was more beautiful than he remembered—her curly brown hair escaping from a twist at the back of her head, her green-hazel eyes fringed with dark lashes. Kim, to whom Ryker had confided the whole story of his and Harper's ill-fated romance, had prickled at what she interpreted as his too-fond descriptions of his teenage girlfriend. "No one is that perfect," she had protested.

But to him, Harper had been perfect. And she had reminded him of how imperfect he was. "Hello, Harper," he said, surprised at how calm and even his voice sounded. "It's good to see you again."

"Hello, Ryker. I heard you'd left town."

He had heard the same about her. "I just moved back," he said.

She was looking at him, but at the uniform, not into his eyes. "I can't believe you're a sheriff's deputy."

"Neither can I, some days." He was trying to make a joke, but the words came off flat. Hannah was watching them, her face full of questions. Did she remember that he and Harper had dated in high school?

Maybe she hadn't known. Harper's rich parents had pitched such a fit about their adored daughter seeing a guy whose father worked at the town's sewage treatment plant that he and Harper had to sneak around in order to see each other.

He had a hundred questions he wanted to ask her: What was she doing back in Eagle Mountain? What kind of work did she do? How had she ended up volunteering with search and rescue?

Was she okay? Could she ever forgive him?

"I have to go," Harper said, and turned away.

"See you around, Ryker," Hannah said. "Jake and I will have you over for dinner sometime."

"Yeah, that would be great," Ryker said, with less enthusiasm than he probably should have. He stared after Harper. She was still beautiful, all shiny hair and soft curves, but more defined now, the blurred edges of youth replaced by the firm lines of maturity. Not that she was old, but she had been through a lot in the past few years.

She had been through a lot, and he hadn't been there with her. One more failure he was having a hard time getting past.

# Subscribe and fall in love with a Mills & Boon series today!

You'll be among the first to read stories delivered to your door monthly and enjoy great savings.

WE
SIMPLY
LOVE
ROMANCE